Colin Macpherson was born in Melbourne, and has lived and worked in a number of countries as a physicist, a teacher, an academic, a computer consultant, a farmer, a boatbuilder, an inventor, and an aid worker. He is also the author of several textbooks and software packages, as well as being a successful freelance writer and editor. He has a PhD in mathematical modelling, and now lives near a beautiful beach on the Queensland coast. This is his second novel.

Also by Colin Macpherson

The Tide Turners

The Holy Well

Colin Macpherson

Mopoke Publishing

First published in 2007 by Mopoke Publishing
P.O. Box 1213, Yeppoon, Queensland 4703, Australia
www.mopoke.com.au

Copyright © Colin Macpherson 2007

Colin Macpherson asserts his moral right to be identified as the author of this work.

All rights reserved. No part of this publication may be reproduced, stored in a retrieval system or transmitted in any form or by any means, electronic or mechanical, including photocopying, recording or otherwise, without the prior written permission of both the copyright owner and the publisher.

This is a work of fiction. Names, places, characters, and incidents either are the product of the author's imagination or are used fictitiously. Any resemblance to real persons, living or dead, or to real organizations, businesses or establishments, is purely coincidental.

National Library of Australia
Cataloguing-in-Publication data:

Macpherson, Colin R. (Colin Robert), 1948- .
The holy well.

ISBN 9780980350104 (pbk.).

I. Title.

A823.3

Cover art by Gerald Brocklesby
Cover photograph by Tony Turvey
Typeset by Central Queensland University Publishing Unit
Printed and bound in Australia by Griffin Press

To Maggy and Al
and
Chrissy and Lok

Prologue – The births

It didn't happen suddenly. There was no earthquake or eruption or even a rumbling from deep under the earth. Rather, it was the result of a slow process – geologically slow. The network of myriad cracks and faults and other underground passageways took thousands of years to form. But, eventually, there *was* notice that something might soon happen on the surface. The plants knew early on – first the long roots of a nearby juniper, and then those of a few of the crowded birches that populated the area. In the year before its appearance, a large patch of grass became greener and, close-by, a small collection of marsh marigolds began to grow – taking advantage of the upwelling moisture. Then, sometime in the season when the snows on the peaks begin to withdraw and the days become longer, it finally occurred. The well appeared. The cool water first greeted the sunshine from the bottom of a small depression in the soil and rock at the base of a steep embankment. A tiny pool formed in this sunken area and then began to overflow and spread out into the almost-flat region beyond. A short distance away was the great river, but the water from the well disappeared back under the earth long before reaching its banks.

A young adult lynx drank from the new source, pleased that she wouldn't have to venture further. Her tufted ears turned slightly as she heard the sound of honking geese flying overhead, and she lifted her face to catch a glimpse of them through the thick tree cover. For a moment, she dreamed a feline dream.

This was an age of vast forests of pine and birch and oak, where bears roamed and wolves hunted. Man was not yet here.

****

Morann had known that the baby would arrive today. Even though the older women had agreed amongst themselves that it would be at least another ten days, and even though this was to be her first child, the girl of fifteen summers had been certain that the new life would emerge from between her legs before the next dawn.

The scoffing of her two aunts had abruptly stopped when, as they were pulling a deer hide from the tanning pit, Morann's waters broke. 'That will give a special scent to the leather,' Kinnow had joked as the prospective mother looked down at the fluid running into the pit from the large flat rock on which she was standing.

Kinnow's more sympathetic sister, Vana, had hurried to the girl's side. 'Don't be afraid,' she had whispered gently as Morann's wide-eyed gaze seemed to look through her to somewhere else. 'Now is the time for us to go back to the crannog and to prepare for this wonderful event.'

'And we will never again question your birth predictions,' Kinnow had said loudly with a chuckle, and in so doing admitted Morann to the circle of mothers even before the labour. This was something of an honour, and the girl had smiled and sung a happy farewell to the oaks that surrounded the clearing where they'd been working, as the two sisters helped her back to the house on the lake.

It was now much later, with the sun no longer in the sky. The early spring was mild this year – the snows having already retreated to the higher realms of the mountains. But still, there was a chill in the night, and this was making itself known to the men and boys who stood or sat on the outside balcony that encompassed the large, circular building. From underneath came the sound of gently lapping water, and from inside, the loud cries of pain.

Morann tried to relax her muscles but she knew that the next rolling spasm would come very soon, and this kept her tense. She was now on her hands and knees in the 'standing dog' position, her enlarged vagina being closely examined by Kinnow. "I think the next thunder roll will cause the clouds to part," her aunt announced to the other women hovering around the sleeping compartment that was normally used for special guests.

Vana softly massaged the girl's sinking back and whispered, "she means the baby will make its first appearance next time."

"I know what she means, I'm not an idiot," Morann answered between gritted teeth, quickly followed by, "I'm sorry, I'm sorry, I'm sorry – it hurts." A drop of sweat fell from the end of her nose into the fur of the great bear skin on which she was kneeling – the dried bracken underneath crunching as she shifted her weight. "Aaaah!" she cried yet again. "I want it to end."

"I can see the head," called Kinnow. Then, in a softer voice, directed just to her niece, "Use your strength girl, push the little one out – it will be over soon. Push!"

Outside, on the part of the balcony that projected furthermost into the lake, Dorvar knelt, looking across the waters to the mountains in the northwest – the crescent moon shedding just enough light for him to see their snowy peaks. Earlier, he had been able to quietly commune with the mountains and the waters – and, briefly, with a salmon that had jumped nearby. They had all given their blessings to the birth. But as the wailing of his young wife got louder and more frequent he had lost his concentration, and with the latest cry of pain two of his helpers, who were standing a little way off, saw him shudder. He desperately wanted this child – someone who might take over the priestly concerns of the clan, and maybe – like himself – also become its leader. But more than this, he wanted Morann to live. Despite the wisdom that had been handed down to him and his people by their ancestors, and despite the new ideas and practices that they had learned from others in more recent times, many women still died in childbirth or soon after. 'Men die in battle, women die in childbirth, but in the end the worms get us all,' his grandmother had once cackled. It was she who approached now. He shuddered again as her stooped form hobbled towards him.

"It is time for you to come inside," she uttered quietly. He could not see her craggy face in the darkness so there were no early hints to be offered by her expression – comforting or otherwise.

As he walked round the balcony to the crannog's entrance he saw a great throng of people standing at the shore end of the elevated timber causeway that crossed the water between the building and the land. The two men guarding the short drawbridge section halfway across had allowed a number of clan relatives and friends to come over to the crannog side. All became silent as the leader-priest briefly looked in their direction before hurrying through the hanging deerskins in the doorway. When he was gone, murmurings of anticipation began – an announcement would surely come soon.

Tears of happiness welled in Dorvar's eyes as he looked down upon his beautiful young wife and the little human form that was already attached to one of her enlarged breasts. She was lying on her back – her eyelids heavy and her skin pale. The baby was wrapped in the fine linen cloth that Dorvar had traded from a western traveller more than a month ago, and both mother and child were partly covered by the large woollen blanket that had been a gift from another priestly family many years past. Morann turned her head in his direction and her lips formed a strange, restful smile. He quickly knelt down and kissed her forehead. He then looked into her sleepy eyes and said, "You are my life. I was so worried, I don't know what ..." She pursed her lips and made a sound to hush him.

"I am dying Dorvar ... I will be leaving you soon." Tears began to trickle down her wan cheeks.

Dorvar sat back, suddenly tense and full of disbelief. He turned to one of the women. "Vana, there is nothing wrong ... is there?" The poor woman was already grief stricken – all she could do was nod in the direction of her sister. He followed her eyes to Kinnow who had lifted the blanket a little. There was some sort of poultice being held between the girl's thighs by a web of leather thongs. It was soaked in blood – much of it bright red. He knew what this meant.

"We cannot stop the bleeding," Kinnow tried to explain. "We have tried everything, but there is something wrong inside. I'm sorry," she said as she lowered the blanket.

The Holy Well

Dorvar's ears were ringing and his hands began to shake. He looked around at the women who were standing near the bed – all had their heads bowed; some already whimpering. He felt Morann's cool hand touch his arm, and he turned his gaze back to her. "Please don't go," he pleaded. "Please."

Again, she hushed him, and in a whisper asked, "What name will you give our son?"

'A son,' he thought. 'A son!' The child was the last thing on his mind at this moment, but he leant towards his wife's ear and softly spoke the name that the waters of the lake had suggested only a short time earlier.

For a moment, the sadness left her face. "Now take him outside and announce him to the world – this you must do. I will still be here when you return." He gave her a reluctant stare. "Go," she insisted, and looked to Vana to help lift the feeding child from her dying body.

Dorvar awkwardly held the baby boy, and for a short time gazed upon his face – noticing that the young mouth was still making sucking movements. He then stood up and marched outside. As soon as the guests and the curious saw him emerge from the great house, they were again quiet.

He walked resolutely to the small wooden drawbridge so that the people on the shore would hear him as well as those on the crannog balcony. He held the tiny bundle above his head and, facing the mountains, he cried out, "This is my son, and his name will be Bren, Bren of the Tull." He repeated this several times – facing a different direction on each occasion. He then lowered the child, who had started to cry, and stared down at it. "I will love you and care for you," he whispered to the howling face. "But if there were any way I could trade your life for that of your dying mother then I would do it without another thought."

As he strode back to the crannog, the crowd had already begun to chant, "Bren of the Tull, Bren of the Tull." On the balcony, people were smiling and some were stepping forward to offer their congratulations. They didn't yet know. But when they saw his expression, they stopped, uncertain. Vana was standing near the entrance. He roughly handed her the wailing child as he rushed back inside.

****

The foreman was such a bastard. He knew that Archie's wife was due any day now, but that hadn't stopped him from continuing his meeting with the architect for another half-hour before passing on the telephone message. To make it even worse, he had yelled, 'Remember ya won't be gettin' paid for this afternoon,' as the middle-aged labourer had rushed from the construction site.

'That foreman's a real prick,' one apprentice plumber had whispered to another after witnessing the incident.

Still, that had been some minutes ago. Right now, Archie was glaring at a red traffic light. "Come on, come on," he said – his fingers dancing on the side of the steering wheel. All he could think of was getting to the hospital in time to comfort Sandra before they whisked her away to the labour ward. He wouldn't see her then until after the baby was born. He liked the new idea of husbands being allowed to be with their wives during the birth but that was a bit too revolutionary for the staff at St Hugh's. Nevertheless, the hospital had a good reputation in regard to care, and it was only a short distance from their home in Brunswick. 'But a bloody long way from here,' he thought as it occurred to him that the lights might be stuck on red. Another car pulled up next to him and he glanced across at the young driver – sunglasses, a shirt with palm trees, hair Brylcreamed back into a ducktail. A sudden impulse hit Archie. "I'm having a baby!" he yelled through the open window. The sunglasses looked in his direction and then accelerated away. The light was now green.

Sandra waddled up to the admissions desk – happy to be alive. She already knew that her mother was possibly the worst driver in Australia, but with the added stress of trying to get her pregnant daughter to St Hugh's before she went into labour, Daphne had probably taken out the prize for the entire planet.

Even before she spoke a word to the woman behind the desk, Sandra found herself being helped into a wheelchair by a young male orderly. When seated, she looked up and smiled at him, and instinctively flicked some of the long, bottle-blonde hair from behind her left ear. Then came a particularly deep contraction. Although bearable, it was the most painful one so far – and they were now getting more frequent.

In the lift, she could smell the orderly's aftershave. It triggered off a rare moment of reflection in Sandra's brain. She thought about sex and love making – which she enjoyed very much. Probably too much. And now here she was – having to suffer the consequences. Despite her best efforts, she occasionally misread the bodily signs that suggested it was safe to have intercourse. And the alternative methods ... well ... they weren't always available; or appropriate. So she was pregnant for the third time – again, unplanned. She rarely saw the other two from her first marriage. 'The Arsehole' had taken them to the farm that he and his sweet little private-school-librarian-with-small-tits new wife had bought with her rich parents' money. Of course the good side was that she wouldn't have a five year-old and a seven year-old to contend with as well as a screaming baby. And at least on this occasion she was sure that the baby was her husband's. Fairly sure anyway.

By the time Archie ran through the gap in the self-opening doors of the hospital's main entrance, the perspiration on his arms and face had mixed with the dust and grime from the building site to give him a wild, almost maniacal appearance. Once inside, he stopped, realizing he didn't know where to go next.

A receptionist beckoned him over to the counter. "Labour Ward?" she asked.

"Yes," he replied, hurriedly.

"Second floor, west wing – over there," she pointed to a lift.

"Thanks," he offered as he prepared to rocket towards the lift door that looked like it was about to close, five or six blank faces staring in his direction.

"BUT, before you go up you might want to have a quick wash." Archie looked down at his filthy arms. "Men's toilets, over there," she pointed again. He ran past the blank faces as the lift door closed.

The cool water on his face felt good. It was the first pause he'd allowed himself since hearing the news that his wife's labour had started and that she was being taken to the hospital. He dried himself on the pull-down towel hanging from the dispenser on the wall, and then looked at the mirror above the sink. "You're going to be a daddy," he said to his reflection, and smiled as he watched it say the same words back. And then he was gone; second floor, west wing.

First he frowned and then he pushed his fingers into the soft area under his ears – trying to get rid of the buzzing sound that had just started in his head. The nurse took one arm, and Daphne, less competently, took the other as they both escorted the large-framed Archie to a chair. "What sort of problem?" he said to the white-clad woman.

"The first thing is that you shouldn't worry, Mr Campbell. Mr Dorovich is one of our most experienced gynaecologists."

"Yes, but ..."

"It's a breech baby," she interrupted, realizing that perhaps she should have started differently. "As well as that, the baby is quite large and your wife hasn't dilated enough."

Archie frowned and turned his head to his mother-in-law. She wrinkled her nose a little and pointed with a moving finger at where her groin was probably located. Archie frowned even more and turned back to the nurse who was continuing her explanation.

"It means that the baby can't get out in the usual way without causing great harm, so the doctor is going to deliver it by caesarean section."

"You mean he's going to cut Sandra open?"

"Well, yes but ..."

"Mr Globovich?"

"Dorovich," she corrected, "he's one of our best, and he has performed hundreds of caesareans." She squeezed his arm. "Don't worry Mr Campbell, your wife is in good hands, and just think, in a short while you will have a beautiful little baby."

Archie sat back in the chair. He was still concerned but he couldn't help dwelling on those words, 'a beautiful little baby'.

Three hours later he was sitting next to the bed where Sandra had been deposited after regaining consciousness. There were only two beds in the room; the other one being occupied by a pretty woman with long black hair and brown skin. She was feeding her newborn. For the first time in his life, Archie noticed the sweet, strong smell generated by the mix of baby and breast milk. He liked it.

Sandra was drifting in and out of sleep. The effects of the general anaesthetic had gone but the operation had left her exhausted and she had to try hard to stop from dozing off. Archie turned from looking at the brown lady when he felt his wife touch his arm.

"Where's Mum?" she asked in a soft, croaky voice.

"They'd only let *me* in for now, so she's downstairs somewhere." Sandra nodded, and then drifted off to sleepland again. Archie stroked her cheek. 'She may not be a young chicken anymore,' he thought to himself, 'but right now she looks wonderful.' While he was still transfixed in admiration, she opened her blue eyes again.

"The doctor said people would hardly notice the scar," she croaked. "He said he would do what's called a 'bikini cut'; sort of following the line of my undies. People ... hardly ... notice," she repeated as her eyelids became heavy. Archie frowned. 'What people?' he wondered. Then the door swung open and in walked a smiling nurse carrying a little bundle.

Archie looked up – his eyes wide. He knew that this was the bundle that would cause his life to take on new meaning.

"Here's your baby, Sandra," announced the nurse, "big, healthy, and hungry." She lifted the blanket and placed the yawning infant to the side where Sandra had already exposed a breast. "You obviously know what you're doing,"

"Yeah, done it before," the mother replied matter-of-factly. The baby quickly attached itself to her nipple. She sighed; it felt pleasant. Right now she was feeling very close to her new child, but she was also thinking about her figure, and really hoped that it would return to normal quickly. Except for her breasts, of course. That was one of the reasons she had decided to breast feed – she knew she would be more attractive to men if her tits were bigger.

Naturally, Archie wasn't aware of any of his wife's thoughts and feelings at this time. All his senses and thoughts and emotions were focused on the little being lying next to her. He got off the chair, knelt on the floor, and placed his elbows on the bed – with his chin in his cupped hands. And he stared in wonder at the baby – his baby – as it sucked and swallowed. At last he was a father.

"So what's the name of this one?" the nurse asked Sandra. The blonde mother looked down at the little face and then opened her mouth to reply, but Archie – without moving – spoke first.

"James," he said quietly. "James Campbell, my son."

Chapter 1

Bren really didn't see why he should be helping the women with their work for a third day in a row. In fact, it didn't seem right that he should be with them at all – on any day. He would soon be celebrating his eleventh spring, and he was clearly almost a young man – even though the dark, wavy hairs had only just started to appear. So, he couldn't understand why it was still deemed necessary for him to accompany Kinnow as she wandered around their lakeside settlement of Ceann Tull supervising the work of the other women, and for him to have to sit with them for such long periods helping with their tasks. For example, by now he was probably more adept at using wooden whorls for the drop spinning of wool into thread than anyone in their clan. 'Keep it up Bren,' some older boys had mockingly encouraged just yesterday as they walked past on their way to the canoes. 'You will soon have enough thread to weave a most womanly skirt.' He had thrown a handful of twigs and soil at them as they giggled their way to the water's edge, carrying lines, hooks, and bait in preparation for a day's fishing. Surely he was old enough to now concentrate all his young energy on the work of men.

He stood next to Kinnow as she spoke to the young woman grinding wild oats between two stones. He wasn't listening – his concentration had lapsed when they started discussing some other woman's pregnancy. Instead, he looked around the interior of the dwelling where the woman was seated. Although small compared to the crannog, its walls were hung with fine animal skins, and a huge set of antlers was attached to the lintel over the doorway. His eyes took in the skins and the antlers and the embers glowing in the central hearth, and then he looked down at the woman as she worked the stones. Although not yet spring, it was warm inside, and she was not wearing a jacket. He dwelt for a moment on the rippling of muscle in her right arm as her hand turned and twisted the large egg-shaped piece of granite. Then he noticed her cleavage and how the visible parts of her breasts moved in sympathy with her arm movements. The two women stopped talking. He looked back at the skins. Kinnow beckoned him to follow her outside.

"What's the matter with you today?" she asked, annoyance in her tone. "You've been drifting with the clouds all morning."

Bren liked Kinnow. She was tough and smart, and she always said what was on her mind. But he didn't enjoy being the subject of her displeasure – her words could slice into you like a newly sharpened dagger. He had long known that being honest and straightforward – just like she would be – was the best approach to take when she was annoyed.

"I'm sorry great aunt," he replied – using the more formal title as a sign of deference. "I suppose I still can't see why I should be spending so much time with the women – given my age – especially when I see Pock-face and the other boys doing manly things."

"You mean like going fishing?"

"Yes, and timber collecting and weapon making and … hunting." He had paused before saying the word 'hunting' because he had already been scolded several times in the last month for harping about it.

"Come with me," the old lady said as she walked away from the settlement and towards a path that led to a small clearing on the edge of the lake. A short time later they were sitting together on a large boulder near the water's edge. They silently watched as an osprey dropped from the sky, skimmed the water and then rose again, but now with a fish tightly gripped in its talons. "I like it here," Kinnow said as she looked toward the distant white peaks. "It's where I sometimes come when I need to be alone; when I want to have questions answered."

Bren glanced across at her lined face. He was no longer worried about being chastised. Although often gruff, her voice was now tinged with understanding and wisdom. "It's natural for you to want to be with your friends, doing the things that you think will shape you into a man. I understand that. But your father has made it clear that while he is away you are to continue your learning of the skills that help our clan to survive, regardless of whether they are deemed man-skills or woman-skills. You and I have discussed this before. He believes, and I agree, that this will help make you a better leader should the clan accept you as such sometime in the future."

Bren drew breath. "I understand that, great aunt, but it's been such a long time. I can now prepare hides, spin thread, tend animals, grind grains, dye cloth, and do all the other tasks normally carried out by women. I've done everything except look after babies."

"That will happen next month."

"What?"

"It's what I was speaking to Yandra about earlier. Her younger sister is big with child, and they are both delighted that you will be helping them care for the little one for a short while." Kinnow couldn't help but smile.

The boy rolled his eyes. "I can already hear the others, 'Is it true that a wildcat nipped off your vital parts, Bren, and that you are now more female than male?'" he said in a mocking voice.

Kinnow scowled at him. "Babies are what keep clans alive, my boy. Knowing how to care for them is one of the most important of all skills – whether it is done by men or women. They are our future."

"But the other …" he began to protest.

"Forget the others, you are Bren Fair-hair of the Tull – and you are special." Her voice was forceful and his respect for her made him think.

"Babies aren't so bad, I suppose," he replied after a short time. "But when do I get to hunt?" he asked – almost rhetorically.

"If all goes well, the day after tomorrow." Her wrinkles grew as her mouth formed a wide smile. "And …" she paused for a moment to give emphasis to her words, "it will be with your father."

Bren's jaw dropped and his eyes widened. He jumped up from the rock, grabbed the old woman's hands, and began dancing to and fro in front of her, singing, "Yes, yes, yes, yes."

Later, as he walked the family's five shaggy cows back to the crannog from their first venture outside since the winter just past, he was still smiling. All during the family evening meal, his happiness was evident – making jokes that had the younger ones sitting in the circle in fits of laughter. Even some of the older folk gave an occasional suppressed chuckle as they passed knowing looks to Kinnow. After the meal, and after Bren and his slightly older cousin, Pock-face, had helped with the cleaning up duties, both boys climbed the ladder to their joint sleeping compartment on the platform that extended around the inside of the crannog.

"Where did you get this?" asked Pock-face as he felt the sharpness of the arrowhead on the end of the shaft that Bren had handed him.

"It was my mother's, along with four others – a gift from her father. You've heard the stories that Kinnow and Vana have told about my mother's ability with the bow; how she was so good that the men let her hunt with them, even though she was only a marry-age girl."

"These are the finest bronze arrowheads I have ever seen," Pock-face commented as he examined all five. "Where did they come from?"

"I think they are Kelti, and maybe from across the great ocean."

"You are lucky Bren," his cousin responded. "All I own are the flint heads I have made myself."

"You still have your mother," the fair-haired boy replied, a sadness entering his expression.

The one with many scars on his cheeks and forehead wasn't sure what to say. He hadn't meant to sadden his cousin – they were best friends. He reached out and touched Bren on the shoulder. "All I mean is that these arrowheads are so much better than mine."

"I know," Bren replied as he drew a breath to cleanse his mood. "But I will be mainly using my flint heads too. These will only be for special occasions."

"Like what?"

"Like if I want to make your arse-crack longer than it already is," he replied with a challenging grin.

Pock-face threw himself onto his cousin, and began tickling him under the ribs. Bren quickly wrapped his legs around the older boy and attempted to stop his hands from performing the dance that was both delightful and agonizing. Soon they were rolling around the platform squealing and laughing. Suddenly, there was a loud bark from below and a thunderous voice called, "What goes on there?"

The two boys stopped their wrestling and peered over the edge of the platform. Below was the great hound Con, sitting at the feet of Dorvar, Bren's father.

The boy stood up and met the old man's angry glare with a steadfast-but-respectful stare. "I am sorry father, we were just …"

But before his son even finished speaking, Dorvar turned away and began chastising the other members of the family. "Why was I not met at the Pass of Rialta as arranged? And where are the other elders? We have much to discuss as a result of my journey."

The inhabitants of the great house on the water were silent – the happy chatter and movement of earlier now gone. Dorvar's younger brother, Elin, spoke. "We all thought you would be entering the pass early in the morning, *as arranged*," he emphasised. "And, so too, the elders didn't expect to see you until tomorrow. Now come, have some hot stew that

Chata has prepared – you must be weary after such a long journey."

Dorvar looked at his sibling and felt his anger draining. Elin always had the knack of bringing him to his senses when he became unreasonably perturbed. He was a fine brother. Were it not for his crippled leg, he could easily have a chance of being accepted as clan leader when Dorvar's days were finally over. The older man paused for a moment, and then smiled as he removed his heavy bear skin coat. "Well, the stew of your wife is what drove me to get here tonight rather than tomorrow." Elin returned the smile, and several girls squealed and clapped their hands – their leader not only commanded respect but could also charm a woman to the point of blushing. Soon, the household was again full of happy noises and activity – but now it was all centred on one person.

Up on the sleeping platform, Bren sat – still staring at his father who was now talking and eating down by the great hearth in the centre of the building. The boy's expression showed a mix of admiration and sadness. "We're fortunate to have such a leader," Pock-face quietly observed. "And you are fortunate to have him as your father."

"Yes," Bren answered absently, lost in his feelings.

"And just think, he will be taking us hunting the day after tomorrow."

This statement shook Bren from his introspection, and caused his eyes to brighten. "Oh yes. My first proper boar hunt where I will be armed – and guided by the best hunter in our clan."

A slight frown formed on the older boy's forehead. "It's strange, but I can't remember you going on other hunts with him ... I mean just to watch ... although I know you must have."

Bren looked defiantly at his cousin. "Well I haven't, and you must know the reason – unless you're an idiot. My father has to look after the needs of both the spirit and the body for all our people. Either one would take up most of a man's time, but he has to do *both*," he repeated. "He just doesn't have time to worry about smaller things. That's what makes him great." He realized that his voice had gotten louder and that Pock-face seemed a little surprised. "Anyway," he said as he playfully threw out his chest and held up one of his 'special' arrows, "the day after tomorrow I shall use one of these on the biggest pig in the forest."

"You mean you're going to kill Fat Gregor?" responded Pock-face with a grin, referring to another boy in the clan. Bren jumped on his cousin again, but this time they rolled among the furry pelts trying to subdue their squeals.

All next morning Bren carried a smile as he went about his chores. While splitting firewood that had come from the nearby Little Forest, he began to sing a hunting song:

"I will stalk you tall reindeer and small hare and wild boar; I will seek you out and spill your blood. And then I will thank you for the food and skins and bones and sinews that you provide. Your death will not be in vain. No creature's death is in vain."

Later in the afternoon he sat with the three other boys who would accompany the men on tomorrow's hunting party. They were at the edge of a large clearing that contained the small stone circle of Chlocht – not exactly a holy place, not anymore at least – but still a place where important meetings and celebrations were held. Bren absentmindedly hummed his song while he watched the men who were inside the circle. He often thought about these stones and the Old Ones who had placed them there so long ago; how they had tried to create a connection with the great powers of the earth and the sky by building these temples. But as time flowed, people found that the great powers had created their own temples – the rivers and forests and lakes and mountains – and that in these were the truly holy places. Just then, Dorvar came striding across the clearing. Bren's roaming thoughts left him, and he stopped his tune as he watched his father enter the circle. The other men stood up and became involved in animated discussion. After some time, Dorvar left with several of the men and hurried back down the path towards Ceann Tull. Bren's friends witnessed this, and as they all turned their eyes towards him – hoping for an explanation, one of the remaining men in the circle made the owl call, which means 'come here now'.

"What's wrong?" Pock-face asked as he ran up to the stones with the others.

"Nothing is wrong," replied the man who had made the call. "We just have to change our plans a little because our party will now be smaller." Bren knew what this meant – and his heart sank. "Dorvar has urgent business with clan leaders from the south; he will not be coming on tomorrow's hunt – and neither will several others." He looked at Bren. "He apologizes and hopes you understand." Bren didn't feel like responding; he simply sat on the grass with his head bowed – wishing that his father had spoken at least a few words to him personally.

"Who will lead us then?" asked Trib, another of the boys. The remaining few men, although reasonable hunters, did not seem eager to take the place of someone of such renown. The uncomfortable silence was broken by Elin, Dorvar's brother.

"I will," he said simply.

※※※※※※※※※※※※※

The forest of Achtar was only a half-day's walk from Ceann Tull, and Pock-face had been grumbling under his breath much of the way. "First he says we won't be using hounds, and now he says we should practise being fast and silent. But look, he can't even walk properly along the track himself," he whispered to the other boys as he scowled at Elin limping up ahead. "How is he going to be able to move quietly through the forest in the afternoon? His leg makes him useless as a hunter."

"That can't be true," Trib replied. "What about all the stories we've heard that describe his feats?"

"The men must make those up so he doesn't feel left out – look at him, he can't hunt if he has to limp like that." He turned to Bren. "What do you think cousin?"

"My father has said that deeds deserve more attention than words – I will wait and see." Pock-face said no more.

As the sun continued to climb in the sky, they reached the temporary encampment where hunting parties from the clan stayed while in the forest. It was close to a stream that descended a gently sloping hill in a series of pools connected by rapids and waterfalls. Because of the sound of the rushing water, Bren could no longer hear the songs of the forest birds amongst the great pines, but in the sky above he caught a glimpse of a golden eagle as it followed the course of the stream looking for prey. A female otter cavorting in a more distant pool with its young saw the eagle too, and Bren knew that it had given a warning cry when he saw the whole family disappear into the banks. The boy closed his eyes and savoured the moment – the water, the trees, the creatures, the sky. One of the men nudged another as they made small repairs to the shelter they would all use this night; he pointed to Bren down at the pool, "he senses the holy," the man said.

"Like his father," his companion replied.

The sun was now well beyond its mid-point in the heavens, not that you could see it very often. Little light was able to get through the dense overcover of pine needles in this part of the forest. Only in the occasional clearings, where there were thickets of heather and bilberry, could the sky be plainly seen. It was one such area that the party was now approaching. Elin was in the lead. Some time ago he had given the signal to be 'most silent'. Since that moment, the leader's limp had seemed to disappear as the group slowly and quietly approached a small thicket near the edge of the clearing. Elin obviously thought that the wild boar he had been tracking might be resting or hiding here. All eyes were now on this man as he stopped and gave the signal to surround the break of matted bushes.

There were eight in the party, a line of four men and four boys, and they quietly forked into two groups in order to carry out the encircling action. There was a slight breeze in the air that they had kept in their faces for most of the afternoon, but because of their manoeuvre some of the party would soon be upwind of the thicket. Bren could feel a mix of fear and excitement enveloping him. He already had the string of his bow set into the nock of a bronze-headed arrow and, as he took almost-noiseless steps, he gently pulled the string back to about a third of its full capacity. Mayflies hovered in the air. In the distance a crested tit called. But all else was quiet.

Bren was in the process of turning his head to look at the others, when suddenly there was an explosion of movement and noise from the thicket. A boar emerged squealing deeply and loudly. It was a huge male, as heavy as a man and with upward-pointing tusks that could rip a person open in an instant. Each of the hunters in the circle was about ten man-heights from the thicket, but the beast covered this distance in little more than a heartbeat – heading straight for Pock-face. The boy bravely stood his ground and attempted to nock an arrow, but he hadn't been properly prepared, and before he could even draw the bow the boar was upon him. He screamed ... and then ... the animal dropped at his feet – a spear protruding from its side.

Boys and men ran shouting to the young hunter who was in the process of slumping to his knees – the boar's snout and tusks only fingers away, its eyes already glazed in death. Two of the men helped Pock-face to his feet; he was obviously shaken but otherwise unharmed. The group crowded around the still-twitching corpse, chattering excitedly. They then stood back in admiration as Elin wrenched his spear from the animal.

"How did you do that?" Trib asked, his eyes wide and his voice high. "It was so fast, yet you dropped him with a spear ... I hope to be a hunter like you ... I ..." The man smiled, and patted the boy's shoulder. He then turned to Pock-face.

"You stood your ground, that was brave," he said calmly.

"And *you* saved my life," Pock-face replied, swallowing heavily and feeling somewhat shameful.

"Not just me," Elin responded. "Roll the beast over."

With the aid of one of the men, Pock-face turned the boar over to its other side. A series of astonished cries leapt from the mouths of the hunters, and they all turned to look at the figure standing a short distance away. In the side of the boar was a broken arrow shaft; its bronze tip had penetrated the beast's heart. Everyone knew from the fletching that it was Bren's.

That night, while the others slept in the small, log lodge – their stomachs full of fresh roast pork – Elin and Bren sat together staring into the flames of the fire that would be kept burning all night.

"You did well today, Bren," the boy's uncle said without turning his head. "You will be a good hunter." The boy nodded, his thoughts seeming to be lost in the glowing dance. "But I think you will also seek other things besides wild game."

Bren turned and faced Elin. "What do you mean?"

"I mean … I have watched you at times, and seen how you study the night sky, and spend time alone by the water or in the woods – you are close to the flow of the world; you are your father's son."

Bren looked back at the flames, and as their reflections played in his eyes, he asked quietly, "And what about my mother, am I her son too?"

Elin showed no surprise at hearing the question, and knew that this was a time for honesty. "Yes you are, Bren." He paused and took a deep breath. "Your mother was not just one of the most beautiful woman I have ever known, but *the* most beautiful," he said, looking at the boy. "And her beauty went well beyond the flesh. At times you would hear her singing as she walked alone along the lakeside tracks – and the birds would seem to sing with her. And on other occasions you would see her chattering with a squirrel as it sat looking at her from a branch, or calling to a beaver as it swam across the lake. Yet she was also a wonderful hunter, outshining many of the men with her prowess. And she was smart; always questioning and putting forward ideas." He sighed. "She was full of joy at being alive – and also close to the flow. But the happiest I ever remember her being was while she carried you in her belly. She called you her 'First Puppy'." He wanted to say more, but stopped when he saw the tears streaming down his nephew's cheeks.

"But it wasn't my fault that she died, was it?" the boy sobbed as he tried to stop the tears with his hands.

Elin's heart went out to his young kin. He leant over and gently embraced him. "No, no it wasn't your fault," he said softly, "you must never think such a thing."

* * * * * * * * * * * *

Most of the trees around the great lake that had always been called the Tull were now in blossom. Even the mighty oaks in the wood above the river that flowed from the lake – and that took the same name – these too were now in flower. It was one of the signs that the ordinary folk used in readying themselves for the spring-birth celebrations. The exact day, of course, was given by Dorvar, because he was the only one in the clan who could read the heavens with such precision. Bren, Trib, and Pock-face were discussing the preparations as they sat against one of the oaks, having just a short time earlier managed to steal honey from a beehive.

"The women will use this to make sweetcakes," Bren smiled. "My mouth becomes wet even as I speak about them – mmm." He closed his eyes and rubbed his stomach.

"And you will get a gift, and be in the honour group," added Pock-face as he spat and blew on one of the bee stings he'd sustained. "I have to wait for another two seasons."

"Well, I can't help it if I was born in spring," Bren replied. "When *your* birth-season comes around, *you* will be in the honour group with all the other autumn-birth folk, and you will get a gift then."

"I want one now," Pock-face replied, grinning as he slowly moved his hand towards the birch-bark-and-wood container that held the honeycomb.

"Be away with you!" cried Trib who had been carrying the container, and who now slapped at the creeping hand. "If you wanted to be a spring-child then your father should have stuck his viper into your mother's hole when the leaves on these oaks were falling."

"I'm sure he did," answered Pock-face as he withdrew his hand. "But he probably pulled it out before it filled her with its milky venom."

Bren laughed, as did the others. It was only recently that he had been taking some interest in such things.

Five days later the celebrations began. The spring birth-season festivities were always bigger than those for the other three seasons. This was partly because the sap of life was rising in all living things during these days – reason enough for joyous dancing and lovemaking. But it was also because the Old Ones had placed great significance on celebrating this period of rebirth. As with many things, the shadowy memories of the Old Ones still lingered with the people of the Tull.

The ceremonial part of the day started in the early hours of the morning – before sunrise. People from the other settlements on and near the great lake had been arriving at Ceann Tull by foot and pony and canoe while the stars were still bright in the heavens. Bren had awoken on six occasions during the night, ready to arise, only to be told by the others that it was not yet time. He was still full of excitement about his gift of a wolf fang that had been solemnly handed to him by his father the previous night. But now everyone in the crannog was busy: women were placing breads and cakes and other delicacies on wicker trays, girls were adorning themselves with garlands of flowers, and men were taking down the carcasses of game that had been hung from roof beams some days earlier. Outside, the visitors and the folk of the settlement – maybe as many as a hundred and fifty – were gathered at the shore-end of the crannog's causeway. They too had items of food and drink, including animals to be slaughtered later. Soon, they would be joined by most of the crannog's occupants, and then, together, they would await the arrival of Dorvar who would lead them to the stone circle of Chlocht.

The eastern sky was slowly changing from indigo to blue when the people saw Dorvar appear on that part of the crannog's balcony that could be seen from the shore. During the noise and movement of others in the lake-house, he had been standing on the farthest-out part of the balcony, silently conversing with the waters of the Tull and the mountains beyond, asking that they help his people in this season and that they give their particular blessings to those who were spring-born. The loss he had suffered eleven years earlier was always with him, especially at this time. He remembered with great sadness how he had been communing with the same waters and the same mountains just prior to the death of his dear young wife, Morann, and how they had given no warning of the tragedy that was about to befall him. But this had never caused him to lose faith in their power and importance. They watched and they provided, but they rarely foretold events, even to those who could speak with them. And now he strode across the causeway, wearing his priestly apparel of a beaver-fur coat, a silver neck-chain, and the ancient bear-skull mask of his clan's forefathers.

Bren was standing with the other spring-born as they waited together on the lakeside. They would be the first to follow Dorvar to the stone circle; and as the leader-priest walked past, his young son stood tall and fingered the wolf fang that now hung from a thong around his neck.

During the procession, people spoke quietly, if at all, understanding that this was a time for solemnity. When they arrived at the clearing they were joined by the men and women who had already been there for some time preparing the faggots for the roasting fires. Dorvar stood at the edge of the stone circle, with the thirty or so spring-birth celebrants – the honour group – sitting on the grass in front of him. The oldest was a leathery-faced, white-haired woman from a settlement on the northern banks of the Tull; the youngest, a baby born only days earlier – now being suckled by its mother.

When the rest of the throng finished placing on the grass the multitude of items they'd been carrying, and were themselves seated or kneeling, the leader-priest raised his hands and began to speak in a loud, deep voice. He spoke about the heavens and the earth, and how the mountains and rivers and lakes and forests and rocks were their older children, with people and animals being the younger siblings who depended on each other through death for survival. He reminded those gathered that the seasons were also offspring of this mystical marriage, and that in celebrating the birth of human children each season, the people were also honouring the wonder of creation – of all things.

And then he began to dance. It was the ancient Dance of the World, and he sang the old words that accompanied it as he shook and twisted his body and stomped his feet in movements that had been passed down through his people since the time that they first came to the Tull.

Bren was one of the first to his feet to copy the movements of his father. Then others did the same. Soon, as many as half the throng were bending and swaying with their arms partly raised and their voices singing in rough unison – the others clapped their hands in rhythm and made shrill shouts of encouragement. Then the tempo increased – slowly at first – and Bren could feel the blood rushing through the veins in his head. As the clapping got faster, he spun his body round with greater speed, and saw the swirling faces and colours in front of him begin to merge into patterns that were both intricate and beautiful. And just when it seemed that the rhythm had increased to the point of being one continuous roar, with the patterns beginning to break up to reveal something else, the clapping suddenly stopped – and the people let out a mighty shout. Bren fell to the ground but the world continued to spin. The strange, flowing forms returned for a short time, and then separated into images of the surrounding trees and the faces of his friends. He felt relaxed but slightly nauseous.

"Did you get beyond the patterns?" Pock-face asked as he pulled his cousin to his feet.

"No, I never do," Bren replied. "What about you?"

"I've never even seen the patterns." Pock-face replied.

"That's because you're too busy looking at the girls as they spin," interrupted Trib who had just walked over to the pair.

All around, folk were now laughing and starting to drink from bladders and cups that held beverages made from fermented berries and leaves. Animal carcasses that had been skewered with hardwood poles waited to be placed above fires. These were already burning ferociously but would soon settle down to the required low, intense heat of burning coals.

Bren and his two companions wandered around the clearing enjoying the merriment. Already, groups of girls were performing the dances they had practised together for many days earlier; the sweet scent of the flowers in their hair and the revealing cut of their garments attracting many young males – and a number of the older ones. Winks and nods and other signs were being passed between the dancers and the observers. Later on, men would show their abilities in contests of strength and prowess with weapons of the hunt, and this time it would be the women who watched. In the afternoon, when the watching and the parading and the flirting was to be followed by sitting and talking and eating together, couples would disappear from the clearing into the many close-by hiding places where a man and a woman – or a boy and a girl – might explore each other's bodies and give vent to the emotions and promises of pleasure that had been welling up inside them all day.

"Hey, there goes Fat Gregor with that girl from the river people," said Trib as he squinted his grey eyes in the direction of the couple who were walking towards the woods some distance away.

Pock-face, who was lying on his back on the grass with a stomach full of meat and sweetcake, turned his head in the direction of the couple. "You have the eyes of a mole," he replied. "That's not Fat Gregor."

"I think it is," Bren said as he sat up, still holding a half-eaten roasted rib of venison.

Pock-face scrambled to his feet and stared harder. "It *is* Fat Gregor – come on, we must go and watch."

Bren was intrigued but he had noticed a young girl of about his age quietly edging towards him and his friends for some time, and he was taken by her long, plaited fair hair and her brown eyes. 'Too young, no breasts,' Pock-face had said when his cousin had surreptitiously pointed her out. "You go," Bren now responded, "I want to finish eating."

The other two needed little encouragement. "We'll tell you if he crushes her," Pock-face whispered loudly as he ran off. "And I still think you're like a mole," he teasingly called to Trib who was close behind.

Bren chuckled. His cousin reminded him of a playful otter. He was about to bite into the roast meat in his hand when he realized that the girl who had been unobtrusively moving closer was now right next to him.

"I see you enjoy eating," she said confidently, and then held out a small wooden bowl containing what looked like rough, rounded duck eggs. "Would you like to try one of these?"

At first Bren didn't look down at what she was offering – he couldn't pull his gaze away from her face. She was even prettier up close than when he had first observed her from some distance away. He saw that her eyes were an unusual light brown and that they were slightly slanted, and long –

like the end leaf on a rowan twig. When she saw that he was staring, some of her confidence seemed to leave her and she lowered her head slightly – but smiled broadly. Bren felt his cheeks becoming warm – and his breath almost left him.

"I call them egg-cakes," she said softly. "They're made from crushed wild grass grains and herbs and honey."

The softness of her voice made Bren feel like he was on the verge of floating off the ground – like a dandelion seed about to be carried off by a wisp of a breeze. But he tried to remain sensible. "And eggs, I suppose," he added.

"No, there are no eggs. I only give them that name because of the shape I make them."

He noticed that she pronounced some words differently to most other people – a little like the wandering toolmaker who had stayed with them for a while during the winter just past. "You're not from the Tull are you?" he asked as he took one of the cakes and dropped the roast rib on the grass.

The girl looked up and, still smiling, met his wide-eyed stare. "I am from a place called Chonardt, far away – beyond the Grey Mountains," she pointed to the north. "But I am staying with the family of my mother's sister down at Sheelog – near where the river leaves the lake." She brushed a tress of her golden hair from her face. "My name is Bodar."

Bren swallowed heavily. "I am Bren … of the Tull," he added.

She giggled. "I know," she said.

He was about to ask more of her when the whole clearing was filled with the scream of a boy. Instinctively, they both looked down towards the woods to see Trib running like a pine marten up the slope towards them. Close behind was Fat Gregor with a branch almost big enough to be a war club. At the edge of the wood was Pock-face, limping heavily. People started to roar with laughter but Trib's face was filled with terror and, as he came closer, Bren could see that he had blood streaming from his nose. The young crannog dweller quickly got to his feet and ran towards his friend, and then planted himself like a risen bear between black-haired Trib and his enraged, red-headed pursuer.

"It's enough," he called as he wondered whether this was in fact a smart thing to be doing. It seemed to surprise Fat Gregor who didn't stop but did slow down.

"I'll kill him," the large lad of fourteen summers said. "And I'll kill you if you get in the way."

Bren quickly turned his head and saw that Trib was now cowering behind him, fresh blood still dropping from his nose. When he turned back, the boy who had the reputation of one who could not control his temper was upon him, the small log in his hands raised. He swung the log in an awkward sideways action while still lumbering forward. "I warned you," he yelled.

Bren stepped backward and felt the brush of a leaf as it swept across his face. He didn't pause. While his opponent was still off-balance from the swing, the leader-priest's son took a step forward and kicked the enraged boy in the groin – with some force.

Fat Gregor dropped his weapon and fell to the ground groaning. "Aah, Aah," he kept repeating as he lay on his side with his knees pulled up to his large belly.

Trib walked over to Bren and they both looked down at the writhing fat boy. "I thought he was going to kill me," Trib said as he kicked the branch away.

"He might have, had he caught you," Bren replied. "But I think you should apologize for whatever you did – just so he doesn't hold any dark thoughts towards you. I like Gregor," he added.

By this time Pock-face had hobbled up to the scene of the short-lived encounter, and a number of the other people had wandered over – several offering words of admiration to Bren. "I saw what you did!" the boy with scars said excitedly, "and so did everybody else. You are going to be a great warrior."

"I'm not sure I want to be a warrior," Bren replied as he looked around at the nearby faces, hoping to see Bodar. But she was gone.

Chapter 2

Storytellers usually came to settlements like Ceann Tull in the early days of winter – before the snows closed the passes. In this way it was more likely that they would be able to find food and shelter in an area for the whole season. In return they were expected to fill the cold nights with tales and news from faraway places, and to repeat favourite stories and legends from long ago.

They would help in other ways too, and become part of the communities that hosted them during those dreary, dark months. But sometimes they passed through in other seasons – only staying for a night or two before moving on to their next destination. In this way they carried their verbal wares – including memorized messages – across the breadth of the land. It was one such storyteller who now sat in the middle of the cleared area of the settlement.

All around were the small, circular, cone-roofed dwellings of the people of Ceann Tull. At the water's edge was the start of the wooden causeway that led out above the lake to the crannog which sat on its array of alder-log posts like the giant progenitor of all the other buildings. Bren was lost in thought as he stared across at his home. Of course he usually took it for granted, but sometimes – like now, while there was still light in the summer sky – he would gaze at its features and try to imagine the massive effort that the clan must have put into its construction all those years ago. It was a fitting monument to their belief in the holiness of watery places and, therefore, an appropriate residence for Dorvar, their spiritual guide, and his family. The young man of sixteen springs was continuing with such thoughts when a sharp jab in the ribs by Pock-face suddenly brought him out of his reverie.

"Bren, he's about to begin, stop thinking about that girl."

"What girl?" Bren responded as he elbowed his friend's hand away – mild annoyance on his face.

"I don't know, but whenever I'm wandering in my head like you just were it's usually with a girl who wants my body."

"Is she that blind girl from across the lake?" interjected Trib, who was sitting behind the other two. Pock-face made a half-hearted attempt to slap his friend, and the three began to laugh, only to be quickly chastised by the other forty or so listeners.

The man at the centre of the gathering was ugly. He had a large wart on the side of his face that competed with his big nose for an observer's attention, and his dark, bushy eyebrows merged together on his lower forehead so that they looked like a single strip of wool from a black sheep. What was left of the hair on his head was cut short in a ragged fashion, and beneath it the skin on his face was brown and wrinkled – like a hide that had been left in a tanning pit for too long. But when he spoke, his voice was loud and deep and full of expression, with an accent that intrigued.

"First I will deliver to you a tale of bravery …"

"Yes!" cried the young men and boys.

"… and of love," he continued.

"Yes!" called the girls and women as they excitedly clapped their hands together.

"And after this, I will pass on to you descriptions of what I have seen in recent times in other places – of events and happenings that may be of interest to you." At this, the older folk nodded sagely, for they knew that great changes were occurring in many regions. But for now they would be just as pleased as the younger members of the audience to hear what would probably be a story they had heard many times before – enjoying it as much now as when it was first told to them. Then he began.

"Far, far south of here, in the land where tin is mined for the making of bronze, there lived a clan leader who had a beautiful daughter called Toora. Her hair was long and as yellow as the flowers of the broom, and her eyes light and brown like the last acorns to fall from the oak."

Already, he had caused the dream-thoughts of his listeners to flow. Some closed their eyes so to better see Toora, while others sat with their jaws slightly dropped, their gazes intent. The effect on Bren was different. The accent of the storyteller, together with his description of the mythical daughter, made the young Tull man think of Bodar, the girl he had met at a spring-birth celebration some years ago – and who he had never seen again.

The story continued as the twinkling points of light in the summer sky revolved around the great Star of the North. There were confrontations between good and evil, a monster bigger than an ox who changed sides, and a warrior called Timot who finally managed to save Toora from the lecherous advances of her captors.

When the storyteller ended the fable, there was a brief pause. As with all his listeners, the people of Ceann Tull needed a moment for their thoughts to race back from the world of tales to the world in which they walked. Then there was a communal sigh, followed by the slow, appreciative clapping of hands on thighs. Bren turned to his friends – inspired.

"I must travel to distant places ... and soon. There are so many adventures to be had, so many things to be seen. And I want to find the answers to all the questions that have visited themselves upon me."

"What sort of questions?" asked Pock-face, not sure whether to follow his cousin with his excitement.

"Like ... is there a purpose for me in this life? Has something already been planned by the great powers of the world – something that will be revealed to me as the years unfold? Or will I create my own purpose entirely, there being no plan? Or will it be a mix, where I will usually walk my own path but sometimes be helped or diverted along the way by the great powers?"

"You've been drinking the fermented blaeberry juice again haven't you?" asked Pock-face, a smile now competing with his earlier look of concern.

Bren narrowed his eyes and sucked in air through a corner of his mouth as he stared at his cousin, trying to be annoyed but finding it difficult.

"... and now, word from the west coast where I have dwelt these last months," the storyteller was saying. "The most important news concerns the coming of more Kelti from the south and from across the waters of the great ocean. Their language is not unlike ours, and some have begun to marry into our families. But many people fear their blood-hungry ways." The audience was silent and attentive; such news was of concern to all members. The storyteller continued. "This shows itself in the way they settle disagreements, and especially in their religious ceremonies – which can involve the sacrifice of fellow humans to their gods. This I have seen with my own eyes ... men, women ... children ..." He trailed off as he saw the look of concern on the faces of some of the young mothers holding infants. He knew that such practices were abhorrent to most clans in this part of the land. Many faces looked towards Dorvar who had been sitting in the shadows to one side. He stood and spoke.

"We must hear more of these things," he said to his people, "so we are prepared for any Kelti who may one day come among us. Already, for many years, we have traded goods that they and their brethren in far-off lands have made." He drew his fine bronze dagger and held it up as an example. "And we have adopted some of their ways as told to us by men like the storyteller." This time he pointed to a young man nearby whose injured arm was wrapped with a poultice made from a combination of herbs and honey that everyone knew as the 'Kelti mix'. "But we must not make the mistake of accepting *everything* that these people produce or use or do. Our ancestors have left us many skills and many truths. We will always be willing to learn from others, but we must never forget who we are – the people of the Tull. Now let us hear more from the storyteller."

With this, he sat down. The older folk nodded in agreement, and many of the women whispered words of admiration to each other. The son of the leader-priest took a deep breath. His chest swelled. He was proud of his father and proud of his people.

✶✶✶✶✶✶✶✶✶✶✶✶✶

Bren was disappointed when Pock-face told him that he could no longer come hunting. Together with Trib, the two cousins had planned this day on the night when the storyteller had enthralled all the people with his tales and his news. The youths were going to not only hunt but also talk of how they might convince their parents that a journey by the three to distant regions would somehow benefit the whole clan. But now the eldest member of their group was being forced to fulfill an earlier (and forgotten) promise to help with the making of a new wooden ard for ploughing the family fields. Bren was ready to call off the hunt – it was only going to be for the day anyway. However, Trib was still keen, mainly because he had a younger relative visiting him from a far-off settlement who he suggested could take Pock-face's place. He also wanted the opportunity to show off his hunting skills to the boy. 'We can talk of our plans for adventure on another day,' he had said. 'My arrows are sharp and I have permission to be away for the day – as do you – so let us take the opportunity.' Bren had admired his friend's logic, so he, Trib, and the boy from the north, whose name was Natach, had begun their walk to the nearby open woodland that eventually turned into the forest of Drumm.

"What shall we find here do you think?" Natach whispered excitedly as they crossed the large clearing that was a common entry point to this part of the forest. Bren could see that the boy was several years younger than Trib and himself, and that he didn't seem to have a lot of experience at hunting. But then he realized that he too had probably given a similar impression when the same age.

"At this time of year there will be fat capercaillie here, feeding and hiding in the understorey of heather and blaeberry. I think they are the tastiest of birds, but the big males will sometimes charge you if you're not careful. And we shouldn't stray too close to the forest," Bren added as an afterthought.

"Why not?" asked Natach, his eyes wide.

"Wolves, bears, and lynx," Trib whispered before Bren could reply.

Shortly afterwards, as they carefully approached a cluster of heather bushes where Trib had thought he saw movement, a red deer bolted and headed up the slope for the forest.

"It was a hind," called Bren from one side of the heather, "There is likely a calf in here somewhere." But as he spoke, he watched in amazement as Natach ran off after the hind. "No, Natach, come back!" he called.

"Don't worry," Trib said as they both watched the boy disappear into the dark green sweep of giant pines. "He'll soon see that his chase is pointless."

Bren felt uncomfortable, and he continued to stare up at the forest while his friend used a stick to push apart the bushes. "If there is a calf in here then of course we won't take it, but I wouldn't mind seeing how old it is."

Bren was about to help, when both young men heard a high-pitched scream. It came from the forest, and it carried the fearful message of mortal danger. Then Natach appeared. He had dropped his bow, and was running for his life towards them – pursued by an enormous brown bear. Trib's first reaction was to run but he glanced across at Bren who was already pulling back on his bowstring, an arrow ready to be sent forth. The dark haired youth felt ashamed, and decided to do the same. But before the beast came within range, Natach tripped and fell, his screams now louder as he squirmed on the ground. He tried to scramble to his feet but the bear was upon him. Bren watched in horror as the animal ripped open the terrified boy's chest with a single swipe of its flint-sharp claws. A sickening, liquid groan came from the poor lad's mouth and then the bear, still ripping at him with its claws, buried its muzzle in the red-soaked cavity where the boy's heart, after fourteen years of life, now ceased to beat.

All this happened in the time that it took Bren to draw in two deep breaths of the summer air. But already he was cautiously running towards the scene of the carnage, with an arrow ready to loose. Trib, however, overcome with rage and remorse, was running faster and was clearly not thinking of his own safety. Although already close to the bear, he continued onward – shouting incomprehensible words of abuse. He loosed an arrow while still moving but in his agitated state he did not take clear aim and it missed. Now the bear reacted. As Trib began to make sense of his situation and frantically tried to set another arrow, the animal left Natach's ravaged body and charged at the boy's fumbling dark-haired relative. This time it used its huge paws to push its victim to the ground and then bit at his neck with its already-blood-stained teeth. Then it roared – not in triumph but in pain. Stepping back from Trib, the bear turned its head, and saw the shaft of an arrow protruding from its huge, muscular hindquarters. Spying Bren, it made a sudden movement and another arrow, intended for its heart, passed through its nose. There was a deep, awful cry of agony and the animal turned and ran for the forest, the sharp edge of a third arrow opening the flesh across its back.

Bren ran to his friend. 'Please be alive,' he thought to himself as he approached the quivering form lying on its back, legs bent unnaturally to one side. "Trib, Trib," he cried as he looked down. The battered youth's eyes were wide open and still full of terror. And he seemed to be trying to speak, yet no sound came from his moving lips. There were terrible flesh wounds on his face and head but it was the blood spurting from the side of his neck that Bren knew he must deal with first. Now, all emotion seemed to leave him as he concentrated on how to save the life of his companion.

"Give me your hand, Trib," he said gently as he took hold of his friend's shaking right hand. "Press your fingers into your neck here … no, press harder." Trib seemed to understand, and as he pressed into his carotid artery the fine stream of blood that shot out of his neck with each heartbeat seemed to stop. But the lad was still bleeding from other wounds – they needed to be bathed. Bren pulled off his tunic and quickly looked about for the bladder of water that he'd given to Trib at the start of their journey. But it was nowhere to be seen. Then he remembered that Trib had ordered his younger relative to carry it only a short while ago. He blinked, surprised that he had momentarily forgotten about Natach. From what he'd seen, the boy was surely dead; it was the main reason why he had run to his friend first.

Now he dashed over to the site of the first attack – and saw that his assumption had been right. Natach's face was also covered with deep gashes, but the bear's claws and teeth had shred his upper garments, and there was a hole in his chest about the size of a small dish. Broken ribs stuck out of the opening at odd angles and Bren could see sections of the lad's partly chewed liver and other organs in the dark-brown mass. There was no life in the body. The water bladder was lying a short distance away, towards the forest. Bren thought

Natach must have dropped it from his shoulder as he tried to run from the bear, although he hadn't noticed at the time. But it was of no use. The wooden stopper at the end of the bladder had come out and its contents had spilled onto the grass. Regardless, he quickly picked up the empty container and rushed back to his friend.

Trib still had his fingers pressed into his neck, and he had somehow managed to straighten his legs. However, blood continued to trickle from his slashed flesh, and as Bren knelt down beside him he summoned his strength and was able to speak – just barely. "Water," he said through lips that were stained and dry. "Water."

Bren tried to collect as much of his own saliva as possible into his mouth, and then spat it onto the tunic in his hand, and proceeded to wipe what seemed to be the worst of Trib's face wounds. But it did little good, and he saw that fresh blood was oozing from under his friend's fingers on his neck, and that his tongue was thick and dry in his now-open mouth. 'I must get water,' he desperately thought to himself.

"Trib, I am going to run to the river – it's not too far – I must get water for you." A new wave of panic swept over Trib's bloodied face and he weakly tried to grip his friend's arm with his free hand. His swollen tongue and dry mouth wouldn't allow words to form properly but Bren understood. "The bear will not return, I promise you, and I will be gone for only a short time." He was certain about the bear but he knew there was the possibility of other meat-hungry beasts catching the scent of death and coming with the intention of feeding. He looked down at the face that he'd known for so many years. Should he pick up Trib right now and try to carry him back to Ceann Tull, or to the river? Or should he hurry to the river alone, collect water, and bring it back? He looked at the mountains, and in his mind asked for guidance. Then he stared back down at Trib, and decided. It would not be good to move his friend right now. Instead, he would go to the river and get water.

Before rushing off, he took Trib's knife from its leather scabbard and placed it in the lad's hand. He then gave a few words of reassurance and ran off towards the mighty Tull.

The closest track to the river was some distance away so Bren decided to head through the heavily wooded area at the foot of the slope they had been walking along. This area was known as Endachni. It was not considered part of the forest of Drumm for the trees were not conifers but mainly downy birch. Oaks were also here, and would one day eliminate their pioneering brethren. Closer to the river, willow and hazel still dominated. A hare ran from a clump of bracken as Bren careered through the woods. People rarely came here because of old stories about monsters and evil magic, but he cared not about such things now.

He estimated that he was about halfway to the river, and had just run down a steep embankment, when he noticed a peculiarly green patch of grass over to his left. Without thinking, he diverted from the straight-line route he was taking and ran towards the patch. Suddenly, his feet sunk into mud and then into water. 'A spring!' he thought. Looking around, he observed that its source seemed to be back towards the embankment, so he took several sloshing steps in that direction, and cursed as his bare chest was stroked by the leaves of the tall stinging nettle plants that crossed his path. Then he stopped, surprised. Ahead, was the source of the water. It was not seepage from the side of the steep slope as he had expected, but a small, deep pool surrounded by several layers of white, moss-covered stones. It was a well; and Bren marvelled at the fact that there were no trails leading to it and that he had never heard talk of it among his people.

He stared at the dark circle of water and watched a fallen birch leaf being carried by the trickle that flowed over one of the stones and into the tiny, short-lived streamlet beyond. The puff of a solitary breeze gently swept over his skin, and for several moments he stood transfixed, feeling something strange and wonderful about this place. Then he blinked, shook his head, and quickly plunged the bladder into the well, manipulating its leathery sides so that it sucked in a quantity of the cool water. He also drank several handfuls himself and without further pause bounded back towards the forest of Drumm. Far above, circling redpolls sang in their distinctive high-pitched trill.

A short time later, Bren was running up the slope to where his friend lay. Several buzzards were sitting in the branches of nearby trees. 'Please be alive,' he thought for the second time of the day. When he knelt down next to Trib a shudder passed through his body. The young man's tongue had swollen more and was now hanging from between his purple lips. His eyes were closed and his hand had fallen from his neck. Little fresh blood seemed to be flowing from his wounds but Bren wasn't sure whether this was good or bad. "Trib," he called softly, but his friend's eyes stayed shut. "Oh Trib, don't die," he said as he lifted the youth's head and poured a small amount of water into his mouth. At first nothing happened but then the enlarged tongue moved, so Bren squeezed out a little more water. This time, Trib swallowed, and then his eyes opened. "That's it, have some more," Bren said as he lifted his friend's head higher. He let Trib take several mouthfuls before pouring some of the bladder's contents onto the now bloodied tunic, which he then used to wipe his friend's face.

Bees buzzed nearby, and a capercaillie called from the woods, but it was a different sound – the baying of a hound – that made Bren suddenly look up. Further down the slope, on the track that he and his companions had used earlier, there appeared four men with as many dogs – he recognised them as being from Ceann Tull. He stood and waved his hands. "Here, here, we need help!" he shouted.

※※※※※※※※※※※※

Back at the settlement, the two men carrying the makeshift stretcher lowered Trib while others lifted him onto his bed of hide-covered bracken. Bren stood close-by, glad that he had insisted on using the hounds' rope leashes to lash together branches for carrying his friend rather than flinging him over the shoulder of the strongest man, as the others had wanted to do. Trib had slipped in and out of consciousness during the journey, and Bren had continued to wipe the youth's face with water from the well – and had given him sips of the cool liquid when the carriers had paused. His bleeding had stopped and he was now sleeping. But had he been curled over the collarbone of Big Godin as they hastened back to the settlement, Bren was sure that his friend would have died.

Three days later, the people of Ceann Tull, and his distraught family who had travelled day and night to attend, bid Natach his last farewell. He had already left this world, of course – shortly after the bear had ripped open his heart. But his body had to be commended back into the great cycle, and those who still lived needed to have a time they could look back on when they had collectively said their final goodbye to one of their own. Bren had been prepared to accompany the body, in its wrapping of birch sticks, to Natach's settlement at the foot of the northern mountains. But the messenger who had been sent with the sad news had returned – exhausted – saying that the boy's family were following and that they had decided to have the ceremony at the Tull because of the lake's importance in regard to things of the spirit.

Dorvar stood in the clearing. Above him was the stone circle of Chlocht. He had spent the entire night at a secret place in the nearby woods; dancing and chanting whilst wearing the ancient bear-skull mask and, eventually, communing with entities of much greater powers than those possessed by men. Now, he looked down at the bundle of tied-together sticks in front of him, and then at the crowd of people a little further beyond. He still hadn't fully recovered from his mystical encounters of the previous night, but this, he understood, was a good thing.

"My people, I have heard the voices of the mountains and the forests, and creatures large and small have spoken with me. All tell me that the one we knew as Natach, whose body lies before me, has moved on to other realms. He has successfully embarked on the wondrous adventure, the mysteries of which we cannot know until our own time comes. And now, to aid him on his journey we shall return his body to the great cycle."

The boy's mother and sisters began to wail – the men folk shedding tears silently, as is expected. Bren saw his father give the pre-arranged signal, so he and three other young men stepped forward and lifted up the bundle. Despite the fragrant herbs and flowers that the women had placed inside, the body was beginning to stink, but it did not cause the four carriers to hurry; they understood the importance of keeping a slow, solemn pace as they walked toward the Tull.

At the designated place in the shallows sat a number of canoes, two of them having been lashed to either side of a small wooden platform. Bren and his companions placed their load on this platform. Natach's parents then tied a circular stone with a hole through its middle around the bundle with a strong piece of heather rope. Others followed, doing the same – the hulls of the two canoes sinking slightly from the added weight. When no more people came forward, Dorvar motioned to Bren that he should take a paddle and sit in one of the platform canoes while he, himself, proceeded to sit in the other. They were then gently pushed out from the bank by the strong hands of Pock-face and Fat Gregor. More canoes followed. No one spoke.

Midway across the Tull, where the crannog could be seen in one direction and the peaks of the sacred mountains in the other, Dorvar held up his hand and everyone stopped paddling. There was little wind this day so the twelve or so canoes barely moved – on other days it could be much different. The small flotilla waited for some time – Bren knew from previous experience that his father was waiting for a sign. Then it came. An osprey, eager to catch a fish for its nestlings, swooped down from the sky and skimmed the water with its open talons. Moments later it was winging its way back up into the blueness, a squirming brown trout in its grip.

Dovar slowly turned his head, looking first at the people in the canoes, and then at the largest of the summits in the northwest. "We arose from the waters of the world, and it is the essence that sustains all living things. So it is fitting that we offer the bodies of those we love and respect back to these, the sacred waters of the Tull." He then leaned over and took hold of a rope on the side of the birch-stick bundle and indicated to Bren that he should do the same from the other side of the platform.

The leader-priest looked across at the two large canoes holding Natach's family members – the boy's mother held her hand to her mouth in anticipation – and then he spoke in a loud and powerful voice. "Natach of Prenor, we return your body to the great cycle, and we wish you well on your journey." Bren understood the meaning of the silent nod his father gave, and both men heaved the body backward off the platform and watched it quickly sink from view under the weight of the many, holed stones.

Saddened cries went out from a number of women and girls in the canoes. And while bubbles still rose from the bundle as it descended to the lake's bottom, people called 'goodbye' and 'we shall remember you' and other utterances of the last farewell. Bren had hardly known Natach but tears now ran down the young man's face as he called out the boy's name and remembered the horror of only a few days past. Despite the teachings of his father and others who were considered knowledgeable about the ways of the world, he could not come to terms with the idea of death – it was outrageous, violent, and full of sadness. He had had it explained to him many times, and he could see the wisdom of what he'd been told. But deep inside it felt wrong. There was something bad about death, and he began to cry openly – as did many of the others.

Later, on shore, he stood and watched the last of the canoes – the one with Natach's mother and father – as it was slowly paddled from where their son's body had been offered to the lake. They had waited at the spot for some time after the other dugouts had left, hesitant about leaving. But now they too returned to the shore. And, as the sun gave its final kiss to the land, a flock of geese high in the sky passed over the vessel, their honking signalling to all those below that this day of sadness was ending.

Bren felt weary but he knew he must now see Trib, to confirm that his friend was still recovering – as he had appeared to be doing since being brought back to the settlement. But it was also to reassure himself that death had, for the time being at least, paused in its dreadful dance amongst the people he knew.

Trib was slumbering when Bren arrived at his bedside. The injured youth was in a specially petitioned-off section of the crannog's sleeping area. Bren had asked that this be allowed, and Dorvar had immediately agreed – both knowing that the spiritual power of the building could assist in the recovery of those who were unwell. The youth's breathing was slow and steady, and he now had some colour in those parts of his face that were visible between the poultices that the women had just recently changed. Bren simply sat and watched and marvelled. Only days ago, this friend lay in a pool of his own blood, seemingly destined to depart the world. Despite the care of those who carried Trib home, Bren had doubted that he would survive the journey. But now he slept peacefully, his wounds healing with a haste that several had commented on. As Bren thought on these things, he heard the rungs of the ladder creak and he turned to see the grey-haired head of Dorvar rising towards the sleeping platform. The young man quickly realized that, except for the sleeping Trib, he was about to be alone with his father – a rare happening.

"How is he?" the leader-priest asked.

"He sleeps, but he continues to recover," Bren replied, briefly engaging the eyes of his father and then quickly looking back at his friend.

Dorvar sat quietly and appeared to concentrate on Trib's breathing. Bren was about to speak when his father turned to him. "I have come here each morning and evening when Vana and the others have changed the dressings on his wounds," the older man said. "And I have been surprised at how fast he is healing – in truth, that he is healing at all."

"Trib has always been hardy, and the power of the crannog is most likely helping," Bren replied forthrightly, but then lowered his head a little as he realized his words may have appeared arrogant to a man of far greater wisdom and experience than he.

"These things are true my son," Dorvar responded, obviously not affronted, "but on the day of the attack, when he was brought back here, his wounds were already clean and the healing – although small – was already evident. It was strange, so soon after the event. I have not seen its like before – nor has Vana, and she has tended many more wounds than I."

Bren nodded, and then recalled the bloody scene that had confronted him when he had run up to Trib. "When I first saw him, I thought he might soon die. And after I returned with water I was more certain of it – I think he already had taken several steps away from our world. But the water seemed to revive him. The more I think about it, the more I am certain that this is what brought him back to us."

Dorvar listened intently to his son. "Tell me again about the spring you found," he said.

Bren had described the events of that awful day to several groups and individuals on a number of occasions, but each time when describing his race to get water for his dying friend, he had simply said he came upon a spring some way from the river. He had not dwelt on it, and had not said anything about the sense of strangeness and beauty that had briefly enveloped him whilst there. But now, sitting quietly with his father – although he rarely had the opportunity to share anything of a personal nature with the man – he felt he could speak more about the interlude.

"To begin with, father," he said as he looked out across the sleeping platform, seeing within his mind the embankment and the flowers and the trees, "it wasn't simply a spring, but a well." Dorvar raised an eyebrow but didn't say a word, knowing that his son was in a state of deep reminiscence that should not be interrupted.

Bren gave a full account of his finding of the well – not just its location and a description of its surroundings, of the white rocks enclosing it and the nettles hiding it from easy view – but of how he had felt great wonder and, somewise, even a connection with it. He struggled for words that might give meaning to his experience.

"Did it feel holy to you, Bren?" Dorvar asked.

"Yes, that's it," the young man responded with relief. "It was … is a holy place. I know there are many holy places in our land – the lakes, the rivers, the groves … and I have felt their sacredness … But this was different, it was stronger and more personal – as if something was reaching out to touch me in a most beautiful way. Yet it was so brief – I had to get back to Trib. It was …" He trailed off as he closed his eyes and recaptured a little of what he had felt that day. It was the first time since then that he had thought so deeply about his discovery of the well.

He felt a touch on his shoulder, and opened his eyes. Dorvar slowly withdrew his hand and studied his son's face for a short while before speaking. "I believe you have found the holy well spoken of by my grandfather, Fion. He described it to me many years ago when he was old and I was young. I remember him telling me one night shortly before he died that there was a well – a holy well – that he and a friend had come across as youths during a search for beehives. Soon after, he went south and was injured in the great battle of Cronamor. His friend was killed there. When he returned, his mind was confused and his body broken. He recovered partly – but never again would he walk more than a short distance from the settlement. He couldn't tell me the exact location of the well but he said it must have been from the time of the Old Ones because who else would have placed the white stones about its rim? I searched for it on several occasions when I was a youth but never found it – I was looking further east than Endachni. After a while I decided that it was a dream or a confusion of places that Fion had described, and that there was no well."

"This one is real," Bren said softly.

"I know," his father responded reassuringly. "And I believe it is of great importance to you Bren. What you have described to me is an awareness, a connection. It is as if a giant, invisible eagle – whose existence you never even suspected – has decided to softly brush your face with her wings. This holy well at Endachni has spoken to you, and you have heard its voice. Even more, it would appear as though it has also provided you with a gift of its power – to heal your friend."

Bren's eyes widened as the significance of Dorvar's words became clear. "So what should I do father?" the young man asked.

"First you must go back to the well and offer your thanks for its gift – and you should spend time there, alone. It will now be your special holy place. Next, you must determine whether the well wants its presence made known to others."

"How will I do that?"

"Listen and watch – it will let you know one way or the other."

Just then Trib stirred and made a grunting noise; a moment later he opened his eyes.

"Is that you Bren?" he asked in a soft voice. His friend leaned closer.

"Yes, it's me, Trib. How do you feel?"

The injured youth stared up at the rafters and took a deep breath; then a smile flickered across his face. "Hungry," he said, obviously pleased that he felt this way.

"Hear that, father, he must be much better …" Bren said as he turned his head. But Dorvar was gone, his large form already stepping from the ladder onto the main floor of the crannog.

That night, as Bren slept, a dream presented itself to him. He found himself wandering through a forest of birch and oak. It was light but the sun had not yet quite risen over the distant hills. He listened to the early birdsong – redstarts and warblers – and then he heard human voices, people singing. He walked further and the singing became louder. Then he saw them – all along an embankment and down at its bottom, there were hundreds of people swaying backwards and forwards as they sang. And at their centre was the well. A woman was on her knees and dipping her head in the water. When she stood, with the water running down her face, she smiled and cried out, 'I no longer feel pain – bless this well and bless Bren for telling us about it.'

Bren awoke earlier than usual in the morning, and he knew what he must do.

Chapter 3

James usually liked Fridays, but this one didn't seem to like him – or anyone else in his grade for that matter. The day had started happily enough: a new joke about copulating dogs being told in the boys' area of the schoolyard, Matthew Hendriksen's big jar of huntsman spiders being shown around, and the record monitor – Charlie Beaumont – putting on Buddy Holly's version of 'Not Fade Away' at the end of morning assembly instead of the usual marching-in music (with everyone knowing that the position of record monitor would be vacant next Monday). A good beginning to the day, James thought.

But then it started to rain, like *really* rain. This meant that the morning sports lesson had to be cancelled. Of course it didn't bother James because he hated cricket anyway, but most of the other boys let out a communal groan when Mr Smith announced the cancellation. The girls in 6B didn't seem to take the news so badly about them not being able to play rounders, but that was probably because most of them thought Mrs Charnet, who would've taken the lesson, was an utter bitch. However, it wasn't so much the not playing of sport that changed the tone of the day, as the effect of the alternative. Now, everyone had to sit quietly in the classroom and be badgered by Mr Smith about how to correctly complete his dreary English grammar worksheet. Clearly, it was becoming increasingly hard for the students to stay interested – or to get interested in the first place – when their internal body programs were screaming, 'you're meant to be outside running around!'

James heard a girl at a desk further back in the room snicker. He looked around and saw Smithy towering above him.

"I see you have circled 'doing' as a verb in the third sentence James."

James was never sure if he was supposed to say anything when a teacher made these sorts of obvious statements, but when the pause lasted beyond about ten seconds he felt he should respond.

"Yes sir."

"Why is that, James?"

"Because a verb is a 'doing word', sir."

"Go on."

James started to feel uncomfortable – he didn't like being singled out, and always tried his hardest to remain inconspicuous. "Well, it's hard to imagine a more doing sort of word than 'doing' itself," he replied.

"Fascinating logic James but you're wrong. Look at the context, remember, always look at the context."

James examined the sheet but couldn't see anything that might possibly be a context – actually he wasn't really sure what a context was, and figured that he must have been absent on the day when Mr Smith showed them to the class. Now he was really uncomfortable because he knew that his large, unhumorous, and pedantic teacher wouldn't leave until this little learning situation was satisfactorily resolved. Salvation came in the form of a loud farting noise from the other side of the room. This was immediately followed by giggles from the girls and guffaws, with a sprinkling of comments, from the boys. Everyone knew that Mr Smith couldn't abide the notion of smutty mirth in his classroom, so they weren't surprised when he strode to the apparent epicentre of the disturbance and used his powerfully deep voice to prevent any further liberties from being taken.

"Stop that at once," he roared. "This is a classroom; you come here to learn, not to behave like idiots."

James thought the sound was probably genuine – it certainly had a liquid component that would be hard to produce by simply using your mouth and tongue. The only confirmation would be if a bad smell was present in the area, and only the children in that part of the room would be aware of this – and Mr Smith, who was now having a quiet conversation with Arnold Cropen, far row, fourth from the front. After several seconds, Arnie got up and promptly left the room, head bowed. "Sounds like he might have done a shit," the boy in front of James whispered across to his friend in the next row.

The effect of this incident, together with the sound produced by the incessant pounding of rain on the roof, was for a sudden spate of requests to go to the toilet to be made. After the first couple of students had left the room, and with at least half of those remaining indicating the same need, Smithy decided to let his charges leave in 'batches'. This could've been a tricky affair, but not for Mr Smith, the consummate organizer. The pupils would be allowed to go to the toilets according to the row their desk was in. When everyone from that row had returned, those in the next row could go – and no one could be away for more than seven minutes or, "there would be trouble," Smithy said as he looked at his wristwatch.

All this seemed fairly reasonable to James who was dying for a piss. The only problem was that the boys' toilets at the Shelley Street State Primary School (No.378) was on the other side of the schoolyard, and only part of it had a roof – the part housing the four cubicles. He and the other boys in his group would have to run through the rain to the small, red-brick edifice, and then, if it was their bladders that had to be emptied, stand at the urinal and get soaked to the skin by the continuing downpour.

As James sprinted across the asphalt with his four fellow rowboys, at first avoiding puddles but then finding it more fun to stomp in them, he noticed streams of other lads heading in the same direction. Most were from the lower grades. Obviously, Mr Smith's colleagues had the same idea about letting groups leave class to attend the calls of nature.

Inside the walls of the primitive structure there was chaos. Kids were jammed together in front of the long, slated urinal – their varying arcs of golden liquid becoming ragged and distorted due to the impacting raindrops. Many boys couldn't find a place in the row and, being desperate to release their internal hydrodynamic pressures, they were pushing open the doors of the cubicles and yelling at those sitting therein to get off their bums. Others had decided to just piss against the wall. It was chaos – maybe fifty kids trying to simultaneously use a facility that was designed for ten. There was shouting, arguing, crying, and cursing, and all the time the rain continued to pour from the sky.

James stood, almost transfixed. As water ran from his now-soaked curly hair down his face and onto his neck, he watched and decided that there was something deeply amusing about the pandemonium that surrounded him, and he smiled. Having convinced his bladder that there was no need for its contents to be ejected after all, he was about to head back to the classroom when he noticed the steel-framed, wire gate at the entrance to the structure. It was open of course, but so too, James saw, was the big, brass padlock hanging from its sliding bolt. Without a second thought, he looked around and, fairly sure that no one was watching, he quickly closed the gate, slid the bolt into its hole, and snapped shut the padlock. He paused for a moment around the corner outside the toilet block. It was just enough time to hear the first cries of surprise from boys who discovered they were trapped inside the overcrowded, urine-stinking facility with ever-increasing amounts of water being dumped on them from above. James chuckled, and ran off alone as the cries became more intense and as other groups sprinted past him in the opposite direction on their way to the now-unavailable relief centre.

As well as being wet and tedious, the rest of the day was also tense for James – the possibility of being discovered as the perpetrator of the prank causing him some concern. Smithy questioned all the boys in the class, and Mr Fisher – the hairless headmaster – even paid a visit to their room, and spoke about the seriousness of the incident. James coolly lied when asked if he knew anything about it, but remained a little fearful that someone might have seen him close the gate and click the lock. The event became a major topic of discussion at lunchtime – most of the grade four boys had become waterlogged – and James really would've liked to tell at least one of his peers that he was responsible. But there was no one he really trusted that much, so he stuck to his normal practice of staying on the fringes of group conversations, saying little. Finally, when the last bell rang at 3:30, without him having been hauled out of class, he knew he was safe.

Ten minutes later, while walking down Shelley Street – alone as usual – James felt happy. He hadn't been found out, the rain had stopped, the sun was becoming visible, and the weekend held promise for more interesting activities than Smithy's uninspiring lessons. He was also pleased with himself because he had managed to unobtrusively dawdle at the school exit as he waited for Anna Popodopoulis to appear with her friend Sharon. They had strolled past him giggling about some girlie thing, totally unaware of his presence of course, and now he was just a short distance behind them. Anna was beautiful: pale blue eyes, long brown hair – usually worn in a single, thick plait – and curvaceous. It was this last aspect of her sweet, pubescent body that James couldn't get out of his mind. In particular, she was one of the few girls in the school who actually had visibly bulbous breasts. Unfortunately, he couldn't see them from where he was, but just being near her, hearing her voice, smelling the perfume she had put on before leaving school, and watching her shapely young hips as they swung down the street – it was almost too much for the boy, bringing a temporary burst of pure delight to his world.

James knew that this interest in Anna – and in girls in general – was associated with his recent, first orgasm. What a startling event that had been. And only a month ago. Playing with himself under the sheets as he pictured the soft skin and white knickers that he'd seen on the young girl from next door earlier in the day. When it had happened – the orgasm that is – he had felt absolutely wonderful, and then confused, and then worried. It had been dark in his bedroom, and something liquid had obviously come out of his dick, but he couldn't see what it was. He had quickly reached the conclusion that it must have been blood, and that he was going to die – in a very embarrassing way. However, when he'd managed to find the torch in his bedside drawer, and shine its beam down to his nether region, all he could see was a small pool of thickish, whitish fluid that was becoming increasingly runny. The fact that there was no blood had made him happier, and although he still had no idea of what was going on, his ignorance hadn't stopped him from repeating the activity fairly regularly since that night.

Then, two weeks later, out of the blue, his father had taken him aside and described all this stuff about vaginas, penises, periods, semen, and babies – and given him a book, with pictures, about all these things. The talk had been a bit uncomfortable for both him and his dad but it had, together with the book, answered many of the questions that had totally mystified James. The most remarkable thing though, was the coincidence of his father giving his talk at exactly the time when James had entered this fascinating new realm of experience. Amazing really.

These thoughts were passing through the backblocks of his mind when he saw that Anna and Sharon had stopped walking and were looking at him as he approached. God, what should he do?

"Hello James, are you following us?" Sharon said in her usual stupid, giggly voice.

"Well ... yes," he replied looking at her with a serious expression, "but only because I was behind you." He meant it as a smart joke but it was wasted on Sharon who just looked at him vacantly and giggled some more. He then transferred his gaze to Anna, and suddenly felt faint. She had the warmest of smiles on her lips, and her eyes were directed straight into his own, and they too had a warmness about them.

"Would you like to walk with us?" she said in her distinctive, low, throaty voice.

James smiled back, and was sure that something – he didn't know what – had passed between them. "Okay," he replied, and the three turned and walked on.

"Me and Sharon were just saying how we were going into the city to the pictures tomorrow," Anna said brightly.

"Oh yeah, what are you going to see?"

"I think it's called 'The Viking'; it's got Kirk Douglas in it. I really like him."

"Uh huh."

"What are you doing tomorrow?" she then asked.

James didn't think it would be appropriate to tell the girls that he intended to visit the State Library. He knew he was already perceived as bit of a loner, and maybe even slightly weird, but he didn't want to also be labelled as a bookworm. "I'm not sure; I think we might be going somewhere," he lied.

Anna turned her head and gave him a second look of warmth and softness. "Well if you don't go, you could meet us at the Athenaeum in Collins Street – the film starts at one o'clock."

James felt his face become hot, and was sure his heart was doing strange things in his chest. "Okay," he replied in a croaky voice.

"Anyway, I live here; see you," Anna said as she and her friend – who had remained strangely silent – crossed the road and headed towards a narrow, two-storey, white, rendered-brick house.

James still had another twenty minutes of walking to do before he got home but he felt like he was floating just a little bit above the ground with every step. Those looks from Anna, they said so much, stirred so much inside him. Had she been observing him? Was she thinking about him in the same way that he thought about her? Did she want him for her boyfriend? He was only eleven years old, but he was tall, and all his female relatives kept saying how handsome he was with his curly, brown hair and grey eyes; but being Anna's boyfriend – that would really be something. The only other 'official' pairing at the school was between Samantha Roberts and John Sandanas – she had breasts too, and John was the much-respected captain of the school footy team. James wasn't sure that he would want all the social stuff that seemed to go with having a girlfriend. And he wasn't sure about how his dad would react – his mother wouldn't care so long as it didn't cause her any trouble. But these concerns quickly faded as he walked on home, and his mind filled with images of Anna, while flooding hormones further strengthened his desire to be very close to her.

He was still feeling happy and light headed – and had decided that he would definitely go to the Athenaeum tomorrow – when he noticed a now familiar van parked outside his house. 'Eric's Electrical' was emblazoned along its side in red, with a horizontal lightning bolt underlining the name. His mother had insisted that their house needed rewiring because the fuses kept blowing. On one occasion he had seen her plug in the vacuum cleaner, a heater, the toaster, and the washing machine all from the one outlet – with double adapters all on top of each other like giant Lego blocks. When he had pointed out that such an arrangement might not be a good idea, his mother had let out a yelp – not realizing he was in the room. But she had quickly regained her composure and had insisted that it was safe. Of course when she turned on everything, the relevant fuse blew in the house's fuse box. James had offered to fix it – he had watched his dad do it on a number of occasions – but she had insisted that he leave it and, for some reason, made him promise not to tell his father about the multiple appliances being run from the same outlet. Anyway, she had convinced his dad that the house was unsafe and that she wouldn't be happy until it was totally rewired. The man from Eric's Electrical (it wasn't Eric, himself) had said he would do the job at a cut rate if he could spread it out over a long period, coming maybe once or twice a week for a couple of hours when he wasn't on other jobs. James's dad said he'd prefer to have the work done faster but had finally agreed to the deal after his mother had insisted that they couldn't really afford the normal rate.

So, when James walked in through the back door, he expected to see trails of wire and a sprinkling of tools, and to hear drilling noises or sounds of movement up in the ceiling – and the electrician's scratchy little radio tuned to that country and western station that he always seemed to listen to. But there was nothing. The house was in its usual untidy state: dishes in the sink, crumbs and food scraps on the table, dirty ashtrays – but no evidence of electrical work, and no sounds at all. Then he heard a muffled male voice, followed by the cackling laugh of his mother.

"Hello wherever you are," he called from the kitchen. The voices stopped and there was a soft bang that seemed to come from the bedroom area. Moments later, his mother came through one of the kitchen doors. He noticed that her strawberry-blonde hair was somewhat dishevelled and that she was wearing one of those short skirts usually reserved for younger women.

"Hello Jimmy, I thought you were going to a friend's birthday party after school today," she said as she quickly ran her fingers through her hair and then adjusted her skirt.

"That was last week, and it wasn't a friend – everyone in the class was invited."

"Well, I am sorry – I'm not your social secretary, you know." She looked over her shoulder, and then back at James – and her tone suddenly changed. "Be a darling Jimmy, and go and buy me some ciggies please."

James sighed, he didn't like his mother smoking, it made the house stink, and her coughing in the mornings was getting worse. He was sure it wasn't good for her. He was about to make a comment concerning her recent promise to cut down on the habit, when the electrician appeared through the door carrying his toolbox. James wasn't very good at estimating the ages of adults but he guessed the tall, dark-haired man was in his late twenties – certainly a lot younger than his dad.

"I'll be off now then, Sandra … I mean, Mrs Campbell," he quickly corrected. "I've done all I can for today."

"Oh, really," James's mother replied. "I thought you could explain to me about those dimmer switches while my son here is down at the shop buying me some cigarettes." James frowned at his mother; she really didn't make sense sometimes. She stared back at her boy, her eyebrows raised. "I mean, then I could explain about them to you, Jimmy – you like all that technical stuff don't you?"

James looked at his mother and then at the electrician – why couldn't he stay and have the man explain about the switches to both he and his mother simultaneously? Surely the cigarettes could wait.

"I … I'm sorry Mrs Campbell, but I really do have to go – I've got another job to get to. Why don't I tell you about your lighting options when I come around next Tuesday." He looked sort of uncomfortable.

"All right, Mr Johnston," Sandra replied with a half smile, "I'll see you out."

A minute or two later she returned to the kitchen where James was spreading Vegemite on a slice of buttered bread. "Give me some money and I'll go get your cigarettes," he said as he lifted the folded-over bread to his mouth.

"Oh forget it," his mother replied, I just remembered I've got some in the bedroom."

* * * * * * * * * * * * *

James liked his workshop. It was only a little room under the back of the house, and being partly below ground level it was always damp and smelling of mould, but he'd been allowed to make it his own. He had set up shelves to hold his jars of nails and screws and nuts and bolts and other little bits and pieces that he'd mainly collected from old appliances, and to one side was a wooden table that he'd picked up from the local wrecker's yard and which he now used as a workbench. An array of both old and new tools hung from hooks along one wall, and against another was a second-hand couch that he'd dragged home from outside some rich person's house during the local council's last 'hard rubbish day' six months ago.

It was on this couch that James now sat, examining what he'd so far completed of his latest project. As he held the object up to the light, he heard a familiar humming coming from outside, and immediately felt a mix of mild irritation blended with a hint of excitement. He raised his head and peered through the louvre windows that looked out across the well-treed backyard. His assumption had been right; it was Cheryl from next door. She was a couple of years younger than James, and had only moved to the area a few months ago, but she was a busy-body sort of little girl who had no reservations about walking into neighbours' houses and making herself at home. James didn't mind her in small doses – she was friendly and playful – but sometimes she stayed well beyond the point when he wanted her to leave. He often had important jobs to do – alone – and he didn't like it when she said things such as, 'go on, you work and I'll just stay here quietly'. Mind you, he had recently realized that she was sort of attractive – for a kid anyway. In fact, it had been *her* thighs and *her* knickers that had popped into his mind during that night of self discovery not so long ago.

"Hello Jimmy ... I'm sorry ... James," she said teasingly, knowing his preference. "Whatcha doin'?"

James remained on the couch while she came and sat next to him. "I'm just looking at this; it's a little pirate's chest," he said as he continued to examine his handiwork. Cheryl didn't reply, which was a bit unusual, so he looked at her. She had a perplexed expression on her face. "I don't mean it's a chest that belongs to a small pirate; it's a miniature version of the big chests that you see in pirate films and history books and stuff – they're usually full of gold and diamonds. I'm making it."

The girl's eyes now widened in admiration as she reached for the small wooden box with the curved lid. "Oh James, it is lovely," she said as she carefully took it from his hands and turned it around. James decided that, today, he liked Cheryl.

"I haven't finished it yet; I still have to do some chiselling to set in the brass hinges" (he pointed to them on the table), "and it has to be sanded and stained and varnished. I might also line it with some red material if I can get any."

"Red velvet would look nice," the girl said as she lifted the lid off and looked inside. "I think my mum's got some – I'll get you a bit if you like." She handed the partly completed project back to its maker.

"That'd be good," he smiled. She really was sort of pretty, he thought.

"Hey, you wanna see me go cross-eyed," she said – breaking his train of thought and emotion.

"Yeah, go on," he replied with a suggestion of a sigh.

After several minutes of watching his young neighbour make weird faces, James had had enough. "Well, I have to get on with this work now," he said while Cheryl was forcing her lips into doing the goldfish thing.

"Okay," she replied. "Can I watch?"

James felt the first pangs of annoyance. "No, I do this sort of stuff better when I'm by myself." He waited for the inevitable pleading.

"All right, see ya then," she said as she stood up and skipped out of the workshop. He remained on the couch – stunned – she *always* pleaded. "I'll try and get you that velvet sometime over the weekend," she called from the garden.

He gazed at the window, still confused. These were indeed strange times for James.

About an hour later, when he had finished all the chiselling and drilling and sanding, and was just putting the last dabs of a dark, walnut stain on the chest's wooden surface, he had another visitor. This time it was his dad.

"Now why did I think I'd find you down here?" Archie said as he stuck his head around the door, smiling. James always enjoyed being with his father – he was smart, sympathetic, funny, and able to give advice on all sorts of things. In a way, he was a best friend.

"Hi, dad," he said as he carefully sat the base of the chest onto four blunted nail points that were protruding from a short plank.

"That is looking very good," Archie offered as he bent down to examine his son's work. "And I see you're using the idea we came up with yesterday for letting the stain dry on all surfaces."

"*We* didn't come up with it dad, it was *your* idea."

"Well, whatever; it's looking very smart, and you're the craftsman who's done it all. Look at those joins, they're just about perfect," he beamed as he looked up at his boy.

"Yeah, I'm fairly happy with it so far," James replied. "I think I'll be lining it with red velvet," he added.

"That would make it very smart." Archie gave the chest a final study and then walked over to the couch and sat down. "Are you intending to keep it for yourself, or are you going to give it to someone?" he asked as he scratched his head and watched sawdust and cement dust drift to the floor – souvenirs from his workplace.

"Well, I dunno. I just wanted to make one. Maybe we could fill it with gold and diamonds and then go and bury it on a deserted beach …"

"... and you could make up a map on some parchment and burn the edges, and write that it's a certain pirate's treasure ... You could be the pirate!"

"Black Humphrey."

"Good name ... but who would you give the map to?"

"Well, there's this girl at school ..." James pretended to suddenly become coy.

"Aha, I bet she breeds parrots."

"Yes, and she's going to give them all to me in exchange for the map."

Archie purposely paused for a moment. "Hang on, she's going to get a chest of gold and jewels and you're going to get a cage full of parrots?"

"Some things are more important than money to us pirates, dad," the boy retorted.

Archie laughed and James smiled. They were both their happiest at times such as these. After a short pause, when their chuckling had faded, James spoke again. This time, his tone was more serious. "Dad, I want to ask you something."

"Yeah, go on," his father replied, trying to change his expression from one of frivolity to one of thoughtfulness.

"It's about girls."

"What, something in the book you don't understand?" Archie replied, referring to the sex-education publication he'd given his boy a couple of weeks ago.

"No, it's not the book – all that stuff is kind of clear. It's ..." James was having second thoughts about going any further.

"Go on, son, don't be embarrassed." His father smiled sympathetically.

"Well, it's just that I seem to be thinking about them a fair bit."

"Anyone in particular, or girls in general?"

"Both really. And I mean … I'm sort of noticing them differently."

"And you're finding that there are a lots around to notice, right?" Archie said, maintaining his gentle grin.

"That's for sure," his boy replied as he puffed out his cheeks and blew a breath from his mouth.

Archie looked intently at his son. "What you are experiencing is very, very natural, James. It happens to all boys. With some – like you – it starts a bit earlier than with others. And it can often be very powerful … at times taking over much of your thinking. The important thing is that you don't worry about it or feel guilty about it – it's part of growing up. And although it can often be confusing, it's completely normal – been happening for millions of years."

James stared back at his father. "How come you always know what to say? You give the right answer even when I don't ask the question properly."

"Hey, I was a boy once you know – I've been through all this too, like most other men in the world." Archie wondered whether he should add some advice about making sure that you maintain respectful behaviour – particularly towards girls – when having these thoughts and feelings, but decided his boy would know this for himself. "So, do you want to ask some more … or tell me anything?"

"Yes," James answered with a mischievous grin. "You know how I beat you at cards the other night …"

"Okay, okay, before you go any further, yes I did remember to buy a box of Chocolate Royals, and if you come up stairs now, I will serve you a cup of tea and two of the biscuits, as agreed."

"Three."

"Good try James," said his father, now smiling broadly as he stood up, "but the agreement was for two – and I'm going to have a couple for myself."

****

The State Library in Melbourne was like a newly-found temple of wonderment and possibility for James. He had only discovered it a few weeks earlier when he'd been on an expedition with Bruce, an older high school neighbour who lived a few doors away from the Campbells. Like James, Bruce was also very interested in science – especially things to do with space and rockets – and he had asked James to accompany him to a special 'space' exhibition at the State Museum, which was housed in the same massive building. Both boys had found the exhibition a bit disappointing, but rather than go home early, Bruce suggested that they visit the library, which was up on the first floor.

James had been awestruck after walking through the second set of unobtrusive swinging glass doors. It was as if he'd stepped into another universe. The huge, copper-covered dome that was visible on the outside of the sandstone, columned building was now straight above him, capping the gigantic main reading room. All around the room's perimeter were dark, wooden bookshelves that extended up the walls for several storeys, there being narrow balconies at each level, and small doorways through which men in grey dustcoats occasionally appeared, collecting or returning books that had been requested from the catalog room. On the ground floor of this vast area was a multitude of stained-wood and leather tables around which four people could sit, and then there were low, panelled dividers that extended like spokes from near the centre of the room towards the outer perimeter, each with a series of single-person tables along either side. And at the very centre was the elevated desk of the reading room supervisor – who sat there godlike, surrounded by an array of mirrors so he could see anyone at a glance – and whose sole responsibility was to maintain the silence and decorum expected of this esteemed repository of knowledge.

Now, for the first time, James was here by himself, and his nostrils took in a deep breath of the musty and polish-scented air as his eyes adjusted to the relative darkness. He focused first on the plethora of books and then on the tables with their little lamp-shaded lights, and then on their human users – some of who sat and read; while others took notes; and still others dozed, occasionally waking with a jolt and looking around embarrassed, hoping that no one had noticed their descent into unconsciousness.

After a short pause he walked as quietly as he could to the catalog room. Inside was a hive of activity – making a contrast with the subdued silence of the reading area. Much of the room's floor space was taken up by stacks of tiny drawers that contained all the catalog cards for all the books in the library – each card containing brief details about a particular publication. James thought there must be millions. People were pulling out drawers, scribbling notes, talking to the men in grey dustcoats, and collecting the small piles of books that were brought down to them from the shelves.

James had decided that today he would see what he could discover about the legend of Atlantis, and what experts and investigators had to say about the whole topic. This sudden interest had been prompted by a recent article he'd read in a *National Geographic* magazine at school. The article hadn't actually been about Atlantis but had mentioned the legend when describing certain underwater ruins in the Mediterranean. The idea of a mysterious civilization that had existed long before ancient Egypt or Greece, and then suddenly to have disappeared without a trace, intrigued James, and he wanted to find out more. He still felt a little intimidated by all the adult action that was going on around him but he wandered over to the 'non-fiction' section of the catalog drawers as calmly as he could, found the one with 'AT – AZ' on its front, and then proceeded to look for the three or four titles that he might request to be brought to him.

Two and a half hours later he was still reading the one book that he preferred to the other three. It was called *Atlantis – fact or fiction*, and it had lots of photographs of places and artifacts, as well as maps and sketches. And the text was easy to read – unlike one of the others, which he found impenetrable. Occasionally, he would stop reading and jot down a note on the back pages of his English notebook from school, which he'd brought along especially for this purpose. He'd had a break some time ago – for a drink of water and a toilet visit – but had again lost himself in his private research after returning.

Now he sat back and ran his fingers through his hair. His neck was a little sore but he felt a quiet sort of elation – he had learned so much in such a short time. He looked around at the other people seated at the tables. He was obviously the only eleven year-old here – and he wondered whether he should feel good or bad about this. Then his eyes focused on the face of the large clock at one end of the room. Oh God! It was five minutes to one. 'Anna; the cinema; I'm late,' he thought as panic quickly overtook his sense of calm self-satisfaction. He grabbed his notebook, stuffed it into his canvas haversack, and ran from the reading room, hoping the elevated chief supervisor wouldn't hear him.

Although it was a fairly mild sort of spring day, beads of sweat were appearing on James's forehead as he jumped off the tram and ran up Collins Street. There were a few people milling around outside the theatre but no one he could recognize. A clock inside the foyer showed that it was nine minutes past one. 'Damn, I've missed her,' he thought despondently. He stared at a large poster publicising the film that was already playing inside, trying to decide what to do. John Wayne stared back at him. 'John Wayne ... John Wayne! He's not in The Viking – it's supposed to be Kirk Douglas!' James thought, momentarily confused. He looked up at the sign above the door, 'Majestic' was written in large, gold letters. 'Bugger, bum, shit,' he thought as he realized he was at the wrong theatre. It was obviously the other one, further up the road and on the opposite side. He was so annoyed with himself. He'd gotten these two establishments mixed up before, and now his stupidity – and his lateness – had ruined what could've been a very important occasion. All of last night's fantasies about touching and feeling and kissing in the darkened back row were dashed.

Then, hope returned. A hundred yards up the street, across the traffic and through the curbside trees, he spied Anna and Sharon – they were in the middle of the footpath, outside the real Athenaeum, looking first in one direction and then the other, but not across to where has was standing. Rather than yell out, he quickly prepared to cross the street but then noticed two boys come out of the Athenaeum lobby and start talking with the girls. They were clearly older than James was, and he saw both girls stop their visual search for him – he assumed they had been looking for him – as they became more involved in conversation with the boys. Just as a break occurred in the stream of cars, he saw the four of them walk back into the theatre. The girls were laughing and they didn't even pause to give a final glance up and down the street.

He ran as fast as he could but by the time he reached the box office they were gone. James was overcome with a deep sadness. Not only had he missed meeting with Anna, but now she was almost certainly sitting in the back stalls next to some older boy who he didn't know – his dreams of passion destroyed. 'All because of bloody Atlantis,' he thought. He considered the possibility of still buying a ticket and of wandering into the darkened theatre alone. Maybe Anna would see him and come and collect him. But by the way she had gaily walked inside with those two big bastards, he would more likely end up sitting alone, wondering where she was and what she was doing – only to be involved in an embarrassing encounter later on when the film was over. No, taking everything into account, James decided to glumly go home, conceding that this was a great opportunity lost.

An hour and a half later, as he walked into the kitchen, he was greeted by his father. "Hello son, you're home early aren't you? I thought you were going to see a film."

"Yeah, I was, but I got there late."

Archie could see that his son was miserable. "Missed meeting someone?" he asked.

"Yeah, sort of …"

It was obvious that the boy didn't want to talk more about whatever it was that was making him down in the dumps – not at this stage anyway. "So how about we stroll down to the shops and buy an ice-cream? Then we can go and watch those fellas with their model aeroplanes in the park – you can hear them buzzing from here."

"Yeah, okay," James replied half-heartedly, then added, "How come you're home so early? I thought you were working all day."

"Well, I was going to, but I got off early – thought I'd come home and surprise your mother; take her out for a drive or something. But she's not here – off gallivanting with her girlfriends at the races. She left a note saying she'll probably be home late, so it looks like beans and eggs again ol' boy."

James sighed. "Okay, let's get that ice-cream," he said as he saw through the happy exterior of his dad's expression.

That night, while in bed, James thought about Anna. He was still upset about missing out on being with her earlier in the day, but now it was dark and he was alone, and he was able to picture her face and the rest of her body – in any way he wanted. Maybe there would be another time and place. In fact, he could see it in his mind's eye right now. They were touching and caressing. And as his hand gently moved under the sheet, he longed so much for the real thing.

Chapter 4

James gazed blankly out of the window as Mr Sherborne droned on about how to solve a particular maths problem. Slowly, a faint sense of nostalgia began to envelop him. He wouldn't be here too much longer – another five months. Then his secondary schooling would be finished. Overall, it had been enjoyable, he thought – especially the later years when he'd finally been noticed by teachers as someone who could actually think. Of course, one of the biggest drawbacks to Strathmore Technical School was that it carried the burden of an old public perception that tech schools were inferior to high schools. This was because the kids who attended them were going to become the carpenters and plumbers and mechanics of Australia rather than the doctors and lawyers and bank managers. After all, the curriculum didn't have subjects like geography or history or foreign languages. Instead, there were offerings such as woodwork, turning and fitting, and welding. As a result, common opinion held that tech school students weren't exactly high on the academic ability scale and that, at best, they were destined to spend their lives in the blue-collar regions of society.

This annoyed James and many other better-informed people because they knew that tech schools were, in fact, strong in the sciences and technology, and that a good smattering of engineers and scientists and similar professionals had come through this branch of the Victorian education system. Also, luckily for James and his peers, over half of this particular school's teaching staff were young and energetic and full of ideas about how to make learning more relevant and enjoyable for students.

A far greater drawback than anything to do with public perceptions or academic profiles though, was the fact that there were no girls at the school. James greatly missed having girls around in his daily life, and so too, it would seem, did most of the other nine hundred boys at the school. Girls were a common topic of discussion at recess, at lunchtime, between classes, on excursions, on the way home, and at any other time when talk was possible – during most waking moments really. A smile appeared on his face as he thought about this.

"So what would you do now, Campbell?" The puffy pink face of Mr Sherborne was glaring down at James. He was one of the remaining old-style teachers, and he'd used a surname – a clear signal that he wasn't pleased. James quickly surveyed the blackboard and saw where the teacher had gotten up to in his development of a solution.

"Well, you can find the gradient of the line because it will be the inverse of the radius's gradient at the same point – since they're at right angles to each other." He hoped this was in fact what the teacher had asked about.

"Yes that's right James ... Arlington! Wake up, did you hear that?" The young Campbell gave a relieved sigh as Sherborne turned his attention to one of the 'trouble-makers' at the back of the class.

Ten minutes later, James's mind began to wander again. He enjoyed maths – and was recognized as one of the school's most capable senior students in the subject. But the day was hot, with little breeze entering the stuffy room through the open windows. And Sherborne had such a monotone sort of voice; no wonder the boys nicknamed him 'Chloroform'. He looked around at his classmates. Freddy Arlington had fallen asleep again, and everyone else seemed to be heading in the same direction. He knew this would lead to some heavy yelling very shortly when the teacher turned around from the blackboard again. 'They should cancel school on days like this,' James thought.

Thankfully, the class was soon jolted from its torpor, and saved from the inevitable consequence, first by a knock and then by the sliding open of the door. Boys shook themselves back into full consciousness as they saw that it was Ron Black, the young and popular senior English teacher. Following normal protocol, he first went and quietly spoke to Chloroform who seemed just as pleased about the interruption as his bored charges. Moments later the younger teacher addressed the class.

"Good morning boys. I won't be seeing many of you until this afternoon so I want to remind everyone that today, at lunchtime, our senior debating team will be having its first debate against the team from Walther Hall." This simple statement seemed to invigorate almost every member of the class, and led to murmurings, snickerings and a few loud 'yeses' being uttered.

"Steady," said Mr Sherborne loudly, but with the hint of a smile.

Mr Black went on. "Remember, it will take place in the assembly hall at twelve noon, and I look forward to a show of support for our team. Thank you Mr Sherborne," he said as he turned to Chloroform – who simply nodded – and he then left the room. The maths teacher looked out on his class, interested but not surprised at how this little interlude had re-animated the twenty-two boys present.

When the lunch bell rang an hour or so later, James went to his locker to deposit his books, and then wandered towards the assembly hall; passing other students as they gulped down their sandwiches and meat pies and pieces of fruit. He had already eaten his hastily-made lunch at recess – mainly because he'd missed out on breakfast earlier in the day. He often slept in – his failing old alarm clock was the usual cause – and today he'd awoken with only fifteen minutes left before having to catch the tram. Anyway, it had all been fortuitous, he thought, because it meant he would now almost certainly get a front-row seat for the debate. He'd actually considered volunteering for the team – over the last couple of years he had overcome some of his natural shyness and was now able to give quite eloquent responses when asked questions in class. But preparing speeches and speaking for long periods in front of his smirking peers – as well as total strangers – was not something that appealed to him at this time.

He ambled down a path that led to one of the huge hall's side entrances. When he opened the door his head jerked back in astonishment. Half the student body already seemed to be there! They were jostling and shouting and laughing loudly as they looked at the rostrum and the microphone and the six empty chairs that had been set up behind two tables just below the main stage. It took less than a second for him to realize that he'd badly underestimated the general appeal of the event.

Walther Hall was the name of a moderately posh private girls' school located about a mile and a half away. Soon there would be actual girls sitting in three of those chairs, and they almost certainly wouldn't be like the ugly, pimple-faced tarts from St Theresa's just down the road (although even that would be quite acceptable, just so long as they were clearly female). No, these girls would be from a school that every tech boy knew harboured some of the prettiest young women in the district. Although they never admitted it openly to any of their students, James got the impression that members of the English department were totally stunned when their counterparts at the girls' school had actually agreed to have their senior students engage in a series of debates with the local tech-school boys. Either the people at Walther Hall were more socially non-conformist than anyone had assumed or they were feeling the pressure of being one of the few private girls' schools in the state that didn't have a 'sister school' of boys. Whatever the reason, James and everyone else in Australia at this time knew that it was extremely unusual for private schools of any kind – with their long history of social elitism – to lower themselves to the extent that they would interact in this way with kids from such a plebeian institution as Strathmore Tech.

A few minutes later, sitting in a third row seat from which a prefect had removed a sullen form three lad in preference for a fellow senior student, James watched as Mr Black walked to the front and, via the microphone, asked for quiet. Almost immediately, a reverential silence descended on the audience. Moments later, the adjudicator came walking down the central aisle. He was followed by the girls of the Walther Hall team, who were followed by the Strathmore Tech team. A soft hubbub could be heard as the two teams seated themselves behind the tables. Like almost everyone else, James focused on the girls. The much-discussed predictions of the previous week had clearly been correct. In fact, the reality was even better. Each of the girls was absolutely beautiful. Two blondes – one with long hair, the other with short – and a redhead whose sprinkling of freckles, together with her penetrating pale blue eyes, surely caused a substantial increase in the average pulse rate of the young, testosterone-laden audience. The question being debated, 'That Australia should markedly increase its aid to poorer countries in the region', would normally have been of interest to James, but not under these conditions. He tried to listen to the arguments – particularly those of the affirmative being put by the girls – but in the end he found himself listening to the distinctive sounds of their voices as much as to what they were actually saying. And he began noticing little behavioural nuances, like how one of the blondes kept sweeping her hair away from the left side of her face. Glancing around, he saw that he wasn't alone in his distraction.

The next day – a Friday – the rarely-seen principal of Strathmore Tech stood before the full student body and congratulated them on their respectful and polite behaviour at the previous day's debate. This was received in silence by the boys. He then said that he hoped there would be more intercourse of this kind between the students of Walther Hall and Strathmore Technical School. Before he'd even finished, pandemonium broke out. Within seconds, hundreds of young male voices were chanting 'intercourse, intercourse,' and students all over the hall were jumping up and making suggestive thrusts with their hips and hands. It took teachers a full ten minutes to restore order, during which time the principal left the stage. 'What an idiot,' James thought to himself.

✳︎✳︎✳︎✳︎✳︎✳︎✳︎✳︎✳︎✳︎✳︎✳︎✳︎

A large yawn eased its way out of James's mouth as he sat on the toilet. There was still an hour and a half before he had to be at the church, so there was just enough time for him to have a shower, get dressed, and run up to the tram stop. The rumbling journey, together with the longish walk at the end, should see him arriving at around nine o'clock. He strained his abdominal muscles and then relaxed. Sundays were something to look forward to. Not so much because of the church service – Reverend Bailey could be a bit boring at times – but because of the youth group meeting beforehand, and the socializing that would happen during the afternoon and maybe even the night. He smiled to himself as he thought about how he and some of his school friends had been conned into attending the Eldewood Baptist Church in the first place.

Way back in form two he had quietly joined in with a group of boys who approached the school chaplain for advice on how they might get girls to come to a form party they were planning – the problem being that hardly anyone knew any girls who they could invite. The chaplain, Mr Derwent (or was it Reverend Derwent?) had come up with an innovative suggestion. He told the boys that the church he was affiliated with had plenty of 'young ladies' in its youth group, and that if the boys joined the group they could ask the girls, collectively, to attend the planned party. He had said he would also privately encourage them to attend.

James strained again, and heard a splash. The deal had worked magnificently. About ten boys had shown up at the following Sunday's youth group meeting; and roughly the same number of girls – all of them attractive in one way or another – had agreed to attend the form party, which ended up being a huge success. Mind you, over the following weeks the number of Strathmore Tech boys attending the meetings dropped significantly. This was probably partly due to the large dose of religious activity that went with membership of the youth group, and partly due to the fairly selective attitude of the young women regarding which males they would continue to interact with. James persisted because he enjoyed discussing and thinking about many of the social and spiritual issues raised in the meetings – and because it provided him with a life beyond his schoolwork and private projects and other solitary pursuits. Also, for some reason that he didn't want to question too closely lest it dissolve away, many of the girls seemed to find something appealing about him. There was no doubt about it, since that first encounter three years ago, the church group had become an important part of his life.

He idly thought about these things as he leaned forward on the toilet seat so as to better check a torn toenail he'd just noticed. This caused him to fart loudly which, via some strange link between body and mind, made him realize that he was now wasting time and that if he didn't get a move on he'd be late.

It was ten past nine when he tentatively opened the door to the small room where the youth group members met for their teenage version of Sunday school.

"Hello James, we've just started – today's topic, in case you don't remember, is 'Whether the taking of life is ever justified'." The speaker was Richard Harrison, a young trainee minister who was in charge of these Sunday meetings and who, unlike most of the elders of the church, didn't seem to be conservative or dogmatic in his view of life, religion, history, the universe, and everything else.

"Kill him, he's late," said a familiar voice from the far side of the room. People chuckled. It was Eddy Atkinson, the only other remaining tech boy from those early days.

"Well Eddy," retorted the trainee minister, "in the context of what we are talking about, you seem to place a fairly low value on human life."

"Not really," James heard his school colleague say as he crossed over outstretched legs and swapped smiles with one or two other members while heading for an empty chair. "I just put a very high value on being punctual."

It was obvious that with this little interruption now over, Richard wanted to get back to a serious consideration of the issue, so he chose to ignore smart-arse Eddy and, instead, addressed the far less cheeky Campbell boy. "What do you think about this issue, James?" he asked confidently.

"Well," James answered as he slowly looked around at everyone in the room. "After thinking about this for some time, I have to …" he paused.

"Go on James," Richard encouraged. "Don't be shy."

"Well … I have to agree with Eddy. Being late for this class is inexcusable and I think we should kill me during communion this morning."

Richard sighed and looked up towards the ceiling. Everyone else laughed. Eddy glanced across at James and gave him a thumbs-up signal. However, five minutes later the tone was a lot more serious. It was how these discussions always proceeded – thoughtful repartee interspersed with jocularity and silliness. They were the highpoint of James's week. But it was only like this because Richard allowed it. The situation had been quite different a couple of Sundays ago when Reverend Bailey had led the group. There had been no humour and no sense of joint exploration and discovery; just the feeling that regardless of how intelligent you might be, there was only one way to view anything, and that was the way defined by the church's teachings. James had felt that Reverend Bailey saw young minds as something akin to sheep, and that they needed mental penning by wise and righteous shepherds like himself. He had hated the feeling.

"All right, we seem to agree that taking the life of someone in order to stop them from almost certainly taking the life of someone else who we care about, is justified." Richard was doing his usual thing of trying to have the group reach consensus on one point before moving on to the next.

"No, I don't agree," interrupted Madeline, one of the older members. "You can always restrain someone who might cause harm – I don't even have a problem with temporarily injuring them, or of locking them away for a long time – but killing is forever. It's removing someone from existence ... and I don't think it can be justified under any circumstances."

"What if some crazy man bailed up your mum in her bedroom and was about to shoot her," said Eddy from across the room, "and you came up behind him and there was an axe leaning against the wall next to you."

"Go on," replied Madeline.

"Well, wouldn't you grab the axe and hit the bloke from behind with it – and probably kill him?"

"I'd hit him with the back of the axe, not the sharp bit; and knock him out."

A smile crept over Eddy's face. "Okay, what if it was one of those double-bladed axes?"

"Then I'd hit him with the flat part."

"What if it twisted in your hand as you swung it and it sliced into his head …"

"Oh yuk!" said Madeline's younger sister.

"… and you killed him?" continued Eddy.

"Well that would be an accident because it wouldn't be my intention." Madeline was obviously becoming annoyed. "Why, what would you do?"

"That's a hard one. Eddy replied with a smirk. "Your mum makes really nice jelly cakes, and I'd really miss them. But I worry about a family that keeps axes in its bedrooms."

Chuckling broke out from around the room, and Madeline glared at her antagonist. "You can be so annoying sometimes, Eddy," she said angrily. Richard decided it was time to take control.

"It might be appropriate at this stage to consider what the bible has to say about the issue." He then spoke for fifteen minutes, mainly quoting passages, and without too much commentary.

James had heard or read about most of this scriptural stuff before – how the Old Testament seemed to condone aggression, with its stories of God's people smiting their enemies; and how the New Testament seemed to take a far more pacifistic view, with love being promoted as the chief weapon against any opponent. At the end of his delivery,

Richard asked if anyone wanted to comment. James looked around and waited for one of the more vocal members of the group to say something deep or entertaining.

"James, what do you think of all this?" Richard asked.

"Umm …" James's face flushed with embarrassment as everyone looked at him. Light-hearted replies were easy; serious ones were harder. He took a deep breath and closed his eyes for a moment before speaking.

"Well … it seems to me that the ancient literature that has been collected into what we now call the bible, has a whole range of points of view about the taking of life – so many, in fact, that anyone might have their personal attitude supported by some quote or another. And this seems to be the case for a lot of other things besides this particular issue." There was total silence in the room. Richard was slowly nodding his head. "But if we just examine this question, then it seems to me that the various Christian churches down through the ages have an awful lot to answer for in terms of life taking. You only need to read about what the crusaders did in medieval times, or what happened during the Inquisition – horrible mass killings of innocent people, and sickening tortures and death – all in the name of Christianity. A little while ago, I read that more people have been killed in the name of Jesus Christ than for any other so-called 'reason'." He paused.

"And your point is what?" said Richard.

"I suppose my point is, that given what has happened in the past, you may not want to place too much value on what the bible has to say about this issue, because it has been used to justify some pretty horrific actions."

Eddy started to slowly clap his hands. A few others followed. Some of the members from long-term Baptist families had worried expressions and seemed to be looking at Richard for guidance.

"Thank you James, that has given us all something to ponder and discuss further but, unfortunately, that will have to be at some other time because it is now seven minutes to ten." He was alluding to the fact that the church service would begin at ten o'clock. "So let me close now with a prayer."

During the service, James sat with Eddy. They were joined by Rhonda – Madeline's sister, who had clearly been making a play for the brash youth for several weeks now – and by her friend, Justine who, unknown to James, was hoping to follow a similar strategy with him. James always enjoyed the singing – it was loud and it enabled him to explore different harmonies without being too obvious. If he made a mistake, then hardly anyone would know. Music had been important to him for years, but actual singing was an interest he had picked up only after becoming involved with the church.

The sermon was boring but the final part of the ceremony, when communion was offered, turned out to be moderately entertaining. Everyone had taken their bit of bread off the tray and their tiny glass of grape juice out of one of the holders that had been passed around, and was sitting in their pew awaiting the appropriate words from Reverend Bailey. James had his eyes closed – trying to get in touch with God.

"A symbol of the body of Christ …" said the black-robed minister, and fifty or so little squares of bread were popped into fifty or so opened mouths. A robed hand then raised one of the tiny glasses.

"… and as a symbol of His blood …" Everybody gulped down their fifty millilitres of dark grape juice. Then the interruption came.

"Arrh fuck, its juice."

Most of the congregation, including James, turned their heads and saw an obviously unshaven and unwashed old man dressed in raggedy clothes storming out of the hallowed building.

"Poor old bastard, he was expecting a shot of wine," Eddy whispered.

James thought about the irony of the incident, and smiled. The literal interpretation of Scripture was a popular stance taken by many members of this and most other Baptist churches, as far as he could see. But wowserism seemed to have precedence when it came to the issue of alcoholic beverages. The fact that the bible tells of how Jesus did a cool miracle by turning water into wine at a party he was attending, and how it was wine that he shared amongst his disciples at the last supper when he spoke about the whole, 'this wine is my blood' thing; none of this was strong enough to convince the people who controlled the workings of the church that wine might be appropriate in some settings. Like in communion for instance. "A fair expectation I would've thought," he whispered back to Eddy.

After the service, standing outside the main entrance to the church, James found himself talking to Justine. The other young people, who normally hung around together to chat and gossip and make social arrangements, had melted away to the opposite end of the path. When James noticed this he thought it a bit strange and wondered whether his critical comments in the earlier meeting were to blame. This train of thought quickly faded, though, when he realized that the attractive young brunette standing before him was just about flirting her knickers off with him. Unfortunately, the spell he felt being cast over him was broken by the approach of Richard, the trainee minister.

"James, look, I hate to interrupt, but I have to leave early today, and I really need to speak to you privately for a few minutes before I go – if that's okay." He looked across at Justine and gave her a marshmallowy smile. She glared back, and then returned the smile – with even more false sweetness.

"Come and talk to me when you've finished, if you want," she said to James with a more genuine expression before walking away.

"I am sorry, James, but …" Richard indicated that they should take a few steps further away from the crowd. "… I need to mention something that has been on my mind for a while now." James didn't respond except by raising his eyebrows. "Look, I've known you for a couple of years now, James. You are obviously a spiritually sensitive person, and I've grown to appreciate your intellect and what I consider to be your healthy skepticism."

"I can't give you any money."

"No, look, I'm serious. The principal of our college was talking about how the Baptist Church needs more theological students and trainee ministers – like me – if it is going to survive and continue to be useful to the community. He encouraged each of us to think of one person in our lives who we thought might be the most appropriate candidate for such a vocation … and I thought of you."

James was stunned. He really hadn't seen this one coming. 'Jesus, I don't want to be a minister,' was a response that crossed his mind, but he didn't vocalize it.

"Well … I …"

"Look, just have a think about it and give me a call if you want to ask any questions or anything – but I'm sure you'd be great in this field."

"Well thanks for the kind thoughts, Richard," James replied, "even if they are completely misplaced."

"I don't consider them misplaced," Richard said as he glanced down at his watch. "But, look, I have to rush off now, so promise me you'll think about it." James nodded in agreement. The young trainee stared into the teenager's eyes, gently squeezed his arm, and then hurried away.

'Well bugger me,' thought James as he stood there alone in the chattering crowd. A daydream-like state then descended upon him as he pondered Richard's words. Moments later, a waving hand some distance away snapped him out of his reverie. It was Justine. 'Well bugger me,' he thought again as he blinked and started walking towards her.

＊＊＊＊＊＊＊＊＊＊＊＊＊

Most people that James knew had Sunday lunch as a fairly important and regular family activity. However, this wasn't the case for him and his parents. Being an only child meant that his family was just about as small as possible, and he considered this to be one of the reasons why his mother had never really accepted Sunday lunch as an event of any consequence. It was fairly common for her to not be home for much of the day, so he and his dad would cook up something and sit around and talk – about all sorts of things. Of course, James and Archie enjoyed these times together, but occasionally they both felt the loneliness of the situation. Maybe if there'd been other kids around things would've been different. It was sad really. James knew his mother was a tart, and that on many occasions she was probably off with other men. He'd realized this some time ago, and he knew that his dad was also aware of it, but it was the one subject that was taboo with his father. His only utterance on the subject had been when James once tried to force a discussion about it. "Your mother had horrible experiences as a child," Archie had said, "and regardless of what she ever does, I will love her till I die." He had then stood up and walked from the room. They never again spoke about it.

"So what was the sermon about today at your church?" Archie asked as he cut into another roast potato.

"Oh, about death and dying and resurrection," James answered.

"Sounds very jolly."

"Yeah, the youth group meeting was about the morality of killing other people."

"So, your morning was focused on fairly light and breezy stuff, huh?"

James gave his father a little smile while reaching for the gravy. He knew his dad didn't exactly revel in the idea of his son attending a church. "They're trying to do what they see as the right thing, I suppose," the boy said, "and death is a pretty important issue."

Not for the first time, Archie felt a little annoyed with himself for his sarcasm – and at the same time, pride in the wisdom of his young offspring. "You're right of course," he said, almost apologetically. "Death is probably one of the greatest issues that we all have to face at some time or another. It's just that, well, you know, I have a problem with people who try to convince others that they have exclusive rights to the truth."

"They not all like that though, Dad," James replied, waving a slice of lamb around on the end of his fork. "I mean, some of the members of my church – like this guy, Richard, who leads our religious instruction group – they seem to be searching for the truth just as much as anyone, and they don't ram the church's teachings down your throat."

"So if you're not going to buy the product they're selling, why go there in the first place? And what's this Richard fellow doing there – unless it's all part of a long-term strategy for getting you to think their way?"

"Well, I go because I like the discussions – they talk about things that other people don't say much about, and ... because of the friendship."

"And the girls."

James grinned. "The *friendship*," he repeated. "And Richard, well, he's a trainee minister, and the only one I know, so I'm not sure if they're all like him or not. But he seems pretty open to different ideas. I get the impression that the Baptist movement is going through a lot of changes and that maybe he's trying to bring in a new sort of openness." He noticed that his father was frowning, and decided not to mention anything about what Richard had said to him earlier. "But what about you Dad?" he then asked. "You've never told me what you think about Jesus, and Armageddon, and life-after-death, and other stuff like that."

Archie put his knife and fork down on the table and looked at his son. "James, I'm fifty years old and I'm still thinking about a lot of those sorts of things. But I can tell you that the argument that something must be true because it comes from some old writings that are supposed to be the Word of God doesn't carry much weight with me. It seems like a convenient way of stopping any debate … and I don't buy it. But like you, it's the questions about life and the universe – meaning and purpose – that I'm interested in. I haven't found too many answers, but maybe you will. You've certainly got a powerful mind. I just don't want you to get drawn into a way of thinking that's got 'bullshit' written all over it."

James grinned.

His father sat back. "What are you smiling at?" he asked.

"And the girls," the boy said. They both laughed.

After lunch, Archie went to have a snooze, and James waited to be picked up by one of the older youth group members who owned a car. Eight of them had arranged to go to the Bulla River, out in the countryside about forty minutes drive away. It was a place that James had been visiting since he was quite young – first with his dad, and then later, when he could ride his bike the distance, he would make the journey alone. It was an almost magical place for him. Surrounded by rolling hills with only the occasional farmhouse to indicate the presence of humans, the small river opened up into a number of wide, deep pools that were connected by stretches of relatively gentle rapids. Tall gumtrees lined the river's banks and these were used by kookaburras and magpies as temporary perches as they surveyed their shared realm. Frequent outcrops of blue granite could be seen not only in the river but also in the fields, thus confirming that most of the land would never be cultivated. In fact, many of the smaller rocks had been used during the last century to make dry-stone fences for separating the old cattle-grazing fields, these adding to the enchantment of the region. Not so many years ago James would search along the banks for frogs, or slide off large boulders that jutted out into the water, or explore the many small gullies and hills that accompanied the river on its meandering journey across the land.

This place was so special to James that he had mixed feelings about being here with other young people who didn't have a similar historical link, or the same instinctive appreciation of the area's uniqueness. But his ambivalence soon faded when Justine joined him on the rock where he had been sitting alone for ten minutes while the others either swam or threw a ball or prepared a fire for boiling a billy. She approached him from behind.

"Hello Mr Loner," she said happily. "Watcha doin'?"

He turned and saw that she was wearing a very brief bikini – and in the short moment that allowed him to stare without it becoming obvious, he admired the smoothness of her olive skin and the curvature of her hips. "Oh, just taking in the scenery," he replied. "I used to come here a lot when I was younger."

"Fond memories?"

"Fond memories and fond feelings," he said as he glanced at her navel – which was about level with his face – and then up at her eyes.

She kneeled down next to him and sat back on her heels. "I can understand that," she said, looking directly at him and ruffling the hair at the back of her neck. "It's such a wild and romantic sort of place ... I would like to have special memories and feelings about it too." She then abruptly stood up and dove into the pool that all but surrounded the rock; her lean body hardly making a splash as it slid under the water. When she surfaced, she called to him. "Come join me."

※ ※ ※ ※ ※ ※ ※ ※ ※ ※ ※ ※

It was early evening when James gave a final wave to the car as it sped away from his house – its remaining load of tired-but-happy youth group members no longer looking back. He turned towards the front gate. It had been a pleasant afternoon, and he was still glowing from it effects. He opened the gate but looked up with a start after realizing that someone was standing almost next to him.

"Whoa! Sorry Mr Woodford, I didn't see you standing there – you surprised me." It was the old man from next door, where his young-nuisance friend, Cheryl, used to live.

"I like to take a stroll in the cool of the evening, young Jimmy, and the night jasmine you've got growing along your fence here – it's a lovely smell. It only makes itself known after dark, you know."

James liked Mr Woodford but it was usually hard to have a conversation with him because he was fairly deaf and he often forgot or didn't bother to use his hearing aid. However, it was always worth trying.

"Yes, I know," James replied. "Sometimes a breeze will blow the scent into my bedroom late at night – it really is wonderful."

"Possibly, but I only watch the Channel Nine news," the old man responded cheerfully. He then leant closer to James and, with a smile, whispered, "I like the look of the weather girl."

It was clear that further discussion was going to be difficult, and James was being bitten by a number of mosquitoes – this being the time of year when they were most active. "Well, I better be going," he said loudly, and then almost shouted, "I'm getting bitten by mozzies." He followed this with the half wave, half salute that meant 'goodbye'.

"Of course we'll beat them, we've got the best cricket team in the world," the old man replied enthusiastically as he waved back. "Goodnight then."

Inside the house was dark and quiet. On the kitchen table was a note from his dad. 'Gone to get Mum, might visit your aunty Jessie after. Stew in the pot on the stove.'

After eating while watching a bit of television, James wandered into his bedroom. It had been a good day; lots had happened; but for some reason he felt a little depressed. Being home alone didn't bother him – in fact he usually enjoyed it – but there was clearly something making him sad. He sat on his bed in the darkened room. Through the window he could see Mr Woodford ambling back from his evening stroll – the street light on the corner casting him in silhouette. And suddenly, James understood why his spirits were low.

The old man had moved into next door just over two years ago. A little while before that, Cheryl had lived there with her mother and father and baby brother. She had continued to visit James almost every day – and after a while his initial annoyance with her had mellowed and then disappeared completely. She became a natural part of his existence and he missed having her around when she went on holidays with her family or to school camps. They would talk about anything and everything: their interests, their fears, their parents, their friends. And they helped each other: sometimes he'd tutor her in maths, or give her ideas for essays and the like, and she became adept at using drills and screwdrivers and spanners as he allowed her to assist him with his various projects. Sometimes – especially on hot nights like tonight – she would show up in his bedroom when everyone else was asleep. She would sit in the chair – in the darkness – and talk about her day at school, or ask questions about why the world is the way it is. James usually fell asleep while she was still there, but she was always gone when he awoke.

At first, when he thought about it, he concluded that she had sort of become the little sister he never had. But on further reflection he realized that she was more than a sister figure. On one of her late-night visits, while sitting in the chair, she had asked if she could come and lie with him in his bed; and he had detected in her tone that the suggestion wasn't entirely innocent. It had been difficult for him, but he had told her that it probably wasn't a good idea. She left the room soon after and he hadn't known whether to feel relieved or not. It was just that if she'd have stayed he would almost certainly have changed his mind; and he wasn't sure where that might've led.

A few days later, his dad came down to his workshop and told him that Cheryl and her mother had been killed in a car crash earlier that afternoon.

No one would ever know the depth of the anger and anguish and pain that tore through his soul during those awful weeks that followed.

And now, as he stood in his room looking out at the blackness of the night, he thought for the millionth time about the young girl from next door who had come so close to him; so much part of him; only to be suddenly wrenched away … forever. She had only been twelve years old – close to thirteen.

He sat down in the chair and wondered if death really was the end of everything. Christianity said that it wasn't – and so did a lot of other religions – but he couldn't see it. Where was the evidence? He knew he would give anything to have Cheryl here with him now – or even to know for certain that she was still happy and laughing in some other existence. But no, he was sure that she was gone ... totally. He closed his eyes and pictured her standing before him. She was smiling – that mischievous grin which perfectly matched the rest of her pretty, tomboyish face. He would never forget her. And through the open window drifted the sweet smell of night jasmine; and down one of his cheeks, a tear rolled.

Chapter 5

Bren yawned. It was a big one – his jaw staying locked open for several paces as he trudged along the path to the well. Of course, arising before dawn was natural to him, but this was earlier than usual – the stars were still twinkling, and the only hint of the coming sun was a weak glow in the southeast. This was just now beginning to silhouette the huge pines on nearby hilltops. Trib was behind him and then came Pock-face, and further back were others – some from Ceann Tull but some not. The three friends hadn't spoken much so far, the solemnity of the occasion combining with the early morning darkness to encourage each to dwell, almost dreamlike, on private thoughts and feelings.

Bren looked ahead and knew that they would soon be in the clearing where only two summers ago the great bear had killed young Natach, and had come close to killing Trib. He turned around and looked back at his dark-haired friend. Even in the limited light he could see that Trib had caught his glance, and saw the nod that signified recognition of a shared thought. The wounds from that attack had healed remarkably fast, and the scars, although clearly visible across the young man's face, were not as ugly as many had predicted.

Bren knew that it had been the well that had saved Trib – and so too, by now, did most people in the surrounding settlements. Once he was sure that the well had instructed him to proclaim its existence, he was diligent in informing all those at Ceann Tull, and beyond, of its power. As a result, many people had already visited it, and now other accounts of its healing properties were also beginning to spread. Furthermore, people no longer simply described it as 'the well at Endachni', but gave it the title of 'The Holy Well of Endachni'. In most ways, all this openness about his discovery had pleased Bren – members of his clan were now able to benefit from the well's power, both physically and spiritually, and also from the prestige associated with its presence in their lands. However, there was a part of him – a selfish part, he thought – that wanted to keep secret everything to do with the well – its location, its properties, and the special touch of magic it had brought to his life; although the last was not something he spoke about, except to a few who were close to him. But he knew that, somehow, he had a deeply personal relationship with the well; that it had spoken to him and that he had heard its voice. It was the clearest contact he had ever had with the great mysteries of the world, and he knew that this would stay with him for all his days, no matter who else became aware of it.

When the three friends arrived at the holy well, Pock-face was clearly stunned to see how many people were already there. "There must be more than a hundred folk here," he said as he stood at the top of the embankment, surveying the crowd. "And look! More are arriving all the time. Have you ever seen anything like it?"

"Yes," replied Bren softly, "in a dream."

Trib had not stopped but continued to walk down the steep, new path that now led to the well. He had been here on several occasions since recovering from his wounds – to give thanks. But even though he believed what others had told him about the holy waters saving his life, he had never heard the voice of the well – not like Bren. Still, he knew that it had blessed him with its powers on that dreadful day two years ago, and today he would publicly demonstrate the reverence and gratitude he felt for it.

People continued to arrive from different directions; some walking, some hobbling with sticks, and some being carried. While Pock-face remained staring at the growing throng, Bren saw the crowd nearest the well spread apart as Trib walked towards them. It was obvious that they recognized him from the scars on his face, and they deferred to him because of his special role in the history of this holy place.

But then a whisper passed among the gathering, and people began looking towards Bren. His association with the well, if not his face, was now known throughout the region. Some of the visitors had already started to edge their way in his direction when the loud voice of Dorvar filled the woods, and everybody stood still.

Bren's father was acknowledged as one of the area's most accomplished priests – that is to say, a person who has both a learned and a natural ability to understand many of the mysteries of the world, and who dedicates his life to using these abilities for his people. So it was appropriate for him to begin the ceremony associated with this rediscovered holy well, and to do so on this day – called *Belnarn*, the start of summer. Standing to one side of the well, Dorvar spoke about his grandfather's mentioning of it, and its links back to the time of the Old Ones – those who probably placed the white stones around its perimeter – and back further to the beginning of all things. He then told the story of the bear attack: of Natach's death, of Trib's wounds, and of Bren's discovery; and how the waters had helped heal Trib. At this point many faces turned in the direction of the two young men, and Dorvar gestured for both of them to come to his side. He then proceeded to tell those gathered that despite the holiness of the well and its willingness to aid some of those who were sick, it would not bestow such gifts on everyone who sought its help. For reasons that no man or woman of this world could understand, it used its power for the benefit of only a few. After death, the meaning of this mystery might be revealed to us, he said. But not now.

When Dorvar had finished, he sat on a fallen willow log next to where he had been standing. The two young men joined him; and then the deep, slow beating of a pigskin drum began to fill the air. Bren looked across to the other side of the well, at the drummer. It was Big Godin. Then, three young women started to play a melody on reed pipes – something new, obviously composed for the occasion. Almost immediately, people began to form into small circles, and to dance – rotating in the same direction as the sun when it moves across the sky. Very gradually, the drumming increased in speed; the repetitive melody of the pipes matching the changing beat. Soon, the circles of dancers were moving quickly, with the people also twirling around individually and crying out words of tribute.

It was then that the sick and injured began to approach the well. Dorvar helped those who could not kneel unaided before its waters, and gently poured small amounts of the holy liquid from his cupped hands over their heads or arms or chest or whatever other parts of their bodies were ailing. Those who knelt offered their prayers to the well, but few others could hear their words because of the music and the shouts of praise coming from the dancers. Bren watched this and knew that for most there would be a wait of many days before they could determine whether the well had helped them or not.

He also knew that this was not a time when he could listen for the voice of the well. For this, he needed to be alone, with only the sounds of the forest creatures and the wind through the trees and the gentle tinkling of water passing over the white stones to be heard. He understood the need for communal ceremony amongst his people, the shared experience confirming their kinship, and he appreciated the strength they drew from each other – and from other entities – on these occasions. But he was relieved when the early morning ceremony finally came to an end and people headed for Ceann Tull or other locations where more celebrations of *Belnarn* would be held. The well would now be left more or less alone for another year and he could concentrate on an event that, although still three days away, was already causing him and his two friends to bubble over like a boiling pot with excitement. At last they were to leave Ceann Tull to begin their great adventure.

* * * * * * * * * * * * *

It was already late as the three young men stepped from the crannog's timber causeway and walked towards the waiting ponies. Bren looked up at The Wolf's Eye, the brightest star in the sky – first and last to be seen – and saw that its light was quickly fading in the glow of the coming sun. He had hoped to be some distance away from Ceann Tull by this time – they had a long journey ahead of them – but this didn't lessen his enthusiasm, or the sudden twinges of sadness that he had just started to feel.

The young boys holding the ponies were smiling as the three approached. And Bren noticed that people in the settlement's common area had stopped their early-morning duties and were also walking towards the animals. He knew that these more remotely related clan members would want to offer their parting good wishes. The youths' closer relatives had already given them hugs and blessings in the crannog, and had agreed not to attend their actual departure. But after turning to see what was causing the clattering on the causeway they saw that this agreement had obviously been revoked. Vana, Kinnow, Elin, Chata, Pock-face's parents and siblings, and Trib's, and an assortment of other cousins and aunts and uncles were all running along the raised walkway towards them.

"We already had the whole clan ceremony last night," sighed Trib, "and then all the tears and well-intentioned admonishments earlier this morning. I thought we would now just quietly ride out of here."

"That, my dark-haired little friend, is clearly not going to happen," Pock-face said through smiling lips – obviously enjoying being the centre of attention.

As they took the reins of their ponies, men clasped their shoulders and wished them a safe and prosperous journey, while women – and some of the more daring young girls – squeezed their forearms just above the wrist and told them they would be missed. Then there was another period of hugging, and as the tears again began to flow, Bren called to his friends, "We go." In a single action they disengaged themselves from the tangle of well-wishers, and jumped over the hindquarters of their ponies, landing in the simple leather saddles that were strapped onto the animals' backs. The crowd stood back in surprise. It was a very swift manoeuvre, and one of the many skills that Bren had insisted they practise over the last three seasons. He didn't know a lot about the world outside of the region of the Tull but he knew it wasn't a safe place and that there would probably be times when they would have to fight and times when they would have to flee. They had trained themselves, and been helped by others in the clan, in both these areas – the call for immediate and swift departure being one such skill. From atop his mount, Bren looked for Dorvar amongst the crowd but could not see him, and assumed that his father was honouring his agreement not to extend the farewell beyond that given earlier in the crannog. He looked over to his companions. Together they gave and received last words of good wishes, and then trotted off along the track to the east. They would follow this along the shores of the lake and then close to the banks of the river that flowed from it. A short distance hence, they would ford the river, and then head north – their ultimate destination being a faraway settlement called Laghana, where a sister of Bren's paternal grandfather went to live with her new husband two generations ago. But this was only to give a physical goal for their roving and, perhaps, to suggest a safe haven in a far-off and sometimes turbulent region. The true purpose of their expedition, however, was to partake of the discoveries and learning and tasting of life that only travel to unfamiliar places can bring.

At the first bend in the track, the three adventurers stopped their ponies and looked back at the small crowd.

"Take in all that you see my friends," Bren said. "For this will be our last view of our home for who knows how long."

Together, they gazed at the distant mountains – the highest being the most hallowed, and at the Tull whose shimmering waters brought forth life and accepted the dead, and at the surrounding forests of great pines with their multitude of wild beasts, and at their small settlement of Ceann Tull – its crannog sitting out in the water and linking the shoreline dwellings to the mystical powers of the sacred lake; and, finally, at the people of their clan – those who had cared for them and nurtured them since childhood. Then, away from the settlement, on the cleared hillside that contained the stone circle of Chlocht, Bren saw a solitary figure standing. Even though some distance away, he could see that it was Dorvar, his father; and at his feet sat the form of his great hound, Con. Dorvar had his left hand raised – a sign of blessing. Bren felt tears forming around his eyes, and he glanced self-consciously at his friends. They paused for another moment, together waving to those they loved, before prompting their ponies to walk on. As they rounded the bend, Bren, who was in front, looked back at his friends. Both were silent, sadness sitting on their shoulders. He felt the same but knew there would be no benefit in dwelling on such things.

"Now it really begins," he said with a smile. "I'll race you to the river."

****

For some time now Bren and Trib and Pock-face had been riding in and out of the shadows of various nearby peaks. At noon, they had stopped in the sunshine at a settlement not unlike their own that sat on the river called the Tuml. Here they had been given the hospitality of food and drink before moving on. This was to be expected – the people in this region being of the same stock as those of the Tull, and speakers of a similar dialect. But now the trio was moving further north, towards regions not often visited by members of their clan. The track they were following took them along the eastern base of what was known locally as the Mountain of the Herds; and as they left its shadow and once more felt the warm rays of the sun, they saw that this would again change before too long.

"With all these hills and mountains pressing on our side it is easy to lose track of the day," said Trib. "See! The sun is already dropping towards those peaks."

"You're right," Bren replied as he pointed ahead and to his left. "There should be a small lake just beyond that rise. That's where the Tuml folk said they had a fishing lodge. We should stay there tonight – and catch fish now for our evening meal."

"That can be Pock-face's responsibility," Trib smiled, "his reward for being last to cross the Tull this morning."

"A fine idea, Trib," Bren replied.

"I hope you both step in pony shit," Pock-face retorted.

Later that night they were inside the small wooden lodge, sitting close to the embers of a fire on which they had cooked their freshly-caught trout.

"That was very tasty," said Bren as he looked across at Pock-face. "You have always been a good fisherman."

"He's from the Tull, what do you expect?" Trib added.

"We are Tull men!" Pock-face shouted in a voice deeper than normal.

"Remember Ceann Tull!" the other two shouted back with the full strength of their lungs – this being the ancient war cry of their clan. Outside, they heard a tawny owl make its own 'kew wit' contribution to the sudden outburst. The ponies at the other end of the lodge continued to munch on the pile of wild grasses that had been cut for them, unperturbed by the shouting. The three young men laughed loudly, then chuckled, and were finally silent.

"Do you think we will ever use that cry in a real battle?" asked Trib.

"I don't know," Bren replied. "Our lands have been free of major confrontations for a long time, but we hear more and more about raids and battles in surrounding places."

"Because of the Kelti, you mean?" asked Pock-face.

"Yes, but not only them," Bren answered. "The seasons have been changing little by little for a generation now. Lands that were once good for growing crops are now useless – some being overtaken by peat. Trees no longer grow in the higher parts of the mountains as they once did. And in many places game is becoming harder to hunt."

"So?"

"So, in some areas, the land is not as abundant a supplier as it used to be. And this is beginning to cause people in those places to look for new, and better land ... and to sometimes fight those who are already there – or to raid the settlements that have good stores of cattle and grain."

"But Ceann Tull is safe, isn't it?" Trib asked, a frown forming on his face. "I mean, the people of the Tull are many and they look after each other."

"Well, there hasn't been a serious raid since we were young children – and it is probably because of strong leadership ..." he thought of his father but didn't mention him, "... and our reputation from the past of being great warriors when necessary. But the world is changing and I fear that we may see fighting before too long."

Trib was clearly worried by these words. "Then should we be gone from our families at this time? Shouldn't we be back with them, preparing to defend our lands?"

Pock-face, who usually interpreted events and situations in a light-hearted manner, now spoke in a serious voice. "My friend, our families, our clan, did not force us to stay with them when we announced our intention to leave. This was because the elders – especially Bren's father – were willing to gamble that we would return wiser and more experienced in the ways of the world, and therefore be in a better position to help the clan in the days and years ahead."

Trib looked at Bren, who nodded in agreement, impressed by his cousin's words.

"And what if we don't return?" asked Trib solemnly.

"Then they will have lost the gamble," replied Pock-face who, after a pause and with a smile added, "Just like *you* will lose if you gamble that piece of breadcake on your dish in an arm-wrestling challenge."

"And what will I get if I win?" said Trib, his mood changing.

"I won't beat you up," Pock-face responded with feigned sincerity. Trib glanced at Bren and then flung himself on Pock-face, tickling the older youth's sides under his tunic. While they were rolling and squealing on the earth floor, Bren smiled; he was fortunate to have these two friends. His smile broadened further as he reached over and took the piece of breadcake off Trib's wooden dish, making sure they would see him eating it.

Next morning they followed the northern track into a mainly forested valley. There were some dwellings near the banks of a small river that flowed through the valley, and in the distance they saw several people in a cleared field piling rocks into an ox cart. But the people did not return their waves – only stared in their direction. So they rode on. They then left the valley and began what they knew would be a long and arduous climb up into the appropriately named Mountains of the Sky.

Two days later, in mid morning, the three dismounted at the highest point of the track they had been following. This was in a wide, treeless area know as the Field of Champions, in memory of a battle long ago between the most skillful warriors of two ancient clans. It was also a major pass for entering (or leaving) this vast mountain range – thus making it strategically important in terms of defence as well as significant to those who would travel across the range. From here the track split in two. One branch went to the northeast and would ultimately take a person to the large settlement of Mora on the shores of the great Eastern Sea. The other, according to the deer-hide map that Dorvar had given his son, and which Bren now consulted, should take them into the valleys of the Grey Mountains. These were wild areas not often visited by outsiders, but many settlements were there – one of them being Laghana, where his grandfather's sister had gone; if in fact it still existed.

"Thank the trees it will be downhill from here," said Pock-face as he finished drinking from the water bladder that hung from his shoulder.

Bren turned to him. "Yes, the ponies are looking a bit tired, and also in need of a drink. My map shows a small stream crossing the track just beyond that hill," he pointed to a small wooded hill not far distant. "There should also be a settlement there where we might be able to exchange some of our goods for food." This excited the interest of the others because it would be their first encounter with people of a different heritage and, perhaps, a different way of doing things.

A short time later they rounded the hill and for the first time saw the full extent of the wide valley that spread out below them. And they were stunned by its beauty. There were large, cleared fields where grain grew and cattle grazed, and a river that meandered across these fields and through the adjoining forests like a great watery viper. On both sides were steep, wooded mountains and so too at the distant, northwestern end of the valley.

While Trib and Pock-face marvelled at this view, Bren was more concerned with a closer feature. About three hundred paces away – across a boggy looking area – was a small, flat-topped knoll with several columns of smoke rising from its centre. He knew from his map that this was where there should be a settlement, but he could see no dwellings. Then he noticed figures appearing at the top of the knoll, as if coming from its inside. His first thought was of magic – he had heard stories about people who lived in such hillocks. But then he realized that the figures were standing atop a circular earthen wall that surrounded the settlement, and that inside, but out of view, must be the dwellings.

Pock-face now joined his cousin in looking at the fortified settlement. "What are those, Bren?" he asked, pointing. "Are they giant ants? – or small people who live under the ground?"

"Neither. I think they're ordinary folk but for some reason they have built a fence of soil around their settlement – look, the grass is new on some parts."

"But it's so high, I can't even see the roofs of the dwellings," Pock-face replied, astonished.

Trib had now also turned his attention to the settlement. "Should we approach it, Bren? They don't look very friendly," he said.

"I think it will be all right as long as we show that we mean no harm. And we do need food. My worry is how to get there; the place looks as if it's surrounded by bog."

"Here," said Pock-face as he took the lead. "This way seems drier."

They were half way to the earthen wall when the ponies' hooves started sinking into the black mud beneath the grassy tussocks.

"There has to be a solid path somewhere, but I can't see where it is," said Pock-face as the others approached him – their ponies also struggling.

Suddenly, a series of screams made them lose interest in the mud, and to look towards the settlement. About ten men were running in their direction from the right side of the mounded wall, while others were racing down its steep face. And all were brandishing weapons.

"We could stay and talk," said Bren as he jumped from his pony and helped it step back to the firmer ground. "Or we could forget about parleying and get away from here right now." Trib and Pock-face didn't have to ask which alternative Bren favoured, and they too pulled their ponies to the harder ground. All three then quickly mounted and rode as fast as they were able back to the main track, and then down further into the valley. The men from the settlement stopped chasing when they saw that their unwelcome visitors were leaving, and shouted curses after them.

"What are they yelling?" Trib called as he encouraged his pony to trot faster.

"Something about your scrotum being small," Bren called back.

"Obviously they know about you," Pock-face chuckled while still nervously glancing over his shoulder.

A short time later they slowed down.

"What was that all about?" said Trib, a worried look on his face. "Those people weren't even interested in seeing what we might want. And why have they gone to the trouble of making a great earthen wall around their little settlement? It must have taken many seasons work."

"Perhaps it is not safe in this region," replied Bren, "But …" He stopped speaking and turned forward in his saddle to see why Pock-face had nudged him. Suddenly, his body tautened.

A man had appeared on the track ten paces ahead. He had nocked an arrow in the large bow he was carrying, but did not have the bow drawn – although this would only take him a moment. He was tall and muscular, and wore a cap made from what looked like beaver fur. And his upper garment was made from thick leather that was laced down the sides. On his side hung a sword – but not of bronze, and on his back was a small, circular shield of wood.

"Step down from your animals," the man said in a heavily accented voice.

Bren looked back at his two friends and then down at his bow which was strapped to the side of his pony. He also wore a sword – a short one, of bronze, held in a finely crafted scabbard of wood and leather. He carefully placed his hand on its hilt.

"Think not that way or you will die," the stranger said as he raised his bow. At this moment two more men appeared from the bushes on the side of the track, and three more came up behind Trib. All were armed with either spears or bows.

"We mean no harm," said Bren as he raised his hands in a sign of peace and submission.

"We shall see," the stranger replied. "Now dismount or I will surely put an arrow through your heart." Bren swallowed hard and then slowly lifted his left leg across the pony's withers and slid to the ground. His friends did the same. What happened next was filled with confusion.

Terrifying screams filled the air as at least ten smallish, dark-haired men ran from a clump of birch trees on the left-hand slope above the track – a similar number ran from behind a rock outcrop on the right-hand side. They were all armed with spears or swords or long axe-like weapons. The stranger and his followers immediately lost interest in Bren and his two companions, and prepared to receive the charge from the frenzied short men. In an instant, the clash had begun.

Bren momentarily tried to think of how he could extricate himself and his friends from the attack. After all, they were visitors to the region, with no prior history of violence toward anyone here. But that train of thought abruptly ended when he was confronted by one of the attackers, a muscular man with a scruffy beard and wild, dark eyes. The man used both hands to swing his large bronze sword at Bren who took a giant step back just in time to feel the breeze of the blade across his face. As this happened, the young Tull man pulled his own shorter sword from its scabbard with one hand, and a dagger from his belt with the other, and as the bearded man swung his sword back, Bren parried it with his own and then thrust his dagger up under the man's ribs. The bearded man dropped his sword and fell back clutching at his wound – the smell of bile filling the air.

At that moment, as he looked wide-eyed at the figure before him, Bren heard Pock-face's distinctive voice call, "Bren, drop!" Responding as he had in their self-imposed training sessions, Bren fell to the ground just as a large axe blade swept above his head. He saw his attacker to one side, the dark-haired man pulling back his cumbersome weapon for a second swing. And in the heartbeat that followed, Bren lunged with his sword at the man's groin. The sharp edges of the blade sliced through leather and cloth, and the axe-bearer screamed as he fell to his knees – blood quickly oozing from around the penetrating metal. Bren withdrew his weapon and his assailant collapsed.

At this point, the young man from the Tull became aware of his own rapid breathing, and for the first time was able to hurriedly take in the scene that now surrounded him. Already, there were many bodies lying on the track and in the nearby bushes. Pock-face was wrestling in the dirt with one of the short men – both had daggers – but he could not see Trib, and a chill went through his body. The ponies were also gone, and where they had stood there were now bodies and several pairs of men fighting for their lives.

As he began to stand up, Bren heard an accented voice cry, "Stranger, your help." He turned and saw the tall man that had stopped him and his friends earlier. Two of the diminutive attackers were hacking at him with their swords while he was reaching for his own that lay on the ground – warding off their chopping with his oak targe. A third attacker to one side had a spear raised and appeared to be calling to his comrades to step back so he could make a clear hurl. They obviously understood, but as they stepped away, Bren quickly grabbed at a large stone that lay on the track near his feet, and flung it with all his strength at the spearer. The stone smashed into the side of the man's head and he dropped to the ground. One of the tall man's other attackers cast a surprised glance at Bren but decided to continue to aid his comrade – probably thinking that it would only take a moment. But the tall man had now regained his sword, and as the closest of his attackers swung a bronze blade down, he swung his dark-metal blade upwards. There was a muffled clanging sound, and Bren's jaw dropped as he saw part of the bronze sword go spinning in the air – cut through by the dark metal. This also clearly shocked its owner but he did not withdraw; instead, he threw himself bodily at the tall man, screaming abuse. This was an unfortunate thing to do because just at that moment the second attacker brought down his blade; but rather than dismembering the tall man, it cut through the spine of his fellow warrior. The remaining small man stood aghast at what he had just done, but the man with the dark sword showed no mercy and thrust it into his attacker's throat. The gurgling sound was loud at first but then quickly faded to silence.

Bren's heart was pounding as he quickly cast his gaze around the bloody scene, waiting for another attack. But it was over, except for the groans and cries of the injured. It appeared that two of the tall man's colleagues had survived with only minor cuts and they were helping a third who had a horrendous gash through his collar bone, his arm hanging

– almost severed. One of the bearded attackers had raised himself to his hands and knees and appeared to be calling for help; his intestines were hanging from his slashed abdomen. The tall man quickly walked over and cut the poor wretch's throat. He looked across at Bren and said, "I do him a favour, disembowelment is not a good way to die." Bren turned away and began to vomit.

He was wiping his mouth when he felt the tall man's hand on his shoulder. "This was your first skirmish was it not?" the man said. Bren nodded as he suddenly realized that he would never be the same – that he had abruptly farewelled his childhood and youth; that he had now killed other men. But then something more immediate struck him.

"Pock-face! Trib!" he called as he desperately surveyed the bodies all around him.

"Your older friend sits over there by the rowan," he pointed to a small tree by the side of the track. "He appears uninjured – but he too brings up his food." Bren saw his cousin spitting out the remains of his retching. He then stood up and waved. There was a dark-haired body at his feet. Panic streaked across Bren's face.

"Trib!" he yelled as he ran towards the body.

"Fear not, it is not your friend," called the tall man.

Bren stopped, his head turning back and forth. "Then where?" he shouted.

By this time Pock-face had hurried to his cousin's side. "Six of those bearded wildcats took him – and our ponies. They were yelling at Trib and would not fight him, even though he slashed at them with his sword. I saw one sneaking up behind him with a club. I called a warning but then I had my own problem to sort out," he pointed at the body back near the tree. "I don't know what happened next, but he's not here."

The tall stranger then spoke. "He was knocked on the head and then thrown over one of the ponies. The group of them then ran your animals back up the track. They will be well on their way to some hiding place in the hills by now."

"But why did they take him?" Bren asked. "And why wouldn't they fight him?"

"They hesitated to engage with him, I think, because he looks like one of their own – a Cattach."

"Were *they* Cattach?" asked Pock-face. "We have heard stories of this tribe but never have we seen them."

Bren nodded, and the stranger continued.

"They are short but strong, and always dark haired and, as you can see, most of the men – except their leaders – wear beards. Some say that they are direct descendants of the Old Ones, the builders of the stone dances. They mainly dwell in the far north, but for a year now they have been raiding and harassing our lands."

"And you think they mistook Trib to be one of them because of his size and his dark hair?" Bren asked, frowning.

"Most surely. And without a beard, they may have thought him of high birth. We have several such individuals that we have captured in recent conflicts; perhaps they mistook him for one, and assumed you were his captors. Indeed, we thought him a Cattach leader and that you were his foreign mercenaries."

"But what will they do when they find out the truth – that he is a Tull man?" said Bren.

"The Cattach are very protective of their kin," the man answered. "They may think he is one of theirs but that he was taken in childhood." Bren and Pock-face looked towards each other, the same thought having crossed their minds. The stranger observed this. "Could this be true? Could he be Cattach?"

"Like I said," replied Bren in a firm tone. "He is a Tull man."

"And we would both die for him," added Pock-face. "So how do we get him back?"

The tall man didn't answer but walked away, looking at the bodies on the ground. Bren nodded to Pock-face. It appeared there would be no help here, so they prepared to leave, to search for their friend alone. But then the tall man called, "Here is your answer." He was standing over one of the Cattach, his sword at the man's throat, and he began speaking to him in an unfamiliar tongue. The dark-haired warrior had blood trickling from a wound on his head and another on his right leg, but he stood up, nodded, and then hobbled away, up the track. "Let him be," the tall man called to his men who already had their weapons raised. He then walked back to Bren and Pock-face. "I have spared his life so that he might deliver a message to his band – that we will make an exchange – your friend for one of our captives."

"How will this be arranged?" asked Bren, thankful for the immediate action of the stranger.

"They will contact us. Do not worry, we have done this before." Bren sighed as he again looked at Pock-face. There was little else they could do but trust this man who a short time ago had threatened to put an arrow through Bren's heart. "We must go now," the tall man said, "in case more Cattach return. But before we move on we must know each other's names. I am Poltan, of the Spey, and that is …" He went on to name his surviving comrades. Bren and Pock-face introduced themselves – and made a point of naming their missing friend, and of stating that he was their kin.

Shortly after this, as Poltan was making preparations to lead the group down the track, deeper into the valley, Bren spoke quietly to him. "Poltan, where are you taking us, and why do you make our concerns yours? With our ponies went almost all our possessions, so we have nothing we can give you, and we will have to rely on your good favour."

Poltan took off his beaver-fur cap and ran his fingers through greasy brown hair. "We go to Ardvortag where my father is chief, and where we will await contact by the Cattach. I offer my assistance because I owe you my life. You did not have to help me when I called – especially since moments earlier I had forced you from your pony. But you did help, and this I will not forget. As for relying on my good favour, it is yours for as long as you wish. All the same, I'm sure we can find something for you to do if you so desire," he added with a smile. "But now, hurry, we must leave here."

"Just one more thing," Bren said as Poltan was turning, thinking the conversation was over. "Your sword …"

"It is made of iron," he replied without looking back. Bren glanced around at Pock-face as they started to run after their new ally. "Iron?" he said with a frown.

Chapter 6

Professor Gerrard's face was well tanned when compared to the pale features of most of his academic colleagues. Sitting opposite him, James wondered whether it was golf or sailing or bush-walking that gave the man his robust complexion. Or whether, perhaps, it was because he sat in his garden at weekends holding a strip of aluminium foil under his chin. James felt a slight smile form on his own face when this thought crossed his mind. It would be entirely appropriate for the head of the physics department to use solar radiation in such a way. He liked this professor. The man was a lateral thinker and an innovator, and the sort of individual who couldn't care less when other people smirked or laughed at his mild eccentricities.

"Now, the note I have here, James, says that you want a reference from me. What, is this for a summer job?"

"No professor. I'm leaving the university, and the country. I'm hoping to be gone even before the graduation ceremony."

"Why, have you committed some dreadful crime? Must you flee the land of the kangaroo because someone overheard you being critical of Australian-rules football?"

"No," James smiled.

"Then perhaps you don't like meat pies and tomato sauce, or you're allergic to koalas and platypuses."

"No, neither of those."

"Then you shouldn't leave here – I can't think of any other reasonable reasons why you should want to go."

James wasn't sure how to respond; the older man wasn't smiling, but then he leant forward across his desk. "Now let me be serious, James," he said with no change of expression. "You are one of our brightest undergraduates. I was sure that you would want to go on to an honours year – and then a masters and probably a PhD." He sat back and opened a drawer. "Do you want a banana?"

"Umm, no thanks," James replied, wondering if this was still serious time. "It's just that I feel the need to find out more about the world. I don't mean like why electron energy states are the way they are, or whether tachyons actually exist; I mean like getting my hands dirty doing different things, being immersed in different cultures, being thrown into situations that would never occur if I stayed here – and seeing how I cope. Does that make any sense?"

Gerrard put his feet up on his desk – one had a sock on, the other not. "It makes complete sense James and, ironically, it makes me wish even more that you were staying here to pursue your studies." He paused and looked at the half-peeled banana in his hand, and then continued. "If, after tasting life in other places, you decide to use your brain to investigate energy states or to chase after tachyons, or to pursue any of the other myriad mysteries open to physics, then please make sure you get in touch with me – I would be happy to be your supervisor."

James was touched. His grades were always good, but he hadn't realized that Gerrard had such a high opinion of him. They had often engaged in lengthy question and answer exchanges in lectures and tutorials, and even had the occasional debate, but James thought that this had probably annoyed the esteemed scholar rather than engendered his respect. For a moment he considered confiding in the professor his other reason for wanting to leave – he could do with some outside advice – but Gerrard was already standing with his hand extended.

"I'm sorry, James, but I'm already late for a meeting with the vice-chancellor and his collection of sycophants. I'd be happy to talk with you further, later, if you want, but I really must go now. I will write you a reference tonight and post it tomorrow. I wish you well on your voyage of discovery ... and don't forget what I said."

James shook his hand, thanked him, and then left the office. As he stepped into the corridor he heard the professor calling, "Miriam, where are my shoes?"

※※※※※※※※※※※※※

The grassy slopes outside the State Library and Museum complex were, and still are, favourite relaxation spots for many Melbournians – particularly around midday, and especially during summer. James found an area between a pair of female students who were reciting passages to each other from a shared book, and a lone, suited, businessman-looking person who was sitting on a plastic shopping bag whilst reading the *Financial Review*. Pigeons wandered around picking up scraps of discarded lunch. James bit into his meat pie and tomato sauce and thought about his brief meeting with the professor. What he'd told Gerrard was true; he did want to extend his wings and discover new people and places.

But the other – unmentioned – reason for wanting leave the university, and the country, was Belinda.

He had only met her eight weeks ago but she had knocked him off his feet. He was totally smitten. And now that she had returned to England he was desperate to join her. He closed his eyes as he recalled their passionate romance. She had come to Australia to visit her married sister who lived in the same street as James. They had met late one afternoon when she was taking her sister's German shepherd for a walk. The dog had broken away from her after spying old Mrs Morrison's cat, and James had helped sort out the resultant commotion. To start with, they had simply gone out together as new friends – a film, a rock concert. He was studying for final exams, and she had family and touristy things to do for a lot of the time, so there was nothing regular, and nothing really romantic.

But then there was the trip to the Botanical Gardens – something he had arranged when he found that they shared an interest in exotic flowers and trees. After wandering around for a short while, she had taken his arm – and laughed at his joke about squirrels gathering nuts. She had continued to hold on – and moved closer – as they walked down the shady paths. It had been the first time either of them had made any sort of provocative physical contact, and it had happened just at the time when he was beginning to see her in a different, softer, sort of way, despite the fact that right from the beginning she had told him about her boyfriend back home.

He opened his eyes and took a bite from his pie, and then closed them again. They had sat on the grass; just like he was doing now. And while she was looking at the ducks in a nearby pond, he had examined her exquisite profile – her long blonde hair; her soft, pale skin – and he had gently touched the side of her face. That had been it. Megatons of passionate energy must have been transferred back and forth during that touch. Tetratons. They had then joined in a long, silky, smooth kiss, and it had taken all their social conditioning for them to not actually slip into serious lovemaking then and there. But this certainly happened later that night in his bedroom, and it was lovemaking like he had never known before; wet and warm and wonderful. Two weeks later she left – family and work commitments back in London being inescapable.

She had telephoned him from Singapore during a stopover and said she loved him and wanted him to come to England to be with her – and that she would immediately leave her boyfriend. This was all James had needed. Belinda was like no other girl he had ever known, and she had appeared in his life just when his sense of adventure was beginning to be stirred in new ways. He opened his eyes, wondering if the two compulsions were related. The nearby girls were still reciting to each other, but the businessman was gone. He stood up, knowing that he shouldn't waste time. There was a lot to do if he was going to Britain – especially since he had almost no money.

****

"Fill out this form and send it to the address at the top. The company will contact you if a suitable position becomes available." James took the form from the bored looking woman. This was the last of the five shipping companies he had on his list. At least this one had a form to fill out. The woman continued, "But without any prior experience at sea, it's not very likely they'll want to take you on."

"Makes you wonder how you're supposed to get prior experience doesn't it?" James replied – friendly but revealing some of the annoyance he was feeling.

"There's no need to be smart with me," the woman snapped, suddenly more alive. "I don't make the rules."

"Yeah, I'm sorry," James responded. "I just want to get to England."

The woman's expression changed – apologies were rare in her world. "No money?" she asked sympathetically.

"Nowhere near enough," James replied.

"A girl?" the woman asked.

James was surprised; such a personal question from a total stranger; but what the hell, she seemed to understand. "Yeah, a girl," he replied.

"Look," the woman said, "the international shipping companies that operate in Melbourne mainly use Asian or Middle Eastern or Pacific Islander crews – they're cheaper. The chances of you landing a job on a boat that is heading for the UK – particularly when you have no training or experience – is pretty remote. And it would take you ages to get there besides. Don't you have anything you can sell?"

"The only thing of any real value that I have is my hi-fi system. It's only six months old and I'd saved for it for ages, but it's made up of high-quality bits and pieces, and your general punter isn't interested because of the price."

"Well isn't that a coincidence," she said. "My husband and I are great lovers of classical music; and especially of old recordings of orchestras from the past. Could your system cope with such things?"

"Like you wouldn't believe," James answered. "It's set up to handle old records and to reduce hiss and rumble and all the rest."

"Then it sounds like it might just be a matter of a demonstration and the price. But I should tell you, we are willing to pay for a system we like." She smiled, and James had the vague feeling that there was more than a straightforward commercial transaction taking place here – like she really wanted to help him.

A week later, he was at Melbourne's Tullamarine International Airport, walking through the doors to Immigration and Customs and the departure lounges. He stopped briefly and gave a final wave to his much-loved dad – his mother had said goodbye at home; an 'important prior engagement' keeping her from going to the airport – and to the one friend who had come to say goodbye. He then turned and walked on.

Sitting in the departure lounge waiting for the call to board the plane, he looked around at the other passengers: suits and ties, off on business trips; elderly pairs, making what might be their last visit back to the old country; people around his age, finally embarking on the year-long adventure they'd been saving for; and an assortment of short-term tourists and others he couldn't categorize. It was a young teenager from this latter group – a member of a family on holiday, he guessed – that caught his attention. The boy was tall and lanky, and had long hair and a face full of pimples. He reminded James of what he, himself, had looked like only five or six years ago.

What a time that had been: girls constantly on his mind – nothing much had changed in that respect except that it was one particular girl who was haunting his brain now; his realization that science and the pursuit of knowledge were things that he was good at and that they filled him with wonder and excitement; and his first steps into the whirlpool of religion. Ah, yes, religion. Frown lines formed between his eyebrows as he thought about his long involvement with the church, and his recent rejection of it. For years, he'd been drawn into the ways of thinking dictated by all the tradition and doctrine. And, for a while, he had tried to put aside his natural skepticism in order to feel as though he belonged to the group. But it hadn't lasted. As he had matured and become more confident in his own ability to think critically, the unanswerable questions about Christianity had caused him to not only reject the dogma but also the trappings that went with it. First he stopped going to bible classes, and then became an infrequent attender of church services.

He and his friend Eddy, and a few other young church members, had started a Sunday activities program for kids in a nearby high-rise estate. No religious stuff, just playing games or going on visits to places like zoos or the beach. Those estates were real shit-holes and lots of the young kids were already aggressive and untrusting and full of hate. Setting up the program had seemed like a good thing to do. But the church elders hadn't liked it. When they had questioned James and the others about it they were disturbed by the fact that there wasn't any religious instruction or attempts to bring the young participants into the church. But it was obvious that they were mainly annoyed because they didn't have control over the program.

The crunch had come one Sunday when James had left the others playing cricket in a park so he could attend the morning service – something that was becoming increasingly rare. Afterwards, one of the deacons had told James that he shouldn't be wearing dirty jeans and a tee-shirt to church services, that he should be more respectful in his attitude, and that what he was doing with the kids was a waste of time if he wasn't 'bringing them to Christ.' That had been it for James. He had lingered on for a short while with Eldewood Baptist Church, but it wasn't long before he gave up his involvement completely. Now, as he sat and thought about it, he realized it had been a passing phase for him – important, but not permanent. It had allowed him access to ideas and beliefs that were stimulating and a joy to ponder but, eventually, to mainly reject. However, the experience had helped him to grow broader intellectually – which was somewhat ironic – and to understand the power that religion can have over people.

His skepticism and rejections had torn away at the basic beliefs that the church had tried to convince him to embrace, so now there was something of a void in his mind about the nature of the universe and his place in it. But that was okay – maybe it was the way things should be. Eddy had summed up the situation fairly concisely when they had spoken about it recently. 'Fuck, I dunno,' he had said. James smiled to himself. Good ol' Eddy – he was the only friend who had gotten up early enough to come to the airport to say farewell; but then, James knew that he still didn't really have many friends.

* * * * * * * * * * * * * *

He eased himself into the economy-class seat and wondered whether he would survive the 24,000km journey with his knees up near his face. The one-night stopover in Bangkok was advertised as an opportunity to 'unwind' after the first part of the journey. James now saw that this was probably meant to be taken literally, especially by long-legged people like himself. He sighed as he glanced at the empty seat next to him.

"You look horribly cramped with your seat forward like that."

He was taken by surprise, and quickly turned his head to see a short, plump young woman standing in the aisle next to him. She had her dark hair tied back in a ponytail, and she looked to be in her mid twenties – and attractive, he thought.

"Umm ..." he said as she bent over him, pointing.

"Here, just press this button and lean back." James did as he was told, and suddenly felt more comfortable.

"Thanks," he smiled. "I'm a bit of a novice with all this flying stuff."

"Well, I can be your private tutor if you want," she replied, loading a bag into an overhead locker. "We'll be sitting next to each other for a long time."

Her name was Susan. She was with a group of five other young travellers who were also headed for England. They had no particular group plans beyond renting a flat together and finding work for six months or so. At the end of that period they would decide whether to stay together and do some joint travelling on the Continent – maybe in a campervan – or go their separate ways. They had met on a farm during the recent fruit-picking season in northern Victoria where they had lived together – with many others – in a bunkhouse. It appeared that Susan had been the catalyst and organizer for the current adventure. She seemed an earthy sort of woman with an easily triggered sense of humour, and James got the impression that she was generous with her affection and concern for those she liked – someone who you would be lucky to have as a friend.

"It's going to be a blast in Bangkok," she said after staring out the window for a long while. "The three boys in our group want to go to a couple of those outrageous strip places you hear about, but us girls mainly want to check out the local foods and handicrafts and clothes. What do you plan to do, James?"

"Well, we're only there for a single night. I thought I'd just get something to eat, go for a bit of a wander … and then go to bed."

"Now that sounds sensible – unplanned, pragmatic, laid-back. Would you mind if I joined you in your wandering?"

James looked across at her, at her dark eyes and soft smile, and got the distinct impression that she wasn't trying to flirt with him but was holding out a hand to someone she thought might be in need of company. At any other time he probably would have made up an excuse for turning down such a request – he was used to being alone – but on this occasion, at this time, he felt that maybe he could do with some companionship. "That would be nice," he replied, and her smile broadened.

Twelve hours later, James was sitting in a bar called 'The Fat Man', across the road from the hotel where he and all the other passengers on his flight were staying. It was just after midnight. He and Susan had started their exploration of Bangkok by joining the rest of her small group of friends as they walked through a late-night market. After that, they'd tried some local food at a small café where they laughed and joked and toasted themselves, and then they went their different ways, but agreed to meet at this place at around 12:00am ... if possible.

"Well, we're obviously the first of our lot here," Susan said as she looked around before sliding into the booth. "We might be the only ones who make it I suppose," she added. "The girls will either be trying on the jewellery and clothes at those all-night places, or fluttering their eyelids at some gorgeous US military hunks in another bar. And I don't want to even think about what the boys might be up to."

"I admire the way you guys can be together but stay independent," James said. "And you seem like a pretty happy bunch."

"A lot of the time, yeah. But we're just like everyone else; we've each got our problems ... our ghosts." She gave that gentle smile again and added, "But we lean on each other from time to time. In fact, I think that's why we've stayed together as a group. There's no romance between us – not anymore at least – but we've all grown very close as friends." She placed an elbow on the table and rested her chin in her palm – and looked James in the eye. "So is there any romance in your life at the moment?" she said. "I get the impression that you're either running away from someone ... or maybe towards them."

James ran his fingers through his long hair and then leant back with his hands locked behind his head – trying to decide what to say. He'd only known this woman for less than a day, but there was something about her that felt secure ... and good.

"That's very astute of you, Susan," he replied. "Do you want to hear my story?"

She nodded, the look in her dark eyes letting him know that she would listen.

Half an hour later, he sighed. "Anyway, I guess I'll see what direction my life is going to take sometime tomorrow – or today, really – or … depends on the time zones I suppose."

Susan had asked questions but had not made any comments regarding James's journey to be with Belinda. Now she reached out and very gently held his hand.

"Stop that – stop that right now you two!" called one of Susan's male friends from the doorway of the bar. He was swaying on his feet, and wearing a strange looking pointed hat. The others in the group were behind him, smiling and giggling.

* * * * * * * * * * * * *

James had collected his luggage – a backpack, a shoulder bag, and a guitar – and was heading towards the Immigration area of Heathrow Airport, when Susan came running up to him.

"I just want to wish you good luck for the last time before you disappear from the airport," she panted. He looked behind her and saw the others standing with several trolleys full of luggage. They all waved. "Now remember, we'll be at the youth hostel in Holland Park for a few days. Leave a message or come and see me if you need anything; somewhere to stay, someone to talk to, a gum leaf to smell – I've got several in my bag. Anything at all."

James grinned. "Thanks Susan; you're a special person and I'm glad we met, but I think Belinda and I will remain in each others arms – constantly – for more than a few days. And I'm pretty sure that's all I'll need for a long, long time."

"But you haven't told her you're coming, right?"

"That's right. She thinks I'm still in Australia trying to decide if and how I should get here. It's going to be a great surprise for her." Susan hugged him and kissed his cheek, and then held herself back at arms length and gazed at his face. She then ran back to her friends who were now in the long, 'foreign nationals', queue.

James moved quickly along the shorter 'British citizens' queue and showed his new British passport to the woman behind the desk. His mother had never had a nice thing to say about the country of her birth – too many bad childhood memories, it seemed – but at least it had enabled James to get the little dark-blue-covered booklet that would allow him to stay in the country for as long as he liked; and to work, and even vote if he felt so inclined. Fifteen minutes later he was on a tube train headed for London. According to the little route map in his hand, it looked like he would only have to make a couple of changes before he'd be walking up the road to his beloved Belinda's flat in Hampstead. For the first time in the long journey, he became aware of his heart pounding, and his thoughts dwelt on images of Belinda's beautiful naked body lying next to him.

****

"I'm sorry, but I can't tell you what dorm she's in," the wrinkly-faced woman said sternly. However, her attitude seemed to mellow when she looked at James's face. "Look, love, why don't you stick your head into the dining hall and see if she's there – it's still early so she might be having breakfast. It's over there," she pointed.

"Thanks," James said without smiling.

Standing in the dining hall doorway, James could see that this was the granddaddy of all youth hostels – among those that he'd seen, at least. The hall was huge, with row upon row of benches and seats. And there was also a sprinkling of tables and chairs for those wanting to be classified as diners rather than eaters. It was at one of these tables that he spotted Susan and her friends. She saw him and enthusiastically beckoned him over.

"James! I am so glad to see you," she beamed – the others nodded and said hello. She clutched his hand. "I thought that we might have been ships passing in the night and all that, but I hoped not. Oh, it's so good to see you! How did everything go?" She was still grinning broadly, but then her expression changed as she looked up at James's face and saw his trembling lip.

"Umm, not so good," he said.

Susan promptly stood up and took hold of one of his arms. "Let's go over here," she said as she led him to a small table with no people around. They sat in silence for some minutes before he spoke.

"I just can't believe how she's changed," he finally said. "When I rang that doorbell my heart was in my mouth with excitement. I was going to grab her and swirl her into the air and kiss her, and we were both going to cry with happiness. But it was her fucking boyfriend who answered the door – in his fucking dressing gown. And then she came down the stairs dressed the same way. Jesus! She'd told me she was going to leave him and wait for me – that I was the only one she could ever truly love. And I believed her. Oh man, I hurt." He shook his head despondently.

"What happened then?" Susan asked.

"What happened then? ..." he responded, distantly. "Oh, she finally convinced Ralph or whatever his fucking name is to go, 'into the kitchen, so we can talk privately.' And then she told me that she had done some, 'very serious thinking,' over the last week, and had decided to stay with her BMW-driving-young-executive, fucking boyfriend. Oh, she still has 'strong feelings' for me," he said with a sneer. "She even knelt down in front of me and kissed my hands and asked me to forgive her. I just couldn't believe what was happening. I said, 'Come on Belinda, this is bullshit. Just think about what we told each other back in Australia; what we felt for each other; what we did together – it was wonderful!' She agreed that it had been wonderful but that on reflection, it had been, 'sort of a holiday thing,' for her. A fucking holiday thing! She said she was sorry and 'still confused,' and that she wanted me to stay in touch with her – as a friend. Then Mr BMW appeared and reminded her that they had dinner guests coming soon. So she asked me to leave! I'd just travelled half way round the world to be with her – because she asked me to come – and given up my studies and my way of life, just to be with her; and after seven point fucking three minutes together she was asking me to leave. She wouldn't even let me kiss her goodbye. She's still so beautiful, though ... Oh man, it hurts."

"James," Susan said as she reached out and held both his arms, "the woman is a bitch, and you are better away from her. Don't even think of staying in touch with her or she'll lead you on a merry dance and keep you miserable. Now, where are you staying?"

"Some dumpy little hotel a taxi driver took me to in Hampstead. I'm not really sure what to do next."

"Well, I'll tell you what you're doing – you're going to come and stay with us. Daniel's cousin …" she pointed to her friends who were still eating breakfast, "… has found us a big flat with accommodation for eight. We're going to check it out at nine o'clock."

"But … the others," James protested weakly.

"Stay here for a minute," she said, and she walked back to her friends. A few minutes later she returned. "It's settled then," she said. "They're all happy for you to stay with us – so long as you pay an equal share of the rent and other bits and pieces, which won't be a lot. And you can stay for as long as you like."

James looked at her. He was tired. "Angels really do exist don't they?" he said.

"What?"

"You, you're an angel aren't you?"

She laughed. "Come on, you look like you could do with a coffee." She took his arm in hers and together they headed back to the others.

※※※※※※※※※※※※

James had the phone tucked between his shoulder and his ear as he simultaneously signed a form that one of the other clerks had put in front of him. "Where did you say the school was?" he said into the mouthpiece. "Perthshire, where's that? … Scotland!" Several of the girls in the office were now looking at him – including Susan who was nodding her head eagerly. "Well, okay, I suppose I could go to the interview and see what happens. I'll just get a bit of paper and you can give me the details."

Moving into the flat with Susan and her friends had been good for James. As you'd expect, they all argued from time to time but there was always this strong feeling of mutual support amongst the group. He still felt like a bit of an outsider, an interloper, but this, he thought, was more to do with his own perception than that of the others – they all treated him as a complete equal.

He'd now been in the UK for five months. But he still wasn't fully over Belinda. His recovery from her sudden severing of their relationship continued to drag on. This was mainly because she had started telephoning him – and even seeing him on occasion – usually to talk about problems she was having with her boyfriend. Susan and the others had tried to convince him to tell her to piss off – that she was only going to play with his feelings, to his detriment. He knew they were right, of course, but the memory of what they'd had in Australia had kept him open to her approaches. Any sort of intimacy with her – even if it was simply her confiding in him – was better than nothing. That's what his heart was telling him at least. Still, his new friends had saved him from the deep sea of depression into which he might otherwise have fallen. He was now just splashing around in the shallows, and felt that soon he would leave these waters altogether.

The job in the props administration section of the BBC had also been of great assistance in his ongoing emotional recovery. And it had been vital in bringing in money, of which he had almost none when he first entered the country. This was still the case, but at least he was now able to survive financially. He had walked many miles and made many phone calls in his attempts to find work, but in the end it had been Susan – again – who came to his aid. She managed to convince her new boss to temporarily employ James – to replace an administrative assistant who was on maternity leave. Just before taking this job, however, he had left his details with a number of employment agencies. In particular, he had approached several agencies that specialized in finding employment in private schools for teachers. Unfortunately, although James now had his science degree, he didn't have any teacher training. But this hadn't stopped the agencies from taking his details. The specialist training was desirable, they said, but not essential for some of their clients. The fact that he'd been a part-time tutor on occasion back in Australia, they said, might convince such clients to give him a chance. Sadly, nothing had happened in this regard – not even a phone call – and no one else seemed to want to employ him, so he had gratefully taken the job offered at the BBC.

Now, one of the teacher agencies had contacted him, and he had agreed to attend an interview tomorrow. It was just after lunch and the supervisor hadn't yet come back from his regular rendezvous at a nearby gay bar. James was the only other male in the narrow office area that accommodated about a dozen young workers. Most of them were aware that he was hoping to find a better paid and more fulfilling job – that he had no intention of being a clerk all his life – and now they all crowded around as Susan acted as their spokesperson.

"Come on, come on," she said excitedly as he put down the phone. "What's happening?"

James had a stunned look on his face. "I have to go to an interview tomorrow, to some place in Essex – it's for a teaching job – mainly maths."

"But what was that about Scotland?" Susan asked while the small sea of smiling faces looked on.

"That's where the job is – in a castle that's been turned into a school – in the Highlands of Scotland," he said, blinking. "In an area called Perthshire."

"Then why do you have to go to Essex?" one of the other girls asked.

"Because the guy who owns the school in Scotland also owns one in a place near …" he looked down at his scribbled notes, "… near a place called Harlow. The train ticket is going to be couriered to me here this afternoon, and someone's going to pick me up at the station." He looked at Susan. "Do you think I should do it?"

"James," she said, "the Highlands of Scotland are beautiful, and they're far away from here. I think this job might be just what you need. Go to the interview and get the position."

The next day, at around noon, he was in the oak panelled office of Mr Michael O'Connor, an Irish educational entrepreneur who had already successfully established two private secondary schools in England, and had recently started a similar venture on the estate of Taroane Castle, in Perthshire.

"So, James," O'Connor said, "the school has only been operating for a few months and we've suddenly lost our mathematics teacher. There are only fifteen students – they're all Americans; many with fathers working on oil rigs in the North Sea – and eight teaching staff. You'll not find a school like it anywhere else in the world."

James sat back. They'd been discussing his background and qualifications for the previous twenty minutes but had now moved onto the job details. He warmed to O'Connor; the man seemed like a bit of a rogue but he didn't have any of the class-based pretensions that James had encountered many times in the last few months. "But how can you operate with so few …"

O'Connor didn't let him finish. "Oh, it's how I started the other schools. Not many students in the first year but substantially more in the second and then twice as many again in the year after that. I expect to have well over one hundred and fifty students in five years – they'll fill up the two hundred rooms in the castle very nicely." He smiled; his white teeth standing out from his freckled face. "So," he went on – obviously enjoying James's amazed expression, "it's a New York curriculum you'd have to follow – all in these books –" he gestured towards a pile on his desk, "and you'd have to be prepared to be the house master for the seven boys; a surrogate father, or big brother in your case. The salary will be modest but the package includes full board – the food is excellent – and you get to live in one of the most spectacular parts of the country."

After more questions and answers, both men were silent for a moment, thinking their separate thoughts. Then O'Connor spoke.

"So, the job is yours if you want it, James. The agency supplied three people for interview. You're the third – and I prefer you. But you'll have to decide now, and if you say yes, then you'll have to be prepared to start within the week."

James blinked. He wasn't used to making these sorts of decisions on the spot, usually preferring to weigh up the pros and cons of the situation. He was nervous about teaching a bunch of American teenagers – but there weren't many of them, and O'Connor had assured him that everything he needed was in the textbooks the school used. And being a housemaster

– he wasn't quite sure what that would involve but it didn't sound too difficult. The salary was reasonable, and the idea of having meals prepared for him every day, and having his own room and study, and his laundry needs taken care of – all seemed wonderful. He would have to leave the secure world of his new friends and the vibrancy of London life but, on the other hand – and this was especially important, he would be well away from Belinda and her dubious influence. He'd be so occupied with his new position that he'd have little time to think about her.

"Okay," he said, "I'll take the job."

O'Connor smiled. "Excellent," he said as he extended his hand. "My secretary will contact you tomorrow with the travel and contract details." And then, hesitantly, he added, "Just one thing, James …"

"Yes?"

"You'll need to have a haircut."

James was surprised. "But I only had one yesterday afternoon – in preparation for this interview."

"Well," O'Connor replied, "I suggest you have another one. Miss Pordosky, the headmistress, is quite fussy about such things."

Chapter 7

Their descent into the valley of the Spey had been rushed – mainly due to the fear of further aggression by the Cattach, but also because there were two critically wounded men in Poltan's much-reduced warrior group. These men would need urgent treatment by healers if they were to have any hope of survival. The party had rested briefly in a clearing beside the river – modest in size at this time of year, but the wide banks showing that in spring it would be a formidable waterway – and then hurried off to the west along a path that stayed close to one of the river's tributaries. Light rain had been falling for a short while when they rounded a bend. Bren was helping one of Poltan's men carry a wounded comrade in a hastily-made birch-pole stretcher when he suddenly stopped.

"What is it?" the man in front said angrily as he turned around.

"That lake … it's … I'm sorry, I didn't know there was such a large lake here," Bren replied. "And there is smoke coming from its centre!" He looked around at Pock-face who had also stopped, still supporting the drooping man with the hideously slashed shoulder.

"That is the sacred lake of the Spey," said Poltan who had come back along the path to see why the others weren't following. "And the smoke comes from where workers build the isle on which our priests will one day assemble for the great rituals."

"They are building *an island*?" Pock-face said, giving voice to Bren's look of surprise as well as his own.

"It seems there will be much to surprise you when we get to Ardvortag. See! A small part is just visible on the left bank," Poltan pointed. Bren was able to discern a few thatched roofs on a small peninsular that was mainly obscured by huge pines. He nodded. The man in the stretcher groaned, and without another word the group continued its hurried journey towards the lake.

* * * * * * * * * * * * *

For a moment, Bren had been apprehensive when the men appeared from the trees on either side of the path – Pock-face had even managed to draw his dagger – but Poltan had quickly assured his guests that these were his people; guardians of the settlement. He then ordered the men to take the two injured warriors from his weary comrades and to rush them ahead to the healers.

Slower now, the party plodded on, and Bren began to hear the familiar settlement sounds of people and animals – voices calling, dogs barking, geese honking. Then, further along the path, the trees thinned and he partook of his first view of Ardvotag. He was stunned. It was so much bigger than Ceann Tull. The flat, cleared area by the lakeside extended some distance back into the surrounding hillocks – and there were more dwellings, although most were small – and more people than he had ever seen together in one place before.

Poltan smiled. "Many are gathered here for the making of the isle," he said. "Half will return to other settlements three days hence to tend their animals and crops. Already they have been here since the new moon." He poked his jaw in the direction of the lake, and Bren's eyes widened further. On the water there must have been more than thirty canoes. Many were bound together with poles and platforms, and all were being used to carry rocks – from those the size of a man's hand, to boulders as big as Fat Gregor's buttocks. On the shore were several large piles of these stones, all sorted by size, with sledges and wheeled carts and a tall log tripod standing in the shallows. Men and women, young and old, were working with the rocks. Some were bringing them along a track that appeared out of the trees, while others deposited them into the piles or lifted them into the canoes. Some worked singly, but most were in groups; working together with ropes and levers and barrows, or in long 'passing' lines. Those in the canoes were either waiting for their vessels to be filled, or were paddling their heavy cargo to a spot near the centre of the lake where there was a tiny, low-lying island with an area not much bigger than that of a modest-sized dwelling. It had a single, stunted tree growing at one end, and a small fire burning at the other. Those in the canoes deposited their stony contributions around the edges of this island.

"How deep is the water out there?" Bren asked without taking his gaze off the busy scene.

"It was about eight man-heights when our parents and grandparents began this great endeavour twenty summers ago," Poltan replied proudly. "You see, the first tree grows there – unplanted by man. And our priests make sure that the fire keeps burning while construction proceeds; the ash is spread with soil on the stones."

"But how long …" said Bren as he looked back at his host.

"Another ten summers and it will be completed, he replied even before the Tull man had finished asking. "It will then be one of the most holy sites in these lands."

Bren suddenly thought about his father, and how he would one day tell Dorvar about this huge undertaking. Perhaps they would then travel back here together, and he could observe as his father spoke with the priests about their work and their ceremonies. But then he shuddered. How could he be thinking about anything other than his abducted friend? The safe return of Trib was all that should be occupying his thoughts at this time. He was about to ask Poltan again about contacting the Cattach, when Pock-face poked him in the ribs.

Turning, he saw an old man with long grey hair and a finely made deer-hide tunic walking towards them. Despite his age, the man looked strong and vigorous, and several muscular warriors with spears and targes had to trot to keep up with him. Without saying a word, the old man wrapped his large arms around Poltan and held him in a tight embrace. A carrion crow flew, cawing, from one end of the settlement to the other before he released his hold. He then stood back.

"How many of the mongrel whelps, and where did it happen?" he said as he focused on the slashed leather of Poltan's vest.

"About twenty. They came at us from either side of the track below Riall." Poltan glanced across to Bren and Pock-face. "The walled settlement you approached earlier," he added for their benefit.

The old man's grey mane swung over his shoulder as he quickly turned his head to look at the strangers. He stared aggressively for a moment and then looked back at Poltan. "And where were your scouts?" he asked, anger in his voice.

"Both killed – we had no warning."

"Twenty!" the old man said loudly. "That is twice your number – you're lucky to be alive." His anger was now showing hints of concern; his brow furrowing.

"We were assisted by these two men from the lands of the Tull," Poltan said. "This is Bren, to whom I owe my life." Bren nodded. "And this is his companion who is called Pock-face."

"I can see why," replied the old man. "Happen in childhood did it? I have a nephew with the same affliction but not as bad as yours." Pock-face looked at Bren, who raised his eyebrows slightly, and then stared back at the grey-haired one and snorted loudly, as a sign of rebuke. But the old man took no notice. He stepped towards Bren and clasped his shoulders. "Saved my son's life, did you?" he said.

Bren held the old man's gaze. "I threw a rock," he said softly.

The old man then embraced the weary Tull youth and whispered in his ear, "Thank you." After this, his mood became more joyous. "Well, now you shall eat ribs of wild boar, and barley bread soaked in fat," he said as he walked over to Pock-face, placing his arm around the young man's neck. "And the women shall prepare the hot bath for you and your ugly friend here."

Poltan laughed – as did the people who had started to crowd around. "May I belatedly introduce my father, Ulvar," he said between chuckles, "chief of our people and Lord of the Spey."

Later, with bellies full of pork and bread, Bren and Pock-face were sitting, naked, in a rectangular, stone-lined pit that was full of warm water; this being inside a small, log-and-thatch hut.

"By thunder, I did not know how soothing this could be," Bren said as he stretched out and submerged all but his head.

Pock-face did the same. "You are most assuredly right," he replied, closing his eyes. "The one we've got back home has only ever been used for old people – to ease the pain in their joints. If I'd known …"

He was interrupted by the opening of the hut door. A large, older woman came in pushing a small barrow full of hot, fist-sized rocks. The two young Tull men quickly sat up – shocked – and placed their hands over their areas of manhood. "No need to bother with that," she said gruffly, "I've seen plenty of those things in my time. Now watch your feet, she added as she tipped the rocks into the far end of the bathing pit. Steam bubbled up from the water, and the added heat soon made its way to the embarrassed occupants.

"Thank you," Pock-face said sheepishly as she glanced, first at him and then at Bren, before pushing the barrow towards the entrance.

"And I've seen bigger," she cackled as she closed the door.

Bren looked at his friend for a moment, and then they both burst out laughing. "Things are certainly different here," Bren said as he wiped his eyes.

"Why do you say that?" Pock-face replied. "There are plenty of woman in Ceann Tull who would gladly walk in on two healthy, young, undressed men – particularly if they were blooded warriors." He then tipped his head back and screamed, "Wooohaa!"

Bren smiled. Although physically relaxed, and allowing himself moments of levity, his mind was still in turmoil – mainly because of Trib's abduction – and he didn't yet share Pock-face's sense of celebration about their earlier experience. "Possibly," he replied in a serious tone, "but I mean in other ways."

"What ways?"

"Well, Ulvar, Poltan's father, is called 'chief', and people bow down to him. And, even though he seems to have an eye for fun, he orders people to do things rather than asks – as though they are all his children."

"Perhaps they are," Pock-face said with a smile. "He seemed to have a lot of women around him during that meal."

Bren half-heartedly splashed his friend. "And there are more priests and warriors and defences than at home ... and a lot of the people seem ..." he struggled for a word, "... poor."

"Poor?"

"Some of those dwellings we walked past; they were so small, and the children outside looked scrawny."

"I saw that too," said Pock-face, "but they seemed happy enough."

Both men sat in silence for a moment, watching drops of condensation fall from the roof beams.

"It must be because of the Cattach," Bren said finally. "In my mind I can see that we at Ceann Tull would have to alter our ways greatly if we were under such constant threat of attack as the people here. My father would need to exert his authority much more strongly ... give more orders rather than spending a lot of time in meetings with the elders. Decisions would have to be made quickly, and people would have to obey – otherwise we would lose everything."

"Ah! What a strange mind you have cousin," Pock-face said, grinning. "If we ever need to defend Ceann Tull then you can worry about the plans – I will simply fight ... for I am now a warrior." He was about to let loose with another war cry when the door to the hut suddenly burst open again. This time it was Poltan. He had not been at the meal – a message being left that he had urgent business to attend to.

"I have been negotiating with a messenger from the Cattach," he said, almost breathless. "They have agreed to trade your friend for one of our prisoners. We journey to the place of exchange tomorrow."

* * * * * * * * * * * * *

The sun had not yet chased away the stars when Bren finally lifted his legs over the edge of the bracken-filled crib on which he had spent the night. Although comfortable, he had not slept well, constantly waking, thinking it was time to arise. He walked across to the large, circular hearth in the centre of the enormous lodge where Ulvar and his family dwelt together with various retainers, friends, lieutenants – and guests. Sitting on a bench, he stirred the embers with a long poker, and yawned; the assorted sounds of snoring and gurgling and slow breathing making him wonder whether he should at least try to get a little more sleep. He looked back at his bed, but then noticed someone moving in the shadows cast by the solitary oil lamp that was burning nearby.

"Don't be surprised young Tull man, it is only me, your host," Ulvar said quietly as he came and joined Bren on the bench. In his hand was a wide leather collar with a sturdy buckle of bronze. Pointed studs protruded from the leather; these also being of bronze.

"That looks to be a fine collar, Ulvar."

The old chief handed it to Bren to examine more closely. "It's new," he said. "It was to be for Teira, the greatest of my hounds – until she disappeared two days ago."

"What happened?"

"There is little to tell. I was hunting boar at a place west of here, with a party of men and several hounds – including Teira – when we disturbed a beast from its hiding place. The hounds gave chase and eventually brought it down – for us to finish off. But when we got there, Teira was gone. We backtracked along the route of the chase, and we called and sent the other dogs out looking but we never found her. No blood, no track, nothing. She was getting on in age, and had put on a bit of weight, but she was my lead bitch, and a great companion. I preferred her to most of my lieutenants," he added without smiling. "I thought I might make one last search for her this morning. She was one quarter wolf you know."

Bren closed his eyes. He had seen his father do this on several occasions. As he held the collar in one hand, he reached out and touched Ulvar, who seemed to know not to speak. Bren saw images of forests and cloudy skies and a large, white hound limping through the understorey of heather. Nearby was a bend in a river. He opened his eyes, noticing that Pockface had joined them.

"Is there a river near where you were hunting?" he asked Ulvar.

THE HOLY WELL

"No, it's on a mountainside."

"In a pine forest though?"

"No, it's mainly ash up there."

Bren sighed, and looked at Pock-face whose grin was about to split his face apart. "And your hound, Tiera, she's not white is she?"

"That is the truth; her colours are grey and black."

"I'm sorry Ulvar," Bren said with a shrug, "I've seen my father do this successfully at times, but it appears I have not inherited the ability. Your dog has probably had pups and is suckling them in the hollow base of an old oak tree."

"You mean you cannot help?"

"It would seem not, but for some reason I thought I should try," Bren drooped his shoulders and handed back the collar. "Truly, I am sorry. I know how important a hound can be to a man, and I hope you find yours."

"And I hope you find your friend alive and well," Ulvar responded as he stood up and walked towards the main entrance of the lodge. "The Cattach can be devious, and not all exchanges go without incident. Listen to my son, and be on your guard." He then disappeared into the darkness beyond the doorway. Bren put his head in his hands and felt a deep shiver pass through his body.

When he looked up he saw that Pock-face, who always had a voracious appetite in the morning, was now standing next to the woman who had supplied hot stones for the bathing pit the previous night. He was holding a wooden bowl, waiting for her to ladle porridge from the cauldron that hung over the fireplace. She was looking about, obviously agitated.

"By the stars! Where is that thing," she said angrily.

"What have you lost?" Pock-face asked, trying to be sympathetic.

"The ladle, the ladle! Do you think I enjoy having you standing here waiting like a greedy goose?"

"Here's an idea," he replied in a loud voice as he looked at Bren. "Why don't you have my friend hold your apron while he closes his eyes. His mind is sure to show him where your ladle is." Bren stood up and charged at his cousin. "... Or, more likely, where it is not," Pock-face shrieked as he dropped the bowl and ran.

A short while later, after a noisy wrestle that woke most of the lodge's other occupants, the two were sitting at a table eating with Poltan and several other men.

"At first light we shall leave for Two Hands lookout. It will allow us to see if there are any large movements of Cattach in the valley before we go to the place of exchange. I don't want us to be caught up in a fight that we can't handle. My feeling, however, is that Drarn is a far more important prisoner than we at first thought, so they are unlikely to jeopardize his life in an attack – at least not while we still have him."

"Drarn," Bren said. "This is the name of the Cattach who we will be exchanging for Trib?"

"Yes. At first we considered him a minor leader – he lacked a beard but his attire was common, not like that of their important chiefs. However, I now think this to have been a ruse; to keep him safer in battle. Last night while you ate, I hurried to a secret location where the Cattach and I have negotiated before. I detected a particular concern for Drarn on the part of the messenger to whom I spoke, despite his attempt at nonchalance. And also, just before we began conversing, I overheard him use a term ... a title ... together with Drarn's

The Holy Well

name, when speaking with his assistant. It was *'toh dirra'* which is close to 'my lord' in our speech. Yet when he spoke to me he only used, 'the prisoner Drarn,' when referring to our captive. If I am right, then they will be sure to keep your friend, Trib, healthy."

"If they have not already killed him," interrupted a giant of a man sitting at the end of the table.

Poltan puffed his cheeks and blew air from his mouth. "I know Gollarg, it is hard to predict what the Cattach might do."

"Stinking, devious toads of shit," Gollarg said as he thumped his huge fist on the table. Bren looked at Poltan whose expression told him that the big man had good cause for bitterness. Others around the table were nodding.

****

Bren looked up at the sky. A bead of sweat ran down from his temple as he saw that it was just after mid morning. The trek to the base of the small mountain had taken much of the time but it had been easy going. The quick pace set by Poltan as the party of ten followed the path up the slope hadn't been arduous either. But now, with the summit in view, the path had become very steep and Bren's heart was beginning to pound in his chest. He glanced behind and saw the top of Pock-face's head, and well behind him was the Cattach prisoner, Drarn; his shiny black hair glistening every time it came out of the shadows. He seemed bigger than the Cattach they had fought only a day ago, and somewhat older than Bren himself – about the age of Poltan. Right now, he was having trouble keeping up with the rest of the party because of the fetter ropes around his ankles and wrists. The two, noosed leashes around his neck – each held by a guard – also tended to limit the speed of his climb. As he looked down, Bren wondered whether the guards would let go of the leashes if Drarn fell; or would they hang on and risk strangling the man – but at the same time ensuring that he wouldn't run off.

Up ahead, Poltan had stopped and was speaking to several men who had appeared from the stunted rowans and pines that grew near the summit. Bren's sharp eyes noticed others lurking amongst the trees; but he did not fear because he knew these were Ulvar's men – stationed here to watch for evidence of Cattach or other invaders in their homelands. However, he himself couldn't see anything much at the moment, except Pock-face's red hair and the stumbling Cattach prisoner; and he wondered how effective a lookout this place could be. A hundred or so ascending steps later he had his answer.

The mountain's top consisted of a roughly flat area with outcrops of grey rock and spindly trees, and as Bren stood there, he caught glimpses the valley of the Spey below. But before he could take it all in, Poltan called him over to the base of the tall, wooden tower that stood at the highest point. "Climb this ladder to the top," he said, "then you will better see the extent and the beauty of our lands."

Bren did this, and as he climbed he saw the nearby obscuring trees drop below. Stepping onto the small, railed platform at the top of the tower he heard the cry of a golden eagle that was slowly circling above. He stared up at the bird for a moment, and then, as his gaze lowered, he felt a sudden affinity with the creature. Both were seeing a vista that was stunning in its grandeur. To the northwest he could see the ragged course of the river as it passed through cultivated fields that sat at the bottom of the vast, forested slopes of the Grey Mountains. To the north, these mountains formed what looked like an impenetrable wall, but further to the east there was an opening into a long, green valley where he could discern the tiny specks of cattle grazing. The Spey passed across this offshoot valley, preferring the lower contours of the land that was even more easterly – with more cultivated fields near its banks. Mountains then obscured his view of the river, but he could see the continuation of the cattled valley as it led south into the forests that surrounded Ardvotag and its sacred lake. Sprinkled throughout the lower regions of this panorama were signs of small settlements; tiny gatherings of round buildings near the banks of the river or its tributaries.

The eagle called again as it flew away and Bren, full of wonder, called back, "Great eagle, I have seen what you see. Your days must be filled with much beauty."

He saw that Poltan was now by his side. "Clearly, you are impressed with what you see," the Spey man said. Bren simply nodded in response and continued to take in details of the wide and spectacular view before him. "We call this place 'Two Hands' because we can see the two main routes into our lands from the northwest and the east. Of course, the Cattach could travel through the forests and at night, but any large movements would most likely be noticed by our people in the nearby settlements, and we have instructed them to give us signals with smoke and fire if danger is imminent."

"What if it's raining?" Bren asked.

"Then we have to rely on runners."

"And what about the south; is invasion from that direction a concern?"

Poltan stared into the distance and scraped his teeth over his bottom lip before answering. "I fear it may be of even greater concern in the future than the current Cattach raids from the north."

"How so?"

Poltan drew his sword and offered it to Bren. "You asked me about my sword after yesterday's skirmish."

Bren nodded as he took the weapon; admiring the silvery sheen of its sharpened edges, but also wondering what would constitute a battle if yesterday was a skirmish. "It feels like bronze but has a colour like nothing I have ever seen before," he said as he squeezed the hilt and felt the balance.

"As I said yesterday, it is made of a new metal called iron. It is much stronger than bronze, and it keeps its edge for much longer."

Bren gently passed his thumb across the blade and noticed a small nick in one of its upper edges. "Is this where it sliced through the Cattach sword?"

"It is."

Bren slowly shook his head. "Truly, I will never forget the sight of that happening – or of the look on your opponent's face. This is indeed a weapon of much power. Was it made by your people?"

Poltan walked to the other side of the platform and looked in the direction of Ardvotag, and then turned. "No, it was a gift from my older brother after he returned from a journey to the lands far south of here. It was made by the Kelti who are numerous along the coast there."

Bren frowned. "The Kelti! Back home we hear more and more about these people, and especially about their blood-hungry ways." He suddenly felt a chill in the air. "If they have weapons made from a new metal like this then who could stand in their way?"

"Indeed," Poltan replied. "My brother not only brought gifts upon his return but also a fever from which he never recovered. He died just days later. His final, distempered words were a warning about the Kelti."

Bren stared out across the valley of the Spey, thoughts about the future rushing through his mind. "I'm sorry he died, Poltan," he said bleakly.

Poltan shrugged and strode back to his new friend. "But let us not dwell on dark things," he replied, forcing brightness into his voice. "Look out there," he pointed to the northwest. "Just above that final settlement you can see near the river – where the large, open field meets the forest; that is where we have agreed for the prisoner exchange to take place. From here, I can see no evidence of large numbers of Cattach, so let us continue on. This day we shall collect your friend."

Bren smiled, and hoped that Poltan's optimism was justified.

* * * * * * * * * * * * *

"Thank the trees that we are on ponies again," Pock-face whispered self-consciously to Bren as the animals drank from the stream. "After the climb up and down that mountain I wasn't looking forward to the walk up into this valley."

Bren grinned and recalled the playful-but-embarrassing words uttered by his friend earlier in the day back at Ardvotag. "The climb wearied you, did it Pock-face?" he said in a loud voice. "Perhaps you should rest here while we go on." A few of the others in the party looked towards them and nudged each other, smiling.

"Sometimes you are lower than a burrowing vole," Pock-face quietly replied from between clenched teeth, his cheeks becoming flushed. "I only meant I did not want to be tired when we made the exchange for Trib – just in case we had to fight."

Bren saw that this was one of the rare occasions when his friend did not want to follow the lead in playful banter. "I know, cousin, you are right; and I suspect it is the very reason why Poltan arranged for the ponies to be waiting for us at the bottom of the mountain."

Feeling that he had now given his cousin an appropriately sympathetic response, Bren had only a moment's warning – via a devious smile – that the normal Pock-face was still alive and functioning. "Well, I can't help it if you have only one testicle," the older youth yelled out while steering his pony away from the water.

By mid afternoon they were at the last settlement that Bren had seen from Two Hands. It was larger than he had anticipated, consisting of about six small dwellings placed around one much larger structure. Inside this building he noticed a number of men with bows and other weapons. "I sent them here last night," Poltan explained, "just in case we need them."

Up the slope was the field where the exchange was meant to take place; and behind it, the beginnings of a broad forest of pines. But Bren could see no movement on the field or in amongst the first few layers of trees. The party had stopped briefly at each of the other small settlements on the way to enquire about Cattach sightings, and to acknowledge the local leader – but had declined any hospitality, because of the urgency of their mission. Now, however, at this final settlement, where the track became steep and climbed up into the mountains where no one lived, Poltan allowed the women to bring members of his party some breadcakes and water. Before this, he had sent several of his men to reconnoitre the area around the field, which is called the Stag Field.

As they waited nervously for the scouts to signal that it was safe to approach the field, Bren walked over to Drarn, the Cattach prisoner. Up until now, he had only observed the man from a distance, wary that his own feelings about Trib might cause him to lash out at the fettered warrior if given the slightest provocation – and possibly jeopardize the whole exchange arrangement. The events and concerns of the last couple of days had made him uncertain about his own compulsions. He had killed men – these men – and they had tried to kill him. A man could be forgiven for acting unpredictably in such circumstances. But now he felt back in control of his emotions, and he squatted down in front of the black-haired individual who was sitting on the ground – still tied by roughly-twined nettle ropes.

Drarn had a partly healed gash on one side of his forehead, and various bruises on his bare arms. The ropes about his neck had also caused bruising and the removal of some skin. It looked painful. Bren stared into the dark, defiant eyes and wondered how Trib was being treated by his captors. On a sudden impulse, he tore his breadcake in half and offered a piece to Drarn. The Cattach's eyes narrowed. He then raised his head and spat in Bren's face. One of the guards was about to kick the Cattach man but Poltan called, "No! They will be observing us you fool." Bren wiped his face with the bottom of his tunic, forced himself to smile at the snarling prisoner, and then slowly walked away. If the Cattach were watching, then the incident would clearly increase Drarn's esteem. But this was of little interest to Bren. His concern was for Trib.

Moments later, a series of whistles could be heard from various locations around the Stag Field, and Poltan said, "We go now, without delay."

As arranged, only four men could accompany each prisoner. Drarn walked ahead of one of the men who had guarded him during the journey. The ropes had been removed from around his neck but his hands were now tied behind his back and his feet were again fettered. The guard carried a spear. Next came Poltan, then Bren and Pock-face. They carried no weapons – except for small blades concealed in their clothing. Bren could feel the tension growing amongst the small group as they approached the edge of the field. He wanted to look across at Pock-face and Poltan but knew he must keep his eyes on the pine trees at the other end of the field, for he feared treachery. They walked a short distance and then, near a solitary blaeberry bush, they stopped.

Almost instantly, figures appeared from the pines. Since none wore head covers, it was clear that they were all dark haired. And each wore the short, brown tunic that was common amongst these people. A single man walked slowly in front of another four who were spread out in a line. One of these others held a spear.

Bren's heart had already been beating much faster than normal but now it began to race as he strained his eyes, trying to discern Trib in the distant group.

"Can you see your friend?" Poltan asked, his speech more urgent than usual.

Bren glanced at Pock-face who had narrowed his eyes to fine slits, but he knew his cousin's sight was not as good as his own. He then looked back at the Cattach group – who had now stopped walking – and concentrated on the man in front. "I am not sure, if we could just ..." and then he noticed. "No!" he cried, "his hair is too long! That man is not Trib." He looked desperately across at Poltan and Pock-face.

The Spey man screamed out something in the language of the Cattach, and grabbed the spear from the guard. Drarn turned and looked at Bren, his arrogant countenance now replaced with one of concern, and the beginnings of fear. Pock-face had already drawn his concealed blade and was waiting for his cousin to give an order – he was ready for bloodshed.

Then a familiar voice called from across the field; compelling, beseeching. "Bren, Pock-face, it is me, Trib! Look, I am unharmed."

Drarn was pointing in the direction of the trees and saying, "Frinda, frinda," as he looked back at the others.

Bren and his comrades momentarily froze their actions, and from across the field they saw not the front figure, but one of the men behind, waving his tied hands above his head. "It's me, Trib!" he called again.

"It is! It is! It's our friend." Bren cried as he looked at Pock-face – who was nodding enthusiastically – and at Poltan and the guard ... and Drarn. Poltan then said something in the Cattach language to Drarn, and the prisoner immediately shouted a message to his people – no doubt a confirmation of who he was.

A few more words were called between the groups – none of which Bren understood – then Drarn looked expectantly at

Poltan who made a lifting gesture with his chin. At this, the Cattach man began to slowly walk across the field.

In the distance, Bren and the others could see the figure with tied hands – still held above his head – walking towards them.

"Wait for him to get to us," Poltan directed as his voice tried to penetrate the rapped attention that both Tull men were giving to the approaching figure. Pock-face began to move forward. "No!" cried Poltan.

Bren quickly reached out and grabbed his cousin by the shoulder. "We must wait," he said. "We must not let them think we are attacking – there is a spear ready for his back, remember."

But as Trib got closer – for Bren could now see that it really was his friend – he started to run in short, stumbling steps, his feet being tied in the same way as had been Drarn's. And Bren could no longer control himself. "Come on," he said to Pock-face, "he is beyond throwing range now." Both ran to their clan brother and embraced him and lifted him in the air – and shed tears of happiness. However, they were still conscious of the danger lurking nearby, and together with back-slapping and cries of joy, they cut through Trib's constraining cordage and quickly escorted him away from the place of exchange. Just before leaving, Bren looked back towards the forest, but there was no sign of the Cattach. They had disappeared into the trees.

* * * * * * * * * * * *

The sun had set some time ago behind the surrounding mountains, yet the summer sky-glow still allowed Bren to see the rugged crags and the long slopes and the pastures and crops and forests – and the river – that made up this wild and beautiful valley. He looked back at the largest of the dwellings in the settlement, and heard the laughter of men who had survived a tense ordeal. Pock-face was in there with Poltan and those of his men who were not on guard in various locations around the settlement. Trib was there too, but he was deep in sleep – something that he'd been deprived of for the last two days. He had been like a chattering finch after they had whisked him away from the field – his words tumbling over each other as he tried to describe all the things that had happened to him. Then he promptly fell asleep after eating from an enormous meal prepared by the settlement's inhabitants. Still, except for a lump on his head the size of a duck egg, and a few scratches and bruises, he seemed healthy. No doubt he would have a lot more to say when he awoke. But he was safe; thank the stars.

Bren turned on the rock he was using as a seat, and looked up at the clearing a short distance away, and he wondered. The Stag Field. An important event took place there today. When they returned to Ceann Tull – whenever that might be – he and his friends would tell the story of the skirmish and of Trib's abduction and, finally, of his safe return. He looked up at the sky and found the Wolf's Eye. But for how long would the story of Trib and the Stag Field be told? Over how many generations? Some of the stories told in the Tull lands went back so far that no one could count the generations. Like those about the Old Ones, the people who stood stones in the ground and worshipped amongst them.

And what other tales about him and his friends might yet be remembered? Were there great adventures still to come that his descendants would one day hear about? Or had the event of greatest importance in his life already occurred? He ran his thumb and forefinger down the sides of his drooping moustache. The Holy Well of Endachni; surely this would be remembered long after he was gone. But would his part in its discovery be forever linked with such a hallowed place? He leaned back and surveyed the skies again. His name would probably be lost – eventually – as the story of the well was re-told. Perhaps the entire story would gradually be forgotten. But the well itself would remain; it would stay for as long as the mountains and the forests and the ever-repeating seasons. And over these many years, would it speak to others as it had to him? Would a distant descendant of the people of the Tull – or perhaps someone else – one day hear the voice of the well? Who might it be, and what effect would it have on their life? Could he ever know of such a person? He sighed. The well was surely one the most important influences in his life, and he felt he would hear its voice again before too long.

He had almost drifted off to sleep when these thoughts were chased away by the sound of a pony galloping down the track. He sat up abruptly as the rider passed him by and stopped outside the large dwelling. "A message for Poltan," the rider called. "And one for the Tull man named Bren."

Chapter 8

James sat back and stroked the leather. It felt smooth and dry; there was none of the tackiness you can feel with that vinyl pretend stuff. And you could smell it – earthy, organic, sort of ... horsey. Ah yes, this was the real thing. But what else would you expect in a Roller? 'Jesus, I'm in a Rolls Royce!' he thought loudly to himself. In a flash of whimsy he wondered whether this was all an illusion – a dream maybe. Here he was, being driven through the most beautiful countryside he had ever seen, in the back of a leather-seated, chauffeur-driven limousine. And he'd spent last night in a sleeping compartment on the train from London – not in a carriage stuffed full of other poor, bored, and uncomfortable passengers who were trying to get some shut-eye in their squashy little seats – but in an actual sleeping compartment.

He touched his nose on the glass and felt the icy coldness that was attempting to penetrate from outside. No, it wasn't a dream. But what a change! It was almost dizzying – like taking on a new persona. He sat back again and ran his fingers through his hair. God! There was almost nothing there anymore – now so short. And all his recently-made acquaintances and friends, like Susan, who had given him so much emotional, not to mention physical, support. Gone. And the busyness of London, with its constant traffic and hordes of people and incessant chatter, chatter, chatter. Gone. What an abrupt uprooting. He remembered a story someone had once told him about an army recruit who, after a solid day of unaccustomed physical activity, fell into a deep sleep on his bed in the barracks. Shortly afterwards – so the story went – his comrades-in-arms picked up the bed and carefully carried it (and him) to a field some distance away. The man awoke the next morning with magpies warbling above him and cows sniffing around his blankets. He was totally perplexed; couldn't comprehend his situation – until, of course, his friends appeared laughing uncontrollably from behind the surrounding bushes.

But there were no friends behind the bushes that the limo was sweeping past. No, this wasn't a joke. James knew he was venturing into this particular phase of his existence all alone; and he was soaring between excited anticipation – of new and wonderful experiences – and the fear that maybe he had made a dreadful mistake and that the experiences wouldn't be so wonderful at all – that he might, in fact, be entering a world where unhappiness would prevail.

"It won't be long now, sir," the man behind the steering wheel said over his shoulder.

Somehow, the chauffeur had identified James at the train station in Perth, and had insisted on carrying his heaviest piece of luggage – the fact that this was an old steel-framed backpack didn't seem to bother the man one bit. He came across as a jolly sort of person but James felt a little uncomfortable about his continuing use of the title 'sir'. The only other time recently that he could remember being addressed this way was when he'd accidently walked into a posh restaurant in London and a waiter had snarlingly asked him if he had a reservation. He'd thought it was an Indian takeaway. The waiter's tone had exuded both arrogance and dislike, and the experience had made James wonder what was actually going through the minds of people who called other people 'sir'.

And now he was being told that it wouldn't be long. Long for what? A new life where everybody addressed everybody else using polite terms, and people took tea in the afternoon, and dabbed the corners of their mouths with serviettes after a meal? Would anyone say 'fuck' or 'shit' here? He shivered – this momentary dive into depression making him suddenly aware of the cold February weather, despite the Roller's royal-sanctioned heater.

The car had turned off the main road and was heading slowly down a winding driveway. There were pines and other trees on the right, and a large field on the left – but then there were wooded areas not far distant on this side too. The whole region was hilly, and James looked down at the rushing water of a stream as the limo crossed over a small wooden bridge. His heart began to race; not only because he was about to face the beginning of his new job, new home, new colleagues ... new world; but also because the landscape had suddenly taken on a different appearance. Moments before, it had been visually magnificent – the snow-covered mountains lining the close horizons, the gentle feel of the surrounding hills, the moss-covered stone fences, the light greens of the grassy fields contrasting with the dark shades of the conifers, and these in turn contrasting with the bare limbs of their deciduous companions. These impressions still remained, but now, as he gazed out the side window and looked into the woods and up at the slopes, James felt he was suddenly seeing things slightly differently – somehow more personal; almost as though the landscape was whispering a welcome to him.

"Now sir, when we go around this next bend, I'll stop for a wee while so you can take in the view of the castle – most people find it very appealing."

Fifteen seconds later, he pulled the car over onto the grassy verge halfway round the curve. They were still on the side of a large, mainly tree-covered hill, but from this position a person had a clear view of what was below. And there, in the middle of his field of vision, dominating all else, was the stark, grey magnificence of Taroane Castle. It seemed to be made up of two different-sized, box-like buildings that were joined together by a lesser structure that housed the main entrance. The smaller box was like a giant cube: three storeys high, with five windows on each floor at the front, and probably the same number on the sides – although James couldn't be sure from this angle. There were crenellations all around the top that gave it a medieval feel.

The main part of the adjoining building, on the right, was also somewhat cubic in appearance, but it had an extra floor; and at each corner there was a large, circular tower with narrow windows and a crenellated peak. And out from the middle of this edifice there rose a large, square tower with two Gothic-arched windows on each wall and its own small, round turrets at each corner. A flagpole projected from the roof of this tower, but there was no flag fluttering from it. In front, was a wide expanse of mown grass, and behind was a hill covered with pines – a little of their rich hues being shared by the castle as the reflected morning sunlight bounced off its dull walls.

James was spellbound. He had never seen anything quite so stunning, and memories of childhood stories about crusaders, and King Arthur, and Robert the Bruce, and fairies and elves – all these flashed through his brain and caused a stirring deep inside him. A short distance behind the castle, just before a hill suddenly lifted the land skyward, he caught glimpses of a river meandering through the valley. He knew from the map that he'd looked at in London and again on the train that this was probably the Tull.

"Like I said," the chauffer smiled, "most people find the view appealing." James simply nodded and kept staring. "But now I'd better get you down to Miss Pordosky, she doesn't like to be kept waiting."

* * * * * * * * * * * *

"What part of Australia did you say you were from?" asked the fifteen year-old New Yorker.

"I don't think I did say," James answered. "But Melbourne is where I was born, and where I did most of my growing up."

"Oh yeah, so where did you do the rest of it?"

"Well, I don't think I've finished yet – it's still happening."

"You mean like, right now – as we speak? Wow, what a cool thought."

"Good night Darren," James replied with a grin and what he hoped was a detectable touch of firmness. "This is the third time now that I've asked you to turn off your light. If I have to ask again then there'll be trouble." The boy frowned. "I'll tell Miss Pordosky that you have a crush on her," James added, thus causing the frown to disappear.

"Oh no, how sick; I think I'm going to vomit."

"Well do it with your light off." James flicked the switch by the door and walked out. "Goodnight Darren."

As he pulled the door shut, the boy yelled, "Goodnight Mr Campbell – you're a cool teacher."

James wandered down the corridor – there were no other tell-tale glows from under any of the other doors except the last one up ahead, and that was his own room.

He sat on his bed and looked at the old clock on the wall. It made a futile attempt to convince him that it was 3:25 but he glanced at his watch and saw that it was in fact a quarter past ten. Over on his desk were the small jars of pebbles, buttons, and paper-clips that he planned to use in tomorrow's grade eight maths class where he'd introduce set theory and Venn diagrams. He smiled. Tomorrow's grade eight class ... just two students – the youngest of the fifteen at the school: lanky Harry and flirty Mary-Jean; both Texans – as were seven of the others – and both lovely kids.

In fact, it was the kids – all of them – who had helped ease him through this first week. They were smart, friendly, and pretty much up-front with anything that bothered them. This latter attribute was mainly displayed in their clearly-expressed hatred for Miss Pordosky. Of course, he had to maintain a degree of professional solidarity when they came to him with disparaging remarks about her, and on several occasions he had asked them stop and to look at things from her point of view. But really, he tended to agree with them. She was a crazy bitch. He'd only been here a short time, but already, he felt fairly confident in this assessment. She seemed to split her time between sitting alone in her huge office, or in her mysterious private apartment in an isolated corner of the castle – where gossipy Morven the housekeeper said she pined for her lover Michael O'Connor, the well-married owner of the school – and making life miserable, or at least depressing, for everyone else.

The other teachers were still pretty much unknown entities. Derwent Peebody, just down the corridor, was a bit older than James, and gave the impression of an upper-class buffoon. He was podgy, wore glasses, and spoke with that R-W substitution thing that is common amongst the English – 'She weally is a tywant,' he would say when talking about Pordosky. He taught languages. The only other male teacher was Geoff White, a PE teacher who, with his wife Adrienne – also a PE teacher – lived in a cottage a short distance away on the castle estate. The rest of the staff was made up of a middle-aged Chinese lady who taught science, a young American woman – who kept staring at James – who taught social studies, an old lady who lived in a nearby village and who was the English teacher and, finally, Miss Pordosky herself who taught a subject called 'religion and philosophy' for two hours a week.

James looked up at the clock and noticed that it had made another attempt at being useful – now showing 3:39. His watch showed a quarter to eleven. He hadn't realized he'd been drifting along with his thoughts for so long. Over on the desk, next to the jars, was the tiny pile of test papers from his 'big' class of eight students. He'd only marked half of them – and was appalled at how little they'd learned from the maths curriculum taught by the guy he had replaced. It was late but he intended going over the four remaining papers. He'd have the class in the morning and wanted to get on top of their deficiencies right away. He stood up, yawned, and walked to the desk. And as he sat down and reached for the pile, he knew that he liked being a teacher – and that maybe he could really be good at it.

Four weeks later – it was a Friday – the staff were having lunch in the Hall of Arms; a room as big as a moderate sized church, with the coats of arms of all the nobility who had visited the castle over the past two hundred years painted on the ceiling or on metal shields that hung from the walls. In the middle of all this grandeur was a large oak table that could probably seat about thirty people. Today there were eight – all at one end. The Chinese science teacher and the old lady who taught English weren't present – they were in a much smaller, adjoining hall supervising the forever-hungry students. However, their places at the staff table were filled. The school accountant, who only visited occasionally, was there; and so too was the school secretary: a local, twenty-something, no-nonsense lady named Jean.

"Tell me Mr Peebody," Jean now said as Derwent fumbled with a small knife and a tiny piece of fruit he'd taken from a bowl in the centre of the table, "do you always peel your grapes individually before eating them?" James grinned as his colleague looked up.

"Well, yes I do, but it's tewwibly twicky with these small ones."

"I don't know why you bother," Jean replied. Then Miss Pordosky, who reigned over each meal as hostess and guardian of good manners, interrupted.

"Etiquette allows Mr Peebody to do such a thing if he is so inclined Jean, and given the amounts of poison that are sprayed onto and taken up by food plants these days, it might be a sensible idea for all of us to consider."

Derwent smiled at the headmistress as she surveyed the others, silently challenging them to contradict her extremely smart pronouncement on such an important issue. James looked at her. She wasn't much older than him – twenty-nine was his guess – and she was quite thin, and very plain. Her eyes were dark and so was her dull, shoulder-length hair. He wondered what O'Connor saw in her – if in fact she was his mistress. Maybe she's great in bed, he thought. He tuned back into the conversation. The sycophantic accountant was going on about how thoroughly he washed his apples, so James drifted off in his thoughts again.

Tomorrow would be the start of a free weekend for him. All the teachers – except the headmistress and the lady from the village – were on a roster that required two of them to organize and accompany the students on a trip to somewhere interesting each Saturday. This meant that on every third Saturday James would have to herd the entire student population of fifteen onto the small school bus – driven by Duncan the caretaker – and take them to some place that, hopefully, they might find stimulating. In fact, James had gone on a couple of these journeys even when he wasn't rostered, partly because he had nothing much else to do, but also because he actually enjoyed the company of the students. It was quite plain that they felt the same about him too. So far he'd joined them on a tour of a distillery, a visit to the Aviemore ski centre – which he had organized, and a trip to Aberdeen. Tomorrow the two PE teachers were going to take them on a climb up a nearby mountain. They assured everyone that it would be a simple activity – no ropes or harnesses or anything, just following a track. But James had declined the invitation. After over-indulging in the company of others, over-indulging for him at least, he now felt the need to be alone for a short while, to make little discoveries by himself – like he'd done for most of his life. Last Sunday afternoon he had, for the first time, wandered around parts of the estate beyond the immediate castle grounds. He'd been fascinated by the landscape; the little things, like the shape of last year's beech nut husks that were still on the ground around the huge grey trunks; and the big things, such as the spectacular glimpses of Loch Tull you could catch over and between the wooded hillsides – with the mountainous peak of Ben Lawers in the background if you stood in the right place. And although he'd had to get back to his room to complete some lesson plans for the next week, he had decided to spend more time in the future investigating the land around him.

The sound of chair legs scraping on the polished wood floor snapped James out of his disconnected state. People were standing; Miss Pordosky was already halfway to the door. Lunch was obviously over.

"Are you two staying?" Derwent asked.

James saw that he wasn't the only one still seated – Cori Chinoza, the social studies teacher was sitting on the same side of the table; a single pushed-in chair separating them. He still caught her staring at him at times. He'd be talking to someone else in a group and out of the corner of his eye he'd see that she was gazing in his direction. If he turned and looked at her she would usually quickly look away, but occasionally she'd give a little enigmatic smile before turning to talk to someone else. At first he'd thought she was coming on to him, but there'd been no real follow-up behaviour to confirm this. She was just friendly and interesting, and not overtly flirty. The kids saw it differently. One or two had taken him aside and informed him that they were positive that Miss Chinoza fancied him greatly. "She talks about you in class – about how funny you are," one had said. Still, James couldn't see it. And he wasn't interested anyway. She was short, skinny, not really pretty in any sense, and wore glasses. He admired her intelligence and sense of humour though – she was a nice person – but he didn't feel any physical attraction at all. "Umm," James said in response to Derwent's question – trying to decide whether to get up or not.

"Yes, we're going to work out how to make the world a better place to live in," Cori answered as James was just beginning to lift his backside from the chair. He quickly sat down again. Classes didn't begin for another fifteen minutes, and a quiet chat with someone sensible might make up for the inane Pordosky-led lunch conversation.

"Well, giving us all a one hundwed percent salawy incwease might be a good start," Derwent said as he walked to the door. "And perhaps a change of hiewarchy here," he whispered loudly before disappearing into the next room.

"She doesn't like him you know," Cori said.

"Yes, but didn't she just stick up for him with his grapes?"

She frowned. "Oh, that. I suppose so, but it must have been the one and only time. She really thinks he's an idiot. She's more or less said that to me."

"You mean she actually talks to you like a real person?"

Cori paused before answering – choosing her words. "She's in a lonely position here – trying to stay aloof but in control, and she has a very conservative view of education. Her father is a fundamentalist Christian minister back in Texas, you know."

"No, I didn't know – but it fits," he felt he didn't have to say more.

"She sees the success of the whole operation here as depending on her, and ... she's got her own personal problems."

A part of James was inquisitive about the nature of these 'problems' but he didn't think it would be polite to ask, and felt that Cori wouldn't tell him anyway. And it was only a tiny part of him that was interested – most of him couldn't care less. "So what have you got planned for the weekend?" he asked, and then immediately regretted it. He didn't want her to think that he was suggesting they do something together.

"I was going to ask you the same question," she replied with a grin.

"Oh. Well, umm ... I'm going to do some investigating around the estate."

"What sort of investigating?"

"Sort of exploring, really. I just think it's so beautiful around here, and I can't believe that I haven't made myself more familiar with the surroundings." Cori looked at him. He was certain she was about to suggest that she accompany him, and he tried to quickly think of a gentle excuse.

"God! I can't imagine anything worse than trudging around here in the mud and rain and having to wipe sheep shit off my boots. I don't mind the countryside as long as it stays out there," she pointed at a window. "One thing that I've discovered while here is that I really am a city girl at heart. I miss all the action – the movie theatres, the restaurants, the live concerts, the galleries, the museums, the ..."

"Okay, I get the picture," James interrupted. "So why are you here?"

"Good question. The answer's a bit involved but it's mainly for the experience ... and to get away from a stifling personal environment back in Philadelphia. But my next job – after I finish this year – will be back in a city somewhere; of that I'm sure. Anyway, I thought that maybe we could go for a drink at the pub in Cranmore tomorrow night – after your bout of exploration."

James felt relieved. He hadn't had to decide between either selfishly hurting her feelings, or having his planned time alone spoilt. But a few drinks at the pub, in the evening, sounded good. "That sounds good," he said with a smile.

* * * * * * * * * * * * *

Straight after breakfast the next morning, James collected some sandwiches from Ethel the cook, "I included three pieces of fruit and a flask of ice-water for you, Mr Campbell", and headed out one of the castle's rear doors.

Three hours later he was sitting on a large boulder next to a small stream – or burn, as the Scots would say – eating the last of Ethel's sandwiches. Already, he had tramped along a number of paths – some of which didn't appear to have been walked on for quite a while – and had crossed fields and entered woodlands. He was sure he had left and re-entered the estate on several occasions, and the amazing thing was that he hadn't seen another person in all this time. There was one place though, where water gushed down from rocks on a steep bracken and birch covered slope, where he imagined pixies and water nymphs might once have dwelt – or possibly still dwelt. He didn't see any and, really, he knew he never would. But he liked the romantic notion that such creatures might once have existed, nonsense as it may be, and if they had, that the little waterfall would've been a likely habitat.

He grinned as he relished a crunchy bit of chicken embedded in the sandwich. The human mind was certainly a strange beast – full of contradictions. Here he was, a dedicated skeptic with a powerful belief that the only sure way of finding the truth about anything was via the scientific process, and yet he had a yearning for the world of Faerie to have once been real, and for remnants of that world to still exist in wild, hidden corners of the planet. But he knew that this fantasy hope would never take on any serious status in his head unless there was evidence. The key to all knowledge systems was verifiable evidence. Maybe a fairy would come and sit on his shoulder one day and give him a supply of magic dust that would allow him to fly. That'd probably be enough to convince him – and most other people. He snorted in self-amusement.

Following the stream back to the castle, he noticed that at a particular curve in its course an earlier flood of water had washed away a little of the outer bank. This had exposed a dark, rod-like object. His curiosity aroused, James crossed the stream on a tree trunk that had fallen between the two banks. As he approached the object, he thought it might be an old piece of metal waterpipe; the diameter was about right, and it was clearly hollow. Using a stick, he dug away the surrounding soil, and was surprised to see that he had uncovered an old enamelled saucepan – what he'd first noticed was the handle. The bluish enamel had broken off in some places and the underlying iron had corroded in black patches, and there was a hole about a half-inch wide in the bottom. It was only a saucepan, but James felt like he'd just discovered a Pharaoh's tomb. He had actually uncovered an object from an earlier time and was now holding it in his hands. The fact that it was probably discarded only a few decades ago didn't matter – it was a piece of history and he had unearthed it.

Over the next few weekends, whenever he didn't have other obligations, James came to this spot on the side of the stream. He was sure that it had been the site of the castle's rubbish dump in former years – perhaps from as early as when this latest version of the castle was built in the late eighteenth century. On each occasion he would borrow a spade and a gardening trowel from Duncan the caretaker, and head off into the woods with these and a hessian bag for carrying any of his finds. He told the whole story to Duncan but made him promise not to mention his newfound interest to anyone else. After about the fifth visit, he had dug up three more rusty pots, a broken china vase, a damaged little candlestick carrier, and a wooden bowl shaped a bit like a Viking ship with a broken off stemhead. There were a lot of other objects that he uncovered but they were mainly fragments or large, rusted and unidentifiable items.

He had been careful to fill in any holes he dug, and to keep the site looking much the same as it had when he first came upon it. However, he got to a point where any further digging would have required him to disturb the bank more than he was prepared to do; so he stopped, satisfied with his little discoveries. But he now spent a lot of time in the castle's small library, reading everything he could about the history of the estate and its people and the surrounding area. In uncovering that first old saucepan he knew that a passion for historical research had also been exposed, and he now felt this merging with his growing affection for the land about him.

✶✶✶✶✶✶✶✶✶✶✶✶✶

James sat back in the chair and rolled his shoulders. He then lowered his head and tilted it from side to side, noticing the spinal clicks. He'd been sitting here for over an hour, totally engrossed. The book that Duncan had loaned him was a real treasure. 'A laddie with as much interest in the area as you should read this,' he had said when he handed it over in his workshop earlier in the week, adding, 'It belonged to my grandfather so I know you'll care for it.' James closed the little book but kept a finger on the page he had been reading. He again looked at the embossed cover; *The Fame of Taroane* by The Reverend Charles Gillchrist, published in 1899.

Most of the other material he'd read about the region and its history had either come from books that gave details about the estate and its former, illustrious owners (the MacEwens) – but that's all, or from other publications that dealt with a much wider area and gave only limited information about this particular region. But the Rev. Gillchrist had focused on both the Taroane Castle estate *and* the land that immediately surrounded it – and in extraordinary detail. For example, he had made careful sketches of 'Pictish' symbols that had been carved into rocky outcrops in the locality in prehistoric times and, although no maps were provided, he attempted to describe the physical location of many of these items that he wrote about.

One such artifact, if you could call it that, was a well that the Rev. Gillchrist mentioned in a number of places in his book. He called it, 'The Holy Well of Endackney'.

> 'The well is clearly of great antiquity and was always associated with the church that once stood nearby. In 1579,

the parishioners of Endackney petitioned the commissioners of the Church of Scotland asking that they be permitted to erect a new church at Cranmore, the reason given being that the church at Endackney was inconveniently situated for the people and was in a ruinous state. The first mention of the church, and the well, is in a charter of 1431 which describes the lands controlled by the MacEwens of Taroane. Even then, the church is described as "most aunciont". It was finally demolished in 1826. All of its stones were either used in building additions to Taroane Castle or for the construction of the new church at Cranmore. No trace of this sacred and ancient site remains, although it is said that soil from under the old church's foundations was used in the consecration of the new church. However, the Holy Well of Endackney remained untouched and much revered, with great numbers of people visiting it on the morning of *Bealtuinn*, the first day of May.'

James was intrigued. From his other readings, he knew that wells were often associated with various gods of the Celts – who appeared in Britain around the time of the late Bronze Age, almost three thousand years ago. He was also aware of the fact that the early Christian church had cleverly endeared itself to new converts by absorbing and transforming pagan festivals and relics and stories into its own system of religious belief and worship. *Bealtuinn* was an old Gaelic spelling of 'Beltane', one of the four major celebrations of the ancient Celts, and one that had more or less escaped this Christianization process. It was still observed – albeit in a modern, romanticized sort of way – by a handful of citizens who were proud of their British ancestry and who pined for a world long gone.

When he had asked Duncan about the well's location, the caretaker was embarrassed to admit that he didn't know of the well, although he was able to vaguely describe the whereabouts of Endackney: "Oh, aye, I believe it was the name given to a section of forest near the river, about a mile out of the village." Other enquiries didn't reveal anything more. The name persisted in some people's memories but that was about all. The Rev. Gillchrist had written:

> 'Endackney is the name of an area of woodland that is between Drummin Hill and the River Tull a short distance northeast of Cranmore. The spelling varies in old documents: *Endachni* in 1431; *Indachny* in 1537; *Endachanney* in 1607; *Endackeny* in 1794; and now *Endackney*. The origin of the name is unknown – it appearing to have a non-Gaelic ancestry. The Holy Well is located in these woods at the base of a steep embankment about four hundred yards north of the two great oak trees that were planted at some time when the old church still existed.'

This was all a bit vague but it didn't matter to James. He was totally captivated with the idea of searching for this almost-forgotten artifact of the land. Finding the Holy Well of Endackney was going to be his great free-time quest, and he was going to make a start tomorrow. Quietly happy with his new sense of purpose, he closed the book and stood up. The clock on the wall showed 5:35. He looked at his watch; it was just after midnight.

He was thinking about a final walk down the corridor – to check that all the boys had kept their lights off since the official Friday-night time of 11pm – when there was a soft knocking at his door. This was unusual. Derwent had already left for London for the weekend, and the boys rarely disturbed James at this sort of hour unless they felt really sick and needed an aspirin or some cough syrup. He opened the door expecting to see a pale-faced youth but his jaw dropped slightly as he was confronted by Miss Pordosky.

"Good evening Mr Campbell. I was doing my nightly rounds and I saw your light on. Can I come inside?"

James was flabbergasted; he had never heard of the headmistress visiting anyone in their rooms. Still, it wasn't as though there was anything wrong with such visits, so he stood aside and beckoned her to enter. As she swept past, he smelt the flowery perfume that she often wore. But she also smelled of brandy – strongly. She walked over to his desk and stood, swaying slightly, next to the chair.

"So this is where you do your preparation." James nodded. She then looked jerkily at his bed. "And that's where you do your sleeping … and other things." She smiled at him. He'd never seen her smile, and was surprised at how pretty it made her appear. It was a shame, he thought, that she had to be slightly pissed to look that way.

"That's right," he replied, not sure of the best way to get rid of her.

"You see!" she said loudly. "I know what young men do." James couldn't help but let a little grin curve the corners of his mouth. She walked up close to him and focused – as best she could – on his eyes. "And I know what girls do too. And you know why?" James gave a little shake of his head. "Because I'm one. Once a girl, always a girl," she said as she blinked several times and then sat down on the chair, sighing loudly.

"Are you okay?" James asked, unsure of how much control she had over herself.

"I'm fine, except that I feel the need to be touched by someone. Not just anyone, mind, just someone who I would like to be touched by."

'Jesus,' James thought to himself, 'What am I supposed to do here?' "Umm," was all he could think of to say. But he did notice that his boss had several of the top buttons on her blouse undone, and he caught glimpses of smooth, creamy skin as she lifted her hands to her temples.

"Don't worry Mr Campbell," she said almost mockingly, "I would just like you to massage my neck and shoulders – I have the beginnings of what could become a nasty headache, and you might be able to stop it from developing." She pulled her blouse off her shoulders and sat quietly with her head lowered.

James wasn't exactly confused, but he knew that there were a number of options open to him, each with a range of possible consequences. There was also the disturbing fact that he was noticing her small cleavage and was beginning to feel a little aroused. What should he do? Part of him said, 'get rid of her now.' However, another part was whispering something quite different. Standing behind her, he reached out his hands, hesitated for a moment, and then gently stroked her neck and swept his palms over the tops of her shoulders. She sighed again but this time with obvious pleasure.

Having made the decision to satisfy Miss Pordosky's request, James found himself enjoying the feel of the woman's soft skin under his gently massaging fingers. Her low groans and words of approval added to his increasing pleasure. For a moment he thought about Belinda and how wonderful it had been when they were together. She was the last woman he'd been intimate with – but he hadn't thought of her for what seemed like ages.

The headmistress raised her head and undid the next button on her blouse. James could now clearly see the top of her small but firm bosom. He kept manipulating the soft tissue on her shoulders with his fingers but he had also started to occasionally brush his hands across the top of her chest.

"You can massage my breasts if you want," she said, her voice soft and no longer sounding affected by drink. "I'm not wearing a bra."

"Would you like me to?" James asked quietly.

"Yes," she cooed without hesitation.

James didn't have to think; another part of his anatomy was now in control. He ran his fingers down the sides of Miss Pordosky's neck, over her thinly fleshed pecs, and around the curves of her protruding breasts. They felt firm – just as he thought they would. Her nipples were small, in keeping with her breasts, but they were already hard. This caught his attention, and he felt sympathetic tingling sensations coming from his own nipples as his shirt brushed over them.

The headmistress was now squirming in her seat and slowly opening and closing her legs, her knee-length skirt riding up her thighs as she did so. She took hold of James's wrists, and gently encouraged their movements. "Tell me what you would like to do to me," she whispered as his hands began to make sweeping motions down from her breasts to the top of her skirt, his fingertips softly prodding under the fabric.

He bent his head close to her ear, "You know I'd like to ..." but he was interrupted by a loud, drawn out 'Bonggg!' sound. They both stopped what they were doing and looked up at the wall. A second 'Bonggg' took place. It was James's clock; showing 6:00. 'Bonggg!' it went again. James frowned; it had never made a sound in all the time he'd been here, so why now? Although he knew it must be simply a coincidence, it did provide a moment for his brain to intrude on the almost overwhelming influence of his dick. He stepped back from Miss Pordosky. She turned and looked at him, dishevelled and almost topless. The clock was making its last 'Bonggg'. She grinned and then started to laugh. So did James.

"Excuse me, I have to go to the toilet," he said between giggles. This made them both laugh even louder. He put a finger to his lips as he opened the door to the bathroom. Miss Pordosky put one hand over her mouth – still laughing – and gave a little wave with the other. When he returned a few minutes later she was gone.

He sat on the bed, and for a few seconds he wondered whether any of this had actually happened. But he could still smell her perfume, and he noticed a button from her blouse lying on the floor near his desk. He looked up at the clock; it showed 6:05. "Thank you," he said. "I think."

Chapter 9

Even though it was summer, the air remained cool – almost chilly. Bren knew that this would change once the sun had shown itself over the eastern peaks, but he also knew that the increased altitude would always keep these high slopes cooler than the valley below.

"That pass we are heading towards must be a place to avoid in winter," said Pock-face, who had guided his pony up next to Bren's.

"I was just thinking the same," Bren replied. "Look how much higher it is than even here … and the blizzards must blast between those two mountains like a hare running from a wolf."

"What a strange time we're having," Pock-face said after a pause. "Only yesterday did we get Trib safely back from the Cattach, when Poltan asks us to accompany him and his men to Laghana – the very place that we had as our ultimate destination when we first left home. Do you think it's simply a coincidence?"

Bren's thoughts drifted back to Ceann Tull. Just before he and his friends had left, one of his aunts had told him about a sister of his paternal grandfather. This woman had gone with her new husband to his settlement of Laghana, 'in the distant north', long ago. The trio had vaguely agreed to find the place at some stage during their travels, but it seemed remarkable that Poltan should now ask them to accompany him to this very same settlement. The message from Ulvar had said he had received a plea for help from the people there – even though it was outside what was considered 'his' territory – and that the party should go and see what support they could offer. Bren wondered whether he still had any distant relatives at the settlement, and hoped that the marauding Cattach hadn't killed all the inhabitants.

"Bren?"

"What?"

"I said do you think it's just a coincidence?"

"Ah ... yes, probably."

"But not what was in the personal message to you from Ulvar, that was no coincidence."

Bren turned to his cousin and smiled. After first delivering words to Poltan, the messenger had come running out of the dwelling and up to where Bren had been sitting. 'Ulvar sends his greetings and his most heart-felt gratitude,' the man had panted. 'This day my lord found his hound, Teira, in the hollow of an oak, suckling a fine litter of pups – just as you had prophesied. And he awaits your return so he may show his appreciation.' Bren had been both stunned and amused. His remark about where to find the dog had only been an offhand comment – his serious attempt having proven an obvious failure. He chuckled now as he looked across at Pock-face. "Just another coincidence I think," he said. But of this, he wasn't entirely sure.

The track narrowed as the ponies and men headed towards the pass – requiring them to move in single file. The valley that had been on their left a short while ago had ended and been replaced by the rocky slopes of another of the Grey

Mountains. There were now steep rises on both sides. Bren could see that this would be an ideal place to ambush a party such as theirs. He looked back at Pock-face who was again behind him, and saw that his cousin was scrutinizing the slopes, as were all the other men. All, that is, except for Trib who was ahead of him – and already beginning to droop on his mount.

Bren had wanted his friend to stay back at the settlement – to get more sleep after his ordeal – but Trib had insisted on joining his comrades. In truth, he probably didn't want to risk being separated from them again. 'If you are to fight the Cattach on the other side of the mountains then I want to be there with you,' he had said. 'And this time, I won't be taken,' he'd added while holding up the sword that Poltan had thoughtfully brought along for him. But now the dark-haired young Tull man looked like he might fall off his pony.

"Trib," Bren shouted, "are you all right?"

Trib's shoulders and head visibly shook and then his posture suddenly changed from that of a limp willow branch to that of an upright pine. "Yes," he called over his shoulder, "Just examining my pony's mane."

"We'll be examining your broken head if you don't stay awake," Pock-face yelled back before Bren could respond.

Just then the column stopped. Up ahead, Poltan was talking with two of the scouts who had been running parallel to the mounted party but higher up on the slopes. Bren knew that they would be telling Poltan whether it appeared safe to continue or not. Moments later they were joined by a rider who had gone ahead some time ago. When Poltan gave the signal to proceed, the silence that had come over the party during their leader's consultation quickly gave way to soft murmurings and the occasional laugh – signs of men relaxing a little when the possibility of battle has diminished.

※※※※※※※※※※※※

They gathered together amongst the stunted trees high above the small valley. Far below, they could see smoke filtering through the thatched roofs of the eight or so dwellings that made up Laghana. A partly completed mound that, from this distance, looked to be made from a mix of logs, stones, and earth, encircled about three-quarters of the settlement. Upright poles seemed to have been hastily stuck into the ground in the open part of this protective barrier, their various angles clearly veering from the vertical. The tiny figures of people could be seen on top of the mound.

"See!" said Poltan as he pointed, "they have not been able to complete their defences, and no one works on them now. They must indeed feel that an attack is imminent."

While the others discussed what they could see within the settlement, Bren cast his gaze to the nearby parts of the valley and surrounding slopes. It was then that he saw movement in a lightly timbered area that was overlooked by a large rocky outcrop high above Laghana on the opposite side of the valley. "Poltan!" he interrupted, "I can see people moving in those woods." The Spey man quickly turned and then looked in the direction of Bren's outstretched arm. As he did so, a party of what appeared to be armed warriors emerged from the distant trees. Some were on ponies but most were running on foot towards the settlement.

"Cattach!" said Poltan from between clenched teeth. "By the heavens I hope we are not too late. "Gollarg," he called across to his huge lieutenant. "They will first set the poles alight and then attempt to scale the mound at the opposite end while the people try to put out the fires. We will use the bull's horn; you to the left, me to the right," he said in an obvious reference to a charging tactic. "You and your friends stay with me," he said to Bren; and then loudly to the others as he mounted his pony, "Prepare for battle. We go to save Laghana."

It took some time for them to get to the valley floor, and then they had to ford a shallow river in order to approach the settlement. By the time they arrived, the attack by the Cattach was fully underway. As he urged his pony forward, Bren could see that Poltan had been correct in his assertion that the attackers would set fire to the timber that the people had used to temporarily fill the gap in their mounded wall. A few Cattach bowmen remained there firing fire-tipped arrows into the assorted poles. He gasped when he saw Gollarg charge up and behead one of these archers before the man had even become aware of the giant's arrival. Without stopping, Gollarg then led his half of the Ardvortag party around the base of the mound to the left – several of his own bowmen dropping the other surprised Cattach.

Bren already had his sword drawn as he followed Poltan to the right. The tumult of battle became much louder as they rounded the curve – men and women shouting, some screaming in pain; metal clanging; hounds barking; and frightened ponies whinnying. Up on top of the mound were the defenders of the settlement; a few armed with spears, others with bows and arrows, but most with nothing more than rocks and clubs. Already, several bodies lay amongst them. And the Cattach – all well armed – were starting to advance up the short incline, obviously confident that they would overwhelm these simple farmers. But the situation was now different.

Poltan screamed a war cry that Bren couldn't understand but which was answered by the others. Then he heard Pock-face yell, "Remember Ceann Tull!" and without looking round he screamed the same words back – hearing Trib do this also. The twenty or so Cattach scrambling up the side of the mound turned and hesitated, their confidence now gone. Their leaders, who were below on ponies, called to their men to retreat, and were making the first moves to ride off, when Gollarg and his warriors appeared across their path. As the Cattach seemed to vacillate about whether to flee or to fight, the party from Ardvortag charged in amongst them, swords and axes swinging; with spears and arrows swishing through the air at those who were now slipping down from the mound.

Following the advice Poltan had given him earlier, Bren singled out a particular opponent – an unbearded Cattach warrior on a pony straight ahead. The man was calling to his warriors and did not see his opponent from the Tull approaching. When almost upon him, Bren lifted his sword ... but then paused, suddenly confronted by the realization that this man, who he was about to destroy, had done nothing to him. In that moment of hesitation the Cattach spun around and saw Bren – first his eyes and then his raised sword. He had a long blade of his own in his hand and with a contemptuous laugh he now thrust it at Bren's chest. But it never found its mark. At that instant, Bren lurched uncontrollably away from the glistening weapon as his pony fell sideways with a spear in its chest – a short, equine scream issuing from its muzzle before the poor creature collapsed completely. As luck would have it, Bren was able to scramble from the animal before being pinned by its dead weight, but when he looked, his adversary had already turned and ridden off.

Just ahead, Pock-face was on foot also, fighting like an enraged badger against two Cattach. He seemed to be in control of the situation, with one of his dark-haired opponents glancing across at his fleeing leaders and obviously unsure whether he should continue to fight. However, a third bearded warrior was cautiously sneaking up behind Pock-face with a long-handled axe in his hand. Without another thought, Bren ran past his cousin screaming and with his sword raised. The surprised Cattach used both hands to lift the wooden handle of his own weapon above his head – to block the imminent blow. But as Bren brought his blade down he swung it at the man's clenched fingers. The Cattach screamed, dropped his axe, and then scrambled off in the direction of his retreating comrades. Bren could easily have slain him, but he did not. On the ground in front of him lay two fingers; both severed behind the second knuckle.

Looking around, Bren saw at least a dozen bodies – most of them Cattach. One lay at Pock-face's feet – it looked like the man who had wanted to flee. Up on top of the encircling mound there were men, women, and children – some crying over the bodies of dead or wounded loved ones, but most shouting words of praise down to their saviours. Some of Poltan's men began to climb the slope, but Bren stood watching as others pursued the fleeing Cattach, cutting down those who could not run or ride fast enough. He walked over to his cousin who was using the grass to wipe the blood and gore from his sword. Pock-face looked up at Bren – his eyes still wild from the battle. But before either could speak, there was a loud scream from behind them.

Suddenly, Trib ran past, calling for help. Close behind, was a young woman; she had a large cudgel in her hands and was shouting, "I'll kill you, you murderous piece of shit. Somebody stop him!"

Bren immediately knew what was going on. He stuck out his foot as the woman ran by. Her feet tangled and down she went – letting go of the cudgel as she fell.

She rolled over on her back and yelled, "You idiot, why did you trip me? Kill that bastard Cattach – they are all murderers," she was pointing at Trib who now stood some way beyond, uncertain what to do next.

Bren reached out a hand to help her up. "He is not Cattach," he said as she lifted her arm – and as Pock-face's laughter filled the air. "He may have the features of those people but he is a Tull man, like I, and he has just helped save your settlement from destruction."

As she stood, she looked at his face and then at Trib and back again. There was mud on her forehead and, although the angry look was still in her eyes, Bren recognized something familiar. She blinked, her appearance suddenly growing softer and suggesting that she too had just become aware of something.

"Bren?" she said. "Bren of the Tull?"

He reached out his hand and brushed a wisp of hair from her face – his heart pounding. "Bodar?" he said.

She held his wrist, and smiled; there was no need for answers.

****

The Holy Well

It was a sad time for the people of Laghana. That some of their brethren had died while defending the settlement was bad enough, but then to also have to decide whether to leave or not, was heartbreaking. After the joy of being saved from the Cattach assault, their mood had changed as Poltan told them that his men could not stay, and that his advice was for them to accompany him back to the Spey valley where they could temporarily re-settle until the menace from the north had abated. But everyone knew that the Cattach threat would not simply disappear, and that the peaceful world they had known for so many generations was now slipping away. They knew it would never return.

Some wanted to stay; to try again to form some sort of allegiance with other settlements nearer the coast – even though none had come to their aid on this occasion – and if not, then to fight to the end for the land of their ancestors. Others saw no point in risking the futures of their children – who the Cattach would have no hesitation in killing – just so they could occupy their beloved valley for a little while longer. In the end, no consensus could be reached, so the elders had advised each family to decide for itself. About half the people sombrely packed what they could carry in ox carts and on their backs, while the rest remained defiant ... but with little hope. Poltan had insisted on speed, he wanted to be out of the valley and in his own lands before nightfall; so the packing was hurried and the farewells brief. But, of course, there was a great outpouring of emotion as the two groups parted – people pleading, crying, embracing, and knowing that they would probably never see each other again.

All this had disturbed Bren and his two friends very deeply. It was a tragic situation. But their sympathy also had a selfish edge. If such events could happen at Laghana then perhaps they could occur at *their* home settlement.

That night, back in the upper reaches of the Spey valley, their concerned mood continued.

"But Ceann Tull isn't alone on the shores of our sacred lake; there are many settlements close-by, and we have good relations with them all," said Trib to the others as they stood guard on a ridge overlooking the camped Laghana refugees.

"Trib's right," said Pock-face, "And besides, there are no Cattach that far south; our people have never had the need to build these ... walls, or mounds or the like around their settlements."

"But neither had these people," Bren replied, "... until now."

"It's not the same," his cousin protested. "Cean Tull will always be safe. And anyway, if it does ever need defending then we will be there." They stood in silence, each thinking about their home.

Bren was still drifting in his mind when his cousin nudged him. "Your woman comes," he smiled, indicating with his chin.

Bren shook the thoughts from his head and looked down at the camp. In the moonlight he could see Bodar had left the group she'd been sitting with and was starting to climb up the slope to where he and his friends were standing. He considered rebuking Pock-face for saying, 'your woman', but decided against it – it would only encourage him to play the weasel further, and anyway, he liked what the term suggested, even if it wasn't true ... yet. He left his grinning friends and walked to meet her halfway down.

There had been little chance for them to talk back at the settlement earlier in the day – except to exchange words of astonishment at meeting again, and in such turbulent circumstances. They had not seen each other since they were children – at that wonderful and memorable spring-birth celebration. It had only been a brief encounter, but Bren had never forgotten this girl who was now a slender, strong, and most attractive woman. And by the way she had looked at him with her rowan-leaf, brown eyes it had been clear – according to Pock-face – that she had also harboured fond memories of Bren.

"How do your people fare?" he said after greeting her.

"The men are sombre, and many of the women still weep," she replied, "But the children were playing before they curled up to sleep, so this is a good sign."

"Ah, it will be an adventure for the young ones, I suppose," Bren replied. "To begin with at least."

She looked at him, a frown on her face. "Do you think they will be playing when the moon is again full?" she asked. "Will it still be an adventure for them?"

"Who can tell?" he answered honestly. "There are great changes taking place in these lands; and much uncertainty." He immediately wished he hadn't said something that was clearly more obvious to her than to him, so he added, "Children have a way of finding pleasure in the simplest of things – as long as they have the love of those around them." Bodar smiled at this, and Bren was pleased with himself. "Let's walk a little," he said, gesturing along the narrow track worn into the side of the slope by many generations of deer and other creatures. "Don't worry," he added, "we shall stay within the guarded perimeter."

After strolling for a short distance in silence, she said, "I am still astonished that we were brought together in this way. I always … wondered … whether we would meet again."

"And I," Bren replied. "But back when we first met, I recall you saying that you came from a place called Chonardt."

"You remembered that?" she said, stopping – and grinning. Bren could feel the blood flushing his face, and was suddenly glad that it was night. She continued, "It's true, I was born and grew up in Chonardt. It is a settlement even further north than here, and it was one of the first to be threatened by the Cattach two summers ago. I came with my uncle and his family to Laghana at that time, we had relatives there." She lowered her head. "Two died today."

Bren looked down at the camp, trying to focus in the darkness on the five tightly wrapped bundles that lay in the oxcart downwind of the sleeping people. Within two or three days they would be lying on the bottom of the sacred lake of the Spey at Ardvortag. He sighed. "And your parents?" he enquired.

"Oh, they died long ago; my mother from a fever when I was still a baby, and my father … he never returned from a hunting trip when I was only four winters old. I have two older sisters; both are with their husbands back at Laghana."

"And you have no man?"

"No."

"And have you promised yourself to anyone?"

"No again," she giggled. "And what about …?"

But before she could finish, Bren replied, "Also no and no." They both laughed, and Bren could see her eyes sparkle in the moonlight.

After a moment, she stepped up to his side and hooked one of her arms around one of his. "Let's walk some more," she said.

The moon moved on its great arc while they talked about many things: what had happened in their lives since they first met, how Bodar's uncle and aunts had been trying to marry her off for several years – and how she had rejected all suggestions, what difficulties her people might encounter in resettling at Ardvortag or elsewhere, and how the three friends had set off on their journey of discovery.

"And you say that one of your grandfathers had a sister who married a man from Laghana?"

"Yes, that's what I was told, and that's why we intended going there sometime during our wanderings. But we never thought it would be so soon ... or in such circumstances."

"The powers of the world do such things all the time," Bodar said, looking up at the stars. "And so, did you find out? Do you still have family in Laghana ... or down there in the camp?"

"Or up here next to me?" Bren said with a serious expression – but with a huge grin lying barely concealed within his face.

"Oh, no! We're not cousins are we?" she asked as her eyes widened. "What was the name of your grandfather's sister?"

Bren had to use all his willpower to maintain his solemn demeanor. "You had better sit down for this," he said as he knelt down himself, gently pulling on her hand. "I spoke to an old lady this afternoon and she has worked it all out for me. What it all means is that you and I are ..."

"Yes, we are what?" she insisted, sitting upright – uncertainty on her face.

"We … are …"

"Yes?"

"We are totally unrelated."

Even before the words had left his mouth, Bren was laughing. Bodar lunged at him. "You slinky pine marten, you cawing crow," she said as she pushed at his shoulders. He toppled back but grabbed at her extended arms, and together they fell, squealing, onto the grass.

"Shhh," Bren said, as much to himself as to Bodar, "We must not frighten those in the camp. He stayed on his back while she adjusted her position and knelt beside him.

"You wanted me to think we were related – you snake," she said as she poked him with a finger.

"Would that have mattered?" he said, smiling.

"No, but you were playing with me," she replied, and then stuck her tongue out at him, as would an angry child – but followed this with a grin.

"I'm sorry," he said as a final chuckle left his lips.

They were then silent for a while; he on his back and she on her knees. He eventually looked across at her. She was staring up at the night sky.

"Bodar," he said, "you know how I told you before that I had also wondered if we would ever meet again."

"Yes," she replied, still gazing up at the stars.

"Well, that was not exactly true." He swallowed with some difficulty as she turned her face towards him. "The truth is I didn't just wonder; I hoped." She didn't smile but her eyes penetrated him and sent a warmth through him that he had not known before. "I have never forgotten you," he said.

She leaned forward and softly stroked his cheek. "And I have been waiting a long time for you," she replied.

The Holy Well

✳✳✳✳✳✳✳✳✳✳✳✳

Their return to Ardvortag was greeted with both relief and insistence. The concern of Poltan's father, Ulvar, for the safety of his one remaining son was obvious; and this was reflected in the faces of the people – Poltan and his father clearly being both loved and respected. However, Ulvar didn't delay in letting his son know that an urgent situation had arisen over the past two days; one that would need all the defensive skills and manpower that the two could call upon. Cattach movements had become more intense in the vicinity, with large numbers being reported from outer settlements and, on top of this, a small party of Kelti – the first ever to be seen in the area – were only a short distance away, their intentions unknown.

Concerns about the arrival of the refugees from Laghana seemed secondary to Ulvar, and after greeting their elders he directed them to one of his lieutenants who was trying to deal with many similar folk who had arrived from other locations. Bren noticed that the island building had stopped out in the middle of the lake, but that a similarly busy and intense work effort was now focused on two forges at the far end of the settlement. From these there issued smoke and the peculiar smell of molten bronze, accompanied by the sounds of pounding hammers and shouting voices. As he studied the scene further, he saw more and more people coming in on the several paths that led to the settlement; bringing grain, cattle, game, and other produce. Ardvortag was bustling and clearly preparing for the possibility of a major conflict. Poltan beckoned to Bren and his friends to join him as he walked towards the great lodge.

"I will go with my people for now," Bodar said to Bren as she helped an old lady lift her few belongings. "But make sure you find me before you run off to do anything brave or foolish."

Bren looked about at the masses of people and activity, and then at her. "Do not be concerned," he said, "we shall not slip apart again." He gently squeezed her arm and strode off after Poltan.

There were about twenty men in the lodge. Most were either priests or senior warriors in the hierarchy that existed in Ulvar's lordship. Bren felt a little uncomfortable at being included in this assemblage; after all, he was only a guest; but both Poltan and his father had insisted, so he could hardly refuse. Pock-face and Trib had also been invited to attend. Noisy discussion had been taking place for some time amongst various groups, when the old man stood on the feasting table. When the others saw this they were soon silent. He then spoke.

"Bands of Cattach have been reported as leaving their lands in the north in greater numbers than ever; and they are heading south. It would appear that the first of these bands are already grouping in the hills above our valleys. I am of the opinion that they mean to either converge on Ardvortag itself, or to draw us into a series of small battles – where they hope to defeat us and wear us down – and thereby take control of the entire region." Several men shouted abusive comments about the Cattach, but most waited for their lord to continue. "So, my first order has been to strengthen the defences around our great settlement, and to extend its guarded borders well back into the surrounding hills and far beyond the ends of our sacred lake. We will send out daily patrols – sometimes of no more than two or three men – to report back on the Cattach movements. Also, most of our craftsmen will now concentrate on the making of weapons. And several of you will be responsible for teaching the men – and some of the women – who now arrive every day seeking safety, how to use these weapons in battle."

This caused some discussion and Bren could see that the general consensus was that this was a desperate attempt by the Cattach to gain new land because of the continuing failure of the crops and pastures in their own, northern regions. But then a young warrior asked a question of the old man. "Lord Ulvar," he said, "What of the Kelti? Do they pose a threat also?"

Ulvar paused as those gathered looked towards him; by the expressions on some faces this question was of as much concern to them as the more apparent danger of the Cattach. "Their party is small, no more than twenty men, and they are moving quite openly; not attempting to avoid detection. They are travelling slowly, and have not caused problems at any of the settlements they have passed through." He then drew breath and looked around at his son before continuing. "Just before I entered the lodge I received word back from a messenger I sent to the Kelti band two days ago." He turned his gaze to a man sitting at the end of the table ripping into a leg of cold meat. "It appears they come to seek me out, saying they have an offer they wish to make."

"What sort of offer my lord?" asked one of the priests.

Ulvar looked at the man with the meat. "They would not say," said the man, "only that it could bring great benefits to both our peoples. They will arrive here the day after tomorrow."

More discussion followed, with Ulvar directing attention back to the Cattach threat, and with Poltan and other lieutenants giving detailed instructions about the plans for dealing with it. Finally, the old man held up his hand to signal silence. Then he again spoke.

"And now I will change the purpose of this gathering from one of concern and challenge to one of gratitude and respect." Amongst the group, questioning glances were responded to with wide eyes and shrugs of ignorance. Ulvar continued. "Every man here knows how much my hound, Teira, means to me. Her fame as a hunting dog, and as a war dog, has spread far beyond these lands; and in recent years many powerful chiefs have made rich offers for her offspring – although she has never been able to conceive. And you know the sadness I felt when I thought she had been taken from me forever. But now I have her back, together with a fine litter of pups – her first. And this is because of the great seeing powers of our guest and friend, Bren of the Tull."

All heads turned to Bren. He felt uncomfortable – no one had told him this was going to happen; and he was sure he didn't deserve such praise. "You didn't *do* anything with the dog did you?" Pock-face whispered; a great smirk on his face.

Ulvar continued. "And because of this deed, he, above all others in my lordship and beyond, shall choose which of the whelps will be his, as a living remembrance of my gratitude." With this, the old man stepped down from the table, walked over to Bren, and threw his arms around him. Whilst in the embrace, he whispered, "Please stay with us my boy, we need you."

Later that evening, while Pock-face and Trib were eating with Poltan and his men, Bren went and sought out Bodar.

He found her with her people just beyond the western edge of the settlement. They were camped in a lightly treed area near the lake. It was a place that the people of Ardvortag had used for many years for festivals and celebrations. Several of the priests had objected to the incomers being sent there – because of the site's association with these mainly-religious activities, but Ulvar had chastised them greatly, pointing out that the immediate physical needs of the refugees should be uppermost in their minds.

As well as the twenty or so people from Laghana, Bren estimated that there must be at least twice that number camped in the clearing who were from other places. He stopped for a moment and surveyed the scene. Small cooking fires glowed in the twilight, outlining the dozen makeshift tents of withes and hide and bark that had already been constructed. People sat in small groups around the fires; some murmuring in quiet conversation; others watching the embers – their hearts heavy with sadness. Bren was glad it was summer; the old and the sick would not survive a winter in such flimsy accommodation. He sighed as he walked towards Bodar and the group of children she seemed to be entertaining, wondering if any of these people would ever be able to return to their home settlements.

Bodar looked up as Bren approached. "Hello," she said happily, as she plucked at the strings spread between a young girl's outstretched hands. She nimbly twisted her own hands around, lifted the strings, and produced a new pattern. The children clapped and cooed their approval.

He squatted down in front of her, and she gestured with her vertical palms – inviting him to play. "It's been a long time," he said, as he cautiously placed his fingers in amongst the strings. "But some things you never forget!" he said with a flourish of his hands. The children giggled loudly as they saw the irony of his proud expression set against the tangled mess hanging from his fingers. "Hmmm," he said, looking down, "there must be something wrong with this string."

"You're funny," said a little girl.

The flap of a nearby tent then opened and a large woman emerged. "All right you young ones, it's time for sleep. Come now," she said in a deep voice.

The children all looked pleadingly at Bodar, but she just confirmed the bad news. "Off you go now," she said, "We will play some more tomorrow."

They all lined up to give Bodar a hug before sauntering over to the tent. The last little boy gave Bren a hug too, and asked, "Will you play with us tomorrow?"

"If not tomorrow, then soon – I promise," he replied, surprised at the boy's show of affection.

"He lost his father to the Cattach a short while ago," Bodar said as they watched the lad disappear behind the hide flap.

A number of other people were sitting nearby, and although they tried to look indifferent, Bren was aware of at least several pairs of eyes that kept glancing across at him, with their owners quietly exchanging comments, and smiling. However, he and Bodar were left alone, and as they talked, the greys of early evening were slowly replaced by the full darkness of the night – the moon being hidden behind a thick bank of cloud.

"I hope it doesn't rain," she said at one point, looking up into the sky. "Some of these tents are not yet complete." Bren remained silent. "You were good with the children earlier," she said, changing the subject completely. "Did you really play 'cat's lair' when you were a child?"

"Oh yes," he replied, "I think everybody does; it's just that I was never very good at it."

She laughed. "You know, I remember where I first learned that game," she said. "My sisters and I were collecting juniper berries for making dye. We were in the woods on the other side of the small lake where Chonardt sits. I was very young, and it was the first time I had gone so far from our home. When we had filled our pouches with berries, my sisters took me to a tiny clearing a little way in from the water's edge. I had to carry a big rock with me and place it with others in a ring that they had been making for the last two years. We sat inside the circle, on the soft green grass, and my eldest sister took some string from her tunic and showed me how to play cat's lair. It was a sunny day, and the birds were singing its praise. You could see our settlement in the distance – through the trees and across the water. It was a wonderful afternoon, and I was enchanted by the clearing with its little ring of stones. I continued to visit there – sometimes with my sisters, and sometimes alone – right up until it became too unsafe to venture so far from the settlement. But it will always be a special place for me."

Bren nodded slowly. "I know what you mean," he said, as he moved closer and lay back with his head resting on her lap.

Bodar brushed her fingers across his hair "Do you have a special place, Bren?" she asked quietly.

He closed his eyes and took a deep breath. "Near my home of Ceann Tull there is a place called Endachni. It borders on the great forest of Drumm where, years ago, Trib and myself and another boy called Natach went to hunt." He told her the whole story and felt himself almost drifting back to the times and places he described, as she gently stroked his head, and listened to his words.

❊ ❊ ❊ ❊ ❊ ❊ ❊ ❊ ❊ ❊ ❊ ❊ ❊

The following night, Bren visited Bodar again. But this time there were many others in the camp. In the late afternoon, the bodies of those who had been killed while defending Laghana – two having been Poltan's warriors – were returned to the great cycle by way of the lake. In the lands of the Spey it was customary to celebrate the lives of those to whom the final farewell had been made, by feasting and song; and much of this had been occurring in the clearing outside Ardvortag as the stars made their slow journeys through the heavens. Poltan and his father were there, as were the families and friends of the slain defenders.

Later still, when many of the guests and visitors had returned to their homes, there were still thirty or so people sitting around the large fire that had been used for roasting the game. Bren was sitting on the ground next to Bodar. On his other side were Pock-face and Trib. Earlier in the evening there had been songs of tribute sung about the men who had died. These had been followed by verses about the places from where they had come; and now a man was singing a song about the sadness of leaving Laghana. There were tears in the eyes of many of the listeners, and gloom sat heavy on the shoulders of all who attended. When the man had finished, no one spoke; the only sounds being the occasional crackle from glowing embers, and the distant calls of creatures of the night.

Then Bodar stood up. Slowly, and quietly, she walked to the small mound from where the others had delivered their words. Everyone there looked up at her as she took a reed pipe from her tunic and lifted it to her lips. The tune she played was unknown to those who sat watching and listening, but it enchanted them all; the soft notes becoming more vibrant as the tempo increased, and then mellow as it slowed down again, with ripples of tone bending into long, sweet, sounds. Then she took the pipe from her mouth and began to sing. Her song told the story of a boy who had run towards a river to get water for a dying friend; and how, before reaching the river, he had come upon a well, a holy well; and that it had offered its life-giving water instead. She sang on about how the boy's friend had been saved from certain death, and how many others had gone on to benefit from his find. But, she sang, it was the well that had discovered the boy, as much as he discovering it.

Bren sat with his eyes wide and his mouth agape. She ended the song with a verse about the enduring wonder of the well and the secrets and gifts it still had to offer the boy, who was now a man.

Tears were trickling down Bren's face when she came and sat beside him. He looked across at Trib whose cheeks were also wet. Even Pock-face seemed ready to weep.

"I don't know what to say ..." he whispered as he wiped at his eyes. "Your song has captured the very essence of ... It was the most beautiful thing I have every heard. It ... you ... spoke to me in a way I've never ..."

"Shhh," she said softly, "it is my gift to you." She turned to Trib, "... And to you, Trib." He nodded, unable to talk.

The rest of the listeners were silent, still captivated by Bodar's performance. Finally, an old man some distance away shouted out, "Bren of the Tull, if you don't marry that woman without delay then you are a fool!" With these words, a great noise erupted as everybody there shouted in agreement.

Chapter 10

James watched as dragonflies swooped and hovered above the small pool by the side of the river. Clearly, finding this bloody well wasn't going to be as straightforward as he had at first thought. The description in the book by the Rev. Gillchrist – which he now opened again for about the tenth time today – described the general area and stated that the Holy Well of Endackney was, '... at the base of a steep embankment about four hundred yards north of the two great oak trees ...' Duncan the caretaker had explained where he thought Endackney once existed, and this conformed with what the book stated, but James had been wandering around in the woods for hours now without success – and he was tired, and had a pain in his head.

He had come across a number of promising embankments but, sadly, no significant oak trees. Of course, there was a strong possibility that the oaks no longer existed. After all, the description had been written way back in the late 1800s. 'Shit!' he thought. Maybe the well didn't exist anymore either – destroyed years ago when new trees were being planted or when land was being cleared. Or maybe erosion and other natural processes had caused it to cave in and fill up. Maybe the river had increased in size and overwhelmed it. The pool he was sitting next to might be all that remained of the well.

However, despite these depressing possibilities, he had no intention of giving up the search. If the well still existed then he was going to find it, and he'd keep looking until he had covered every square centimetre of ground in the area. If it was going to take him a year of weekends then that was fine.

He stood up, his resolve overruling his weariness and his developing headache. Ahead was the decaying old footbridge that spanned the river. Disregarding the warning signs about not using it, he crossed to the opposite bank, and turned left. A short distance away were the woods that he had already investigated from the other direction, the tall pines and firs offering a dark and gloomy alternative to the bright sunshine. But just before this dense assembly of trees there was a grassy area of about half an acre, and this is where he now stood. Looking across at the river, he saw that it was very wide here and obviously shallower than in most other places. Also, as the land gently sloped to the water's edge, the grass gave way to a carpet of small pebbles that seemed to continue on under the swift-flowing Tull and re-emerge on the far bank. This made James' pulse quicken slightly. He remembered another passage in the Rev. Gillchrist's book that described, 'a place where cattle could ford the river', as being close to the old church of Endackney.

He lifted his gaze from the swirling water and studied the clearing. It was then that he saw it. A short distance away – set against the dark background of conifers – was a giant of a tree that was covered in buds, and which already had young leaves in its upper branches. It was an oak. There were no other trees of this size in the cleared area but there was a large, jagged trunk nearby – its thickness and texture similar to that of the giant tree. James made a loud, excited whistle. He was sure he had found the two oaks mentioned in the book, and therefore the place where the ancient church had once stood. But now for the well.

'Four hundred yards north,' James quoted to himself as he stood between the living tree and the stump of its long dead sister. He pulled a cheap hand-bearing compass from his pocket and waited for its needle to settle. To the north, the clearing ended and more trees rose up from the undulating land, except for a small field that bordered the woods and extended across to the banks of the increasingly distant river. It was along the western border of this field that he now began to pace out four hundred yards; 'a yard is a bit less than a metre,' he kept cautioning himself as his strides began to increase, matching his growing excitement.

At the count of four hundred he stopped. On his right was the field, and on his left were trees and bushes. He wandered into these woods for about twenty metres but he could see nothing of significance. The ground was beginning to rise when he decided to turn around and go back to the edge of the field.

He looked up and down the line of trees – mainly birches – that formed the natural border. There was nothing to indicate … Suddenly he stopped and focused on a patch of grass about fifteen metres ahead. It was a slightly darker green than the rest of the field. He hurried to the spot, and felt his boots sink into mud. Looking directly into the woods he could see the glistening wet surface of a small, boggy area that wound its way amongst the trees and shrubs. On either side were yellow wildflowers which didn't seem to be anywhere else close-by.

Careful not to step on the flowers – or in the mud – James followed the bog. A little way in, he was temporarily stopped by a fallen tree. As he climbed over its fungi-covered trunk he looked ahead and saw that the gently rising ground he had noticed on his first entry had now turned into a steep slope. He remembered the Rev. Gillchrist's words: '... at the base of a steep embankment ...' Then he saw it, just to his right. The Holy Well of Endackney.

Several minutes passed before James could even begin to calm down from the thrill of his discovery. But when he did, he tried to be objective about what he could see. For instance, the well was far more modest than he had imagined. Only a couple of feet in diameter – if that – it was basically a hole in the ground that was lined with white stones. Where these stones protruded above the surface – for no more than a foot or so – they were mostly covered with moss of a most vibrant green. Various small fern-like plants grew around it, and water trickled over one of the encircling rocks and dropped down to form a tiny brook. This meandered for only a short distance before turning into the narrow bog that had signalled the well's existence. But the more he looked, the more he was stunned by the simple, natural beauty of it all. And he knew that this relic of the land was very, very old.

James squatted next to his discovery, elated, but also noticing the increasing pain in his head. He looked into the water, surprised that it could simultaneously appear so dark but also be quite transparent – the bottom being clearly visible. He touched the mirrorlike surface. It was cold. Standing, he took *The Fame of Taroane* from his haversack and opened it to one of the pages he'd marked with a strip of paper. This section listed items from the region that had been reportedly given to the National Museum of Antiquities by various 'donors' over the years. He read the relevant entry:

> 'Endackney; from the Holy Well, several old coins and pins, and a rudely-made stone cup; provided by the estate of the late Marquis of Taroane. The ages of these items are unknown.'

He squatted down again but as his head began to thump he decided to sit. It was certainly peaceful here. He listened to the 'chirrup' sounds of several unseen birds and looked up at the blueness filtering down through the branches from the sky. Closing his eyes, he rubbed his temples, trying to dismiss the pain that threatened to distract him from his fascination with the place. He thought about the stone cup and wondered what features it possessed that had caused it to be described as 'rudely-made'. Who had made it? And how long ago? Who had drunk from it? And why had it been removed? It saddened him to think that the cup may have been an important accompaniment to the well – that it may have been here for hundreds of years, with nobody ever dreaming of stealing it – only to have it appropriated by some Victorian aristocrat who thought it would be better in his private collection than remaining at its original site where it could be used by the common folk. James leaned forward, cupped his hands, scooped up some water, and drank. It was cool and cleansing, with no noticeable taste.

As the ripples settled, he gazed into the well, trying to see if there were any objects of interest on the bottom. Finding an old pin or coin would really be something. Feeling a little guilty, he gently placed his left hand in the water and reached down until he could feel the bottom. It was deeper than he thought, requiring him to roll up his shirtsleeve to the very shoulder. There was a thin layer of mud under his fingers and he slowly sifted through this until he felt something flat and round. Bringing the object to the surface, he could see that it was a coin, about the size of the old copper pennies which he remembered from childhood. Unfortunately, it was badly corroded as well as being encrusted with a patchy layer of some sort of hard substance – probably a product of the corrosion process. A few vaguely-shaped letters were discernible near the rim, and maybe a tiny part of an image – but that was all.

He ran a finger around the edge of his find. If it had've been the stone cup, he would certainly have used it, but then left it for those who might come later. So shouldn't the same principle apply to the coin? He thought on this and was about to return the piece of corroded metal to the well, but then suddenly changed his mind and slipped it into his pocket. Strangely, he felt no guilt. In fact, he had the overwhelming feeling that on this particular occasion it was the correct thing to do. He did, however, take a fifty-cent piece from his wallet – he'd been carrying it around since leaving Australia – and dropped it into the water, whispering, "This is for you." He then stood, looked around, took a deep breath, and walked out of the woods. Ten minutes later, after carefully stepping over the gaps in the old bridge, he stared back in the direction of the well. For the time being at least, he would tell no one about it – it would remain his special secret. He blinked and looked up into the sky. He felt good, exhilarated even. And on top of this, his headache had gone. He walked on, smiling. High above, an eagle circled.

The Holy Well

※ ※ ※ ※ ※ ※ ※ ※ ※ ※ ※ ※

It had been many months since what James called 'the visit' had taken place. He only used this term in his own thinking and in an occasional diary he kept – very occasional – and it referred to the brief but erotic encounter he'd had with Miss Pordosky. To be honest, it had sparked some interest in him, and he had often thought about that night, but he'd not pursued the matter with her. This was partly because she hadn't given the slightest indication of wanting anything further to happen between them, but mainly because he felt that any close relationship with her would lead to disaster. She was now more unstable and aggressive than ever – the tiniest thing going wrong being enough to make her fly into a fury. And she was isolating herself to such an extent that several days might go by before any of the students or teachers would see her.

With this in mind, James now felt uneasy as she approached him outside the castle.

"Good morning Mr Campbell," she said in a flat tone, without smiling. A short distance away, one of the students nudged her partner.

"Good morning Miss Pordosky," he replied, hoping he was prepared for any verbal abuse she might throw at him.

"Can you give me one good reason why these students are outside in the grounds rather than in their classroom?" She was glaring.

"Because there are no trees in the classroom," he answered.

"I beg your pardon?"

"There are no trees in the classroom," he repeated. "The mathematics curriculum for this topic and grade level requires students to use measurements and trigonometry to calculate the heights of very tall objects such as trees and buildings." She looked at him aggressively. "There aren't any buildings inside the classroom either," he added for good measure.

She continued to stare at him for a several seconds, but he observed that the harshness was quickly draining from her face and was being replaced by something more unusual – the beginnings of a smile perhaps. However, before the transformation was complete, she turned and without saying another word, walked away.

"God! I hate her," said a voice from behind.

James swung around and saw one of his students, Dianne Swanston. Her bouncy black hair glistened in the sunshine, and the frown on her face couldn't detract from the youthful sparkle in her azure eyes. Her beauty didn't go unnoticed by James. "Hey," he said with a smile, "the sun is shining, you're surrounded by friends, and in a week the summer holidays begin – you shouldn't be hating anyone."

"We say 'vacation', Mr Campbell," she replied with a smirk.

"You mean people from Texas?"

"Yes, and those from every other state in the union."

"Just as a matter of interest," he asked with his eyebrows lifted, "would Scotland happen to be one of those states?"

"No."

"And where are we now – like, right at this point in time."

"Scotland," she said, wrinkling her nose in a gesture of mock petulance.

"And ..." He decided not to continue – she obviously got his point. God, she was pretty. "So how are you going with the worksheet?" he asked, clearing his thoughts and getting back into teaching mode.

"I'm finished; and I think everyone else is too. We were just wondering whether we could do the rest of the lesson out here rather than back in that dreary classroom."

He glanced over at the doorway that Miss Pordosky had walked through minutes ago. "Yes, why not," he replied. "We'll all sit on the grass over there."

A short while later, the eight teenagers were sitting in various positions in front of him. "Okay," he said, "I'm going to skip all the earlier questions because I checked those with you individually before. So let's start with question four." Most of the students looked down at their jottings and calculations – except for Ronald Tolridge who was squinting at the sun, and Dianne who was staring at James. She was doing this while leaning back on her elbows, with her legs stretched out towards him. He could see the bottom of her knickers. At first he was going to say something, but decided not to – she would be embarrassed, and that was the last thing he wanted. Instead, he would make a discreet gesture for her to adjust her leg position. But then he decided against that too – for different reasons. Quickly, he turned his attention to the others.

"Now, rather than going blind by looking at the sun, Ronald, can you point out which tree you and Dorothy chose to calculate the height of?"

"It won't be the sun that makes him go blind," interjected one of the school wags, Barry Libowitz. Everyone laughed except Ronald who was a rather serious young man.

"We didn't do a tree, we did the tower on the corner of the castle over there," he pointed.

"Excellent. What angle of elevation did you get, and what distance back from the wall?"

"Fifty-five degrees and thirty-three point six feet."

James wondered when Americans would start using the metric system. "And what trig function did you use?"

"Well, we used *cotan* to find the extra ground distance because of Dorothy's height – she was using the inclinometer – and then we used *tan* to …"

"Mr Campbell, can I interrupt for just a minute? It's important." It was Barry the wag.

"What is it?" James asked as he held up a hand to Ronald, indicating he should stop for a moment.

"How old is this castle? The brochure that convinced my parents to send me here said that it was built in seventeen eighty something, but then someone heard a guy in the village saying it was much older; so what's the story?"

All the students could see that James was about to chastise Barry and steer the discussion back to boring Ronald's measurements, so almost with one voice they supported the sudden enquiry. "Oh come on Mr Campbell, tell us about the castle," said one of the girls, "We can get back to the math later."

"No, we'll let Ronald finish and we'll talk about the technique – and everyone will be really interested – and then I'll answer Barry's question. How's that?"

Fifteen minutes later James stopped all the math talk – yet again pleased with his students' progress. He still enjoyed teaching them and, unlike some of his colleagues, he hadn't tired of living with them. Really, they had grown pretty much to be his new, extended family. And even though he was looking forward to the coming break – in which he planned to travel around Europe – he knew that he would miss these kids, who weren't too much younger than himself, and that he'd be happy to get back to the castle after the holidays.

"Okay, the castle," he said as they closed their notebooks. "What we see around us was indeed built in the late eighteenth century, so it's not really that old as far as castles go. But part of it stands where there was once a much older and smaller fortress – one that appears to have been built in the fourteen hundreds. And even before that, there is a suggestion that a series of other defensive-type structures stood here – maybe going back as far as the Dark Ages."

"Whoa," said Barry, "What are … or were, the Dark Ages?"

"They were from about AD 500 to AD 1000. The start was when the Romans left. They took all their organization and culture and control with them. Different tribes then tried to take over different areas but this led to fighting and marauding and general mayhem across the land. Eventually, some semblance of order again arose, and the period ended. As you'd expect, there are very few records from these times, so our knowledge is pretty limited."

"What about the stone circles around here Mr Campbell?" Everyone turned and looked at Ronald. "Like the one in the field when you come here from Abercrombie." The students nodded; they had all seen the stones he was referring to.

"Well, they go back a very long time – probably to what is called the Neolithic period. The word means 'New Stone Age' – before people discovered how to make metal. Although some also seem to have been put up in the early Bronze Age."

"When people had found how to make things out of bronze, right?" said Barry. James nodded.

"So how long ago was that?" asked Dorothy.

"Thousands of years, Dorothy. In Britain, the Bronze Age lasted from about 2200 BC until about 700 BC; and the Neolithic period was before that."

"And are there any books or records or stuff from then?" Barry asked.

"No books, no inscriptions, no writing – not in Britain anyway."

"What about the Celts, where do they fit in?" It was Ronald again.

"That culture originated in Europe, and the people and their customs seem to have got here over a long period, beginning around the late Bronze Age and into the next epoch, called the Iron Age – and their influence was enormous. You know, all the 'native' languages of Britain, like Welsh and Cornish, and up here, Gaelic, are Celtic."

James was wondering if the students were still interested; they were all so quiet. Then Dianne spoke.

"And what about prior to the Celts? There must have been people before them. What did *they* speak, and what was their culture like?"

James was impressed. It was a question he had just recently started to ponder, and to investigate. He smiled at her and she smiled back. "It's a great mystery to us, Dianne. There are a handful of placenames that we know aren't Celtic, and we have some building foundations and artifacts like jewellery and other items, but that's all. We really know almost nothing about them."

"I wonder what they sang about," she said as she looked towards the hills. "I wonder what they knew."

James shivered as he stared at her stationary profile. Then the fire alarm bell rang for five seconds. It was time for lunch.

❋❋❋❋❋❋❋❋❋❋❋❋

That night, James sat at his desk, and for the umpteenth time he examined the coin he had found in the well all those months ago. He knew that it was probably less than a hundred years old and that he wouldn't see anything more on its corroded surface now than he had on each of the other times. But he liked handling it; it helped him to remember – no, to *taste* – what it had been like when he discovered the ancient site.

Of course, he'd been back on a number of occasions, but not as often as he would have liked. In fact, it had been more than six weeks since he last sat by the well with his eyes closed, listening to the forest sounds and the tinkle of the water as it passed over the white rocks. The extra-curricular responsibilities he'd taken on seemed to occupy most of his free time these days; like the sound-proofing of the old store room so that Barry and some of the others could play their electric guitars without causing Miss Pordosky to go apoplectic. All those polystyrene tiles. It had been hard enough tracking them down in Perth, but then he and his small team had to carefully cement the whole bloody lot to the walls and ceiling. It had taken them ages. Even the making of the little electric hot-wire cutting tool had taken two weekends – mainly because of the journeys he had to make in the school bus just to find the right size transformer and nichrome wire. Accessing such things wasn't easy when you lived in the countryside. Still, that project was over, and although he had others on the boil, he was determined to keep this weekend free, and to visit the well again this Sunday.

As he fondled the coin, his mind drifted over the day's activities. Those guys in the class just before lunch had genuinely wanted to hear about the castle and the former inhabitants of the area. It had surprised him. And Dianne Swanston; what magical thoughts had come from that young, intelligent head, to be so poetically expressed by those pretty lips. He tipped the coin slightly so the lamplight made the tiny crystals in the corrosive layer sparkle; and he repeated to himself her words regarding the pre-Celtic people, 'I wonder what they sang about; I wonder what they knew.' It prompted him to reflect further on the well and the thousands of people who must have used it.

Through the early Christian period it appeared to have been considered quite sacred; it was, after all, called the *Holy* Well of Endackney. And he was now fairly sure, as suggested by the Rev. Gillchrist's writings, that it had spiritual significance in the Celtic era, long before Christianity took hold in the region. But did it go back even further, before the Celts; to the time of an unknown people who spoke an unknown language? What significance might the well have had for them? The question intrigued him, and he decided he would think about it when he sat alone at the site on Sunday. Maybe he would be inspired with some sort of answer, or the beginnings of an answer.

He placed the coin in the little matchbox he'd covered with aluminium foil – so it wouldn't be accidentally thrown away – and prepared himself for bed.

A short while later, as his feet explored the cool areas between the crisp, freshly laundered sheets, he closed the book he'd been reading, and then closed his eyes. Sleep began to descend quickly, but in that brief, twilight period when wakefulness is giving way to dreams, he pictured Dianne lying on the grass. He saw her speaking; her angelic face; her lips. And the last thing he saw before slipping into the gentle chaos of images were her long legs and the whiteness of the material that covered where they merged.

The next morning, he was sitting on a park bench in the small town of Abercrombie, about fifteen minutes drive from the castle. You could actually buy things like shirts and dictionaries and apples from the dozen or so shops here; unlike the village of Cranmore which you could walk to from the castle but which only had a pub and a little general store. Most of the students had come to the town so they could buy gifts for the family and friends who they'd soon be seeing back in the States. James himself had already purchased a few items that the town had to offer for his planned trip across Europe – a tiny portable gas stove being his best find. He was examining this when a familiar voice made him look up.

"Now I believe it; you really are going camping aren't you?" It was Cori Chinoza, the social studies teacher.

"Yep, the tent I ordered arrived on Thursday, and now with this little cooker and these little pots and thingies ..." he opened up a bag for her to see, "... I'll be fully self-contained."

"You'll be hot and bothered and eaten by midgies," she said.

"No," he replied as he reached into a bag and pulled out a small bottle, "I'll have my 'extra high potency Buzz-off' insect repellent."

"You'll still get hot," she said, crinkling her nose at him.

"Water bottle," he responded, pointing at yet another bag.

"Bothered?" she said hopefully.

"I might enjoy being bothered – depends who's doing it," he smiled, raising his eyebrows in a Groucho Marx fashion.

"You're incorrigible," she said with a grin of her own.

"Australian actually," he replied, repeating the Groucho gesture.

"That's it, I'm leaving," she said. "I've got heaps to buy before the bus goes. Do you want to join me? – there could be a coffee in it for you later."

"No, I'm going to sit here in the sunshine and quietly read my newspaper, but thanks for asking."

"Okay, I'll see you later," she said as she walked away, and after glancing over her shoulder, added, "But I don't think you'll get much reading done." This remark mystified James until he turned his head and saw the approaching figure of Dianne. He found his mouth suddenly becoming dry as he watched her walk towards him. She was gorgeous … 'but she is also a student,' he told himself, 'and you are her teacher.'

Ten minutes passed in pleasant chitchat while they looked at each other's purchases and talked about what they'd be doing over the summer break. But then a moment seemed to arrive when they both wanted to end the lightness of the conversation – happy as it was – and move onto something deeper that they both felt the need to explore. James knew he had to be careful here – he could feel his heart pushing for control over his actions. However, it was she who broke the silence.

"You know how we were speaking the other day about the people who lived around here in ancient times?"

"Yes."

"Well, you're a math teacher, and you've studied science and technology and all that sort of stuff, so I was wondering how come you knew so much about history and the different ages and things like that?"

He looked at her briefly and saw that she was staring at him. He wanted to stare back but, instead, found himself lowering his eyes. "I'm just interested in that sort of thing I suppose. I've read a fair bit in the last six months, but I really don't know much. It's just that …" He wasn't sure what to say next. He suddenly felt like he wanted to share a deep and personal part of himself with this girl. But his brain told him it would be pointless – she was too young to understand, and it was such a private feeling.

"You love this land don't you?" she said. He looked at her – totally surprised. "I know you do. The way you talk about it, the way you sit and gaze at the hills and the sky. I've watched you from my window. And I've seen you go off on your walks – always alone." Now she lowered her eyes. "I even followed you a little way once, when you set off along the river bank with one of your books and your compass – as though you were searching for something."

Without thinking, he reached out and touched her hand, astonished by her perception. "You're right," he said hesitantly, "a very special … I don't know … bond, has grown between me and the land around where we live. It's really strong and … wonderful … but I find it hard to explain. And on the day you mention, I was in fact looking for something."

"Did you find it?" she asked softly.

"Yes," he replied.

She sat, looking at him. She was so beautiful. "It was a well," he continued, "a holy well; from very ancient times. It is the most special place I have ever been to. That's why I've not mentioned it to anyone. You are the first."

"Please tell me about it," she said quietly, and for the next thirty minutes he did – sharing his sense of excitement and wonder; and at the same time gently falling ... She was in the middle of asking a question when Barry's raucous voice filled the park.

"Hey Mr Campbell and the Swanston chick, Duncan's waiting for you; everyone else is in the bus already." He was running towards them.

James looked at Dianne, saying, "About what I've told you ..." and placed a finger to his lips.

She nodded, and in the few seconds before Barry arrived, said, "Please James, take me to the holy well. I want to see it, and to be there with you."

He blinked, and then quickly squeezed her arm, but before he could answer, Barry was with them.

* * * * * * * * * * * * * *

That evening James had trouble concentrating on any of the things he tried to set his mind to. There were school jobs to do – like marking the final tests of some students, and preparing revision classes for others who were yet to have their tests. And there were personal things he wanted to finish. For example, he had started a letter to his parents two weeks ago and it was still sitting, only half completed, on his desk. Also, it had been ages since he'd been in touch with Susan down in London – and a few other people in Australia. He hoped to rectify this situation tonight, and had bought a handful of postcards in Abercrombie earlier in the day as a preliminary step.

But it didn't matter what he started at, his thoughts kept drifting back to Dianne and their time together in the park. God! Why was she one of his students? Why couldn't she just be a girl he'd met in the town? – like someone who had picked up something he'd dropped; one of these bloody postcards for instance – and they'd just got to talking. But he knew that wouldn't have been the same. He and Dianne had lived and worked and had fun together – albeit with all these social and moral barriers that limited their interactions – and they had slowly developed an affinity for each other; appreciating the little nuances of behaviour that … 'Oh shit!' he thought, 'I have to get her out of my mind. Nothing can come of it.'

He put down his pen, having only written 'Dear Susan' at the top of one of the postcards. Looking out his window, he saw that the moon was close to being full. It gave the landscape an eerie quality, with the trees and hills silhouetted in many dark shades against the dull glow in the sky. He thought about the holy well and decided to include his Dianne dilemma in his thoughts when he sat by it tomorrow. It was strange, but he often found himself walking away from the well with new ideas or with solutions to problems he'd been thinking about. He had sometimes thought that maybe, in a way, the well 'spoke' to him about such things. But this was clearly anthropomorphizing the phenomenon. It was obviously just the relaxed state that the surroundings induced that made his unconscious mind come up with answers and ideas that were not available through conscious processes.

But there was Dianne again – in his mind. She had shown such empathy for what he had described to her about himself and the well. He really wanted to take her there. But how could he, without jeopardizing his – and her – position at the school? Damn it. She would be a student for another two years – an awful long while to wait without actually doing anything 'unethical'. He rested his chin in his hands and stared, unseeing, at the school timetable on the wall in front of him. "Fuck!" he said to himself before standing up and walking over to his bed.

This dream was weird – like most – but, at the same time, it was becoming increasingly pleasant. He had been walking through a field, and was wearing a dressing gown. He felt warm and comfortable as he ambled along. In the sky above, a large bird lazily drifted in circles that got lower and lower. It made muted tapping sounds with its beak as it slowly descended, and then it began to call his name, 'James, James.' He sat on the grass and looked up at the bird, and then he lay back. Eventually, the bird landed at his feet and opened its shimmering, rainbow-coloured wings. Then, in an instant, it changed into a beautiful, young, naked woman. It was Dianne! She knelt down next to him and undid the cord on his dressing gown. He felt a slight chill as she opened up the garment, but then warmth returned as she lay beside him, the dressing gown now having grown bigger so as to envelope them both. She whispered to him in a strange but familiar voice, "I know you want this; so do it now; I am moist and you are hard; come inside me."

Without saying a word, he rolled over on top of her and began what she had asked for. It felt good, so, so good. But in the midst of this extraordinary experience he suddenly felt something was amiss. Was it the voice? Or maybe the perfume he now noticed? Or was it the squeaking sound? ...

He opened his eyes. The dreamscape quickly melted into oblivion and he realized that he was in his bed ... but so was someone else – a woman – and she was gently squirming as he rhythmically pushed into her. "Oh Dianne," he said softly but intently, no longer caring about the consequences of what she had obviously initiated by coming to his room.

"What did you call me?" said his love-making partner.

This comment promptly removed any remnants of sleep that still clouded James's head. He focused on the face of the woman whose open thighs were cyclically gripping and releasing the sides of his buttocks. It was Miss Pordosky! "Oh God!" he said. He knew that it would only take a few more thrusts before he would come, but some drive even more powerful than physical desire took over, and he withdrew himself. "I'm sorry," he said. "I ... I didn't know ... I can't do this."

Miss Pordosky made an attempt to reach up to him but he pulled back. She then forcefully swung her legs to the side of the bed and reached down for a dressing gown that lay on the floor. "Thought I was a student did you?" she said as she put on the gown. "I should have known. I've seen the way you two look at each other – you bastard." And with that, she stood up and promptly left the room.

"Great, just really great," James shouted at the door.

Next day he skipped the communal breakfast, preferring the tea and dried biscuits he prepared for himself in his bedroom. Although still a bit stunned by the previous night's happening, he was more concerned with getting his marking and lesson preparation done so he could have the rest of the day to himself – away from the castle.

It was just after eleven o'clock when he looked across at his window and saw a car in the distance disappearing behind trees as it passed up the driveway and out of the castle grounds. He walked over to the window and surveyed those parts of the estate that were visible. Down below, to the far right, he saw the back end of a white Rover – the same as that driven by the owner of the school, Michael O'Connor. James hadn't heard that he was coming, but assumed it was something to do with new enrolments for next term – or to see his mistress. He winced as he thought about last night again. "Jesus, what a crazy woman," he said to himself.

Just then there was a loud knock at his door. It was Duncan. "Good morning Mr Campbell," he said.

"Hello Duncan, what's up?" James replied, wondering why the caretaker had used 'Mr Campbell' rather than his usual 'Jamie'.

"Mr O'Connor is here and he asked to see you right away," Duncan said in a tone that definitely lacked its usual warmth.

"Oh, okay. Do you know what it's about?" James asked.

"No, I've no idea," Duncan answered, but James was sure this was untrue; Duncan always knew everything that was going on. They walked along the corridor in silence.

As they began to descend the elaborate staircase that led to the small library O'Connor used as an office during his occasional visits, James tried to make conversation. "That car I just saw driving away, Duncan, who was that – anyone I know?"

Duncan didn't look at him. "It was Mr and Mrs Swanston and their daughter, Dianne. The girl's parents had planned a big surprise for her – to take her out of school early so she could join them on a holiday in the Caribbean."

James stopped walking, feeling a blend of bewilderment and sadness sweep through him. But Duncan was already at the library door, knocking.

Ten minutes later James was walking back to his room. But now he was in shock. O'Connor, the man who had been so friendly and encouraging when he had first offered James the teaching position – and who had seemed happy with his work when he last saw him two months ago – had just told him his contract would not be renewed, and that even though he'd be paid for the approaching holiday period, he would need to vacate the premises when school ended in a week. 'I've found someone more qualified,' he'd said when James asked for a reason. 'And more suitable ...' he had cryptically added.

Back in his room, James sat at his desk, his head swirling. The castle had become his home; he loved it here ... and he'd been doing a good job. But these appeals had meant nothing to O'Connor. When he had left the library and stood for a moment outside the door, he'd heard the school's owner talking to Miss Pordosky. She must have been waiting in one of the little anterooms. James knew she was behind this, but he also knew there was nothing he could do about it.

So he'd be leaving in a week. He looked at the pile of test papers on the desk, and at the class timetable hanging in front of him. Over on the right was *The Fame of Taroane* by the Rev. Gillchrist, and on top of it was his little foil-covered matchbox containing the coin from the well. He reached over and picked it up. On the wall, the old clock started to make a noise, like it was going to ring out with one of its rare 'Bongggs'. But nothing happened.

Chapter 11

The most noticeable thing about the twenty or so Kelti who first came to Ardvortag was that many had red hair. Everyone commented on it, and it brought forth a number of comments about Pock-face and his own distinctive, flame-coloured locks. Of course Trib pounced on this opportunity for getting back at his friend who still made gibes about stolen Cattach babies. "Your mother travelled a lot when she was younger, did she?" he asked with feigned innocence as the Kelti rode past. This led to an attack by Pock-face, and a memorable wrestle amongst a flock of geese at the edge of the watching crowd; the wild squawks of the protesting birds mixing with the shrieks of laughter and mock curses coming from the two rolling bodies.

As well as the profusion of red hair, the other feature that made the Kelti stand out was their colourful and unusual apparel. The older women of the settlement were particularly vocal about the blue and yellow chequered trews that most of the males wore under their flimsy tunics. "They wouldn't want to be in a rush to do anything with what lies underneath," one cackled loudly to her sisters as they watched the party go by on their larger-than-usual ponies.

"Perhaps they enjoy the feel of something wrapped around their legs," another called back.

The men of Ardvortag, on the other hand, became keenly – albeit less noisily – interested in two of the riders who were near the centre of the group. They had not been singled out for special attention at first because they could not be fully seen – the outer riders obscuring the view. But as the party slowly headed towards Ulvar, who was standing with Poltan and others outside his lodge, it became obvious that the two partially-hidden Kelti were female. They wore similar clothes to the men but their loose-fitting top-shirts and open jackets revealed the unmistakable upper curves of women. Both were young, but one – with blazing red hair drawn back into a single, thick plait – was clearly of a higher social rank; her white pony being taller and adorned with a fine bronze cap, and she herself wearing an open collar of some sort about her neck. It was obvious that this adornment was made of gold. Bren, who was standing with Bodar, had never before seen so much of the glistening yellow metal in one piece of jewellery.

He was also acutely aware of the grey, silvery spearheads attached to the long, wooden shafts being carried by some of the warriors. Clearly, the material was iron, and he assumed that the scabbarded swords resting across the backs of the men were made of the same remarkable, and worrying, substance. Bodar squeezed his arm.

"Why aren't you over with Poltan and his father and the rest of the reception group?" she asked.

"Because I'm only a guest here," he said with a smile, but quickly saw from her expression that she wasn't satisfied with this explanation. "Ulvar asked some of us to mingle with the people – and to be watchful. He didn't want all his lieutenants and other special folk in the welcoming party – in case something goes wrong."

"So, I'm holding the arm of a 'special folk' am I?"

His grin returned, but he didn't reply.

The crowd followed the Kelti to the great lodge but stayed a moderate distance away from the strangers as they dismounted. The rider who had led the group into Ardvortag – he was tall, young, and had unusually short-cropped hair – approached Ulvar with another man. This other man must have spoken both the people's tongue and that of the Kelti because he waited for each of the leaders to speak and then spoke himself. Bren was close but not close enough to hear the words. Ulvar and Poltan and the two foreigners then entered the lodge, but not before several of the Kelti warriors had spent some time inside – obviously checking that it was safe for their leader to enter.

Some of the crowd drifted off at this stage but many stayed to further observe the strangers as they stood together by their ponies. A number of Ulvar's female retainers walked amongst them offering drink and pieces of breadcake. After a long wait, the Kelti leader emerged from the doorway. He walked over to the two female members of the party, conversed with one of them briefly, and then all three entered the building. There was another considerable wait before someone else appeared just inside the lodge's entrance. This time it was Poltan. He called to a number of his men, said a few words to each, and then disappeared back inside while the men either scurried out into the crowd or approached members of the welcoming party who were standing nearby. One of these messengers ran up to Bren and Bodar.

"Bren of the Tull, my Lord Ulvar asks that you join him in the great lodge," he said, after bowing his head slightly.

"I really can't get used to all this rank and power thing," he whispered to Bodar.

"Oh, I'm sure it's not too hard after a while," she replied as he kissed her cheek and then strode off.

As usual, it took time for his eyes to become accustomed to the darkness inside the huge building, but he could discern Ulvar and his son standing at the farthest end of the long feasting table; they were talking with the head priest. Closer by, at the nearer end of the table, stood the two Kelti women and their two male companions. They nodded as Bren slowly walked past. The taller woman, the one wearing the gold collar, was standing in such a position that the light from the doorway illuminated her whole body. As well as her long red hair – which was now unplaited and hanging loosely down to her waist – he could see that she had eyes the colour of the sky, and slightly freckled skin. She was solidly built, and quite beautiful – but not as much as Bodar.

"Bren, we require your special counsel on an important matter," Ulvar said, breaking from a conversation with the others. Bren watched as several senior members of the clan hierarchy entered the building and walked towards them. He also saw that Poltan was staring wistfully in the direction of the strangers.

"If I can help," he replied.

The Lord of the Spey then beckoned the group to gather close, and in a low voice said, "These Kelti have come with a proposition."

****

Bodar had been standing for what seemed like half the afternoon when Bren finally stepped out of the great lodge. He was behind most of the others who had been inside. Ulvar was in front, and next came Poltan with an arm locked around that of the gold-collared Kelti woman. They were both smiling but they separated from each other when Ulvar addressed the crowd.

"People of the Spey," he said, "I present to you Etain, the eldest daughter of a great Kelti chief known as Ruadan, who rules over much land in the south," There was not even a whisper from the crowd. "And this is her cousin and head warrior of his people, Diarmid."

"Young for a head warrior," Pock-face muttered to Bodar; both he and Trib having joined her.

"He's older than you, and you've done a fair share of fighting already," she murmured back.

"Ochar! I could be the head warrior of the Tull folk," he said to Trib who was straining to hear the rest of what Ulvar was saying.

"Oh yes, keep dreaming," Trib replied, "But be quiet." Bodar gave a supporting frown.

"… and so I want everyone to welcome these people and to treat them as honoured guests during their time here," Ulvar finished. He then began introducing Etain and her cousin to others in the welcoming party. At the same time, lesser members of the hierarchy, together with many people from the watching crowd, began to mingle with the remaining Kelti. Bodar and her two new friends, however, held back as Bren approached.

"What is happening?" she said quietly as he came up to her side, "Why are they here?" Pock-face and Trib also gave him expectant looks.

Bren placed one arm around Bodar's shoulder and the other around Trib's. "Come with me," he said softly, "there are too many ears in this crowd."

A short time later they were at the lakeside, standing amongst the boulders that would be ferried over to the holy isle when construction again began.

"Well?" said Bodar after Bren had finally decided where to sit.

He looked at the others, grinned for a moment, and then took on a more serious countenance – as though, on reflection, an initially mirthful thought had been revealed as something more grave. "They want power and land – although they have not stated this directly – and they are offering to trade for this with blood ties and bodies ... and knowledge."

"Ah! Now everything is clear," Pock-face said, "Just like the muddy water over there." Bodar gave him a dark look. Trib waited without expression.

"What has happened," Bren continued, "is that the chief of these Kelti, Ruadan, has offered his daughter – the tall redhead, Etain – to be Poltan's bride." The others looked like stunned salmon. "Also, he has offered to supply warriors to fight with Ulvar to stop the Cattach intrusions into the lands of the Spey; and to share the knowledge of his people's culture – even the means by which to make iron."

"And why would he do these things?" Trib asked. The other two looked at him and nodded in agreement.

"Because in return, the Kelti want Ulvar to allow some of their people to move into the lands that he controls. In the south there is much fighting between the Kelti and the original inhabitants – and, apparently, even amongst different Kelti tribes. This particular chief now wants to try a different, and more peaceful approach to gaining power and influence ... and land; a bringing together of two peoples without hostility."

"And why should Ulvar accept such an offer?" said Bodar, her brow still wrinkled.

"Because the situation of his clan is far more desperate than he is making known," Bren replied, shaking his head with concern. "He speaks of vanquishing the Cattach, but in truth he fears that his people will be overwhelmed by them. Reports coming in just today tell of large numbers entering nearby forests. The Kelti are reputed to be great fighters. To have them assisting in battle would certainly be a benefit. And the idea of learning how to arm his own warriors with weapons of iron, and of having other Kelti secrets revealed, is very tempting to Ulvar at this time." He paused for a moment before continuing, "And there is another reason ..."

"Go on," Bodar encouraged.

"It's Poltan; he seems to be utterly besotted with the woman being offered."

"What!?" Pock-face said loudly, "He has only looked upon her for a short time. How can he be so taken?"

"I do not know," Bren replied. "According to his friends – as well as himself – he has never been much interested in women ... until today when he saw Etain."

"She is quite beautiful," Bodar said. "I wonder what her thoughts are about Poltan."

"She smiled nicely at him during the deliberations in the great lodge," Bren replied, "and it was she who took his arm when they walked towards the doorway. Anyway, both sides have agreed that the two should have a week to decide whether they wish to marry."

"By the mountains, that's a bit …" Trib bit his lip before finishing as both Bren and Bodar stared at him.

"Sometimes the heart can see truth in an instant," Bren said with a grin, knowing that Bodar's eyes were now casting an affectionate gaze towards him.

Trib nodded, embarrassed. Pock-face broke the ensuing silence. "The big redhead uh?" he said, running a hand through his own tangled mane. "I'd give her one," he half whispered to Trib from behind a cupped hand.

"You'd give one to a goat," Trib replied.

Pock-face paused, seeming to deliberate on the suggestion. "Only if she was attractive," he said.

Moments later, their discussion was interrupted by the approach of one of Ulvar's personal messengers. "Men of the Tull, my Lord Ulvar urgently requires you to join him at the great lodge." There was unease in the man's eyes.

Bren stood, stepped over to Bodar – whose face showed her own uncertainty and apprehension, and kissed her gently on the cheek. "This may take a while," he said. "I shall see you back at the encampment later." And then he ran off, with Pock-face and Trib close behind.

Back at the lodge, the scene had changed from one of gaiety and welcome to one of turmoil and concern. The settlement people had been sent away – to return to their work – but the Kelti remained, huddled together outside in intense conversation. Guards were now at the entrances to the structure, and messengers and others kept entering and leaving in hurried succession; and warriors were beginning to assemble in a nearby field.

Inside, there were many men and a few women standing in various groups. They were talking softly amongst themselves but clearly remaining alert to the quiet deliberations of Ulvar and his lieutenants at the far end of the main chamber. Messengers constantly ran to and from the edges of this elite group carrying their memorized information. Poltan saw Bren and called him over.

"What has happened?" Bren asked. "Is it the Cattach?"

"Yes, they have overrun two of our outlying settlements and slaughtered all the inhabitants. There is a host of them; perhaps as many as two hundred. And more seem to be joining as they head in this direction."

"You mean they're approaching Ardvortag itself ... now?" Bren said, astonished.

"It would appear so. They wouldn't do this unless they had what they considered to be superior numbers."

"And with desperation driving their intentions I would guess," Bren replied.

Poltan nodded. "I really didn't think it would be like this. Neither did my father – not so soon." He looked into his friend's eyes. "Will you and your comrades join me as I go to meet the Cattach in a great battle – probably somewhere in the upper reaches of the Spey valley?"

"It's from there that we've just returned!" Bren said lifting his eyebrows, "But if that's where we must stop the Cattach then so be it. And you know I will join you – as will Pock-face." He then paused for a moment before continuing. "However, as a precaution, I will ask Trib to stay here to personally guard the love of my life."

"Ah, the fair Bodar; of course. I understand," Poltan replied. "When this is over, I intend to marry Etain – if she will have me. You and Bodar could marry at the same time – in one huge celebration of victory and affection."

"We shall see," Bren replied, now more concerned about the approaching conflict. "What of the Kelti party? Are they to depart now and observe from a distance?"

"No, my father and I have prevailed upon them to join us. Ulvar has agreed to allow up to fifty of their people to settle in our lands in the next year, and I have made my intentions regarding Etain clear. Although she has not said anything yet, I believe she is as keen as I. Anyway, it is enough of an agreement for them to abide by their original proposal, that they help us fight the Cattach. Ten of those warriors outside will be with us when we leave tomorrow. The rest will remain here with Etain and her servants."

Bren looked across at Ulvar; he was talking to Diarmid, the leader of the Kelti group. He then spotted Trib laughing at some utterance Pock-face had just made. And a shiver passed down the young Tull warrior's spine.

* * * * * * * * * * * * *

That evening, Bren sat with Bodar and Pock-face by the fire that was stoked into life midway through the afternoon of each day. It was outside the hide tent where Bodar and her relatives slept, and was essential for providing heat for cooking. At night it deterred wild beasts, but it also served as a gathering point for family and friends – its embers and flames providing warmth and security and, if you looked into its wavering glow, that strange inducement to ponder things large and small – and, sometimes, to see things. All people have known of this power; even those who existed before the Old Ones.

Bodar felt the tremble in Bren's hand. "Bren, what's wrong? What do you see?" she said with her mouth close to his ear.

He looked up from the flames, and blinked. "Nothing I understand," he murmured back. Then, straightening his back, he looked around the clearing. "Where is Trib?" he said, slightly annoyed. "He told me he'd be here by the time the Wolf's Eye had risen above that peak," he looked up at the star that was now clearly above a close-by mountain.

"Here he comes," said Pock-face who had appeared to be asleep. "Ayar!" he called as their friend approached. "Did you get lost in the dark?"

Trib scooped up a pinecone and threw it at Pock-face – barely missing his friend's groin. "I'm sorry, I took longer than I thought," he said as he looked down at the bundle of cloth he was holding.

"Ah," said Pock-face, "you've brought some of the roast duck from the lodge – a good reason to be late. Here, share it around, my hunger has returned."

"It's not food," Trib said dismissively.

"What then?" asked Pock-face. "I'm sure I smell duck."

Trib sat down next to his antagonist. Pock-face could see that his friend was in no mood to play so he sympathetically placed an arm around his shoulder.

"I'll show you later," Trib said. "First, I wish to hear from Bren about our expedition to meet the Cattach."

On the opposite side of the fire sat two of Bodar's male cousins and one of her uncles. They had not joined the others, thinking the Tull men and Bodar wanted to be alone. But Bren knew that tomorrow they too would be carrying weapons against the northern enemies, and that the possibility of death must be the subject of their thoughts at this time; so he beckoned them to now join him and his friends.

"As you know, we leave at first light tomorrow," he said after first cautioning all present that they should not reveal his words to anyone else. "We shall cross the stream at the eastern end of the lake and then walk the path that leads north-east around the base of the Hill of Otherfolk, and then follow the Spey, keeping on the western side of the valley – in the trees where the slopes begin. Somewhere below, we hope to find the Cattach. They will be expecting us to arrive from the other side of the river – where we travelled just days ago."

"How many of them are there?" asked one of Bodar's cousins, a worried expression on his face.

"At least two hundred – maybe a lot more, we can't be sure."

"And our warriors," asked the uncle, an old man of maybe forty summers, "how many?"

Bren rubbed his forehead. "About a hundred and fifty from here, including ten or so Kelti. We expect to meet up with more of our warriors from outlying places during our trek up the valley, so our numbers should swell. Some of the Kelti will remain here to protect their chief's daughter; and the same reasoning is behind Ulvar's decision to leave fifty warriors here to guard Ardvortag – although there is now general agreement that the Cattach will not directly threaten the settlement."

He paused for a moment, feeling guilty about not being entirely open. It was important that he inspire confidence in these men from Laghana, but in truth he was worried about the safety of Ardvortag. As he'd walked to the clearing after sunset he'd heard the shrieking of a white-faced owl, and for a moment it had sounded like the screams of women and children. And in the fire, just a short time ago, he had seen ... forms ... like writhing bodies. Maybe it was just his mind playing with the ever-changing dance of the flames, but it had made him feel even more uneasy.

"Which brings me to a request I wish to make of you, Trib my friend," he said, looking across to his fellow Tull man. "I want you to stay here as Bodar's protector while I am away with Pock-face and the others."

Bren had expected some argument from Trib, and thought he would have to justify his decision to accompany Poltan and Ulvar into battle. He had also anticipated loud objections from Bodar, for he knew that she feared for him; and he was ready to explain that if they were victorious in the coming conflict then it could mean the end of Cattach intrusions for a long time – maybe for good – and that the people of Laghana, for instance, might be able to return to their homes.

But neither of them said a word of protest. Trib simply nodded, and Bodar fixed him with her eyes, and sighed. In their faces he saw not so much deference as understanding; and he felt his chest swell with a deep happiness. What more could a man desire than to have companions who loved and understood him this way.

It was at this point that Trib lifted his cloth-wrapped object from the ground and, reaching across Bodar, handed it to Bren. "Now seems like a good time to give this to you," he said.

Bren unfolded the rough flax cloth and revealed what appeared to be a large, half-round stone. It was lighter than he expected and, upon turning it over, he saw why. The stone had a natural dip on its flat side, and rough markings showed that this had been hollowed out further by some form of grinding or chipping. The result was a small bowl or cup that fitted neatly into his hand.

"Thank the trees I won't have to lug it around any more," said Pock-face as Bren ran a finger around the smooth rim. And looking at Trib, he added, "You're lucky I had agreed to carry it in my shoulder bag on the day you were taken by the Cattach, that's all I can say."

"But I don't understand …" Bren said, looking at his friends.

"It's for you," Trib replied "… a cup; to commemorate the day you brought water from the holy well and saved my life when we were still boys. I began working on it long ago, and brought it with me when we left Ceann Tull. Like Pock-face said, good fortune caused me not to be carrying it on the day I was abducted. I did the final grinding yesterday and today. It's why I was late tonight."

"Why do you give it to him now?" asked Bodar softly, sensing some embarrassment – or was it uncertainty – in Trib's manner.

"Because it is finished," he replied, "and because it seems like the right time. But since you're leaving tomorrow, I'll keep hold of it until you return. It's not the sort of object a warrior carries into battle."

Bren stood and walked over to a water bladder hanging outside Bodar's tent. He filled the stone cup from it and then came back to the group. He sipped from the cup and then handed it to each of those around the fire. Finally, he stepped in front of Trib and beckoned him to stand. "This is a fine cup," he said, "and a fine symbol of our friendship – both shall survive long after we are gone." And with this, he embraced his dark-haired comrade.

"I never exactly thanked you for what you did," Trib whispered, as they held each other.

"You don't have to thank friends," Bren replied. "Besides, I had help."

"All right you two, you'd better separate now before Bodar here gets suspicious," Pock-face said amid giggles from the others. "And give me another look at this artful piece of stonework; I'm thirsty now as well as hungry."

* * * * * * * * * * * *

"Are you ready?" Poltan said to Bren as he looked at the men grouped behind his friend from the Tull.

"I am, and Pock-face even more so." He looked back at his cousin whose eyes were already wide with anticipation. "And if you're right about the others being willing to follow a stranger into battle, then they're ready too."

"Believe me, you are no longer considered a stranger. And like me, they see you as a valiant supporter of the Spey people. Now remember, this is a dangerous manoeuvre." He looked out from the trees at the massed Cattach far beyond, on the other side of the river. "It all depends on timing. I will take the main body of our warriors to the riverbank – to a place where it is only ankle deep at this time of year – down from the fork you can see. The Cattach may immediately cross when they see us coming, in order to meet us head on. Or they may prefer to stay where they are and wait for us to cross, thinking they can cut us down as we emerge on the far bank. But there is hardly any bank at all where I will be taking my men, so the Cattach would have little advantage. Ulvar will be with me, and we will decide what to do when we see how the Cattach respond to our presence."

"But I will wait until you have engaged in battle?" Bren asked, still reluctant to follow what seemed to him like a tactic involving great risk.

"Yes. It is a plan that the Kelti say they have used successfully in similar circumstances, and one that Ulvar and I agree with. We want the Cattach to feel confident that their numbers are far superior to ours. They will use the bull's horn movement and attempt to surround us, but at that point you will appear on the right flank, and the other group, led by Gollarg, on the left. You will then complete your own bull's horn – with the two groups surrounding the Cattach; they will find themselves fighting an inner knot and an outer circle."

Bren bit his lip. "My concerns are that we may not get to you in time, and we may not have enough men to effectively surround the Cattach."

"That is why you must run like a wolfhound when the fighting begins with my detachment. And whether you and Gollarg have enough men ... we shall just have to hope. Between you there is half of all the warriors; I daren't give you more for fear of having too few for the knot."

Bren looked down at the Cattach but felt Poltan's eyes staring at him. He blew a breath between clenched teeth, and then looked around. "I am ready," he said.

Moments later, he watched as Ulvar and Poltan and one hundred men rushed from the trees down towards the River Spey. The small Kelti troop was with them – their colourful clothing and painted faces making it easy to follow their movements within the throng. They uttered no war cries at this time, but offered each other shouts of encouragement as they first walked and then jogged in the direction of the slowly-moving Cattach horde. Bren knew that the cries of ancient tradition would be heard as the warriors got closer. He became aware of his heart beating faster.

Pock-face was at Bren's side when they saw the fighting begin. After a brief pause, Ulvar had ordered his men to cross the river. This seemed to surprise the Cattach, who were of a far superior number at this stage, for they only began to head towards the shallows after most of the Spey warriors had already crossed. In fact, it was the Kelti who crossed first, and this too must have added to the Cattach consternation – to see such strangely clad fighters, and their devastating iron weapons.

Bren stood high and looked at his waiting men. "We go!" he shouted, and then turned and ran from the trees, Pock-face still by his side. As he pounded through the tall pasture towards the increasingly audible clang of metal and screams of men, he caught a glimpse of the giant, Gollarg, and his charging group. They were some distance away but remained more or less in line with his own men. By the time they stormed across the river, both groups were screaming the war cries of their ancestors. Many of the Cattach had not seen them coming, and still had their backs to these new additions to the battle – pushing to engage the men they had surrounded. Bren thought that Ulvar and the others must be almost overwhelmed by now.

"Remember Ceann Tull!" Pock-face yelled as he brought his sword down on the neck of an unsuspecting Cattach fighter. He was then immediately confronted by several of the fallen man's comrades. Bren quickly assessed that his cousin would be able to handle the situation, and continued to lead his men in the agreed-to circling movement. However, it wasn't as straightforward a manoeuvre as planned. They were too close to the Cattach to get around them without having to do battle with those who saw what was happening. Bren knew that if he had more men this wouldn't be so much of a problem but, as it was, he didn't have enough momentum to continue the encircling movement. He was about two thirds the way round his half of the inner battling warriors when he looked behind and was shocked to see that all his men were already engaged in fighting. There would be no more encircling.

Three Cattach stood before him – all with swords and small targes; their beards plaited and their faces snarling. Suddenly, Pock-face was next to him, and together they screamed, "Remember Ceann Tull!" as they rushed at the Cattach, their swords flailing. Blood spurted onto Bren's cheek as his weapon cut through the carotid artery of the Cattach directly in front of him. Then there was another, bringing an axe down so hard on Bren's oak and bronze targe that the Tull warrior fell to the ground. But he held on to his shield, and as the Cattach desperately tried to dislodge his imbedded weapon, Bren thrust his sword up into the man's lower abdomen; the blade stopping when it hit the spinal column.

There were many bodies on the ground, and the screams and groans of the dying mixed with the shouts and curses of those still fighting. But Bren was not aware of any of this – surviving from moment to moment being his only concern. Then, suddenly, there were no more Cattach confronting him. Instead, he saw the blue-dyed faces of three Kelti warriors. Like him, they were spattered with blood and other bodily fluids, and Bren's eyes widened as he saw the swathe of dead or dying Cattach behind them. It was as if a wide path had been cut through the grass and then lined with dismembered bodies. But he quckly noticed there were also dead Kelti amongst the corpses. He lifted a hand in recognition, and then turned to rejoin the battle; one that was now clearly going their way.

He saw Pock-face a short distance off, typically engaged with more than one opponent, and was about to rush to his aid when Poltan appeared from the fray with Gollarg and another warrior. This cheered Bren because it meant that the giant man had also broken through the Cattach who surrounded the central knot of Spey and Kelti fighters.

"Bren," Poltan called. "We have won this battle, but may have lost more than we know." Bren frowned, wanting to hear more but concerned about Pock-face. Poltan understood and nudged Gollarg who raced to Pock-face's side – utterly demolishing one of the Cattach with a great club he was carrying.

Poltan was now at Bren's side. "My dear friend, here we have been successful, but Ardvortag is under attack." He glanced across to the other man – a messenger – who nodded. "Ulvar lies injured and I cannot leave his side ..." But Bren was already running towards one of the few ponies standing near the edge of the bloody scene.

"A few can go with you now, and I will follow soon," Poltan shouted after him. "We shall stand a stone here to commemorate today's great battle, my friend, and your name shall be long remembered as part of it," he added as Bren galloped off.

※ ※ ※ ※ ※ ※ ※ ※ ※ ※ ※

The pony was close to exhaustion as it cantered down the main path to Arvortag. Its coat glistened with sweat, but its heart was big, and Bren knew it would follow his urgings until it dropped.

He could now smell the smoke that only a short time earlier he had seen rising above the treetops as he rounded the Hill of Otherfolk. He had let out an anguished cry at its sight and had ridden down the steep slope like a boulder bouncing down a mountainside – caring little for his own safety. Getting to Bodar as fast as possible was all that mattered.

He knew that the six or seven Kelti who had survived the huge battle were some distance behind him – the safety of their chief's daughter being of greater concern to them than the final stage of the conflict. And Poltan had released twenty or so of his own men to hasten back and help defend the settlement. But most of these warriors were on foot; many of the ponies at the battle having become casualties. Bren realized that, for the moment, he would be the sole reinforcement for the defenders of Ardvortag.

As the pony swung around the final curve in the path, the young Tull man could hear the screams of women and the cries of children. Upon entering the settlement he was stunned by what he saw. The roofs of most dwellings were afire; bodies lay amongst the buildings and on the path – some calling for help, but most lifeless; and a few small groups of Spey men, grossly outnumbered, fought with Cattach on the slopes of the surrounding hillocks. The great lodge of Ulvar was now just a pile of smouldering cinders; it had clearly been singled out for early destruction; and the smell of burning flesh filled his nostrils. But he didn't stop; he had to find Bodar, and the first place to look was the clearing where her people were camped. He knew that Trib would be at her side wherever she was, with his sword in his hand; but how much could a single man do against such overwhelming odds? He dug his heels into the side of the pony.

As he galloped through to the outskirts of the settlement, a dwelling with its roof still intact came into view. Near its entrance lay the body of a man and those of two small children; their heads staved in. Close-by, a woman screamed as two Cattach warriors held her to the ground. The front of her garments had been sliced through, exposing her bare skin and dark fur. A third warrior knelt between her kicking legs with his tunic raised.

Bren diverted his pony and raced towards them with his sword lifted high. The kneeling Cattach was dead before he knew of his change in circumstances – blood and grey matter spurting from the cleft in his head and onto the poor woman's naked body. But Bren didn't stop to take on the remaining warriors. He had noticed two Spey men running towards the scene and hoped that they would discourage the ravagers from having their way. He had to find Bodar.

His heart sank as he entered the clearing. The tents that had been standing there just yesterday were now nothing more than strips of hide and bark and hazel wands on the ground; their contents strewn about the grass. But he saw no bodies, and for a moment he felt hopeful: maybe the inhabitants had run deep into the surrounding forests, and were hiding there right now, waiting until it was safe to return. Then he looked up; and gasped; his fear returning like a lightning bolt. High above, hanging from ropes tied around the branches of a single oak, were the inverted bodies of five adults – a profusion of Cattach arrows imbedded in each. Two of the poor creatures were women, but Bren thanked the stars that neither was his loved one.

He had dismounted and was about to venture into the woods when a faint but piercing cry penetrated the surrounding trees. He stopped and listened. It came again ... from the direction of the lake ... it was his name that was filling the air! Bodar was calling to him!

Crashing through the pines and bushes like a wild boar, he arrived at the shoreline, and immediately saw a small group of people on the tiny, man-made isle in the middle of the lake. A canoe load of about six Cattach had just landed and were doing battle with two or three men at one end of the rocky protuberance. At the other end stood two figures – clearly women. The rich red hair of one showed her to be the Kelti woman, Etain. The other was alternating between shouting abuse at the Cattach and crying out Bren's name. Bren could see it was Bodar. And just in front of them, as a last line of defence, stood the recognizable form of Trib, sword in hand, long dark hair tied back as a pony's tail.

Nearby was one of the many small canoes used by the isle-making workers in better times. Bren dragged it into the water, jumped in and, with the power of ten men, began paddling towards the tiny nipple of land. His heart had made less than a couple of hundred beats when the canoe hit the tops of the barely submerged rocks. But already, there was only Trib left defending the two women. Three Kelti lay face down in the shallows, with more than twice that number of Cattach bodies spread about the near end of the island. A further two or three bearded bodies lay in front of Trib who now, alone, was attempting to fight off another four Cattach.

The Holy Well

The women were trying to help by throwing rocks at the murderous invaders.

Bren jumped from the canoe and roared like a charging bull as he ran across the stones and dark soil, his sword raised and ready to devour the Cattach. "Remember Ceann Tull!" he screamed. Two of the bearded warriors turned, and he saw a familiar grin cross his friend's face just before an already bloodied bronze blade slashed across his neck. Bren screamed with rage and swung his sword like a giant harvesting sickle, opening up the chests of the two closest Cattach in quick succession. A third came at him as he completed the mighty swing, but didn't reckon on the dagger in Bren's other hand; the enraged Tull warrior ripping open the shocked Cattach's abdomen from his navel to his sternum. Then there were no more; the fourth Cattach lay dead on the end of Trib's blade.

Bren knelt by his bleeding friend. Bodar was already there, gently stroking the face of the dark-haired defender with her fingertips. They could both see that Trib was still alive, but that the life force in his eyes was quickly fading. He coughed; his blood and saliva and gastric juices spraying into the air. Clasping Bren's wrist, he made the merest of movements with his face, bidding his friend to come closer. Then, in a voice only barely audible he whispered, "Remember Ceann Tull." Next, he closed his eyes, gave a final sigh … and died.

"No, please no!" Bren cried as he looked up at the sky. But he knew Trib was gone. He then cradled his friend's head in his hands, and began to weep.

Bodar also wept. "He was so courageous," she said as tears ran down her cheeks. "How much I wanted you and I to grow old together with Trib as our friend."

Bren was unable to utter a response; his sadness so deep. But he raised his head a little and, despite the tears pouring from his eyes, he saw something on the ground just behind where Trib had fallen. It was a small bundle of cloth, partly open. And sitting in amongst its folds was a rudely made stone cup.

Chapter 12

'October at Balnakeil Bay. And no fucking commune anywhere along the way!' James jabbed the pen into his diary to make the exclamation point.

He was tired and disappointed, and worried about his immediate future. That priest he'd met on the train from London to Inverness had been so friendly, and had appeared so sincere. 'Yes, the leader's name is Bobby MacGillivray,' he had said, 'And the commune he started is on the way to Durness, right up at the top of Scotland. There's about twenty of them on as many acres of land – they even use horses for plowing.'

At first, James hadn't really been interested in hearing about this group of young people who, according to the priest, were attempting to find their way back to, 'a way of life that is more harmonious with nature.' But as the middle-aged, Irish-accented clergyman had enthusiastically described what this group seemed to be up to, he had become more intrigued. Unfortunately, when he'd had time to think about the possibilities of such a lifestyle – enough to want to have a first-hand look at what was going on – the priest had already disembarked, taking the details of the commune's location with him.

So, James had made an on-the-spot decision to catch the regular bus from Inverness to Ullapool. Next, he caught a ride on the Post Office bus that passed first up through the bleak terrain of Wester Ross, and then further north over the strange, treeless, fairy-mounded landscape of Sutherland, to the village of Durness. Sadly, the P.O. driver, who was a fountainhead of knowledge regarding almost everything in this relatively remote region, hadn't heard a word about any newly-arrived hippy farmers. Or that's what he'd said, at least. So James had gotten off the bus at Durness loaded down with his backpack and tent and shoulder bag and guitar, and had headed out of the village along a track to the northwest. An hour later, he was sitting alone on the beach of Balnakeil Bay writing in his diary and feeling the day's final rays of sunshine on his face.

He took the last of the Greek cigarettes from the packet he'd bought a week ago on the island of Skiathos, and lit it. Smoking was an occasional habit he'd picked up while hitchhiking around Europe – mainly because of Arnie, the American guy he'd met in Austria and with whom he had travelled down through Yugoslavia and on to Athens. But he knew this would probably be the last time he'd indulge in the practice. Someone had offered him an English cigarette on the train, and it'd tasted horrible; not like the lung-cutting harshness of 'Papastratos' which he'd grown to enjoy in a perverse sort of way. Still, English or Greek – it didn't matter, there'd be no more after this.

He popped apart his lips and blew an almost perfect smoke ring, watching it quickly dissipate despite there being no breeze. His eyelids drooped and he thought about the last fourteen months in Europe; the countries: Holland, France, Spain, Germany, Austria, Yugoslavia, Greece; and the jobs: picking cherries, coaching in English, crewing on a fishing boat, tending a bar; even singing Bob Dylan songs in a Munich restaurant. What a time it'd been. He'd met so many people, and even made a few friends, but he doubted whether he, or they, would write. Just the memory of their time together would be enough. Writing might even spoil it. And regarding sex ... well, there had been some, and at times it had been great, but it had never been accompanied by anything that was deep or lasting. There'd been warmth and fun and desire – but no real love. His barriers were still up in that regard. He opened his eyes and glimpsed the sun as it began to touch the horizon, and then closed them again and thought about Taroane Castle School.

Leaving the school had been such an awful experience – especially telling the kids that he wouldn't be back for the next term. A number of the girls had cried, and several of the boys had looked like they might too. And they all wanted to know why he wasn't coming back. 'They've found someone who they think is better qualified,' was his standard reply. Some had actually gone to see Miss Pordosky to convince her that he should stay. 'They couldn't find anyone better than you,' Barry Libowitz had protested. 'They're fucking crazy.'

But the headmistress had dismissed their protestations and had angrily responded that it was she and Mr O'Connor who ran the school, not them. Some said they would spend the summer holidays working out how to kill her when they came back. He had discouraged such talk but understood how they were feeling. The other teachers – except Pordosky – had turned the little end-of-term celebration at the pub in Cranmore into a send-off party for him. And before he left, every student had given him either a little gift or a personal note of thanks. Everyone except Dianne Swanston of course. By the time he quietly departed in the taxi on that final morning, she was already somewhere in the Caribbean – probably oblivious to his situation and, he was sure, looking forward to seeing him again when she returned.

Yet something had gone wrong in that respect too. The first letter he'd written to her when school began again – just to let her know where he was and what he was doing – had been returned to his forwarding address – 'return to sender' scrawled across it. He'd used a false name on the back of the envelope in case Pordosky still examined the mail (as she was reputed to do) – knowing that she would never pass on any message from him. So he hadn't been sure what to make of the return. But then the same thing happened with his second letter a couple of weeks later. However, this time someone had written on it, 'No longer at the school – address unknown'.

He had sat in a dirty little café in the south of France staring at that second envelope, wondering what to do. Back then, Dianne was still only sixteen, and nothing – he tried to convince himself – had actually happened between them. Nothing physical anyway. God! she was still part child. He had no right to mess with her head and heart – even if that was what she wanted. In the end, he had walked out of the café having made the decision not to try to contact her further. Another beautiful memory to be kept safe from attempts to extend and develop it into a new reality in a different context. But he still thought about her; achingly.

And he thought about the well. It was strange, really. Often, when on the Continent, he would come across old ruins, or standing stones – particularly in Brittany. And if he was alone and sitting and trying to picture what life must have been like in those ancient times, images of the Holy Well of Endackney would often slip into his mind. For instance, he'd be imagining how a local megalith must have been put in place. He'd close his eyes and see large numbers of people with ramps and logs and ropes attempting to lift the huge slab of granite upright. And then this would fade, and he'd see the well with its surrounding white stones and overhanging trees – peaceful and secluded – just as it had been when he discovered it. But once, only a short while ago, he'd imagined seeing something else there – a person, indistinct. At first, he thought it must be Dianne, because she had asked him to take her to the well, and he had dearly wanted to do that. But … it wasn't her … and the clothes were of fur and leather … a man. For some reason it had disturbed him; he wasn't sure why. He knew that the images were simply the product of his fertile imagination, but this particular impression had seemed somehow different. For a while now, he had found himself becoming less certain about such things; less dismissive.

And now no commune to have a look at. 'Bloody priest,' he thought. 'You just can't trust religion.' It didn't really bother him though. The idea of taking the best from the past and of weaving it into what we have today, in an attempt to create a more 'nature-sensitive' way of life; it all sounded very attractive – especially the study of past practices. And it wasn't just theory; people were actually doing things, trying things. Or so Father What's-his-name had said. Still, if it wasn't here then too bad. He'd head down south – and maybe even visit the well – but only if he could get over the hurt and embarrassment and reticence that he associated with the area because of his final school experience. His more immediate concern though, was lack of money – there was almost none left. He'd been used to sleeping in his little two-man tent for much of the summer and autumn, but it was already October, and the nights were getting colder. Soon he'd need to have a bed in a heated room – if he was to stay in the UK. And that meant finding work – quickly.

The sun was now far below the horizon – only its fading glow spreading across the ocean in front of him. He stubbed the cigarette butt into the sand, and walked back to his tent, slapping at the midgies that were beginning to find his blood highly agreeable.

* * * * * * * * * * * * *

James looked up from his map and gazed about the youth hostel's eating room. It could probably seat about fifty people – and most likely did at the height of summer; and winter. But tonight there were only a few other travellers with him there: the couple cuddling and giggling softly at the table next to the door; and the young guy standing at the nearby stove stirring something in a saucepan. It wasn't the first time he'd been to Aviemore – he had selected its well-known winter sports centre as a Saturday excursion destination back in his days at Taroane Castle. The kids had loved it. Of course, there was no snow yet, but that wouldn't be too long in coming. And, if he was right, now would be the time that the hotels and restaurants and other facilities would be looking for casual, ski-season workers.

Getting a lift from the top of Scotland had been a real bastard, but after two days he had managed to arrive back at Ullapool on the west coast. This had really lifted his spirits; the little town was in such a beautiful setting on the shores of Loch Broom, and people there had again been friendly and helpful – just like when he'd been travelling north. Then a single lift all the way across to Inverness and down to here.

That had been lucky, even if he did have difficulty conversing with the German couple who had picked him up. So despite only having enough money to last another couple of days – with limited eating and staying at the hostel, or a bit longer if he camped outside in his tent – he was hopeful that such simple good fortune might remain with him.

"Would you like some tea?"

James had drifted off into one of his reveries – imagining himself knocking on doors, offering to chop firewood or to make a kennel for the household dog or to sing and play guitar while the family ate, or to design a nozzle for the combustion chamber of a solid-fuel rocket engine that the lady of the house might want. He blinked his way back to reality, and saw the guy who had been at the stove.

"Pardon?" he replied.

"I've just made tea, would you like some?"

"You boiled it in the water didn't you?"

"Yes."

"It's not the usual way of making it, you know." He remembered how disgusting stewed tea could taste.

"It's the only way we do it back home."

"Where's that?"

"Kansas."

James looked at the youth's face – he couldn't have been more than sixteen or seventeen years old. His eyes suggested a certain melancholy, and he obviously wanted to talk to someone. Although tired and ready for bed, James smiled. "Yeah, thanks. I'd love a cup," he said.

The next morning was wet and windy. It was eight o'clock and he was alone in the kitchen-cum-dining room. The young guy he'd spoken to the previous night – Billy was his name – had said he would be leaving early, and it looked like he had. Poor kid; he'd run away from home – far away; it wasn't as though Scotland was next door to Kansas. It was parent trouble. He and they just weren't compatible he'd said – despite their pleas to the contrary. James had spoken with him well into the night, mainly about love and conflict and self-discovery and understanding ... and of taking a lead. He hadn't really behaved like a big brother to anyone since being at the school, when students would sometimes come to him for advice or to just talk about life. Even then, he was never sure whether he had much to offer. But Billy had seemed happier after their conversation – as though new light had been shed on his problem. Of course, his way of making tea remained revolting.

At nine o'clock, James, with his scruffy long hair, stained T-shirt, and multi-patched jeans, was standing next to Mr Buchanan, the well-coiffed, silk-suited staff manager of the Aviemore Winter Sports Centre who, despite his appearance, had obviously taken a liking to the young Australian. Also there in the kitchen of the 'Schwarzwald' was Mrs Forbes, the maître d' of the restaurant. She was a silver-haired woman in her late fifties who seemed to eye with condescending concern this newcomer that had been foisted upon her. Whenever she wasn't speaking she would pout her lips into the tiniest possible circumference. This, James thought, was intended to add to her air of superiority, but it actually made her look like a goldfish.

"So James," she said as she looked down her well-hooked nose, "have you worked in a restaurant kitchen before?"

"Only briefly," he replied, remembering back several years to when he'd helped out his Aunt Jessie in her little café for a couple of nights.

Mrs Forbes gave a daggered look at Buchanan – forget any management structure, this was obviously her domain.

"He heard about the dishwasher job from someone he met at the youth hostel last night," the staff manager said, almost apologetically. James smiled and nodded in agreement, briefly wondering where Billy-from-Kansas might be by now. "And I knew how desperate you were for someone to replace Huey …" There was that daggered look again. "And James here has a university degree, so …" but the woman cut him short as she regally turned her head towards the smiling graduate.

"I hope it's not in hair-dressing or clothes design," she said, finishing with the characteristic pout.

"Then your hopes are fulfilled mon maître d'," James replied with a melodramatic bow of his head. "For my time at university was spent studying far more important things." As he looked up, he saw a distinct twinkle in the woman's eyes, and her mouth shape change ever so slightly so as to suggest a smile. She turned to the staff manager and nodded.

"Yes, I suppose he'll do," she said.

"Excellent!" Mr Buchanan replied. He then looked at James. "I'll get someone to bring you the key to the house where you will be staying in the village – after I've telephoned the landlord and arranged everything. Unfortunately, there's no room in the centre's male dormitory, but I'm sure you'll find the village accommodation adequate. Mrs Forbes will talk to you about your duties and the rules and tips, etcetera." And then he left.

James was happy. Hungry, but happy. He looked out the servery window to where Mrs Forbes was talking to the first of the waitresses to come in for the evening shift. They had ended up getting on famously after their initial introduction; her snootiness obviously being a facade that she did away with if she liked you. On the other hand, she still behaved that way towards Tony – or Anthony as she insisted on calling him – the young English chef. But then Tony clearly had little time for her either, seeing her as continually trying to undermine his authority in the kitchen.

James looked up from the pot he was scrubbing, and smiled. This job was going to be his financial salvation. Of course, it'd be a week before he saw any money, so he wouldn't be eating very much until then, but when it did come, he'd also be getting a share of the restaurant's tips – which, according to Mrs Forbes, could sometimes be more than what you receive in your pay packet. And on top of this, he now had a cosy little room in the village. What a bonus. He hadn't realized that the Centre provided accommodation for its workers. It was another load off his mind. Money had never been of great importance to him, but being in a foreign country with no real friends or family and without any money at all; this was not a state he wanted to remain in. It seemed like this might be yet another case of 'outside' help.

Over the last twelve months or so he had started to feel that maybe there was some sort of benevolent entity or force or power or something that intervened in his life at critical times. He knew this didn't sit comfortably with his well-honed skepticism, and it was certainly nothing like the Christian God that he'd had pushed in his face as a teenager. He wasn't sure about it at all, really. But enough unusual events had occurred to make him wonder if there was something other than just random chance operating in his life. Ostensibly little things, like a car picking him up when there should have been no one on the road at the time; or meeting someone in unexpected circumstances who turned out to be instrumental in resolving a difficulty he was facing. It had led to a sort of primitive faith – that everything would be all right; always. When he was alone, which was much of the time, he would use the term, 'the gods', when he thought about this helpful intervention – if that's what it was. Suddenly, his contemplation was disrupted by a voice.

"Hey James." It was Tony the chef, standing in the doorway of the larger-than-necessary storeroom at the end of the kitchen, beckoning.

James put down the scrubber, wiped his hands on a towel, and walked over to his young boss. "What is it?" he asked.

"See, this is the cupboard I was talking to you about before." Tony opened one of the doors. "And these are the fresh apple strudels that you'll sometimes be responsible for getting if me or Rosie-the-kitchen-hand are busy. They're simple to serve – I'll show you how to do it when we get our first order tonight."

James's stomach gurgled, and he swallowed hard. "They're big aren't they?" was all he could say. The sight of the slabs of golden pastry enclosing the hugely thick layer of apples and sultanas, and the sweet smell of cinnamon ... He swallowed again.

"To get them off the tray, all you do is slide a piece out with this lifter, like this ..." Tony demonstrated, "... and put it on a plate – we'll use this paper one for now – and then ...

Oops!" he cried as the paper plate fell from his hand onto the floor, still upright. "Damn! We won't be able to use that one," he said, smiling at James. "Seems a shame to throw it away – you can have it if you like."

James looked at the young Englishman, his eyes wide. "Can I have it now?" he asked.

"I think that would be a good idea," Tony replied. "I'll just close the door so Madam Muck won't see you." And as he was leaving, added, "It's funny you know, we often seem to drop those strudels – must be something in the air." James just nodded, his taste buds having an orgasm.

A short while later – just before the first customers started to arrive – Mrs Forbes formally introduced James to the waitresses. There were four of them: two sisters from New Zealand, a South African, and an English girl – but no Scots, which Tony said he always thought was a bit strange, and gave the maître d' a mildly contemptuous look as he said so.

"No more strange than having a German name for a highland restaurant," James said happily in an attempt to break the moment of tension. But Mrs Forbes wasn't going to let the chef's comment pass.

"As you well know Anthony, waitressing positions at international tourist destinations are often filled by visitors from other countries – particularly if the location is well away from large local population areas." She pouted, obviously pleased with her small triumph.

"Excuse me everybody, but I would just like to point out that the two most important people in this establishment are me and Mrs Forbes – and we're both Scots."

Everyone looked across at the storeroom from which Rosie-the-kitchen-hand was emerging. Tony rushed over and put his arm around her young shoulder. "Isn't she lovely," he said as she shrugged him away.

"You shouldn't be standing around like this, we're going to have our first customers through that door any moment now," she said in her delightful Inverness-shire accent.

"Quite right," said the older lady as she clapped her hands. "Girls, back to the dining area."

Just then, the side door to the kitchen flew open and in rushed a fifth waitress – at least James assumed this was the case, she was wearing the same stylized frilly white blouse and black pinafore as the others, except she hadn't yet put on the funny little cap. He wondered if she could yodel.

Before speaking, the latecomer looked at James, and paused for a second – a tiny smile forming at the corners of her mouth. Then she quickly turned to her boss. "Oh, Mrs Forbes, I am so sorry. The power went off in the dormitory again and I hadn't finished ironing my uniform." Her accent sounded American, and James was glad everyone was looking at her, otherwise they would've noticed the effects of the blood rushing to his face when their eyes had met. Then he saw that Rosie had observed his blush, and that she was grinning at him. On an impulse, he quickly poked his tongue out at her; which made her grin even more.

"Well Karen, each of the other girls seemed to manage – and to get here on time. I'll speak to you about it later," Mrs Forbes said dismissively as she held the door open and waved her charges out into the restaurant, but as an afterthought added, "Oh, and this is James, the new dishwasher. James this is Karen, our Canadian representative at the Schwarzwald."

Karen turned and made a little curtsy. James chuckled and responded with a formal bow. When they'd all gone, he saw that Rosie was still looking at him with that knowing smile of hers.

"What? ... What?" he said as she turned to lift a bowl of batter, her expression unchanged.

※※※※※※※※※※※※

"Come on you ditherer, we'll miss the bus if we don't go right now," Karen shouted up at James's bedroom window. Fifteen seconds later he came bounding down the stairs and out the front door – pulling it shut behind him.

"Did you call me a deliverer?" He asked as they ran towards the bus stop. But before she could answer they had to make an extra effort to get to the old green and gold vehicle that had just closed its doors and was preparing to pull out onto the main road. Five minutes later they were sitting together, arm-in-arm, and heading south.

"It was the maps," James said.

"What was?"

"I mean, that's why I took so long in my room; I couldn't find the right map. Mrs McNaughton is a lovely old thing but she insists on periodically tidying up everything, and she moves my stuff around."

"Can't you lock your door?"

"No I can't. I did think of balancing a big metal bucket of water on it so it would fall on her the next time she entered the room – you know, just to give her a hint. But then I thought it'd probably kill her, which would mean I'd have to shift to somewhere else ... and she does leave me biscuits and milk at night."

"You really are weird aren't you?" Karen said as she looked at his smirking face. "Now show me where we're going."

He liked Karen. In terms of appearance, she was sort of ... substantial – some might say fat even – but he preferred to think of her as 'big boned'. It wasn't as though she had a bulky stomach or gigantic hips, she was just ... largish everywhere. However, she did have a particularly sizeable bosom which, James thought, was most becoming. He also considered her pretty, and those pale blue eyes of hers often conveyed the humour and intelligence that was at the core of her personality.

They had slept together, but just the once. Physically it had been vigorous and enjoyable, even though her loud groaning had almost got him caught by the female-dormitory supervisor – no male visitors being allowed. But afterwards, even though he tried to suppress it, she had detected in his manner a hint of sadness – and of regret. Eventually, she managed to glean from him the story of Dianne; of how he was still haunted by the memory of his former student, and how he had finally decided that it wasn't right to pursue her; that she was too young, and needed to grow into a woman without him disrupting her life. Karen would've been justified in severing their relationship right there and then, accusing him of insincerity, maybe even of taking advantage of her. But she didn't. Instead, she had shown great understanding and sympathy – and had become his friend.

The restaurant was closed on Mondays, and the winter weather was slow in arriving this year. For James this had meant he could go trekking around the countryside on at least one day a week, and even stay overnight at a bed-and-breakfast if he needed to. A month ago he'd told Karen he was going to check out a place called Nethy Bridge and a nearby forest. She had asked if she could accompany him, and he had agreed. There was no more sex between them – even though they'd had to lie about being married, just so they could stay in a cheaper single room – but they'd enjoyed each other's company, and had been going somewhere different together each week since.

This time they were heading for a small village called Laggan. James had seen it on one of his maps; it was at the beginning of what was now a little-used road that had been originally constructed by the famous army engineer, General Wade, in the early 18th century. It more or less followed the upper reaches of the River Spey until diverging and crossing through the Monadhliath Mountains. The bus would take them as far as Newtonmore but then they'd have to try hitching a ride along a more westerly minor road to Laggan. He looked up at the grey clouds and hoped they wouldn't have to wait too long for a sympathetic driver.

As it turned out, he needn't have worried. He and Karen had only been standing at the junction for five minutes – outside a museum dedicated to one of the traditional clans in the area – when a car pulled over.

"Not many people have even heard of Laggan, let alone want to go there," the driver said as they sped down the road through lush green fields on one side and timbered hills and grey crags on the other.

"So, you're obviously from around here," Karen said.

"Oh, you can tell from my accent that I'm not a native – I grew up in England – but I've been here for ten years now; I'm the local doctor." He introduced himself as Brian Handelson.

"Actually, we're not that interested in the village itself, but mainly the old road that goes up through the mountains and then down to Fort William."

"Well, I hope you aren't planning to go any further than Drummin," he said with a note of concern. "The road deteriorates badly past that area, and at this time of the year the weather can change very quickly. People have died in snow storms up there in the past you know."

James looked across at Karen. It still hadn't started snowing in the lower regions through which they were driving, but he could see glistening white caps on the peaks to the south and on those up ahead. "We were hoping to book in at a nearby bed-and-breakfast – if there is one – and to follow the road for a few hours and then turn around and come back."

"Oh, there's nowhere to stay in Laggan itself – it's just a little one-shop place. There are a few B and Bs around about but they're not close to the road you want to follow." James looked at Karen and forced his mouth into a 'let's-think-about-this' gesture.

A short time later, Dr Handelson slowed down. Opposite was the single shop. "I'll tell you what," he said, "you can stay the night in my bothy up at Drummin. There's no power – just paraffin lamps, and a fireplace in which we burn peat – but it's just off the old Wade road and is surrounded by some stunning vistas. We use it in the summer as a little getaway. In fact, I'll take you halfway there now if you like, and then you can walk the rest of the distance. You'll be able to visit the standing stone near the bothy."

Karen looked across at James, her eyebrows raised. He smiled and nodded. "That sounds wonderful Dr Handelson," she said.

Fifteen minutes later they were on the side of the road, waving goodbye to their new benefactor. "What a nice man," James said as he watched the old Landrover cross the bridge over the river.

"And he's even going to pick us up tomorrow morning. I can't believe how lucky we are," Karen said, her eyes sparkling with excitement. "And look at this country; it's so wild and rugged and beautiful. And that building on the other side of the bridge – what did the doctor say it was called? Glenshirra Lodge – wouldn't I love to see the inside of that."

"Yeah, I bet it has some stories locked up in its stone walls," James replied. "And with its own fairy hill looking down on it," he gestured towards the steep slopes that the doctor had pointed out to them. "According to this map, there's a track that goes around the base of that hill and then eventually drops down towards Loch Laggan – which is supposed to be really beautiful. There's a place on its far bank called Ardverikie where legend has it some ancient Scottish kings are buried; and also a couple of islands in the middle of the loch that are considered man-made."

"And what was that other big hill that we passed a little way out of Laggan? I was too interested in the deer running away from the road to hear what he was saying."

"Oh, what did he call it? ... sounded like *'Dun da Larve'*. He said it was Gaelic for 'Fort of the Two Hands'."

"Why that name?"

"I don't know; he was going to explain but then you started squealing about the deer, and we never got back to it. Anyway, let's head up the road, we'll freeze if we stand around for too long."

They walked on in silence, each entranced by the landscape in which they had been deposited. There were relatively few trees here, except for the sporadic plantations of conifers; their neat, rectangular boundaries making them look like little dark-green patches that had been sown into the lighter grassy fabric of the valley floor. The lower slopes of the huge, dominating mountains that defined the valley had a sprinkling of native trees – mainly birch – but for the most part, there was just rock and heather and grass. According to Dr Handelson, the mighty forests that had once been here – and that were, ironically, still named on the maps – had been removed centuries ago. And down through the heart of this glen ran the River Spey, its meandering here being less pronounced than in the lower, well-cultivated region they'd driven through on their way to Laggan; and its secondary banks suggesting that in the spring, when the winter snows began to melt, the modest stream would become a wide, fast-flowing torrent.

But there was something else that gave this landscape its peculiar presence – its mix of grandeur and foreboding. James stopped walking, and gazed around, trying to figure out what it was. Up ahead, on the side of the road, were the remains of a network of stone dykes – probably an old sheepfold. And close-by was what looked like the foundations of a small dwelling. Then it occurred to him. The valley was empty. Not of wildlife – there seemed to be plenty of that – but of people. Yet even this wasn't quite it. He'd been to lots of places that were devoid of people, and none had had this feel about them … He looked across to the river, less than half a mile away. Near its farthest bank was the tiny form of an abandoned bothy. Then it struck him. This was a region that had once rung out with the sounds of men and women and children. Cattle had been here, and goats, and sheep, and the folk who tended them. Tiny hamlets had dotted the sides of the road, and of the river. People had put down roots here, had lived here for countless generations. But no more. They were gone. And in their place – fused in with the spectacular beauty of the land – was a great sadness.

Karen, who had continued walking while James had stood, drifting in his thoughts, now came running back to him. "There's Dr Handelson's bothy up ahead – behind that clump of pines, just like he described. But ..." she said, pausing to impress, "I think I can also see the standing stone that he was talking about." She pointed towards the river.

"Where?"

Ten minutes later, after leaving the road and crossing the tussock-covered flats, they were examining an unassuming piece of granite that stuck up less than a metre from the boggy ground. Their helpful host had made a point of describing its location after they had accepted his kind offer of accommodation. "It doesn't look as impressive as I imagined," Karen said as she tilted her head to one side. "Not like others I've seen."

James nodded as he unfolded his map. "Yes, but it is the only visible stone for quite a distance – and close to the river. It was obviously put here to mark something of significance."

"That first story the doctor told us, about it marking the place where the chief's men had killed the guy who had run off with their boss's daughter ..."

"... only to later find that he was an Irish nobleman."

"Yeah, I don't buy that – it seems too Mills and Boon."

The Holy Well

"That appeared to be the doctor's attitude too. The second story, about it marking the place of a great battle in the twelfth century; that sounds more credible. This map has it marked as 'Clach Chatail'. I know *clach* means 'stone' but I've no idea what *Chatail* means. The doc said they used to be called 'catstanes' and were put up at sites of big battles, but …" he walked over and ran his fingers down the side of the ancient memorial.

"But what?" said Karen, frowning.

He looked across the river. "… but I wonder if this was put here much, much further back in time … in memory of something or someone long forgotten." He sighed and looked down at the stone. "If only it could tell us," he said.

"Well there's something I can tell you," Karen replied, breaking the philosophic mood. "I'm cold and I'm starving; so let's head for …" but she stopped and turned back towards the road as a small, red car came speeding up the rise. It pulled over at the closest point to them, a couple of hundred metres away, and an anorak-clad figure emerged, waving and calling.

Karen hesitated, but James strode off towards the gesticulating stranger. As he got closer, he realized it wasn't a stranger at all: first the silver hair and then the characteristic trill voice. It was Mrs Forbes. James ran the last thirty metres to the road.

"What is it Mrs Forbes? What's wrong?" he said as he arrived next to her, sucking in the cold air.

"Now don't worry," she said reassuringly, "there is nothing wrong. You told me last night that you intended coming up here, so I took a chance and hoped I'd find you …"

"But why, what …?" He turned to see Karen step up onto the road. Mrs Forbes nodded to her but then turned back to James.

"Oh, I hope I've done the right thing, James. But she has gone to so much trouble to find you, and from what she told me, you would want … Oh my goodness, I hope I …"

James had never seen her in such an irresolute state. He gently took her hands in his and looked into her worried eyes. "Mrs Forbes," he said, "what, exactly, are you talking about."

She didn't respond in words but simply turned and pointed towards the car. He hadn't realized there was anyone else in the vehicle, but now the passenger door was opening and another person was getting out. He stared across at the dark-haired woman in the lambswool jacket. She smiled uncertainly; but within a moment he had rushed across the short distance separating them and was embracing her. Tears flowed from both their eyes as he repeated her name, "Dianne, Dianne."

"I tried so hard to find you, James, and I was so frightened you might have forgotten me," she sobbed.

"Never, ever could I forget you," he said as he held her away and looked into her wet eyes. Glancing over her shoulder he saw the two other woman – old and young – standing close together. Both were crying, one was smiling. "You did the right thing Mrs Forbes," he said. "A great thing."

Dianne pushed the side of her face against his chest and held him tight. He stroked her hair and looked across to the Clach Chatail and then up at the mountains. He knew there was something going on here even though he didn't understand it. "Thank you," he whispered. "Thank you."

Chapter 13

Bren leaned so far forward over the pony's neck that his forehead was almost touching the animal's ears. He grabbed at its mane with his free hand while still loosely holding onto the reins with the other. The small mare twitched a little at this unusual behaviour by its rider, but remained steadfast in following the other animals on the narrow track. Bren groaned despite his utmost effort not to. The pain was now much worse than it had been when they started out two days ago. Earlier in the morning they had passed what Pock-face had reckoned to be the halfway point between Ardvortag and Ceann Tull. If he could just continue to ride ... they ...

He lifted his head and saw the tender face of his girl child, asleep and innocent, her little head held from rocking about by the leather sides of the harness strapped on Bodar's back. He smiled, and wished that he could take a turn in lessening his wife's load. It was just that the pain ... He saw the trees beginning to move ... and the mountains and the sky – all starting to sweep around in a great arc.

"Mind you there my friend." It was Pock-face's voice. Bren felt the strong arms of his cousin holding him; and then there were others; and Bodar's voice crying out; and the smell and feel of grass. The pain was still there but it was now more distant from him – less intrusive. It was a sensation that he had felt before – the result of a thinking technique for lessening pain that the Kelti had shown to a number of warriors at Ardvortag. Some of the healers' medicines had a similar effect. But this was different. It had been many days since he'd been able to concentrate enough to employ the Kelti method, and the various brews from the healers no longer seemed to work. Still, for some reason it was happening …

The grass felt cool even though the sunlight was filtering through the birch branches and warming his cheeks. He saw faces and heard voices but the words were indistinct, as if mumbled through the double-layered walls of a dwelling. That sunlight was very warm now – or was it heat from somewhere else. He felt wet. He smelled Bodar and heard her voice, clearer than the others, close to his ear. Then a coolness across his brow. And his hound, Culann, was there, its head resting on his thigh. And then darkness.

"Do not fret Bodar, his breathing remains strong," Pock-face said as he touched her shoulder.

"Do not fret? Do not fret!" she repeated angrily as she shrugged his hand away. "My husband is dying you big oaf; what do you expect me to be doing?" She continued to wipe Bren's hot face with the water-soaked cloth while Haldad, the healer who was accompanying them, removed the linen dressing from the warrior's upper abdomen. Pock-face bowed his head, and Bodar turned to him. "I'm sorry cousin," she said tensely, "but how can I not worry? We must get him to his holy well soon. It's the whole reason why we took him from his bed at Ardvortag – his body was clearly losing the battle with this wound. Yet in trying to make haste in our journey, his remaining strength is drained even faster. We are trapped like deer in a blind valley." She reached out and squeezed Pock-face's hand. He nodded, and she turned back to her love, her eyes first glancing across at little Pettah – still asleep but now being held by the nursemaid.

She flinched a little as the healer removed the final layer of pus-and-blood-covered linen. It stank, even worse than rotting meat on a carcass. She bit into her bottom lip. "It's worse isn't it?" she said to the healer, an old man and – according to Poltan – the best in all the Spey region. He didn't answer but proceeded to gently squeeze the pink and yellow liquid from the centre of the gash that crossed from under Bren's right rib to the left ilium of his pelvis.

Fortunately, none of his internal organs had been penetrated or exposed. In fact, at the time, he had kept on fighting, but had dropped to his knees a short while later because of the loss of blood. Haldad's senior apprentice had been with the warrior band that day, and he had quickly washed the wound and then applied an ointment of honey and oil and lime before using fine beaver gut to sew the sides of the deepest parts together. When Haldad had inspected the wound two days later at Ardvortag, he had approved of his apprentice's work. But already there had been signs that things were amiss; reddish streaks were visible, spreading from the gash like a network of tiny streamlets, and carrying toxins to every part of his body.

In fact, after a detailed examination, the healer was of the opinion that the bronze Cattach blade that had made the gash had been wiped with human faeces, a sickening practice that the dark-haired warriors had recently initiated as a desperate response to the increasing use of iron weapons by the men of the Spey. The number of even minor wounds that had become badly infected, and often led to death, had increased greatly since the Cattach had begun doing this. Poltan forbade his warriors from copying the practice, but responded by no longer showing the mercy for enemy prisoners and wounded for which he had become widely known.

Bren emerged from the blackness that surrounded him, and so then did the rest of his world. He floated through a strange forest populated by trees and other plants that were unfamiliar to him, his feet not quite touching the ground. He could hear birds calling and insects buzzing … and the regular sound of waves breaking on a shore – just as they did when the wind was strong across the lake of Tull. But still he seemed to be hearing these things from far away, as though his ears were a long distance from his head.

At times the floating sensation took over all his other senses – he did not mind though, happy to drift into the beckoning nothingness. But then he became aware that he was now leaving the forest and was on a sandy beach, with a vast body of water spreading out from it – he guessed that it was an ocean, and smiled when he saw the long lines of waves singing their messages from far-off places as they fell apart and rushed up onto the sand. Some distance away there were two men – together – approaching him. They did not float, but walked. Looking down, Bren noticed that his feet too were now pressing into the surface of this strange land.

As the men moved closer, he recognized one. It was Trib! Suddenly his heart swelled up with emotion and he ran to his old friend and threw his arms around him. "Oh Trib. Oh brave, brave Trib, I have missed you so much," he said. "So many times I have wished for you to be with us once again; for us to laugh and talk and hunt together."

The Holy Well

Trib stepped back and looked deep into Bren's eyes, and locked his hand in that of his friend, in the way of Tull folk when they are greeting or farewelling someone dear. "I am always with you," he said with a smile. And then he was gone, vanishing like a wisp of smoke caught up in a breeze.

Bren blinked and saw that the other man was still on the beach, standing a little way off. He was dressed strangely and was clean-shaven. He did not smile but nodded in acknowledgment of Bren's presence. But then he too was suddenly gone.

Bren sat on the sand, and then lay back. He didn't understand what was happening but it didn't vex him. What would happen would happen. Turning his head to one side, he saw a hound running towards him along the water's edge. It looked like his dog, Culann. It was still some way off, so he closed his eyes – just for a short rest. When he opened them again, he was no longer on the beach but inside a hide tent, and Culann was licking his face.

"Argggh! Be off with you Culann, you sloppy mongrel," he cried as he pushed the great brindle-coloured hunting dog away. At that moment, the tent flap opened and in rushed Bodar, quickly followed by Pock-face and the old healer.

"Oh thank the mountains and the stars," she said, "the fever has broken."

"Culann, get outside and guard the camp like you're supposed to be doing," Pock-face said to the dog, whose mouth flaps lifted a little as he defiantly planted his hind quarters on the ground next to his master's bed of bracken and goat skin.

"Outside," Bren commanded weakly, and the hound immediately got up and left, growling softly as he walked past Pock-face.

Bren knew that he didn't have the strength to raise himself so he just lay there smiling at his beautiful wife. Sadly, the more he became aware of his surroundings, the more he felt the return of the pain – but it bothered him less than before. "Where are we?" he asked, "And how long is it since I sat upon the pony?"

Bodar smiled at him with her eyes as well as her mouth. "We are close to where you almost fell from your mount, still some distance from Ceann Tull, and you have been here for three days – sometimes talking deliriously to invisible beings, but mainly silent,"

Haldad was on the far side of the makeshift bed feeling the pulse of life in Bren's neck with one hand and the heat from the warrior's forehead with the other. "Remarkable," he said. "I must check the wound; but first give him more of the water."

Bodar helped her husband raise his head, and then lifted his treasured stone cup, full of water, from beside the bed to his lips.

"I saw Trib," he said. "He is with us now." Then, as if being jolted from a different reality, he moved his tongue around in his mouth. "This water …" he said, "… it's …"

"It is from the Holy Well of Endachni," Pock-face interrupted. I returned from there with a goat's bladder full of it yesterday – before the sun had risen."

Bodar stroked his face. "We understood your conviction that you would have to visit the well yourself if its water and its power was to have any effect in healing you – after having

The Holy Well

been absent from it for so long. But, Bren my darling, you were dying, and we feared to move you any further. So, shortly after laying you out here, your cousin rode like a swooping eagle to the woods of Endachni and to its holy well."

"And returned even swifter," Pock-face added proudly, "As if the eagle had its arse feathers on fire." Bren smiled.

"Did you see anyone from our homeland?" he asked as he lay back, still holding onto the stone cup.

"No one – no person, no beast; although there were many wolves about. The full moon that encouraged their cries also helped me and the others to see through the darkness."

"Others?" Bren asked.

"Your cousin took two of our escorts to accompany him."

Bren was puzzled for a moment but then the fog in his brain cleared a little more. He remembered that back at Ardvortag Poltan had insisted on providing not only the best healer in his land to accompany them, but also a band of six accomplished warriors. 'If his only hope is this holy well, then you must get there safely,' he had heard the new leader of the Spey folk say to Bodar. 'He is a hero to our people, and I would go with him myself were it not for the urgency of our continued defence against the Cattach hordes.'

He closed his eyes and took in a deep breath – and thought about Poltan, now responsible for so many people. He would cope with it – just as his father, the much-loved Ulvar, had done. It had been sad seeing that proud old man die in agony amongst the ruins of his beloved settlement; another case of a wound being more serious than at first believed. Still, he had lived a full and happy and courageous life, and was now at peace somewhere within the great cycle.

Bren sighed, and then felt a small grin appear on his face. The new Lord of the Spey had certainly needed all his reserve energy for his new bride, the lovely Etain. They had stayed in bed for three days after the huge marriage feast. When they had finally emerged from the partly-rebuilt lodge, Poltan had expressed his astonishment to Bren that there could exist in the world something that was at the same time so delightful and so tiring. They too now had a child – a boy. Etain had insisted that the little one be named after Trib, the Tull man who had fought so valiantly to save her and Bodar on the holy isle in the middle of the lake. In the Kelti way, this adoption of such a 'foreign' name was a means of bestowing great honour, and Bren knew that his dead friend would be remembered in the stories of at least two different cultures for many generations.

He opened his eyes and looked from Bodar to Pock-face. "I saw Trib," he said for the second time.

"Tell us about it when you are a little stronger," Bodar replied, concerned that he might slip back into the darkness if he became too anxious about anything. Pock-face simply nodded, but Bren knew that his cousin missed their dark-haired comrade as much as he did.

During this time, Haldad had been using a spluttering pig-fat lamp to examine the Tull warrior's wound. He was a practical man, and had little time for priests and lofty ideas about the nature of the world. "I think you are now on the path to recovery young man," he said. "But I have to say that I believe it was my poultices that brought about the turnaround in your condition. To give the credit to drinking some water from a remote well seems unjustified to me. Although …"

But it was too late for any rider to his arrogant words. Pock-face leaned across his sick cousin and grabbed one of the healer's shoulders in his strong hand. "Old man," he said, "you may be respected for what you have done in your trade over the years, but let me give you this advice: never offer pronouncements on things of which you know nothing, and never take credit for something that is not due to you." The healer looked fearfully at Pock-face's angry countenance, and saw that Bodar was also glaring at him. He bowed his head, acknowledging his conceit. And below them all, breathing heavily, was Bren – smiling, his eyes shut.

* * * * * * * * * * * *

Their arrival at Ceann Tull was an event that would be remembered for many years to come. The settlement was tiny compared to Ardvortag, but people from all over the region had dropped their tools and stopped their planting and their hunting and had rushed to the place of the crannog in order to witness the arrival of Bren and Pock-face. Three years earlier, these sons of the Tull had left as young adventurers, but now they were returning as battle-hardened warriors of great fame. In fact, the stories that had filtered from the tumult of the north down to these relatively peaceful lands had been embellished to the extent that both men were given credit for turning the tide of entire conflicts, and of having skills and powers far beyond those of other warriors. It has always been the way with such stories.

Up until yesterday, Bren hadn't even thought about his party's entry into the settlement, and now, with all these cheering and waving folk … it was like the great birth season celebrations he remembered from his youth. He tried hard to sit tall in the saddle, and smiled as he waved back to the people who thronged both sides of the path. But the pain was strong, and he remained weak – having only been helped onto the pony a short while earlier. Prior to that, he had made the slow journey down through the hills lying on his back in a small wagon pulled by an ox. Despite finding it hard to remain fully upright for any time, he had insisted on at least giving the appearance of good health when entering his home settlement. From what he'd heard, his people were already uncertain enough about the future without him needing to add to their concerns. He had always hoped that returning would be a happy affair. Clearly, this could never be entirely the case now because of Trib's death. But he didn't want sadness and apprehension to be the dominant emotions amongst his people – Trib would have understood – did understand.

He knew that he was still ill and that the water Pockface had brought back had only postponed his succumbing to the infection. Of course, he was grateful that his friend-and-cousin had taken that action, otherwise he would be entering the settlement wrapped in a blanket of birch sticks. But he had been aware for some time that his only chance for a full recovery lay in him visiting the well in person. He didn't know from whence this conviction came, only that it was strong. So for now he would continue to smile and enjoy what he could of his return.

"Are you all right?" Bodar said as she guided her pony next to him along the widened track. Her voice was hard to hear because of the shouts of greeting from the swelling number of welcomers.

"I am fine," he lied. "And look at this reception – the cheeriness of the people would be a tonic for anyone." She frowned, but then turned and smiled at the crowd.

On his other side rode Pock-face who was obviously revelling in his people's show of affection, calling out to those he recognized, and winking at any female who took his fancy. However, he kept glancing across at Bren, and the injured warrior knew that his cousin would again reach out with his powerful arms if necessary. Their eyes met for a moment, and Bren smiled. The tall redhead saw the smile and, with a grin of his own, quickly looked down at his groin. Then, with eyebrows raised, he nodded his head in the direction of a group of waving girls. Bren chuckled; Pock-face was a rare and true friend.

Their party consisted of three of Poltan's men in front; then Bren and Pock-face and Bodar. Next came the wagon – now carrying little Pettah in the arms of the young nursemaid who had insisted on accompanying Bodar; and in the rear, three more guards – including a Kelti warrior named Lachlann, a cousin to Poltan's wife. All now stopped in the settlement's clearing, in front of the causeway that led across the water to the crannog. Seeing this grand building, the home of his birth, made Bren's eyes moisten. Details he'd forgotten about hastened back to his mind: the angle of cut at the end of the thatch, the slight wobble in the line of the causeway, the smallness of the entrance. But much more than the building, was the joy at seeing his family members: Kinnow, Vana, Elin, Chata, and all the others, smiling and standing together – some with their arms outstretched in expressions of joy. And there was his father, standing in front of the group, a solemn expression on his face.

Bren took a deep breath, gritted his teeth, and dismounted – maintaining his smile through the stabbing pain. His father stepped forward. He knew of his son's continuing illness – special messengers had seen to that – but most others believed he was fully recovered from his wound.

"Bren, it is good to see you; good to have you back." Dorvar said; uncertain, it seemed, at how to display any affection he might feel towards his son.

Bren, on the other hand, had grown in many ways during his three years away, and was confident about taking the initiative. In different circumstances, he would have embraced his father, but to do that now would probably cause him to fall faint, so instead, he bent his arms in front of his chest, and crossed them. It was a style of greeting that Dovar had once told him was used by warriors in the days of his grandfather. The older man understood immediately and, after crossing his arms in a similar manner, he clasped his son's hands and held them tight – at the same time nodding his head and smiling.

The people of the surrounding crowd had fallen silent while the two men approached each other, aware of the distance that had always seemed to separate them, and waiting to observe what form their greeting would take. Now, seeing the old form of salutation being formally revived by their favourite son, they let out a spontaneous cheer and continued with calls of welcome to all those who had just arrived.

Next, Bren quickly greeted his other family members and friends, but then excused himself as he tapped Pock-face on the shoulder – he being lost in a series of embraces – and walked back to those of the party who were still standing by their ponies. He held up his arms, indicating a request for silence, and spoke loudly. "People of the Tull," he said. "We have returned." He clasped one of his cousin's hands and held it high in the air. The pain across his abdomen suddenly increased. Everyone cheered, unaware of his suffering. "You already know that we lost our dear friend Trib, a true son of the Tull. But you will also know that he brought great honour to us all because of his bravery." The crowd was silent for a moment, except for the soft crying of some women, and then Trib's name was called out, and people began to chant it with increasing vigour and loudness until Bren again raised his arms.

"And this," he said, lifting his love's hand, "is my wife, Bodar." Again there was cheering and the repeating of her name. "And ..." he shouted as he took the inquisitive looking little bundle from the nursemaid, and held it up, "this is our daughter, Pettah – and Dorvar's first grandchild." The crowd roared its approval; and the little girl began howling.

Much later, inside the crannog, Bren lay on the new, large bed that had been prepared for him and his wife. As was the case all around the sleeping platform, hanging deer hides partitioned off this area and offered some privacy. Although he wasn't sure he wanted to be alone right now. The great building had few others in it – most having gone to the celebrations. He could hear the sounds of voices and music from across the water and up at the stone circle of Chlocht. Bodar had remained with him up until a short while ago, but then one of his great aunts had come to collect her, insisting that she be introduced to other folk. He sighed. He would rather she had stayed but, of course, he had encouraged her to leave; the respite from worrying and from being his nurse would benefit her; she needed some lightness in her life.

The celebrations had started even before he and his party had arrived – the people unable to withhold their exuberance. It seemed they held the conviction that he would be able to help his father in guiding them through the increasingly troubled times they were witnessing. When he had left three years earlier, peace had been abroad throughout the region. But now the disquiet that had started in the north and the west was affecting even these previously safe lands. Intrusions into pastures by outsiders and their cattle, the stealing of grain and animals, strangers taking game and berries from the forests, and the rise in power of certain families – using the sharp edge of the sword as their authority; all these were now happening. From what he had heard, it was like a sickness spreading across the Tull countryside, and he wondered whether he would live long enough or have the strength to do anything about it. He felt so tired and weak. Dovar was still much respected as a leader and a priest, but earlier – at the welcoming – it was obvious that he had aged greatly since Bren had left. The strains of leadership and his reluctance to share his emotions had brought a greyness not only to his hair but also to his face. It concerned Bren, and he hoped he would be able to assist his father in restoring stability to his people's lives.

But his own survival in the world as a man, a warrior, a husband, a father, a friend; clearly, this had not yet been decided. He tried to distance himself from the bout of pain that was mounting an attack on his weary body, but found it difficult. At these times, the rolling spasms in his partly severed muscles would merge with the deep, focused throbbing along his wound, and leave him almost breathless. The water had helped – had saved his life – but as the pain mounted, he knew that tomorrow's journey would be his only chance for continuing in this part of the great cycle.

※ ※ ※ ※ ※ ※ ※ ※ ※ ※ ※ ※

Most of the inhabitants of Ceann Tull were still wandering through the world of dreams when the small group emerged from the crannog – but not all. Rumours of Bren's illness had spread very quickly during the celebrations, and although they were dismissed by many – tiredness and the need to attend important discussions being the reasons given for his early departure – some had seen the physical torment behind his eyes. So, despite the darkness and the lack of morning birdsong, a few people had already arisen and were waiting to offer their personal blessings to the young warrior. They knew that he would be making an early trek to the place that, because of him, was now part of Tull-folk lore.

He had crossed the wooden causeway without help, holding onto the rails when necessary, but now he needed Pock-face and Bodar to assist him in mounting the pony. He didn't speak but nodded in acknowledgment of the kind words that were offered to him, and he squeezed the hands of those who reached up to him. To one side, stood a man and a woman and several young children; they were Trib's parents and siblings. Bren had sought them out the night before and had secretly asked them to accompany him today.

Dorvar was also in this small group that headed off east to the woods of Endachni, and so too was Haldad the old healer – on his own insistence – but that was all; except for Culann who loped ahead of his master's pony, sniffing the pre-dawn air.

"The man is too ill to be riding," said Haldad to Bodar as they both walked behind the lone pony. "It would have been better to carry him on a stretcher – the distance is not great I am told."

"One will be following a short way behind," she replied, "Just in case it's needed. But my husband knows his body better than you or I and, as you are aware, succumbing to the notion of being an invalid can often make it so." The old man nodded, and wanted to qualify her point, but thought better of it. In the saddle, Bren did not hear their words; the tiredness already spreading through him and dulling his senses.

There was a glow in the eastern sky when they arrived at the new junction, the sun still hiding just below the horizon. They were on the main track alongside the forest of Drumm but to the right was the path that many feet had made in recent times; it passed down through the strange woods of downy birch and oak to the Holy Well of Endachni. At this place, several people waited. Bren recognized them as being from a nearby settlement, and he nodded in their direction, and forced a smile. They joined the rear of the band that had also picked up a few others along the way.

A short while later, at the beginning of the embankment that he remembered so vividly, Bren asked Pock-face and Dorvar – both of whom had been leading his pony – to stop. He was in pain but it wasn't overwhelming, and the weariness he'd felt earlier had begun to dissipate during this final leg of the journey. He cautiously turned his head (for twisting his body was not wise) and looked back at Bodar. She smiled warmly and dipped her head slightly acknowledging that she understood the well was just ahead – even though she had never seen it with her eyes. Behind her stood Trib's close family – sad faced, as would be expected. But behind them he was surprised to see that a small throng of about fifteen people had gathered, with several more appearing out of the trees. Beckoning to his cousin and his father, he sucked in a lungful of the cool morning air, and then prepared himself to be helped down from his mount. This was accomplished without a great deal of pain but he still required the support of Pock-face's shoulder as his legs reacquainted themselves with the task of holding his body upright. He took another breath. On the ground near his feet were patches of wood sorrel, the white flowers contrasting in the early half-light with the rich yellows of nearby primroses. He then looked up at the growing blueness filtering through the many overhead branches, and heard the harsh calls of jays interspersed amongst the melodious songs of redstarts. The sun would soon show itself above the distant hills. It was a good time to be here.

As he approached the well – with Bodar holding his arm, and the others nearby, ready to assist – he felt again the sense of enchantment and wonder that had always filled him when visiting here in the past. And there was the feeling of closeness and familiarity; as though he was somehow part of this place. He knelt beside the ring of moss and lichen-covered white rocks, and looked into the darkness of the water. The others also knelt, or sat, except for Dorvar who was obviously preparing to officiate. But before he started, Bren beckoned him over and spoke to him in quiet tones. Dorvar listened, nodded, and helped his son to his feet; he himself then sitting on a fallen branch. Bren looked around at those assembled, holding his side with a hand.

"My friends, I thank you for being here with me at this holy well on this fine summer morning," he said. "I expected no one beyond our small band but, of course, you are all welcome." He then went on, "There are two purposes in me coming to this sacred place today. The first is to dedicate to the well an object that is of great importance to me." He signalled to Trib's mother and father that they should come to him. This they did, and as he continued to speak, Trib's mother held aloft an object that Bren had given her the previous night.

"What Meerim is holding above her head is a stone cup that was made for me by Trib, her son and my dear friend. He did this in remembrance of the day his life was saved by the water I had brought to him from this holy well. I now dedicate the cup to the well, and to all who will use it. May the name of Trib stay with the people of the Tull far into the future. Whenever stories are told about friendship and sacrifice let him be remembered. And whenever a person sits by this holy well and partakes of its water, may they recall the story of he who fashioned the cup which they hold in their hands." Both parents placed the roughly-made cup on a rock next to the well, and then each gently embraced Bren before stepping back to where they'd been sitting.

"The second purpose in me coming here," Bren said after a pause, "is to make use of the well's healing properties. I know these exist – as do most of you here today. But the well chooses who it will help and when it will help; the choice being forever beyond our influence or understanding." He closed his eyes and wondered whether he would be saved from the slow death that was obviously working its way through his body. And he felt the well speak to him – not in words or even thoughts, but it spoke all the same.

When he opened his eyes, Dorvar was standing in front of him with the cup, full of water. Bren took it and drank deeply. After returning the vessel to his father, he nodded to Haldad who, with Bodar, helped him to remove his jacket and topshirt. The healer then took away the dressing and exposed Bren's wound for all to see. Some people gasped. Others craned their necks to see more clearly the red and pusy and still-not-healed gash. Dorvar poured water from the cup onto a cloth, which Haldad then used to wash the long line of infected flesh and muscle.

After the washing, and a suitable period of silence, most people left – the original party eventually being all who remained; except for the person who Bren saw standing some distance away, partly obscured by a cluster of young birch. He was strangely dressed, and at first Bren thought it was Lachlann, the young Kelti warrior who had been part of his escort from Ardvortag. But it wasn't him, the clothing was different and the hair the wrong colour. Yet for some reason he seemed familiar. A little while later when Bren looked again, the stranger was gone.

* * * * * * * * * * * *

On the seventh evening after his visit to the well, Bren was standing on that part of the crannog's balcony that protruded most into the sacred lake. There was still light coming from the direction of the great mountains in the northwest but the sun had been gone from the sky for some time. He watched as a pair of tufted ducks swam by, producing two ever-growing vee-shaped patterns on the smooth surface of the water. Overhead flew a night hunter – probably a white-faced owl. From inside the crannog came the sounds of women singing as they went about some evening chore; Bodar's sweet voice was obvious among the others.

He had forgotten how peaceful it could be in Ceann Tull, and was glad that circumstances had brought him back. He had grown into a man in the far-off region of the Spey, and had, of course, re-discovered the love of his life there ... he paused in his reflection for a moment and listened to her sing ... but Ardvortag and the rest of the embattled north was not the place for little Pettah to grow, or for the other babes they hoped to produce. No, this would be their home.

He breathed in the twilight air, and felt glad to be alive. The speed of his recovery had astonished everyone. The holy well had smiled upon him, as he had hoped it would. Poor old Haldad the healer, after a lifetime of cynicism about such things, had finally accepted that the well at Endachni possessed a wonderful healing property. Nothing else could explain the rapid mending of Bren's wound and his return to good health. Of course, the Tull folk were always sure of the well's power. Bren stretched his arms; there was almost no pain. Soon he would be able to take on some of the responsibilities that were expected of him.

He heard the moving of the small side door that opened onto the balcony, and saw Dorvar emerge from inside the crannog.

"I thought you might be out here," he said, walking over to his son.

Bren was pleased that his father had sought him out. Since his return, Dorvar had been visiting him at his bedside every day, and they had spoken about many things: problems in the region, recent hunting expeditions, new farming ideas. But with each discussion, the aging leader-priest seemed to reveal a little more of himself – as if he were attempting to tear down the hurdles that he'd set up between them so long ago. On the days just past he had started to talk about his own youth and the lessons life had taught him. They had laughed together – for the first time – and Bren had revelled in the closeness that was evolving. However, he couldn't help but feel that there was something pressing that his father wanted to tell him – something he'd been circling around like a high-flying falcon, but was not yet ready to reveal. "It is a good place and a good time to think," the younger man replied.

Dorvar didn't respond immediately, and Bren noticed that his father's hand was trembling slightly as he placed it on the rail. Together they looked out across the water.

"It is the same place where I knelt many years past, awaiting your birth," Dorvar said, keeping his gaze on the distant shore. Bren swallowed deeply but said nothing. His father had never before spoken of this time.

"Your old great grandmother – now long gone – came and told me of your arrival in our world," he continued. Bren felt a long-hidden sadness welling up from deep inside him. Dorvar took a slow breath and went on. "Then, full of happiness and relief, I walked through the waiting crowd to your mother's bedside." His voice began to quaver, and Bren's mouth became dry. "My first sight of you was of you drinking from her breast. I will never be able to describe the joy I felt at seeing you there. At that moment, I thought my heart would burst with the love I felt for you both … and then …"

Bren turned and saw his father was now looking at him, his eyes watery and his words faltering. "And then *what* father?" he said gently, feeling a great sympathy, and instinctively reaching out a hand.

"And then ... she died," Dorvar said, bowing his head. "My beautiful Morann bled to death before me." He blindly reached out his arms, and Bren quickly embraced him. "I held her hand as she slipped away," the older man continued through tears. "And I could never come close to you because your birth and her death were so closely tied together – like the strands of a knot."

"I know, I know, and I am so sorry," Bren said, his own tears now trickling down his cheeks. "I know how much you loved my mother, and the sadness I feel at being the cause of her death will remain with me forever. I love her too," he said haltingly, "just as I do you."

Dorvar held his son at arm's length, and bent his head so as to look into the young man's lowered eyes. "Bren ..." He shook his son's shoulders to force his attention. "Bren, you must never feel responsible. I was wrong – so, so wrong – to keep you at a distance all these years. I should have been showing not only my love but that of Morann too. Instead, I have dwelt in my own sorrow. You were not the cause of her death. She left us because it is the way of the world, of which we are all part. The events that led to that tragic moment might be followed back to the falling of a leaf in the forest one spring morning, or the splashing of a wave on the lake in the winter sun. Many things lead to any happening; this is how the world is. It is something I have always known and understood, but in my own life I could not see it – could not feel it – until I heard of your wounding in battle, and that you too might die. At that time I knew how wrong I'd been, and I resolved that if given the chance, I would show you the love and affection that I have hidden for so long."

Bren wiped his eyes on his arm, and then looked at his father. The old man was staring back, concern on his tear-streaked face. Bren smiled and nodded gently, and Dorvar held him close. They stayed that way for some time.

＊＊*＊*＊*＊*＊*

Later in the season, when the flowers on the oaks were in full bloom and the fluting whistles of the visiting golden plovers could be heard, Dorvar passed from this world. Bren sat by his side and held his hand, and heard him whisper Morann's name.

Chapter 14

"You sure you don't want a beer?" asked Tevita, lifting a stubbie of Fiji Bitter from the plastic carry bag.

"No thanks, I'll stick with caffeine," James replied holding up the Coke bottle, "It'll be safer for my frail brain after all that kava you lot had me drinking this afternoon."

Tevita grinned, his perfect teeth shining out from his dark face. He then looked across at the solar panel array that he'd been helping James set up and test over the last week. "It was an important ceremony," he said as he put the stubbie back in the bag. "Our people and our ancestors needed to show their gratitude for what you and your organization have done. That power supply will save our community a great deal of money; money that we sorely need for other purposes. And the benefit to the environment is an added bonus."

"No more rusting diesel-fuel drums on the beach, huh?"

"And no more smoke and noise from the generator."

They both gazed out across the Pacific. Down below, naked children were frolicking in the waters of the lagoon. Closer to the reef, several outrigger canoes drifted while the occupants waited for the evening meal to tug on their fishing lines.

"What did you mean about your ancestors showing their gratitude – how can they do that if they're all dead?"

THE HOLY WELL

James kept staring out to sea; he wasn't totally ignorant of Fijian culture – not after working with the people on so many occasions – but he wanted to hear the explanation from the young, articulate, chief's son.

"Come on, James, you know what we believe. We feel the presence and influence of our ancestors all the time. The plaited cord with all the cowry shells that was stretched from the kava bowl towards you during the ceremony; its purpose was to connect you to our ancestors."

"Symbolically you mean?"

"Maybe ... or maybe not."

"What, are you saying that the plaited cord might actually connect living people with those that lived in the past?"

"All I'm saying is that I've felt the presence of the *vu* – our ancestors – on several occasions during *yaqona* ceremonies."

"Yes, but drink enough kava and you'll see and feel all sorts of things," James said with a grin, but then quickly changed his expression when he saw that his host was deadly serious. "I'm sorry," he added. "I didn't mean any disrespect."

"Don't be sorry," Tevita replied, "you're right. The drinking of *yaqona* – or kava, as you call it – has been debased a lot over the years; and it's like any narcotic: have enough and you'll end up with some pretty unusual perceptions. But I tell you, in our world – on our island – the *vu* remain a subtle part of everyday life. Did you know that Fijian people once believed that certain hilltops and boulders and the like – they were called *yavutu* – that they were the dwelling places of the *vu*. The Methodist missionaries, in their zeal to discourage ancestor worship, knocked down and dug up and flattened many *yavutu*." He paused and took a swig of beer. "We're sitting on one right now," he said as he looked out across the water.

James shivered in the late afternoon sun and gazed down the slopes from the top of the small hill. There was a stirring deep inside him.

"It's something that you westerners will probably never understand," Tevita continued as he drained his stubbie. "Not in the same way that we do."

* * * * * * * * * * * * * *

The boat journey back to Viti Levu hadn't been very pleasant. They'd had to endure several squalls as well as an already boisterous sea. Even the islanders had been sick. James couldn't remember too much of the second half of the voyage, except that his stomach had kept trying to eject food that was no longer there. For much of the afternoon – between dry retches – he had sworn to himself that he would never again step aboard a boat. But that was more than a day ago. Things were brighter now. He'd slept soundly last night in the hotel – even though that dream had been a bit strange – and here he was, sitting in the best seat in economy class with his long legs stretched out next to the exit hatch. Another three hours and the plane would have him back in Melbourne. God, it'd be good to see Dianne again. And little Hamish probably would have grown ten centimetres in the two weeks he'd been away. That was the worst part of this job – the constant travelling. But there'd only be one more off-shore visit at the end of the month and then it'd be mainly design and administrative work for at least half a year – he'd made that clear, given that Dianne was due in another seven weeks.

The Holy Well

He sipped on the airline coffee, and looked out the window, vaguely wondering how the dark liquid in the cup could smell okay but taste so bad. He thought about the photovoltaic power system he'd just set up on Onagu. It would last for years, as long as it was maintained properly. And Tevita would see to that. He was obviously an intelligent and reliable man.

Turning from the window, he glanced at the woman sitting next to him. She was asleep, but the magazine she'd been reading was still open on her little fold-down table. Amongst the text was an image of some Aboriginal kids playing in a waterhole that was surrounded by desert. It prompted his thinking. Australia's indigenous people seemed to understand about being connected with the past via places in their landscape. That's why their traditional land is so important to them; it links them to their ancestors, to the Dreamtime of creation, to the universe. It's similar to what Tevita had been talking about, although the Fijian view seemed to put more emphasis on the *spirits* of ancestors. But it was the idea of being connected, to both the landscape and to people from long ago ... this had haunted James for years.

He looked out the window again, at the endless blue, and thought about Scotland and the well. It'd been almost fifteen years since he'd experienced the peace and ... what was it? ... joy? of sitting by the Holy Well of Endackney. The last occasion had been with Dianne, just before he accompanied her back to Texas to meet with her parents. He frowned; what a confrontation that had turned out to be. But not a month would go by when he wouldn't think about his days in the Highlands, and of the well. So many times he'd wanted to return – and maybe even check out the possibility of staying there permanently. But events just seemed to take him in a different direction.

And Dianne, despite her loving nature, didn't feel the same pull from that faraway place. She was totally happy with the life they'd made together in Australia, and had clearly set down roots in her adopted country. He sensed that, in a way, she might actually be fearful of them ever going back to Scotland – even for a visit – in case he never wanted to leave; which could, perhaps, be true. So he didn't bring it up any more – just to keep her happy. And, of course, he was happy too – who wouldn't be? Dianne was as close to an angel as he'd ever get. He loved her so much. Still, that faraway land, and the holy well; they had never stopped calling to him. Tevita might've been right for now about him not understanding such things; but one day he would return to the Highlands, and seek to know more of that mystery of the landscape and the past which had touched him so profoundly in his youth.

It was late in the afternoon when he emerged from the customs hall at Tullamarine International Airport outside Melbourne. Besides a couple of bottles of duty-free liqueur for his old mum and dad, his trolley included some Swiss chocolates and a little electronics kit that was supposed to be suitable for kids aged from seven up. There were lots of people watching and waiting, and then many little cries of recognition as other travellers matched up with their friends and families. But where was his wife? And where was Hamish with his customary squeal of 'Daddy'? Then he saw her, kneeling next to one of the seats in a nearby row. In front of her was Hamish, taking long, deep breaths as his mother stroked his forehead. When James saw the familiar blue puffer

The Holy Well

in his son's hand, he knew what had happened. He left his trolley and ran.

"Hey big fella," he said gently as he knelt next to Dianne. "The nasties got you again huh?" using the young boy's own term for whatever it was that brought on his asthma attacks. Hamish forced a little smile and nodded but kept on with his attempt at relaxed breathing.

"He'll be okay," Dianne said. "I think the trigger was the jet exhaust fumes; the wind usually blows the stuff away from the terminal, but not today. We hadn't even got to the main entrance before the attack began."

"Did he do the four puffs, etcetera?"

"Yes, we knew what to do, didn't we sweetie?" she said to her son in response to her husband.

Hamish then reached out and gave his father a hug. "Hi Daddy," he said, now breathing easier and looking happier.

James stroked the back of his seven year-old's head, again admiring the little boy's resilience and bravery. "My goodness!" he said as he then held him away. "You've grown an awful lot in the last two weeks. And stronger looking too," he added as he gently squeezed one of his son's biceps. Hamish beamed, and proudly bent his thin arm, its muscles taught.

"Yes, and so have I – grown a lot that is," interrupted Dianne, still on her knees. "And I think you two strongmen might have to give me a hand if I'm to get on my feet successfully." Father and son grinned at each other and then jumped to the fair madame's aid.

* * * * * * * * * * * *

James lay in bed. Ostensibly, he was reading the first newspaper that he'd seen for the last couple of weeks.

But it was hard to concentrate while Dianne kept wandering into the room fiddling with things in the wardrobe and then walking out again. It was, however, an increasingly delightful distraction.

Really, the foreplay had started in the airport car park when he had gallantly opened the passenger door for her, and she had brushed her nose across his cheek and then given him a soft but prolonged kiss on the lips. And now, as she appeared to be busy with some domestic chore, moving her enlarged body around while wearing that flimsy maternity nightdress that buttoned up at the front – it was quickly becoming too much for James. He put down the paper, and watched her hang several dresses. Her profile had indeed grown – and not only her abdomen. Even when she wasn't pregnant, her breasts were quite large; now they were … James looked down at the small model of a conical mountain that had formed in the topography of the blanket.

"If you don't come to bed sometime within the next thirty seconds, I fear there's going to be an explosion in this bed that won't be good for anyone," he said.

Dianne looked across at the blanket. "More like a volcanic eruption I would've thought," she said with a smirk, and then put on her best waif-like expression and, fondling her nipples through the thin cotton fabric of the nightdress added, "you could come and get me, you know."

James jumped from the bed, the cause of the mountain obviously travelling with him; and Dianne made a soft yelp, her own miniature twin peaks having started to dampen their covering.

Half an hour later, after both he and Dianne had secreted a good proportion of the fluids available to their bodies for lovemaking, James began to fall asleep. His arm was still under Dianne's neck. She was already in the land of dreams, on her back, with the nightdress still unbuttoned. He roused himself and carefully removed his arm from under her. She stirred, and he leaned forward and kissed one of her breasts before pulling the blanket up over her. God, he enjoyed making love with her; they were so good together. And with her pregnant it was even nicer in some ways. As he curled up on his side and again began to drift off, he felt the relaxing glow of satisfied sex and the deep happiness of reciprocative love. Soon he was snoring.

Several hours later he knew there was something wrong. The dream had been peaceful, with images in his memory from long ago being manipulated and merged: the field, the track, the ring of white stones around the water – and that glimpse of another person, not from memory. All that had abruptly changed when he smelled the smoke, and his dream relocated him beside a Grand Prix race circuit with cars screeching around a sharp turn. But that had only lasted for a moment before he suddenly awoke, the smell of burning rubber remaining real and present as the dream images abruptly disappeared. "Jesus!" he said as he sat up and swung his legs from under the blanket. Through the window he could barely make out the glow of a fire in the direction of the big tyre warehouse about five kilometres to the east – sirens were wailing in the distance, and all around was dark smoke, it even obscuring the nearby street lights.

Dianne was already gone, and just as he was stepping towards the door, she called from down the hallway, "James ... JAMES!" He knew immediately where she was, and didn't even have time to shudder as he ran to his son's room.

The light was on and Hamish was sitting on the side of his bed wheezing badly. Dianne was sitting beside him with an arm around his shoulder. With forced calmness she looked up at James. "I can't find his puffer. Would you please check under the bed – I know it was on his table when we kissed him goodnight."

James dropped to his knees and looked under the bed. There was an assortment of books, low-allergenic stuffed toys, tiny wheeled vehicles, and plastic blocks – all residing in the darkness. He raised his head and reached over for the torch that Hamish kept on the bedside table. "Check his speech," he said, knowing that Dianne was aware of this method for determining the severity of an attack. If their son got to the point of only being able to say single words, then it was time to call an ambulance.

"It's okay … Dad … I just need … my puffer," Hamish said as his wheezing became more pronounced. It was obvious he was already at the 'phrases' stage. James passed a worried look to Dianne.

"Don't worry big fella, I'll find it." He ducked down under the bed with the torch, lifting and moving the closer objects in his increasingly desperate search. 'Where the fuck is it?' he thought. If the blue, plastic puffer had simply fallen from the table then it would have to be somewhere nearby; it wasn't as though it was of a shape conducive to rolling or bouncing. He pulled the little table away from the wall and surveyed the floor. Hamish's wheezing now seemed even more severe, but maybe his own growing sense of panic was colouring his perception.

"Mum … I think this … is getting … pretty bad." Despite his age, Hamish had learned to control his anxiety to a large extent when having an attack, but they all knew that on this occasion things were getting worse than ever before – especially the little boy whose eyes were beginning to show signs of fear.

James was aware that he was running out of time to find the small device that could spray measured doses of Ventolin down his son's trachea, to be inhaled more deeply into the constricted bronchioles that were not allowing enough air into the lad's lungs. "Go to the bathroom and turn on the shower – hot as you can, no fan, window closed," he said to Dianne as he scooped up Hamish in his arms. "I'll follow."

Dianne rushed ahead and turned on the hot water. She knew that this was an old-fashioned procedure that would probably be of no value, but there was a small chance that it might offer her son some relief.

James gently deposited his boy on the bench next to the sink. "Dad ... I'm scared ... help me," the words cut deep into both parents.

"I'll call the ambulance," he said quietly to Dianne as she took his place beside their child. As he closed the bathroom door, above the sound of the shower blasting a stream of hot water onto the surrounding glass, he heard his wife urging the sick little boy to relax and to take slow breaths. He ran to the phone, noticing that the smell of burning rubber had diminished a little. Then he suddenly stopped. The toilet! He hadn't checked the toilet! Sometimes – only occasionally – Hamish would get up in the middle of the night to go and relieve himself. Once or twice they had found him asleep on the seat, his torch in one hand and his puffer in the other. It seemed that even in a semi-conscious state he felt compelled to take the device wherever he went.

James rushed back down the hallway and pushed open the toilet door. There it was, the missing puffer, sitting on the floor. He grabbed it, and burst into the nearby steam-filled bathroom. "Here it is," he cried triumphantly, as he handed it to his wide-eyed son. "Okay big fella, four big breaths and puffs – you know the deal – and then we'll do it again if we have to." Somehow, the little boy found the strength and presence of mind to follow the emergency procedure; they were good inhalations. James knew that the drug wouldn't alleviate any inflammation that might have flared up in the boy's respiratory system, but it would relax the surrounding muscles that were squashing his soft air passageways and thus restricting the life-sustaining exchange of gases in his lungs.

Five minutes later the change in Hamish's condition was remarkable. Colour had returned to his face – he'd not gone blue around his lips thank God, but had grown pale – and his wheezing had all but ceased. And, importantly, he was smiling.

Twenty minutes later, both parents were satisfied that their family emergency was over. Hamish had joined them in their bedroom and now sat in his father's arms staring out the window at the distant glow that had been responsible for his physical and emotional distress. James sighed, thankful that a breeze had obviously replaced the earlier evening stillness, and that it was now carrying the pernicious smoke away from their home. As the glow diminished, Hamish turned to his dad and said, "The firemen have beaten the nasties." He paused for a moment and then added, totally unaware of the irony of what he was saying, "I'm going to be a fireman when I grow up."

James nodded, "Sounds good to me," he said.

"Mum, I *am* gonna be a fireman, and Dad said it's okay," Hamish called over his father's shoulder – seeming to refer to an earlier conversation of which James wasn't a part. But there was no reply. Dianne had lain on the bed while the two men of the family were looking out the window – and now she was fast asleep.

"Okay, time for bed; your room or here?" James asked his boy. A few months ago the answer would've been obvious, but in recent times he'd observed Hamish becoming more ambivalent about such things.

"Hmmm ... the nasties won't be back again tonight will they Dad?" he asked.

Since his return, James had noticed that 'Dad' was now frequently replacing 'Daddy' in his son's speech. For the briefest of moments he confronted the fact that his boy would one day leave, and that he himself would grow old. He promptly dismissed the thought and its associated sadness. "I don't think so," he replied, "I'm pretty sure they're gone for the night."

"Well ... if you come and tell me a story, and don't go until I'm asleep, then I think I'll stay in my room."

"Done!" replied James, and he quickly kissed him on the forehead, and carried him out the door.

A few minutes later James was propped up in Hamish's bed; his son nestling into a pillow next to him. He reached forward and pulled the blanket with the tiger print a little further over the boy's pyjamaed body. "So what story would you like; one from a book or one that I make up?"

"No ... neither of those. Tonight I want to hear a true story – about when you found the magic well in Scotland."

James was surprised. He'd mentioned the well to his son once before when giving a summarized account of how he and Dianne had first met – and then re-met – in the Highlands all those years ago. But Hamish usually preferred hearing the crazy stories that his father made up on the spot – such as 'Another Adventure for Herbert the Stick'. Lately, however, he'd started to show some interest in tales from his family history; especially his dad's early experiences.

"Okay," James said, "But I have to tell you, I'm not sure about it being a magic well exactly; people preferred to call it a holy well."

Hamish frowned. "So what's the difference?"

"Good point, big fella, let's see if I can explain," James replied, realizing that his seven year-old son's question had cut to the core of what was probably an important general theological issue, and that ultimately the only difference might be in the semantics. As a result, he dealt with the two terms briefly – saying that one usually related to the idea of God or gods, ideas that Hamish was vaguely familiar with, and that the other didn't necessarily relate to any explanation at all. Hamish listened but then shrugged his shoulders and said he wanted to hear more about the details of his father's discovery. So James settled back and told the story, recalling images and impressions from that wonderful day so long ago when he found the well near Taroane Castle. Typically, Hamish asked lots of questions but then became silent, obviously thinking about what he'd just heard. He looked across at James.

"But who built the well, Dad?" he asked. "And how was it used? And why?"

James rubbed his chin. "I don't even think we can say it was actually built," he said. "It seemed to be a sort of natural spring that people from long, long ago simply put white stones around. And I'm not at all sure what people did when they visited it. The book I told you about just said that it was very special to them and that many went there – especially on the morning of the first of May."

"That's when they used to have the big party?"

"Yeah. And people had been having that party for a long time before the church was in Scotland."

"So the well goes back millions and millions of years – when there were dinosaurs?"

James grinned. "No, not that far back, but before there were knights and kings and fair maidens in distress."

"So why did they do all this stuff around the well? Why was it so important? Why was it called a holy well?" James was about to give what he thought would be reasonable answers for a seven year-old, when Hamish gave his own answer. "It was because it did magic, wasn't it?" he said staring at his father, a smile on his face.

James nodded, his eyebrows and mouth contributing to an expression of acknowledgment, "I think you're right big fella; that's probably how *they* saw it anyway."

"I'd like to visit that well at Enducky one day," the boy said as he rolled onto his side, his head resting in an elbow-supported hand.

James grinned at his son's pronunciation. "I never had a camera when I lived in Scotland so I can't show you a photo of it ... but I did a sketch of it once, you know," he said. "Would you like to see it?"

"You bet," Hamish replied, not showing the least sign of being tired, despite the time.

James walked to the spare room that would soon be a nursery but currently served as a study for Dianne and himself. He rummaged about for a few minutes and then returned to his son – fairly sure the boy would be asleep by now. But he wasn't. Instead he was now sitting up in bed looking at a children's book about a paleolithic cave dweller named Og.

"So here's my pretty bad drawing of the Holy Well of Endackney," James said as he sat down beside Hamish.

His son examined the sole sketch in the old quarto pad. "What's that?" he said, pointing.

"It's moss; it was growing on the side of some of the rocks."

"And are these flowers?"

"Not exactly; they're young nettle plants. They grow quite tall in the summer and can sting you if your skin touches them." Hamish sat back in mock apprehension and made a face with an inverted smile.

"And who's this hiding behind the trees?" he said, peering back at the pencilled drawing.

James turned his head to get a better look at where his son was indicating, at the same time saying, "There was no one hiding anywhere. Like most times, I was alone on the day I did this sketch." But as he examined the paper – which he hadn't viewed for over a decade – he became aware of Hamish staring at him.

"Yes there is Dad, look, there's his face, and an arm, and a sword ... and ..."

"Mmm, I see what you mean, but they're just lines and squiggles that make up the background – just a coincidence. Believe me, I would've known if I was drawing someone." But it was a little unsettling. He'd never before noticed how the almost random strokes could be perceived as representing a person amongst the trees, and for a moment he marvelled at the imaginative power of young children. Then, without thinking about it further, he moved onto something that he knew would engage his young son even more.

"But besides this drawing, I've got something else you might be interested in seeing." He handed Hamish the matchbox that was still clad in the aluminium foil he'd glued around it many years ago.

"What is it?" the boy said excitedly.

"Open it and see."

Hamish carefully pushed at the inner part of the little box with his small fingers. "It's the penny coin you told me about!" he squealed. "You kept it!"

"I did; and I only came across it a few weeks ago when I was cleaning up the study – just before I left for Fiji."

Hamish lifted the corroded copper disk from its tissue paper bed and held it up to the light. "There's a bit of writing on it and part of a picture," he said. "Did the people who made the well leave it there?"

"No, I think it's just an old British penny – probably from not too long ago; maybe a hundred years, but I'm only guessing."

Hamish kept turning the coin, his eyes fixed on its mainly crystallized surface. "I don't care what other people say, I think you found a magic well, Dad; and I think this is a magic penny – much, much better than pirate treasure." James knew that this was quite a commendation for the small piece of chemically degraded copper, given his son's love of all things to do with pirate treasure.

"You never know big fella, there are lots of things in the universe we don't understand," he replied, not wanting to spoil the boy's sense of wonder – and no longer as skeptical about such things as he once was.

Hamish nuzzled up to his father. "Daddy?"

"What?"

"Can I keep this magic coin for a little while? I promise I'll look after it." He then moved his head back so he could see James's response.

"Sure you can. Just be sure you do take care of it though – it holds a lot of memories for me."

For the first time in half an hour, Hamish yawned. "Thank you Dad," he said as his little mouth stretched to its limit.

* * * * * * * * * * * * *

The next morning was a Sunday. James had already been weary because of the multi-stage journey from Fiji, but then last night's episode with Hamish had given his body an extra reason to remain unconscious and in the restorative clutches of sleep. So when he did finally wake up, it was very late; close to noon. But even then, it wasn't a natural awakening; it was Dianne – using her insistent voice.

"James … James darling, you have to get up and see this," she said, giving his shoulder a little shake.

"Mmmfff."

"Come on darling, you can go back to sleep later, but you really must see this for yourself."

James rolled onto his back and opened his eyes. "Whassisst?"

Dianne kissed him on his mouth and then made a sudden raspberry with her lips on his chest. "Just get up and follow me," she said, standing above him.

He blinked and wriggled his shoulders as he walked behind her. She led him to the balcony at the front of their house, and pointed. Across the road was a small park where kids of different ages often played impromptu or loosely organized games of football or cricket or baseball or anything else that required a bit of grass-covered space. As James's eyes began to focus on the bodies that were running around, he saw that on this occasion the game was soccer. He recognized some of the kids from the neighbourhood, and thought about his son. Hamish loved soccer, and he'd often sit on the balcony or go down to the park itself and watch the other kids play. Sometimes, he'd even join in as an assistant goalie – where he didn't have to do hardly any running. He and the others knew that anything more exertive might bring on an attack. James turned to Dianne and sleepily scratched his pubic region; the sounds of boys yelling to their teammates filling the air.

"So what am I looking at?" he asked as he squinted from the sunlight coming over her head.

Surprise filled her face, and she quickly glanced from him to the park. "Look again sleepyhead, over there; the kid with the ball is your son!"

James was suddenly awake. "Jesus!" he said as he looked, mouth agape. Hamish, their child, their asthmatic child who could never run far without suffering the wheeze-and-cough-ridden consequences, was speeding along the grass with the ball at his feet. Seconds later he paused and then kicked. "Jesus!" James said for the second time as he turned to his wife. "Our son just kicked a goal."

Then concern replaced astonishment. "Shit, we'd better stop him," he said, heading for the door.

Dianne grabbed his arm. "James, he was already playing when I got up half an hour ago," she said. "I've been over to him and he seems fine. He wasn't showing the slightest hint of distress – just the opposite in fact. He seems to be on top of the world."

James stepped back onto the balcony and, frowning, looked from his wife to the boys running and yelling in the park. "But …"

"I know what you're feeling, James, but I think it's worth the risk. In fact, I think something has happened. Look at him."

James stared across at the exuberant children – his son was again in the thick of the play, running and calling for a pass. He'd never seen the boy so active. "What do you mean, 'something has happened'?"

"I don't know – he seems different, confident … and he said to me when I ran across to the park that …"

"What?"

"He said that the nasties had gone forever."

James's brow furrowed as he looked at his wife. "Dianne, he's seven years old! Just because he feels good on a particular day doesn't mean that he's suddenly gone into some miraculous remission."

"I'm only telling you what he said, seven years old or not; and you know how cautious I am with him. It's just that … I feel we should let him continue playing; that it'll be all right."

THE HOLY WELL

James sighed through his nose – this wasn't like Dianne. He was about to express his concern further, when she spoke again.

"There's something else I want to show you – before you run over to the park." She took his hand and led him back into the house and along the hallway to Hamish's room. They stood next to the bed, and she pointed to the pillow. "Lift it up," she said. James hesitated. "The pillow, lift it up," his wife repeated.

James reached down and raised the special hypoallergenic pillow. Underneath, sitting on the patterned white sheet, was the corroded penny that he'd loaned his son. He turned to Dianne. "I gave it to him last night – to keep for a little while. He wanted to hear about me finding the well."

Dianne's expression gave no hint of her inner thoughts or feelings. "You didn't tell him it was magic, did you?"

"Of course not," he said angrily. "*He* called it that – but that's just a kid's fantasy."

"Because he told me that it was your magic coin that chased the nasties away," she said, maintaining her inscrutable countenance. And before he could respond, she added, "And I'm willing to hold my judgement until I see what happens."

"But you can't believe that a piece of …" and then he paused, the distilled essence of years of thinking and experience spurting through his mind: the internal arguments he'd had with himself about evidence-based knowledge and the possibility of shortcuts around scientific method for finding meaning and mechanism; his loosening of the constraints imposed by his skepticism; his memories of the Holy Well of Endackney, and the strange and beautiful hold it had kept on him over all this time. "Okay," he said. "Let's see what happens. But if it turns out that our son has gone into remission, then there may be things we have to do."

He didn't need to explain, she understood completely.

※※※※※※※※※※※※※

James sat in front of the fire, the small pine logs he'd just put in amongst the embers were beginning to crackle. Dianne stretched out her legs on the couch and rested her head in his lap, the thick novel she'd been reading on the plane now almost finished. He twiddled with her hair as he stared into the flames.

From the single bedroom came the sound of Hamish making a hummffing sound as he rolled over, this being followed by an abrupt-but-loud fart from his little sister Morag who was asleep in the cot. "Bean salad," he said, referring to Dianne's choice of evening meal.

"Mmm," was the singular reply – and he realized that attempts to strike up a conversation with someone who was lost in the last few pages of good novel were unlikely to be successful. Still, he didn't mind; it gave him a chance to think about the past week. And what a week. Travelling halfway across the planet in the cattle-truck environment of economy class – with a baby, and with little sleep. And then that muck-up about the connecting flight from Heathrow to Edinburgh, and the drive to Cranmore, and the emotionally tense visit to Taroane Castle – only to find that it was no longer a school and not open to the public. No wonder he was now happy to relax.

Of course, finding the well again had been an exciting time – not only for him, but also for Dianne and Hamish, and even wee Morag. At one point, he feared that it might somehow have been obliterated, their difficulty in locating it being so great. But then, after hours of searching – and overcoming the distortions that can creep into geographic memory – he had found it. And what jubilation. They had danced around on the nearby grass, and Dianne had read aloud a little poem that she had written especially for the occasion. They had then joined hands and stood beside the small pool, and he had said some words. By the time they left, they all felt invigorated and happy – although this was hard to confirm in the case of Morag who had fallen asleep halfway through the impromptu ceremony.

But it was when he went back by himself later in the day ... that had been something that would stay with him till the end of his life. And maybe beyond. The earlier visit had been a wonderful mix of excitement and fun and solemnity, but he'd only felt an inkling of the personal connection he remembered from the past. However, it was enough to make him realize he had to come again – soon, and alone. It was a message. And when he had once more ventured through the bushes and trees, and had sat quietly next to the ring of white stones, and heard the sounds of birds as they bid the sun goodbye for the day; this was when he again experienced the emotions and feelings that he recalled from fifteen years earlier. It had been like awakening from a heavy slumber that had lasted for an age. Again he heard the well – but now more clearly than ever before. And then there was ... the new thing – something that he felt and saw – but in the strangest of ways; a further development in his peculiar relationship with this ancient relic – at the same time confusing and wondrous ... and utterly compelling. It had helped make him absolutely certain that his idea – one that he'd already discussed with Dianne – was justifiable; was the right thing to do.

He yawned. Of course, he'd have to think a little more before taking any sort of action, but at least he now knew where he was going with it all. For the time being though, there was more travelling to do; all the locations up north that he wanted to visit with his family. Some would be places from the past for Dianne, and most would be the stuff of family legend for Hamish. The lad would certainly remember this journey – so happy and healthy and full of life. Little Morag wouldn't recall anything – not consciously anyway. But maybe something would stay with her, simply because she'd been present – a brief part of the landscape. Who knows? All things were now possible as far as he was concerned.

There was a sudden 'bang'. He glanced at the fire, but the cause hadn't come from there – it had been Dianne, slamming shut her book, "Finished," she said as she took his hand. They both stared into the flames, and after a long pause she added, "I think it's time to move onto something else."

Chapter 15

"It's ... it's so beautiful ... and ... and at the same time, frightening," Pettah said as she gazed from the hilltop at the distant sea. You could tell who in the group had never seen an ocean before; their eyes were wide with wonder, and their mouths open.

"Why frightening?" asked Kian, the young Kelti man on the pony next to her.

"Because all that water goes to the very edge of the world – look! There is so much of it! What if a giant wave came? What if the land began to sink?"

Her betrothed laughed. "You are a strange girl, Pettah," he said. "You grow up in a dwelling that sits above the water, and yet you are afraid of the sea."

She half smiled, her hazel eyes bright. "That's different. The sacred lake of Tull is big, but nothing like that," she pushed her chin in the direction of the coast. And then, after a pause, "It really is a thing of great beauty isn't it?"

"Like you my love." He leaned towards her, but she pulled away.

"Not here," she giggled softly.

Bren looked across to his wife and sighed. It was good to see that their first-born was happy, but he was weary after travelling for so many days. Of course, he understood how some of his party felt – the first sight of the sea was always a special event. He himself had only gazed upon such a vast body of water twice before; and he wanted to allow the others time to relish the view. But he was also eager to get down to the coast before dark, and to sit by a fire with some food and drink and, he hated to admit, to sleep in a soft bed.

The leader of the escort group that had met them the previous morning guided his mount over to Bren. "My lord, the smoke you see near the coast, in line with the small island …" He pointed. "That is Feochan, where Kian's father, my Lord Eremon waits for you.

Bren nodded, and again looked across at Bodar. She knew he didn't like the elevated title that the young Kelti warrior insisted on using when addressing him. He had been disturbed when he first heard it used all those years ago in Ardvortag, and the fact that it was now fashionable in other areas, and that it also fitted in with the Kelti idea of social hierarchy, hadn't altered his attitude. Still, at the moment, he was a guest of these people, and he didn't feel like making an issue out of it. There were more important things to think about. He heard a cough from behind.

"Shall I tell everyone to prepare to leave *my lorrrd*?" Bren didn't have to turn his head to know who it was. "Yes cousin," he called over his shoulder. "And remind me to jab you in the side later this evening." Bodar grinned, and the Kelti warrior frowned.

The sun was close to the low peaks of one of the offshore islands when the fifteen or so riders entered the enclosed settlement of Feochan. It wasn't exactly on the coast but by the shore of a small sea lake whose waters merged with those of the great western ocean via a narrow entrance. There were many dwellings here, made of stone and timber and thatch, but they were different to those of the Tull folk.

"They use a lot of stone here don't they?" Bodar whispered to her husband as they rode past the staring and mainly unsmiling Kelti who watched from their doorways.

"There's lots of it around," he answered. "Still, the wall that encircles the settlement must have taken years to build."

"And the dwellings are smaller than ours, and their roofs aren't as steep …" Bodar continued, pausing as her eyes darted about; "… and they don't have any heather in their thatch, and …" But she stopped suddenly as they turned to the right.

Ahead was a huge roundhouse; its walls of stone almost as high as a man, and with an entrance passage that had its own gabled roof and a wonderfully decorated door of oak and iron. On either side of the entrance were several posts embedded in the ground. Carved into them were the representations of strange-looking people – some male, some female – naked and hairless, with staring eyes of quartz and smirking mouths of red ochre.

Bren noticed that his daughter had come up beside him. "This place frightens me," she said.

"Don't worry," he whispered, "We will only be here for a few days, and then we'll return home – back to your brothers and sisters. You'll be able to tell them they've been carved in wood here on the west coast." She forced a tiny smile.

The riders stopped at the building's entrance, and Kian jumped from his pony and ran to the outstretched arms of an aging woman. "His mother," the young escort warrior said to the Tull leader. Bren didn't respond but looked back at Pock-face who was clearly about to say something. However,

Bren gave a slight shake of his head, and his cousin's sharp tongue remained inactive. The Kelti were smart people but irony and sarcasm was not something they fully understood or appreciated.

Formal greetings were offered from Kian's family and other senior members of the clan to Bren and his wife and daughter and their small entourage – the speaker being Kian's mother. Her words were translated into the language of the Tull folk by her son. The Tull leader then surprised his hosts – and no doubt impressed them too – by responding in the Kelti tongue.

After this, as guests and hosts enclosed hands in the common form of salutation, it was plain that the male Kelti were appraising the strength and likely warrior skills of the native men from the east. But even more obvious were the judgements being made by the richly dressed Kelti women as they studied the features and attire of Bodar and her daughter. Bren sighed silently while still smiling politely. Marriage between their two cultures was always accompanied by concerns, but the unusual arrangement in this case, whereby the man would live at the home of the bride, was clearly not popular with many of these folk – even though their sick chief was the one who had insisted on it.

As if to underscore this smouldering antipathy, Kian's mother looked across at Bren – just until she gained his attention – and then addressed the Tull leader's daughter. Everyone fell silent, and the other Kelti women began smirking, for she loudly observed that Pettah's hair was short – it was only to her shoulders – and asked, using the blunt humour of her people, whether the young woman might not in fact be a boy. Pettah glanced at her parents, and then stared into her future mother-in-law's mocking eyes. She responded in perfect Kelti.

"My lady, your wit is clearly sharp, but let me assure you that despite the length of my hair, what I have between my legs is in no way boyish. Indeed, I believe it is most capable of providing you with many grandchildren." Bren raised an eyebrow but felt proud of his daughter of fifteen winters – 'just like her mother,' he thought.

Pettah's Kelti antagonist however, was clearly taken aback, her mouth agape, and her companions no longer grinning. But then the older woman started to laugh; chuckling at first and then breaking into mirthful cries. All around soon followed suit.

"I think I'm going to like you after all," she said as the laughter subsided, "My son is obviously to marry someone who is an astute warrior in her own right. And your use of our language is excellent – as good as any Kelti girl." With that, she took one of Pettah's hands and, reaching out to her son who was standing nearby, joined it with one of his. Spontaneously, everybody cheered, and she looked across to Bodar and Bren. "Now, my lord and lady, allow me to take you to my husband who lies awaiting you in his bed."

Bren had been inside Kelti dwellings in the past but he'd never before noticed so much illumination. There were reed torches and sea-bird lamps burning in many parts of the *taighri* (as the Kelti called their leader's great lodge); all carefully placed, it would seem, to show off the many fine furs and works of metal and wood and cloth. These mainly hung from the partition walls that protruded from the outer rim of the structure to create separate sleeping and working areas.

"Is it always this bright inside their dwellings?" Bodar whispered to her husband.

"I think this is intended to impress us," he replied quietly.

"I wonder why they don't use sleeping lofts like we do," she said as they crossed the large, open central region with its great hearth, above which pots of rich-smelling foods were cooking. "It seems like such a waste of space; not like …"

Bren turned his head to see why his wife had suddenly stopped speaking, and saw that she had just noticed the human skulls sitting on top of the inner stone wall; one on either side of each giant rafter, just under the thatch. In the flickering light they seemed to almost come alive, their black eye sockets blindly staring, and their toothy, lipless mouths grinning, leering. He looked back at Pettah; she too had seen the skulls.

The people of the Tull kept a few skeletal relics of ancient ancestors, but that was all. What they saw now, however – and they all knew it – were once the heads of Kelti enemies, killed in battle or sacrificed in religious ceremonies. A tremor passed through his body as he hoped – for the hundredth time – that his decision to not only allow this marriage but to encourage it, would be right; first for his daughter, but also for his people.

Inside the partitioned area that they now entered, was Eremon, chief of this Kelti clan. He was propped up in a large, raised, box-bed that stood on short legs. His plaited, mostly-grey hair framed a ruddy face that was dominated by intelligent, if not weary, blue eyes. Kian knelt down and kissed the man, and spoke briefly in whispers with him. He then stood up and walked over to Pettah.

"Ah, Bren of the Tull, at last I meet you," Eremon said with a voice that was obviously once strong and powerful but was now tinged with tiredness and pain. "On many occasions I have heard of your prowess – first as a brave young warrior in the north, and then as an adroit leader of your people around the great lake of Tull to the east. And soon, if the gods wish it, our two families will come together in marriage – a prospect that not all my advisers find favour with but one that I have supported ever since I heard of my son's attraction to your …" He reached out a hand towards Pettah, and she walked over and took hold of it, her face radiant. "… to your obviously beautiful daughter." The young escort who had led Bren's party to the settlement now translated for Bodar while Bren answered.

"You do me kind Eremon. Your own fame reached the banks of the Tull long before the arrival of your son and the traders he accompanied. And, as you know, there have already been a number of couplings between our peoples."

Eremon looked Bren in the eye. "It is something from which we should both benefit," he said. "You, for instance, will gain the support of a powerful Kelti clan; a useful commodity in these uncertain times …"

"And you," Bren quickly responded, "will be gaining access to land which has far more to offer than any I have seen over the last three days … and without the drawing of a single sword."

"From what I've heard, you would be a worthy opponent in battle," Eremon said with a thin smile.

"As would be every last one of my people," Bren replied in a gentle tone but without returning the smile.

"And I understand you still have friends in the north."

"Poltan of the Spey would not hesitate in sending warriors south if I asked."

"Then I hope you never feel the need to ask."

"That is a hope I share."

Eremon continued looking into Bren's steadfast eyes for a moment and then turned away and sighed. "I have also heard that the land of the Tull is full of great forests and hunting grounds, and that the fishing is good and the pastures rich; and that the fertile soil leads to bountiful crops. Ah! Would that I could see it for myself."

Satisfied with their initial, testing exchange, Bren now felt some sympathy for the bed-ridden Kelti chief. "You will surely return to good health soon, and then you and your wife will be our guests. We shall hunt and fish together, and have these young puppies carry our bows and spears," he nodded in the direction of Pettah and Kian.

"No, good Lord of the Tull, I fear I will never see your fair land …" He wanted to say more but, instead, started to cough – shallow at first and then deep and wet and painful. His wife stepped over and began to rub his back while a young woman held a bowl in front of him. Eventually, the coughing subsided and, between heavy breaths, he spat into the bowl. The phlegm was streaked with red. "What I intended to say before my lungs tried to climb out of my mouth, is that even though I will not see the lands of the Tull, I would enjoy talking with you about them … and about other things … Two aging warriors reminiscing about life – what do you think?"

Bren's feelings were further stirred. Clearly, the man was dying. But he aroused more than just compassion; there was a certain sincerity under his cagey exterior. "I will look forward to it," the Tull leader replied honestly.

The Holy Well

❋❋❋❋❋❋❋❋❋❋❋❋

The twists and turns in the relationship that was developing between the visitors from the Tull and their Kelti hosts were more than those made by a hare running from a mountain cat. On one day Bren would hear nothing but praise for the Kelti from amongst his people, and the next, nothing but criticism. The early reticence that existed on either side had largely broken down, and Bren's party had shown genuine interest when the people of Feochan proudly displayed their achievements in everything from art to agriculture and from medicine to weaponry. They were clearly a clever people, with devices and ways of doing things that, in many cases, seemed superior to the approaches of the Tull folk. But then, most showed little interest in the ideas and techniques of their guests, and this tendency to arrogance hadn't endeared them to the people from the east.

Bren had dealt with various Kelti clans over many years now, and he was certain that the similarities between their two cultures were capable of bringing them together and, he hoped, of slowly causing them to merge into something new and lasting. The only alternative would be bloody warfare, where one group would eventually be obliterated. This, he knew, was already occurring in some regions, with the Kelti always proving to be the victors. But there were also important differences in the views the two cultures held of the world, and of other men. Bren and Eremon were both aware of this, and it was a topic that they had been circling around in their early discussions. For Bren it was important because his people's future might depend on their understanding of Kelti thinking; for Eremon it seemed important for more personal and immediate reasons.

"Ah, this sickness Bren. Sometimes I feel like my body has been invaded by an army of evil little creatures which is slowly breaking down the defences of my own miniature warriors. There is definitely warfare of some sort going on inside me – and I'm losing – have already lost." Eremon leaned back into the soft goatskin pillows, bitterness tinging his general tone of resignation. "Still, the priests tell me that my soul will be reborn into this world at some time – they say they have seen this written in the stars."

Bren was seated next to the bed. He stroked his chin. "Your soul?" he said.

"Yes; my essence; the spirit that powers and directs my body and my thoughts; that which is truly me." He saw Bren frowning. "And after death, some are able, with the help of the gods, to enter the body of a newborn child, and to partake of the joys of life once again. Do you not know of this truth?" he said, surprised.

"We see the great cycle of life and death differently," Bren replied, knowing already that the differences were vast.

"But you know of the soul, and you have your gods ... don't you?"

Bren spoke carefully. He didn't want to upset Eremon but he had to remain true to what he knew, and to what his father had taught him. "My people have never seen the need for such ideas – although they have long been aware of them in the beliefs of other tribes."

Eremon seemed shocked. "You have no gods?"

"No."

"But my son has told me that you are a profoundly religious people, that you commune with the spirits of the wild beasts of the forest ... and with those of the forests themselves. By the cruaich! You speak of your sacred lake and your sacred mountains – we also believe in the holiness of such places, where spirits dwell and gods reside – but now you deny all this! Do you mock me?" He was clearly agitated, and began to cough. Bren quickly helped him drink a calming potion from a bronze cup. This had the desired effect, and the Tull leader stood up, preparing to leave. "Please, Bren, do not go. We are a proud people who maintain strong beliefs; beliefs handed down through many generations; and on many occasions our priests have demonstrated the power of our gods. But your knowledge has come from a different past, and …" He paused and took a rattling breath, "… and since I will soon be staring into the dark abyss of death, I would like to hear what you have to say about such things. And I will endeavour not to become riled again." He motioned with his hand for Bren to sit and to continue. The Tull leader obliged.

"You are right Eremon, we, like you, consider many places to be holy, but not that they are inhabited by spirits. They are as they are, just as we are what we are – flesh and bone and blood. However, we also believe that we are all linked – like far-removed members of the one great family. And, on occasion, some of us are able to commune with these distant kin: a forest, a mountain, a lake, a salmon, a bear, an eagle. In this sense, all things are holy. Yet, a few we hear more loudly or more often than others; or they reveal their interest in us in uncommon ways, and therefore become especially important." He paused for a moment and looked at Eremon. "There is no need for a spirit behind a thing, just the thing itself."

"But what about life and death? What do you believe happens when a man dies?"

"We talk of 'the great cycle' – a looping path along which all things journey; merging and separating and merging again. Life as a person is just a small part of the journey. After death, our bodies eventually disappear – eaten by fish or birds or worms; or sent up as smoke into the sky. The fish is eaten by a bear; the bird by a wildcat; the worms feed an oak; the smoke settles on a pasture where cattle graze. Eventually, we become part of all things, just as we are made from all things. And the great cycle continues."

"So nothing of the person's life – his memories, accomplishments, feelings, ideas – none of these continue, you say?"

Bren sighed. He knew that what he was about to utter wouldn't satisfy Eremon – the Kelti preferred clear and definite answers. "That is part of the wonderful enigma," he said. "For we know that somehow, something of the person does survive. Whether it is simply in the minds of those he left behind, or whether in some way he is drawn together from the trees and rocks and rivers that he becomes part of, we don't know."

Eremon sat back. "You don't know?"

"So much of our existence – of the workings of the world – is a mystery."

"Spirits, gods, souls, these are the solutions to your mysteries, Bren of the Tull."

"I think not Eremon – they are the creations of men. They solve nothing."

The Kelti chief was silent, his eyes studying his counterpart. "I cannot decide whether you are a fool or whether you have hold of a great truth," he finally said.

"Perhaps a little of each," Bren replied with another sigh.

Eremon chuckled briefly but then continued. "Tell me, Bren – and with no embellishment – what is the most profound encounter you have ever had with … with something holy?"

Bren leaned back against the partition wall, and ran his fingers through his silver-streaked hair. "For me, that is not a difficult question," he said, looking up at the rafters. "In a wooded area called Endachni, not far from my home settlement, I one day found a well …"

As the lamps burned, and as women at the hearth of the *taighri* began preparing the evening meal, Bren told Eremon the story of the well – how it had spoken to him without words, how it had saved Trib – whose name was already legendary even amongst these people, and how it had played a crucial role in his own remarkable recovery when Pettah was still a nursling. The sick chief listened intently without interrupting, and when Bren had finished, he allowed moments of silence to pass before speaking.

"And no spirit of the well has ever revealed itself to you?" he asked.

Bren snorted; he wasn't sure whether Eremon was attempting to goad him or whether the ailing leader just couldn't let go of his Kelti beliefs – not even for a short time. But then, he decided, the man might simply be looking for the truth. "No spirit, just the well," he replied, "… although …"

Eremon's eyes narrowed slightly. "Although what?"

Bren wondered whether he should proceed. He had rarely spoken to anyone about this before – not in this way at least. He hadn't even considered the possibility. But this sick Kelti chief was obviously steeped in his people's understanding of the world – even if it was inhabited by demons and blood-hungry gods. Perhaps his views on the matter would be of value. "On occasion, when at the well," he said, "I have caught glimpses of a man standing amongst the trees." Eremon nodded slowly while Bren continued. "Always, it is fleeting; he is there, some distance away, and then when I look again, he is gone."

"Does this stranger ever speak to you, or signal you with his hands?"

"Never. He is just there, and then he's not. At first I thought he was a visitor from a far-off settlement – his clothes are strange, of fine cloth, and he is clean-shaven, with very short hair – but now I think he is somehow linked to the well."

"Why?"

Bren took a deep breath. "Because I first saw him in a dream. He was with my great friend, Trib, whose life had been extended by the holy water from Endachni."

"And did he speak in the dream?"

"No, it was the same as later, at the well; just a passing moment."

"Spirits can take many forms, Bren; their propensity for doing this is described in many of our stories and beliefs."

"The stranger is not one of your spirits, Eremon, he is something else."

"Another wonderful mystery?" the Kelti replied, a grin brightening his face.

Bren laughed. "Yes, another wonderful mystery."

For a short time the two men discussed other, lighter matters, both tacitly agreeing to a break in their exchanges about the true nature of things. But Bren felt the need to return to the subject one more time. He could not let this man whose son was to marry his daughter cough away his life without offering some help.

Eremon had just finished telling an entertaining story about a man and a woman and a badger, and was laughing loudly – as was his guest.

"But why did the badger bite him *there*?" Bren asked as tears trickled from the corners of his eyes.

"Because, at the time, it was the most prominent part of his body," Eremon hooted. His chest then started heaving and Bren promptly knelt beside him and massaged his back while the poor man's lungs tried to expel the toxins that lay within. When the coughing had ceased, and Eremon was again settled, Bren spoke.

"Eremon, there is something I must ask you, must offer you, before I leave Feochan."

The Kelti chief smiled weakly. "You want to offer me water from your holy well."

"Yes," Bren replied. "Your son told me that you would not hear of it – for reasons to do with your religion – but I brought some anyway, and I am compelled to ask you myself. There is never any certainty that it will help a particular person, but it has helped many – I still live because of it."

"Bren," the sick leader said quietly, "I greatly appreciate your offer; you are a good man, but you must have heard of the term *geis* in our language." Bren nodded but remained silent. He knew the word, and felt annoyed. "There are *geis* in all cultures," Eremon continued, "… things that just cannot be done under any circumstances. Men being unable to marry their sisters is a common *geis*, for example. But with all Kelti, there are also personal *geis* – things that are forbidden to that person alone. For my youngest brother it is simple; he must not cross a bridge after sunset. For Kian, my son, it is that he must never refuse an invitation to feast. My personal *geis* is more profound: I must not partake of cures that are not Kelti."

"Then make it Kelti," Bren said, his brow wrinkled.

"That would require us to inhabit the land where your holy well is situated – to take it from you and to settle there. And our gods would have to give their blessing."

Bren's annoyance overflowed into his words. "Who tells you these things?" he said emphatically. "Who determines the *geis* for a man, and who decides whether a bladder of holy water is Kelti or not?"

"The priests," Eremon said resignedly. "They determine all such things; to act against their words could bring misfortune to my whole family. And don't worry," he added, smiling, "I don't intend fighting you for your land."

But Bren's irritation was turning to anger. "So what have your priests done for your illness?" he asked.

Eremon sniffed and then reached over to a long piece of cloth that was draped over a bench on the opposite side of the bed to which his guest was sitting. He pulled the cloth away, and Bren flinched as he saw the five dried, leathery faces with no eyes. "They have sacrificed three men and two women so far, but I don't think it is doing any good," the dying chief said matter-of-factly as he again began to cough.

※ ※ ※ ※ ※ ※ ※ ※ ※ ※ ※ ※ ※ ※

They were watering their ponies on the bank of the Black River when the attack came. Bren and Bodar were admiring the splendour of the three mountains to the south

– the largest being called The Mountain of the Calf-one by the Kelti – when they heard the shrieking voices of the men who came running from the trees.

Pettah was the only member of the Tull party who remained mounted but she was also the closest to the raggedly-dressed attackers. One of them already had hold of her pony's reins and was quickly leading the animal back towards the forest. Several others ran by its side pointing spears towards her and shouting at her not to dismount.

Bren instinctively ran to the aid of his daughter, drawing his sword from its scabbard on his back. Pock-face had appeared from further down the river. He was carrying his battle-axe and was sprinting diagonally, clearly hoping to get ahead of the abductors before they reached the pines. As he ran, Bren briefly wondered why there was no one else with his cousin.

The Tull leader reached Pettah first, and saw that she had grabbed one of the threatening spears below its bronze head and was boldly attempting to wrestle it from its owner.

One of the attackers turned on Bren and thrust his spear towards the determined father's face. Bren quickly moved his head, and at the same time swung his iron sword to the side, splitting the spear's wooden shaft. He then advanced on the man. At the same time, the attacker who had been holding the pony's reins screamed, Pock-face's axe having chopped into his left scapula. The other attackers beside the nervous animal shouted to Bren and Pock-face to stop or they would immediately kill Pettah. One had already snatched the reins from his companion who was now writhing on the ground, while two others had their spears at the girl's throat. They looked fearful but intent, and the words they shouted were Kelti.

Both Tull men froze, then slowly lowered their weapons. Bren glanced over his shoulder and was horrified to see that one of the dishevelled attackers was holding Bodar from behind with the point of a dagger pressed under her breasts. The two other women in their party were also thus held. All the men had dropped their weapons and were surrounded by six or so spearmen. All, that is, except for young Kian who had somehow managed to mount the largest of the ponies further up the bank and who, at this critical moment, had raised his bright sword high above his head.

"You shameful outcasts from the south who would take these women for your pleasure or for trade," he shouted. "Let me warn you, I am the son of Eremon of Feochan, the most powerful Kelti lord in these lands, and if you do not leave us now – with our women unharmed – then I promise you, you will be hunted down like the swine that you are, and every last one of you will be slow-roasted over the fires of Lugh." The attackers now looked fearful and shouted across to each other. "Go now," Kian called, "and we will not give chase."

Suddenly, the man holding Bodar sheathed his dagger, pushed her aside, and ran towards the trees. On seeing this, his companions quickly released their captives and followed – including those who surrounded Pettah.

Bren felt his hands trembling as he ran to his daughter. But even as he helped her from her mount, he heard the strange whooping battle cry of Kian's clan as the young warrior rode after the fleeing attackers, his assurance to them forgotten. Pock-face looked at Bren, his eyes questioning. Bren nodded, and Pock-face let out his own familiar cry as he headed towards the trees, followed by most of the other screaming Tull men.

Bren hurried back to the riverbank with his now quivering daughter, and re-united her with Bodar, herself pale and anxious. Next to the older woman were two young warriors, the only ones to have remained by the river. They now knelt in front of Bren with their heads bowed.

"Bren of the Tull," one of them said formally, you gave us the honoured task of protecting the persons of your wife and daughter. We should have been at their sides but were not. They could have lost their lives because of our carelessness, so we are now prepared to forfeit ours – as punishment."

Bren felt a new anger mixing with that which had been aroused by the attackers. "By the stars, you are right," he said sternly. "Despite your reputations as fine warriors, your laxity today is hard to forgive. But let me hear no more about the forfeiting of lives. You have only been amongst the Kelti for a short time and already you're sounding like them." Both men kept their heads bowed. "Now get up and assure me that you will never again leave the sides of your charges."

Both men jumped to their feet and grabbed at their leader's hands, offering promises and gratitude at allowing them to keep their positions. He waved them aside and stepped over to his womenfolk. "It wasn't their fault," Bodar said quietly.

"There was little they could have done," Pettah added.

"I know that," Bren replied.

They stood there together for a moment, not speaking. The steady sound of the river's rushing water being punctuated by the triumphant shouts of the returning Tull warriors and, less audible, the cries of pain from a few of their hapless victims at the edge of the forest.

"So much for our peaceful journey home," Bodar said, relieved that her loved ones had survived unharmed. Bren stood beside her, preparing to welcome back his men and the skillful young Kian. He held up one hand in salute, but the other he held behind his back – it was still trembling.

❊❊❊❊❊❊❊❊❊❊❊❊❊

Their return to Ceann Tull was greeted with some relief by the clan. They had been gone for more than half a lunar cycle, and the temporary leadership provided by Bren's uncle, Elin, had left a number of people nervous. Elin had always been respected, despite his lame leg, but he was now an old man, and some clan members had concerns about how he might act under pressure. Still, Bren hadn't been too worried; there were now many young warriors in the clan – most trained by himself and Pock-face – and Elin was quite capable of directing them if necessary, despite his age and personal affliction.

However, several matters had arisen to which Bren gave a higher priority for action than had his uncle. The most important of these was a dispute between two prominent families regarding the use of a particular piece of cleared land near the settlement of Sheelog. He had gone there with Pock-face and Kian and a small escort only two days after arriving back from the west. Both parties had accepted his adjudication in the dispute – for the time being at least – and he and his small band had headed back to Ceann Tull. However, their route passed close by the woods of Endachni, and Bren had bid the others wait while he walked to the holy well, to pay personal homage. He now returned.

The Holy Well

"You weren't gone long," Pock-face said looking up at the afternoon sky.

Bren also turned his eyes towards the heavens. High above them, a small flock of geese crossed the underbelly of a cloud, their distant honking barely audible. Turning his head, he saw the dark, spreading crowns of the great pines in the nearby forest of Drumm, and then – behind him – the tall, domed outline of oaks, their light green leaves fluttering in the breeze, and their branches playing host to cooing wood-pigeons and busy squirrels.

"Our world has great beauty cousin," he said as he lowered his gaze. "Will it always be like this I wonder?"

"I don't see why it shouldn't be," Pock-face replied, recognizing that his kinsman was in one of his thinking moods. "But if we don't get back to the settlement before sunset with little Pett's future husband – as you promised – then she and Bodar will take much of the beauty out of your life."

Bren smiled. "Ah, the arrangements for the wedding feast," he said as he began to walk, "I remember something about that."

Pock-face chuckled as he indicated to Kian and the others to follow. "It's all we've been hearing about for the last month," he called after his leader.

The sun was close to the mountain peaks when they decided to take one of the lesser-used tracks down to the lakeside. Bren was with Kian, behind Pock-face and a young spearman who were in the lead. A further two men were at the rear. Suddenly, Bren's cousin stopped – his right hand raised, and the other pointing to the trees on the left. Bren drew his dagger, and Kian beckoned to one of the men behind to pass him his spear. No one moved their feet. All were listening.

Then, the sound that Pock-face had first heard was repeated – like the shaking of a bush, overlayed with tiny yelps.

Quietly and carefully, the two older men stepped away from the others, using hand signals to indicate that the younger warriors should secrete themselves on the opposite side of the track. Kian either didn't understand these signals or chose to ignore them, for he followed his future father-in-law into the trees – creeping softly.

Only a short distance in, the three stopped. Bren pointed. Ahead, was a thicket of blackthorn; the branches of young suckers mingling with those of an old, gnarled parent plant. At first, all was still and silent, but then part of the thicket vibrated, the movement being accompanied by the sounds of a creature in distress. Stealthily, the men moved to one side to better view the area of agitation. And then they saw the cause.

Caught up in the needle-like thorns, a short distance above the ground, was a wolf pup. Its neck was at an awkward angle and its small front paws seemed to be permanently pinned in a splayed-out pose. It was motionless. Then, as they watched, the little creature of no more than four months made scurrying movements with its hind legs. But these bloodied limbs seemed to have lost contact with a nearby branch, and so they kicked against nothing except the sharp ends of the protruding thorns, causing it to yelp with pain.

Kian stood up. "Looks like he's pinned himself out to dry," he laughed. "Although why he tried climbing a blackthorn is a mystery – he must be a stupid wolf."

"His intentions were good," Pock-face replied, pointing to the almost-hidden bird's nest just above the pup's head. "There'll be eggs in there."

"Then let me make the birds happy," Kian said, lifting his spear, "and let me show you the accuracy of a Kelti hunter."

Pock-face stood back, but Bren stepped forward, placing his body between the spear and the struggling pup. "No," he said firmly. "We shall release the animal and send it off to its mother." He pointed up the rise to a rocky outcrop. On the top of a large boulder stood a she-wolf, silently observing. "See, her snout bleeds and tufts of her fur cling to the thorns – she has been trying to rescue her offspring."

Kian, however, didn't lower his spear, but began to argue with Bren. "Better that we kill them both," he said. "Are we not hunters?"

Pock-face instinctively reached over his shoulder for his sword.

Bren walked forward and with an open palm, gently pushed the spearhead to one side. "Learn something today, Kian. Help me release the pup, and then think on what you have done."

The young Kelti warrior maintained his position for a moment, before placing the spear on the ground. Pock-face's hand dropped back from his shoulder. Bren then led them to the blackthorn bush, and together they spent some time untangling the frightened creature from its spiky deathbed. Finally, while Kian held the pup, Bren pulled at the knot in the twine he'd wrapped around its muzzle, and quickly they both jumped back. Without a second thought, the young canine ran off in the direction of the rocky outcrop. Kian looked at Bren. He was still puzzled, but he smiled. The older man nodded, and then led the way back to the track.

Later, as they rounded the final bend in the lakeside path, Bren stopped, and so did the others. From here they could see

Ceann Tull; the sun's final rays making long shadows of the crannog and the land dwellings. Children ran and played in the open area, and smoke drifted up from the evening fires. And behind, the sacred lake glistened.

He turned to Pock-face. "It is a world of great beauty," he said earnestly.

They were silent for a time, and then Pock-face came up close to his cousin. "That which happened before – with the wolf pup – it's to do with the well isn't it?" Bren didn't answer but kept his gaze on the playing children. "You saw the stranger again didn't you?"

Bren turned his head and smiled. "… a world of great beauty," he said.

Chapter 16

James had eventually fallen asleep with the sounds of cars and buses and trucks roaring and rumbling outside. And those same sounds greeted him now as his old body roused itself into consciousness. It took more than a few seconds for him to realize where he was: not in his own bed; not even in his own hemisphere; but in Edinburgh, at a bed-and-breakfast on Minto Street – noisy, noisy Minto Street.

"So much for double glazing," he said as he turned and looked across the blankets. But even before the last word had left his lips, he knew no one would be there. The great sadness that was always close-by at such moments threatened to cast its shadow over him, so he dismissed it by yawning and stretching his arms – long and hard. Sitting up, he ran his fingers through his grey hair – still relatively thick over most of his head, except at the front where bare scalp on the sides now surrounded a peninsula of growth in the middle. He smiled briefly as he remembered how Dianne used to twiddle his hair with her fingers. Then he promptly threw his legs over the side of the bed and stood up.

Later, down in the dining room of the large, two-storey Georgian house where he was staying, James sat at a small, single-person table. There seemed to be settings for another seven or eight guests. He was soon approached by the owner-manager who had greeted him upon his arrival from the airport the previous evening.

"Good morning Mr Campbell," the man said cheerfully, "I trust you slept soundly?"

"An apt use of words Mr Ferguson," James replied with a smile. "The room you put me in has caused me to become an even stronger advocate of electric-powered vehicles than I was before." The owner-manager looked confused. "I wonder if you could shift me to a quieter room for tonight," James continued. "I did request such a room when I booked the accommodation back in Australia."

"Oh, indeed," the man responded, his dark, slicked-back hair and white-shirt-with-tie causing James to think of used car salesmen and born-again preachers. "Unfortunately, there was nothing else available at the time, but as it is, the Finnish couple are leaving prematurely today, so I can transfer you to their room – it's at the back of the building, and very quiet."

"That will be fine; thank you," James replied as he glanced down at the small, printed menu.

"The only trouble is that it is a bigger room, so the charge is more."

James looked up, and studied the man's face. "How much more?"

"Fifteen pounds."

"Fifteen pounds!" James said – much louder than he'd intended. "Do I get a free massage thrown in?"

"No, but I can give you extra tea bags," Mr Ferguson replied, his smile as slick as his hair.

James didn't feel like debating the issue – or of continuing the exchange. "In that case, I'll take it," he said, "and if you could serve me one of your 'full Scottish breakfasts' then I will be delighted."

As Mr Ferguson almost danced his way out to the kitchen, James looked across at the young woman sitting alone at the table next to his. He hadn't seen her when he first came into the dining room, but then, he missed a lot of things like that these days. He nodded a greeting to her. She gave a sort of smile from her pale face and then lowered her head, seeming to stare at the bowl of hardly-touched cereal in front of her.

Halfway through eating an oily piece of black pudding, James asked the chirpy Mr Ferguson how he could best get to the city centre by public transport – having forgotten most of what yesterday's taxi driver had told him.

"Oh, there are lots of buses you can get … the most frequent are the Lothian 3 or 3A and … here, let me write them all down on this wee tourist map you can keep," he said as he reached over to a pile of pamphlets on a nearby mantelpiece.

While listening to the owner-manager's descriptions, James saw that the young woman at the next table was leaning forward, and that she appeared to be copying down the same information. When she noticed him looking, she quickly turned away, and then stood up and left.

She was also at the bus stop just down the road when he emerged from the residence fifteen minutes later. The day was mainly overcast, but patches of blue sky were visible. The few trees that struggled to grow from the narrow strips of soil in front of the houses were just starting to show off their new-season leaves, and the air was still chilly enough to cause tiny fog clouds to form around people's mouths as they walked past. James stuck his hands into the pockets of his jacket.

"Early morning cold, but I'm told it will get warmer," he said to the woman as he ambled up to the lamppost on which the various bus schedules were bolted.

She gave that hint of a smile which he'd noticed in the dining room, but again said nothing. He'd long become used to the disheartening idea that some younger folk just didn't like talking to old farts like himself, so he didn't persist. She was pretty, he thought, probably in her mid-twenties; but sad. Her dark shoulder-length hair was pulled back into a limp horse's tail, and the lids of her large brown eyes drooped a little. She seemed distant and dispirited, and he wondered what had gone wrong in her young life to make her appear this way.

In the distance he saw a bus approaching. Its number was becoming visible, so he reached into his back pocket for the map that the bed-and-breakfast man had scribbled on. It was then that the pain struck; like a knife being thrust into his sternum. He let out a muffled grunt and buckled over, dropping the map. It didn't last long – only a couple of seconds – and as the pain dissipated, he felt a hand squeezing his arm.

"Are you all right?" a gentle voice inquired. It was the young woman.

He straightened up, slowly – not wanting to induce another stab – and took a deep breath. "I ... I think so ... yes ... I'm okay," he replied. "I get this pain sometimes, but it always goes, almost as quickly as it comes. I'll be fine."

She looked concerned, and kept hold of his arm as the bus pulled into the curb. "This is a number 69, it'll take you down Princes Street in the city if that's where you want to go – it's where I'm going," she said in an accent from the south. James nodded, glad that someone was taking control for a moment while he gathered his wits. She guided him up the steps of the vehicle, told the driver their intended destination, and then threw some coins into the funnel-shaped device just under the 'exact fare' notice. James was still fumbling for his wallet as she escorted him to a vacant double seat.

"Thank you so much," he said once he'd regained his composure. "Here, how much do I owe you?"

"Let it be my treat," she said. "Are you sure you're all right?"

"As healthy as any seventy-one year-old – more so in fact," he said, "and I really can't let you pay my fare."

"I insist," she replied.

He grinned. "In that case, I accept," and he held out his hand. "My name is James Campbell … from Australia."

She paused for a moment and he felt her eyes studying his face. Then she took his hand and shook it gently, "And I am Sophie Anderson, from England."

They chatted amiably while the bus went through its routine of collecting and depositing passengers on its way to the centre of the nation's capital. James explained how he'd been to Scotland many times over the years but had never actually visited Edinburgh – always just passing through the outskirts as he headed north, where he would again be venturing tomorrow.

Sophie had holidayed here as a child – when she was mainly carried around the streets by her parents. But she remembered little of the place – only that it had been an immensely happy time. On saying this, she became quiet again, stepping back from the more cheery state that James's little incident had seemed to encourage. He stared at her delicate profile as they passed by the houses of Nicholson Street and headed towards the shops and offices of South Bridge. She was a complete stranger, but she had helped him, and he wished he could make her happy.

Glancing out the window, he saw a man in a tweed jacket and woolen cap striding vigorously along the pavement. He was puffing just as vigorously on a large pipe, sending up sizeable plumes of grey smoke at regular intervals. The bus had slowed down in the traffic, and as the man strode past, James nudged Sophie and pointed out the window. "Human locomotive – traditional design," he said.

She looked and smiled, but still seemed preoccupied. Then, as she was about to turn away, another man – dressed in a similar fashion and also sucking on a full-firing pipe – came marching towards the first. They passed without the least acknowledgment of each other, but with their cloudy emissions mingling momentarily, as if this was recognition enough.

James found the scene profoundly amusing and grinned broadly. Next to him, Sophie snorted as she tried to restrain a giggle.

"We *are* about to cross over a major rail system," he said, still smiling.

"And Waverley Station *is* just around the corner," she responded.

"Is it?" he said.

"Yes – according to my map."

"Then that explains it."

She now allowed herself to laugh and then, suddenly, to show her amazement as they crossed over North Bridge. The dark, intricately-worked spires of the Scott Monument had just come into view and, further back to the left, the high, dominating beauty of Edinburgh Castle was revealed.

"Oh, how stunning," she said, gazing through the glass. "And look at the trees and gardens all around – such lovely greenery in the middle of a bustling city. I think I remember this." She turned to James, her eyes now sparkling.

Minutes later, he was stepping off the bus behind her, silently accepting the offer of her hand as he cautiously placed a foot on the concrete pavement. They walked to a nearby seat but neither sat down. James was uncertain what to say. He was beginning to enjoy her company, but understood that she would have better things to do than trying to put up further with a silly old man.

"I suppose this is where we say adieu," he said. "I intend to do a bit of wandering – as much as my old legs will allow – and a bit of sitting and observing; preferably in the sunshine or in a warm café."

"What, no museums or art galleries or castle tours?" she asked, surprised.

"No, that sort of thing has always been a low priority for me – perhaps I'll make some such visits when I get back here in a couple of weeks, if there's time."

"Well, I thought I'd visit the National Gallery," she said. "And maybe take one of those open-top bus tours."

"Do the latter when the sun is higher in the sky is my advice," he replied. "Otherwise you'll freeze. Perhaps I'll see you back at Mr Ferguson's esteemed establishment later."

"Yes, perhaps," she said, looking at him with what seemed like a mix of concern and … uncertainty.

Before turning to go, James decided to cross into territory that is normally forbidden in such brief encounters; but he was old and therefore could be forgiven; and anyway, he knew that sometimes such intrusions were worthwhile. "And Sophie," he said.

"Yes?"

"You know, the world can deal out much sadness at times, but there is also great beauty out there, and wondrous things." He paused and looked into her young face with his watery old eyes. "And there is hope; always, there is hope."

She was staring at him, her expression serious. He nodded in farewell, turned, and walked away.

He had sauntered up to the next intersection and was preparing to cross the road when he felt a gentle tug at his arm. It was her, breathing heavily from running.

"Mr Campbell ... James ... would you mind having me for company? Maybe we could talk and ..." but she trailed off without finishing.

He smiled. "I would be delighted," he said. "Here, let's cross over the road and begin our personalized tour right now."

****

James couldn't have wished for a more amiable companion. Sophie didn't appear to mind where they wandered, and she seemed genuinely interested in the sites that caught his attention, and in the conversations he initiated with local inhabitants. Even his daughter, Morag, back in Australia, sometimes cringed when she was with him on a stroll somewhere and he would boldly ask total strangers what they thought about this or that – not like the reserved youth of bygone years. But Sophie didn't appear to care; she had actually joined in the discussion with the traffic inspector when James had asked for his views about the huge, locked, private gardens in the middle of the city.

Furthermore, she didn't walk too fast, obviously appreciating that even a fit seventy-one year-old needed to move at a slower pace than most other people, '... except, perhaps, for fit seventy-two year-olds ...' he had joked at one point when they were deciding where to wander next.

That was another thing, she appeared to be amused by the same silly observations that delighted him. When they'd looked at the plaque under the imposing statue of William Pitt at one of the street intersections, they had seen: 'Born MDCCLIX Died MDCCCVI Erected MDCCCXXXIII'.

'A great man,' James had said.

'Yes,' Sophie had replied, and then added. 'Do you think he was any good with numbers?'

'Excellent question,' he had answered, enjoying her company even more.

And now they were at a café called 'Tum Tums' in the popular promenade known as Rose Street. James could've walked a little more but his young companion had grown subdued again and he sensed that she might want to sit and talk for a while – or that maybe she was simply hungry. They had ordered some food, and their drinks had just been placed on the table – hers a coffee, his a pot of tea. She had said little for the past few minutes, and a frown was slowly forming on her face. James looked at her, trying to figure out whether he might be causing a problem.

"Well, Miss Sophie Anderson," he said (she had told him she wasn't married – or attached). "I've had a wonderful morning with you," "But if you want to go your own way after lunch then I won't be in the least bit offended."

"Oh, James," she sighed. "It's not that. I've had a great time too – you remind me of my grandad; what I remember of him. And you've somehow managed to take my mind off other things, but … those other things just won't go away – they're waiting for me whenever I …" She wiped at the tears forming in her eyes. "I came here to escape from all the sympathy and concern that was choking me back home but …"

James reached out his wrinkled hand and touched hers – he was surprised at how cold she felt. "Go on," he said gently.

"It's just that … what you said to me this morning when we got off the bus – about there always being hope. Do you really believe that?"

He nodded, "Yes I do."

"Even when a series of doctors tell you that you're going to die in less than a year?" She looked mournfully at him, her eyes swimming in tears.

He held her hand more tightly. "Listen to me, Sophie," he said. "Hope is a strange and powerful sentiment which is capable of bringing about great change. But sometimes we discover that maybe we've been hoping for the wrong thing."

"How do you mean?" she said, looking at him sadly.

"I mean, sometimes, for instance, we might be hoping for good health, when what we really want is a sense of peace, or to be happy despite our afflictions."

"I'd settle for either of those," she said sniffing, "… and I would really like to stay alive …" Tears trickled down her pale cheeks. James made a decision.

"Sophie," he said, "this may not be of any help to you whatsoever, and you may not even want to consider what I am about to suggest – just the ramblings of a strange old man perhaps. But let me tell you about a place I know of, to the north …"

* * * * * * * * * * * * *

It was a few minutes past one o'clock when James entered the village of Abercrombie. It seemed to be bigger every time he came here – more buildings, more people. Some of the quaintness remained, but it wasn't the same as he remembered from his castle years. Passing up the rise from the old village square, he looked for somewhere to park the hire-car. There were several simple little private ceremonies he now performed whenever he came to this land of hidden mysteries that had so influenced his life – and soon he would carry out the first of these.

He had some difficulty reversing the car into the space he found, and held up the traffic while making a second attempt – the spaces seemed to be shorter here, or maybe it was the stiffness in his neck that stopped him from being able to turn around properly. The restrictions of age annoyed him at times, but not as much as they used to.

He walked down to the gate that allowed access to the small public gardens. The air remained cool but the sun shone brightly overhead, with the songs of birds adding a further dimension of splendour to the day. Sitting on a bench under a large oak, he looked up – as best he could – at the sky. Of course, the tree had been smaller all those years ago, and it had been a different season – you wouldn't have seen much sky back then because of all the leaves. In fact, he couldn't remember whether he'd actually looked up during their encounter here. But Dianne's beautiful young face – he certainly remembered that; her long dark hair and big brown eyes, and her lips that could curve into the most vivacious smile … And her Texan accent that hadn't yet been influenced by all those later years in Australia … "Good morning y'all", he quietly quoted to himself with a grin.

It was here, right on this bench, that they had both conveyed messages of love to each other – not so much in words, but in looks and touches, and in the hints behind their words. It had only been a brief meeting, but even now he could feel his old heart swelling with the same powerful emotions – of desire and affection. On this occasion, however, they were also accompanied by a great nostalgia.

Ten years ago this June, that's how long it had been since she was taken from him. At first, he didn't think he was going to be able to continue, his desolation so vast. The kids had been hard hit too, but they were already young adults – Hamish married, and Morag about to be – and they had their own network of friends to support them. James recalled how they had tried to help him through his grief. But really, it had been the trip back here to Scotland – to the holy well – that had finally pulled him out of his depression. And he would be going to that magical place again tomorrow, to hear what it had to say to him this time, and maybe to feel the strange presence of his fellow visitor – the one from long ago; the one who had, in some mystical way, given him hope.

He stood up and walked behind the bench, looking at the ground. The big oak didn't yet have any fully-grown leaves on its branches – just a smattering of early, green shoots – so he knelt down and picked up two of last season's leaves, brown and crisp but still intact. He had difficulty getting back to his feet but a passing woman gave him a hand, and after thanking her he slowly walked to the edge of the tiny stream that ran through the gardens on its way to the nearby Tull. He held out his hand and dropped the leaves into the gently flowing water. At first they were together, drifting side by side, but then they separated – one caught up in a tiny side current and the other not. A tear dropped from each of James's eyes as he whispered, "I will always love you Dianne." He then turned and walked away.

He didn't see it, but further down the stream, the two leaves met again, the water pushing them together, their edges overlapping. And they stayed like this, all the way down to the great river.

After a brief lunch in the little café across from the gardens, James headed off for Cranmore. It was only a short drive – about twelve kilometres – with the narrow, tree-lined road passing by the main entrance to the Taroane Castle grounds. In fact, the old stone wall that surrounded part of the estate ran alongside the eastern side of the road for some distance. He'd been driving slowly anyway but he reduced speed even further as the castle turnoff approached. He had intended to visit his old home and place of work either tomorrow or the next day, but decided that viewing it from a distance for a few minutes right now wouldn't hurt – it wasn't as though he had a tight schedule or anything. So he turned to the right.

As far as he knew, the castle was no longer in use; locked up and still for sale, as it had been for years. But the gates across the private driveway remained open – no doubt to allow access to patrons of the golf course that existed in a section of the estate. He followed the winding path to a familiar bend, and then stopped the car.

Through the windscreen he could see the old, stone edifice, its harsh greyness standing out from the surrounding range of greens provided by the various conifers and budding deciduous trees. It was just as he remembered it when he'd first viewed the castle from this same point almost fifty years previous. 'My God!' he thought as he realized how long ago that really was. He sat there for a while, recalling events – and wondering what had happened to all those people he'd lost contact with: that teacher who had fancied him, and the clownish kid, what was his name? – Dianne always remembered – and, of course, Miss Pordosky, the school witch. His brief reverie was suddenly broken when two large vehicles came speeding around the bend, golf bags and buggies in their rear compartments. He started his car and turned back towards the road.

The next day, James awoke in the old schoolhouse at Achlocht, the name of a little gathering of buildings on the southern side of Loch Tull, a couple of kilometres from Cranmore. It wasn't a schoolhouse anymore, of course, but a comfortable bed-and-breakfast run by a widow, Mrs McGowan. It had become his regular place of abode when he visited this part of Scotland, and the old lady (she was actually a few years younger than James) took care of him. She also charged a reasonable tariff and didn't ask too many questions about his activities. On one or two occasions he had almost taken her into his confidence, but had decided against it. Perhaps she already knew what was going on anyway.

After a light breakfast – one 'full-Scottish' a week was more than enough for him at his age – and a convivial chat with

The Holy Well

Mrs McGowan about local happenings, he drove down the single-lane road towards Cranmore. Along the way, he pulled over opposite the 'Crannog Reconstruction Site', a small parcel of land on the edge of the loch where an archaeology group from one of the universities had set up a dual research and tourist facility. There were several transportable rooms on the site that were used for displays and work activities, and visitors could play with a range of recent copies of ancient artifacts, such as weaving looms, grinding stones, and fire-making devices.

But the most noticeable – and spectacular – feature of the centre was the large, round structure that sat on log pylons out above the water. This *crannog*, with its railed balcony and steep, conical thatched roof was connected to the land by a raised wooden causeway. It had taken several years to complete, and its design was based partly on underwater ruins that had been discovered nearby, and partly on assumptions and intelligent guesswork. If it wasn't for the extraordinary ability of alder wood to remain preserved under water, then little of the ruins would have been found. Evidence suggested that the original site had been occupied since the late Bronze Age.

Specialists still debated why people would've gone to all the trouble necessary to construct these buildings out in the water. Some structures, like the ruins up in Loch Laggan to the north, were built on man-made islands, which must have taken an enormous effort to establish. The most popular theory was that they were for protection – from either wild animals or other people. James smiled as he put the car into gear. It wasn't for protection; he knew the real reason.

Passing over the bridge where the river exited from the loch, he drove up through Cranmore. It had changed little, still just a pub, a church, a few shops, and a small collection of residences. There were few visitors around at this time of year, but he knew that would change once summer got into full swing. He passed out of the village and turned right and then another sharp right as he entered the driveway of Robbie MacIntyre's farmhouse.

Robbie's family owned the land that encompassed the site where the old church of Endackney had once stood, and where the holy well still existed. James had found this out many years ago and, over a period of time, had promoted a mutual understanding of the well's historical significance – first with Robbie's father, Angus, and then, when the old man had retired, with Robbie himself. He had never given them any details about the well's personal importance to him, or about the powers it seemed to possess. But he had convinced them of the need to keep the site unpublicized and to retain its wild surroundings – while still making it accessible to those who went to the trouble of seeking it out.

The family had been in the area for many generations, and the young farmer and his father seemed to appreciate James's sentiments despite him being an outsider and despite the fact that they also owned a caravan park that hosted hundreds of sightseeing-hungry visitors every year. He had a great deal of respect for the two men because of this, and he sometimes wondered whether they understood more than they let on.

"Mr Campbell; welcome back to your adopted home," Robbie said as he stepped from the back door holding a mug. He reached out his other hand in greeting. "I was just finishing my coffee when I saw you drive in. Can I offer you one?"

James saw that two farm workers were obviously waiting for their employer to join them. "Thank you Robbie, but I'll let you get on with your work. I just wanted to let you know that I have arrived, and that – as usual – I will be around for a short while."

The young farmer lowered his voice. "I received your letter two weeks ago about you coming, and I checked the site just the other day. Everything was still intact – still secluded and wild. Someone had dumped a bit of rubbish further along the main track, and there were a number of footprints in the mud near the well – but nothing to be concerned about. As usual, I've kept a regular eye on it."

James nodded and touched the young man's arm – there was an understanding. "Thank you Robbie," he said.

The farmer's voice then returned to its normal volume. "So, can we look forward to you joining us for dinner tomorrow night?"

James grinned. "That sounds good to me," he replied.

Fifteen minutes later he was walking down the track that led from the small field where he had parked the car. In the old days, when he was younger, he always preferred to approach the site from the other direction. That way, you could walk close to the riverbank, and then through the dark pinewoods that opened out to the clearing where the old church had once stood. The ancient oak still grew there – the one that had helped him pinpoint the well on that magical day in his youth. But it was a long walk, and he'd had that blasted pain jab at him again earlier in the morning, so he thought it prudent to take the easier route on this occasion.

There was no clearly-visible path that led directly to the well, so he used his memory to determine where to leave the main track. He knew he was becoming increasingly forgetful, but not about the things that really mattered and, in this case, his powers of recall were perfect – or so he thought.

"Now where are you?" he said to himself as he searched around the leaf-strewn ground. Then, looking back up the embankment, he remembered it being steeper and higher, so he walked further along near its base watching the slope increase. Less than a minute later he saw it, and the old excitement flooded back into his aging body. "The Holy Well of Endackney," he mouthed.

Robbie had been right, there was no change that he could notice. It was still just a simple hole in the ground encircled by a ring of white, moss-covered stones. And the surroundings were as he remembered from last time – as he remembered from the first time – a tangled assortment of trees looking down on the well with its gently overflowing water that soon turned into a small bog, and the scattered patches of grass and wild flowers.

He sat on the thick branch of a fallen tree – it bridged the short streamlet of trickling water – and he closed his eyes. Close-by, a lone bird sang. James felt the peace descending and enveloping him, and with it came the thoughts and the feelings. It was in this way that the well quietly spoke to him. His great loss, his children, his future, his past, the plight of the world and his part in trying to help; all these things were dealt with; not individually but together – somehow.

He also felt the presence of the other visitor. If he opened his eyes, he would see no one – or perhaps just catch a fleeting glimpse, as he had done on a few occasions before. But the man was here nonetheless, and James recognized him as being from a period far earlier than when history had begun to be recorded. A hunter maybe, or a warrior. They didn't speak, not in words at least, but it was clear that they both heard the well, and that sometimes, in some way, they also heard each other. He had come to know so many wonderful things because of this – and he knew that it was part of the well's great gift to him.

Of course, there was the possibility that it was all just an elaborate fantasy; images and impressions unconsciously conjured up by an overly creative brain. But James had dismissed that notion long ago. And anyway, the fact was, the well really seemed to help some people.

He wasn't sure how long he had stayed sitting there, but eventually he opened his eyes and then spent a little more time taking in the simple and natural beauty of the ancient site. True holiness is like this, he thought. He then stood up and walked over to the ring of stones, peering down at the small, dark pool. At the bottom he could see a number of silver coins, glinting in the broken sunlight. He smiled; others had been here.

Driving back along the lochside, he felt good – refreshed, light-hearted, full of ideas and intentions. As he turned into the little parking area of Mrs McGowan's B-and-B, he noticed another car. He had been the sole guest during the previous night, so he idly wondered who the new arrival might be – someone other than the old lady to chat with over tomorrow's breakfast perhaps. His curiosity was soon put to rest. As he walked across the driveway, the front door of the house opened and out ran Sophie Anderson, the young woman he'd met in Edinburgh. She flung her arms around him but didn't utter a word.

"I wasn't at all sure that you would come," he said. "I wouldn't have blamed you if you hadn't."

She released her grip on him and stepped back. Her eyes were brushed with tears and her mouth was formed in that sad, half smile that he'd seen before. "So, here I am," she said.

He looked at her intently. "No promises, you understand."

She nodded. "I understand."

They stood gazing at each other for several seconds, and then he took both her hands, not at all concerned that he was about to make a return journey. "Let's go then," he said.

****

'You love this land don't you?' That's what Dianne had once put to him, back when they were at the castle school. And she had been right, he did love the Scottish Highlands, and he still looked forward with great anticipation to his visits there. He paused for a few seconds and thought about the trip of three months ago. But it was also good to get back to the familiarity of his little home up in the hills overlooking Melbourne.

He and Dianne had shifted up here after the kids had moved out of their old suburban house, and the place was redolent with pictures and artifacts that now acted as prompts for his faltering memory. Which was why he was down on his knees at the bookshelf in his small study trying to find his 'special' photo album. It was the one that he'd made up a few years ago with copies of pictures of particular significance from other albums; a sort of brief, pictorial summary of his life. 'My life is only three centimetres thick,' he had joked to Hamish and Morag.

Hamish and Morag; he was pleased they would be coming to see him tomorrow night – or was it to be the next night? No, they did say Thursday ... God! Surely jet lag can't last this long, he mused. Then he found what he'd been looking for; squashed in between the wedding album and the giant atlas.

Still on his knees, he shuffled over to the desk and put the book of pictures on top. He then used the desk and his swivel chair as aids for getting to his feet, and then ... 'Oh shit!' he thought as the pain dug down into his chest. He managed to slump into the chair, and that's where he remained until the sharpness faded to a more general soreness. He took a calming breath and resolved – against his better judgement – to go and see that young smart-arse doctor down at the medical centre sometime during the next couple of days. A few minutes later, he stood up and carried the album into the bedroom, and placed it on the faded blankets.

Down in the kitchen, he waited for the kettle to boil. He usually just had a glass of water before going to bed, but tonight he was cold, despite having several heaters turned on, and he thought a hot drink might chase away the chill in his bones.

On the little breakfast table was the pile of personal correspondence that he never seemed quite able to get through. But that would be one of tomorrow's main jobs – together with some gardening. The actual answering of the various letters would probably take the better part of a week. He made the tea and then carried the steaming mug back up to his bedroom.

He was still a little cold, and that soreness hadn't properly dissipated, but he had no doubt that a restful sleep under the pile of blankets would remedy both problems. For now however, he was happy enough to sit up in bed wearing his woolen dressing gown while he opened up the photo album.

There he was as a baby, being held by his dad; his dear old dad, what a fine man he had been. And there, the only picture he had of Cheryl, the girl from next door, her cheeky grin stirring feelings from way back in his childhood – including the hurt he had felt when she died. Further along was a school photo. Had he really been that young once? And what was the name of that boy on the left – the one with the girlfriend? He flicked through the pages. There was his favourite picture of Dianne, just after she had found him up in the Highlands – her youthful face glowing with the promise of times to come. And here she was again, with little Hamish and baby Morag – during their first family visit to Scotland. What fine young people they had grown into. He felt a surge of pride and happiness.

The next page showed a picture of the holy well. He couldn't quite remember on which trip he'd taken the photograph. It was written on the caption underneath but that appeared a little blurry for some reason and he couldn't quite make it out. He leaned back and looked up at the ceiling and then out through the window. The drapes weren't drawn so he could see the night sky. There was the moon – a crescent – and a multitude of stars.

The holy well; it seemed to be linked to so many of the important happenings in his life. This was certainly the case after he had discovered it, but sometimes he wondered whether it might even have been calling to him before that time – all his life perhaps. He closed his eyes, and saw the trees and the water and the ring of white stones. Dianne was there, young and beautiful; and over by a tree, the man – the stranger – in his ancient garb of animal skins and roughly woven cloth. They were both grinning at him, and beckoning; and there were others there too. He could hear the songs of birds – sweet and high, and smell the fragrances of the forest – delicate and beguiling.

He sighed as the album dropped from his hands. And while the stars twinkled in the outside darkness, he took his first steps on a strange, new journey.

Epilogue

Morag stood shivering in the half-light while her brother locked the car. "That's probably not necessary around here, you know," she said, moving her legs up and down in an attempt to generate some extra body heat.

He looked across at the other cars parked on the strip of land next to the track. "Yeah, you're probably right, but there are obviously other people around and …"

"And you're just a suspicious city boy – I understand," she replied, a small grin on her lips.

Hamish had been aware of his sister's subdued manner ever since they passed through Abercrombie yesterday. He understood why – they were here to say a last goodbye to their father, not something you do every day. Still, he was glad to see the hint of brightness on her face. He took a letter from his jacket pocket and briefly examined it. "Dad's map shows this is the route he preferred, even though you can get much closer to the well if you go further down the road."

Morag wandered over, the plastic container under her arm. She looked down at the map – they'd both studied it yesterday, as well as in Edinburgh, on the plane, and back in Australia. But she wanted to glance over it again; to see the notes her father had jotted around the neat sketch. 'Best way', he had written along the dotted line that represented the track they were about to take. Attached to the map and folded behind it was the rest of the message the old man had left with his children shortly before he passed away. 'To be opened after I die', he'd printed on the envelope. She looked up.

"How long do you think before the sun will actually rise," she asked, referring to her father's direction that they should spread his ashes at dawn on Beltane, the first day of May.

"Probably another thirty or forty minutes," Hamish replied staring at the glow in the east.

"Then let's get a move on," she said as she took his arm and headed away from the car.

They walked along the main track without speaking – listening to the birdsong and the soft roar of the nearby river. On either side of them were huge beech trees, their smoky grey trunks just beginning to cast long shadows in the gathering light. Morag watched a red squirrel run along a lower branch, and she recalled a similar moment many years ago. "These trees aren't native to the UK, you know," she said. Hamish looked across at her, his eyebrows raised. "Dad told me when we were last here."

"I'm surprised you remember," he said. "You must have only been about ten."

"Nine," she replied. "I was nine."

Moments later, they carefully negotiated the slope on the river side of the track and dropped down to a much narrower trail that was only metres from the water.

"How did you know to come down here?" Hamish asked as he stepped from amongst the bushes behind his sister.

"It must be marked on the map," she replied, continuing on.

The trail and river began to part company as the two walkers approached a dark gathering of tall conifers. They quickly walked through these gloomy and silent woods, and soon emerged into the open, lightly-treed area beyond.

"I remember this place," Hamish said. "I think this is where Dad said the village and the church used to exist way back in the past."

"And there's the old oak." Morag pointed, but saw her brother was unsure. "Not the birch or the willow," she said, still pointing, "… that big scraggly tree without any leaves but covered in buds."

Hamish nodded, and was again surprised by his sister's apparent knowledge about the place. He pulled the map from his pocket. "Now let me see … according to the map, we should head …" He looked up but saw that Morag was already tramping off to the north.

A little further on, the land rose up slightly and they passed by the old decaying bridge with its aged warning signs. From here they could see a large field with the river bordering one side, and a narrow, wild, wooded area bordering the other. "The holy well is just in from the fence line," Morag said, "… near where that juniper is growing. Come on."

Hamish put the map back in his pocket without even glancing at it. "How come you know so much about Northern Hemisphere trees?" he said as she hooked her arm about his.

She shrugged, and then looked him in the eye. "We're quite close now," she said, and he knew she was suggesting that they proceed more slowly, and solemnly.

They chose to walk along the edge of the field rather than follow the main track that had again come into view. There was no trail, and it was muddy underfoot, but Morag remembered

James telling her that this was how he had first discovered the well, and she wanted to follow the same route.

At the tree, they stopped. There was a wire fence they had to climb through, and while Hamish was stretching apart two of the strands for his sister, he looked back towards the old bridge and saw a woman coming towards them. He mentioned it to Morag, and so they quickly stepped into the cover of the surrounding trees and bushes – both knowing that the holy well was close-by. They had only moved ten or so metres when it became obvious that they were not alone.

Morag tightly grasped her brother's arm as they stood and looked in amazement. She could see the ring of white stones and the water and the bog – and a patch of wild irises that she remembered from her childhood. But there was also a gathering of people here – about twenty of them! They were dotted around the well and amongst the trees – some standing, some sitting on logs or on patches of grass. A few more arrived as they watched. "Hamish, what's going on here?" she whispered – astonished.

"I have no idea," he said. "Perhaps it's a local custom."

A woman – a bit younger than Morag – approached them. "Hi," she said in a friendly voice, but quietly. "My name is Sophie." She then paused and looked from Hamish to his sister. "Were you helped by James Campbell?" she said.

Morag blinked. "We are his children," she replied, totally perplexed.

The woman turned and called out to the others, "It's them, they have arrived."

She led the stunned siblings closer to the well as the people gathered round. There was a little boy being carried by a big, powerful looking man; and an old lady navigating her way between the trees with the help of a young girl and; Hamish couldn't help noticing; a man of about his age standing a short way off with two beautiful, grey-eyed women who appeared to be identical twins.

"Your father was a wonderful person who shared a wonderful discovery," an elderly gentleman said as he leaned on a walking stick.

"I owe my life to him for bringing me to this holy place," said someone else.

"He never took any credit or payment … just helped those he thought the well might cure. He was a saint!" said yet another member of the group, with many voices uttering words of agreement.

Morag glanced across to her brother, and then around at the many faces. "But how did he … and how did you …?" Her voice trailed off; she still couldn't fully comprehend what was happening. An aging woman with silver hair tied back into a bun came to her rescue.

"He never told you about us, did he?" she said.

Morag shook her head.

"Your father was very protective of this place," she went on. "He knew the well had the power to cure some people of their illnesses, but he was always afraid that if it became too popular – like a tourist destination – then it would lose that power. And there was something else about it, something more personal, that he never really discussed. I suspect it was a constant dilemma for him to balance the need for secrecy with his desire to share what he had discovered. He helped each of us individually, but we had to agree to not tell anyone else about the place." She smiled. "Sometimes, though, we would suggest to him others he might consider helping. We kept in touch through the little network he established."

"Is that how everyone found out about his passing away?" Hamish asked.

"Yes," she replied. "After one of us found out, the word spread. And James had told several of us on different occasions that he would like his children to scatter his ashes here on the morning of Beltane. He said it would be appropriate. So we knew to come here on this day; to honour him. Folk have travelled from all over the world, and there were quite a few more who couldn't get here for one reason or another."

They spoke with the people for some time, listening to stories of how their father had reached out the hand of hope to many sick and troubled individuals. At first it shocked them – to think that there had been such a secretive aspect to his life, a part of his existence that they knew nothing about. They'd been aware of the holy well's importance to James, and that it might have had something to do with Hamish's recovery from childhood asthma, but not that he'd been using its apparent powers for so long a time to help so many people.

Still, the more they heard, the more they understood. "He knew we would find out on this day," Morag said to her brother after hearing yet another tale. "It's a surprise, but a wonderful surprise – maybe a gift. Our dad was an unusual, and amazing, man."

Hamish nodded. "The letter makes more sense now," he said. He looked at his sister, and then at the faces around him. She smiled and lifted her eyebrows in approval, so he took the letter from his pocket and held up his hand. "Everybody," he said, "I would like to read to you a part of the letter that our father wrote to my sister and I." The small crowd became silent as he turned to the appropriate page.

'And now, my dear children, I shall tell you a little about the Holy Well of Endackney. There are many mysteries associated with this special place. Some you will find out about soon enough, and others will require you to read through my diaries and notes and general ramblings. I suspect that a number of your questions shall then be answered. Indeed, I feel honoured that so much has been revealed to me. But the big mysteries will, I think, always remain – as perhaps they should. Let me just say here that I have learned two great things from the holy well.

'The first, is that there are places in the world – wild places – that can speak to you. You may not always hear them clearly, but if you listen with your heart, the murmurings will come to you there. Furthermore, some locations are special for some people, and can offer gifts of wisdom and peace and health – as was the case for me with the holy well. This has always been so, but it is a lesson that we have largely forgotten. Now we seem hell bent on destroying the very things that can offer us the help we so sorely need. Rivers, lakes, forests, mountains, and all their wondrous inhabitants – they have so much to say to us – they are part of us and we of them. It is right that we should preserve such kin and listen to their voices.

'The second, is that these wild places – these artifacts of nature – have been heard by those who came before us. There were times in the past – going back many thousands of years in some cases – when the whisperings of the land and the water were more clearly understood. I believe that through places like the holy well, we can somehow connect with these ancient, and special, people. I know it may

The Holy Well

sound foolish, but I really believe that in some mysterious way, we can gain from their knowledge and strengths and insights and, stranger still, that perhaps they can gain from us.

'I will understand if you think that these are the mental meanderings of an old man whose brain is losing its hold on reality. But it seems to me that for some unfathomable reason, I was selected – that the Holy Well of Endackney chose me to show that the universe has many hidden treasures, and that there is purpose and reason and great wonders still waiting to be uncovered. I have been given but a brief view of these things, and I have tried to do what I thought was right with what I was shown. But now I leave – have left – and it is time for you to make discoveries of your own.'

Hamish lowered the letter and smiled. "And now for the ashes," he said. "My father wanted them to be scattered here – where he did the same with my mother's ashes over a decade ago."

* * * * * * * * * * * * *

Much later, after everyone else had gone, Morag and Hamish whispered a final farewell to James, and then walked out of the woods and up to the main track. They didn't speak for a while, but eventually Hamish broke the silence.

"That woman did give you the list of names and addresses, didn't she?" he asked.

Morag patted her jacket. "Here in my pocket," she replied.

"What an extraordinary day," he said. "And what an extraordinary bunch of people. I wonder if any one of them will be able to pick up from where Dad left off – if any have what appears to have been his gift?"

Morag nodded but said nothing. She was still thinking about the stranger she had glimpsed amongst the trees back at the well – his hair had been fair and long, and his coat made of animal skins.

Acknowledgments

This story began not so much in my head as in my life – reaching a focus some years ago when I lived in Scotland. But numerous gaps in my knowledge and understanding, especially regarding that country's prehistory, had to be filled before I could even to begin to write. The research involved a lot of reading and field work, as well as meeting with various specialists who were willing to answer my many questions and offer their expert guidance. In particular, Piers Voysey talked and walked with me through woodlands and fields, and helped educate me about tree species and other plants in the Highlands. Barrie Andrian and Alan Torrance provided keen insights regarding the structure of timber-framed crannogs, and the technologies – and enigmas – associated with the people who built them. Pat Sandeman taught me about relevant bird species: their appearances, calls, habitats, behaviours, and histories. And Dr Peter Rowley-Conwy came to my rescue when I desperately needed to know about the domestication of horses in pre-Celtic Britain.

Some of the key written resources I used included: *Scottish Prehistory* by Richard Oram; *Wild Harvesters: The First People in Scotland* by Bill Findlayson; *Farmers, Temples and Tombs: Scotland in the Neolithic and the Early Bronze Age* by Gordon Barclay; *Settlement and Sacrifice: The Later*

Prehistoric People of Scotland by Richard Hingley; *Ancient Scotland* by Stewart Ross; *Highland Man* by Ian Grimble; *Lost Beasts of Britain* by Anthony Dent; *Celtic Myths and Legends* by Charles Squire; *Celtic* by T. W. Rolleston; *Picts* edited by Christopher Tabraham; *Celtic Scotland* by Ian Armit; *The Man in the Ice* by Konrad Spindler; *Scotland's Place-names* by David Dorward; *Dictionary of Place-Names in the British Isles* by Adrian Room; *Wild Flowers* by Francis Rose and R. B. Davis; *The Scots Herbal: The Plant Lore of Scotland* by Tess Darwin; *The Lomond Guide to Birds* by Jim Flegg and Martin Woodcock; and *Field Guide to the Trees and Shrubs of Britain* edited by Michael W. Davison and Neal V. Martin

Three people deserve special mention because of their support in this endeavour. Jenny Barry read the manuscript a number of times and provided encouragement and criticism when I needed both. Maggy Macpherson's contribution can't be overstated. Besides knowing more about the underlying truths of this story than almost anyone else, she read and commented on endless versions of chapters, paragraphs, sentences, and words, and supported me in so many other ways that this book's existence is as much due to her efforts as to mine. And finally, there is a man whose name I cannot give, for reasons I cannot say. A landowner, he listened to me, a total stranger, when I asked for his help. He understood, and did what was right. *Tapadh leibh.*